A Total Waste
of Makeup

A Total Waste
of Makeup

KIM GRUENENFELDER

ST. MARTIN'S GRIFFIN ≈ NEW YORK

www.stmartins.com

ISBN 0-312-34872-X
EAN 978-0-312-34872-4

D   15   14   13   12   11

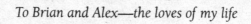

To Brian and Alex—the loves of my life

Acknowledgments

Thanks to Kim Whalen, my brilliant literary agent, and Rebecca Oliver for introducing us.

Thanks to Jennifer Good, my awesome film agent, who encouraged me to take a break from writing screenplays for a few years to try my hand at a novel.

Thanks to Jennifer Weis, my wonderful editor, who won me at auction (something I never thought I'd be able to say), and her assistant, Stefanie Lindskog.

Thanks to my family: Carol (Mom), Ed (Dad), Janis, Jenn, Rob, Jake, Jean, and all of my wonderful aunts, uncles, and cousins.

Thanks to the friends who got me through turning thirty: Rachel, Lauren, Cookie, Ashley, Patrick, Dave, Doug, Laurie, Jeff, Karen, and Stephanie. And, of course, Anjani. Another thanks to sister Jenn and friend Laurie, who both made me maid of honor at their weddings. When I was twenty-nine and single. Which sucked. (I'm kidding.)

And to "the wine tasters"—my female pack: Jen, Dawn, Gaylyn, Christie, Marisa, Missy, and Dorothy.

One

Don't wait by the phone.

Okay, so when my great-grandniece reads this, it's probably going to be, like, 2106, and by then there will not only be pagers, cell phones, e-mail, and answering machines, but some necklace that can reach you at any time, day or night. Which really just means that women will be perpetually waiting by the phone—painfully aware that no one is calling, even while they're out shopping, or at the gym, or doing whatever else they can to try to get their minds off the fact that the guy they're waiting for still hasn't called.

I am sitting on my living room sofa, an empty carton of Ben & Jerry's by my side, trying to give advice to a great-grandniece I've never met. Why? Well, I'm turning thirty soon. And I recently started thinking about all of the things that I wish I had known when I was younger. Basic universal laws that don't change from year to year, century to century.

I started out writing to my great-granddaughter. But the way my love life's going lately, the poor dear is nothing more than a pipe dream. I'm now betting on my engaged sister's chances of procreation—hence, the great-grandniece.

What am I writing? Pretty much anything I wish I had known at sixteen, and wish I could force myself to remember at twenty-nine.

Things like:

Never chase a man. Let him chase you.

Exceedingly simple. And yet, how many times have we women bought into the lie that some men "just need a little prodding," then done something stupid, like ask him out?

If someone has a SORRY, IT WAS A SENIOR MOMENT bumper sticker on their car, stay at least three car lengths behind them.

Because, really, every teenager should know that.

And my favorite:

Don't wait by the phone.

Or course, as I write this, I wait in desperate hope for Dave to call. We've had three dates. No sex yet. I wonder if that killed the deal.

My home phone rings. Hallelujah! My prayers are answered!

I pick up, putting on my cheeriest voice. "Hello."

"I think your father's gay."

Oh, for God's sake. Now here's the type of conversation I'm pretty sure our foremothers never had. "Mom, Dad's not gay."

"Don't be so sure," Mom says. "Jeannine kicked him out again. He asked if he could stay at my house tonight."

My parents are divorced, but they're best friends. Yes, I am from Los Angeles. How'd you guess? "Well then, he's not gay," I insist. "If he were, he'd be staying with a guy named Steven tonight."

"Oh, sweetheart, you're just so naïve," my mother declares. "You want to cling to the illusion that your father's straight so that you can go on to be a happily married woman. We discussed it in therapy."

"We?" I ask, a little alarmed. "Who's we?"

"My therapist and me."

"Mom—you're not supposed to pay a therapist to talk about me—I'm supposed to pay one to talk about you."

"I blame myself," Mom continues, ignoring me completely. "I was always a fag hag. So open-minded, so understanding. Naturally your father couldn't help but be drawn to me." As my mother begins some sort of monologue, I tune out, choosing to write the following in my journal of advice:

Don't wait by the phone! Ever! If you do, the guy you like won't call. Your mother will!

". . . and then there's his love for musicals!" Mom continues. "I mean, how many times can a guy see *Annie Get Your Gun?* And for God's sake, an English major???? What was I thinking?"

For the record: It was the seventies, free love reigned, and I doubt either of my parents were thinking. I doubt they were talking. I'm going to go out on a limb here and say I think they were just having sex. Oh. . . .

If you are a teenager when you read this, let these next words of wisdom be the most important: boys your age desperately want to have sex. They will say and do anything to get sex. They will pretend to love you just to get sex. Girls, on the other hand, desperately want to have a boyfriend and be loved. They will sometimes use sex to get that love. This is why you should wait until you're sure a man really, really loves you before you cave in. . . .

I erase that.

. . . before you give yourself to him.

In other words, a fifteen-year-old male would fuck a snake if someone would hold it still long enough. By thirty, they've matured, and will only do it if the snake is still hanging around the bar after last call. Hmmm. Perhaps I'm getting bitter in my old age.

And remember, even when those boys do grow up—the sex thing never completely goes away. This explains a phenomenon in my generation called Pamela Anderson.

. Well—what am I supposed to say? They never get better? That people make entire careers out of trying to translate between men and women? That if I could figure them out even vaguely, I'd be happily married by now, or at least happily in a committed relationship, or at least not still waiting by the phone just weeks before my thirtieth birthday?

"Are you listening to me?" my mother screams into my ear.

Shit! I hate it when I miss my cue. "Yes," I lie.

"And . . . ?" she asks.

"And Dad's not gay. Believe me—we live in Los Angeles; we'd know by now."

"Well, of course you'd have to defend him. He's your father."

As my mother continues babbling, I pull my cell phone out of my purse, and call my home phone. I wait for the beep.

Beep. "Mom, that's my other line. I gotta go."

"Tell them you'll call them back."

"It's Drew. I gotta go."

"Do you think *he's* gay?"

"Loveyoubye," I say in one rushed word, then abruptly hang up.

Oh boy, do I have a few bits of advice to write on parents:

Hide everything from your parents.

Particularly if they are ex-hippies who think that they're "understanding." My mother is a fifty-five-year-old party girl who still sneaks off at parties to smoke pot. She thinks she's my best friend. Why is it every mother in the world thinks her daughter is her best friend, and yet everyone's mother makes them crazy? Oooh, that's good.

Your daughter is not your best friend. And no, your relationship's not different!

My home phone rings again. I answer. "Hello?"

"I need to talk to you about the wedding," my sister Andrea (Andy) says in a rushed tone. She refers to all of her wedding plans in a rushed tone—despite the fact that she quit her job the second her fiancé proposed, and has had nothing to do but plan the wedding for the past month. Okay, it's in only three weeks, but still.

And, to answer your next question, she says no, she's not pregnant. But we're thinking they'll announce the heir apparent as soon as the wedding's over.

"How do you feel about salmon?" Andy asks as though the fate of the free world depended on my answer.

"Depends. Alaskan King or farm-raised?"

"To wear."

Did I mention I have the dubious distinction of being the maid of honor?

I immediately write in my book:

In the 21st century, no woman in the world ever wore her brides-maid's dress "a second time"—except to a Halloween party.

I manage to stumble out a "It's not one of my best colors."

My phone beeps. "Hold on." I punch the button, then say, "Hello?"

"Tell your sister you're a 'summer,'" my mother says sternly. "Salmon is a 'spring.' And I'm not paying fifty thousand dollars for a wedding so she can dress you like a fish."

"Mom, where are you calling from?"

"The bridal shop. I snuck into the alley. Andy thinks I'm smoking a joint."

"Summer. Got it. Bye," I say, then click back over. "I'm back."

"It was *her*, wasn't it?" Andy uses a tone with me like I was talking to my mistress.

Beep. "Hold on again," I say, then click over. "Hello?"

"Who's your Daddy?"

"You are," I say.

Don't get excited—it's not Dave. It actually is my father. He heard the expression on T.V. once, and he's a little unclear on the concept.

"I'm not gay," Dad assures me.

"I know."

"Your mother's crazy as a loon."

"I know that, too."

"I mean, this is, like, the thousandth time she's accused me of this. I'm tempted to go over to her house right now and prove to her how straight I am, but of course that's how you got here in the first place."

Wow! Was that ever too much information? "Dad, Andy's on the other line, and . . ."

"She wants to put you in a salmon taffeta monstrosity with

pouffy sleeves. I suggested a beautiful silver Vivian Tam you could actually wear again."

"Well, that's sweet but . . . Dad, are you sure you're not gay?" I joke.

"Right now, I wish I was. Women think too much. They always want to define everything. . . ."

As he starts lamenting about his problems with Jeannine, his second wife, I hear the holding call click dead, then my cell phone rings the cancan song. "Dad, that's Drew," I lie. "I have to go." I know it's Andy calling my cell impatiently.

"Love you," he says, then hangs up immediately. One advantage of Dads over Moms—they always let you get off the phone.

I pick up my cell. "I'm sorry. That was Dad. They're fighting again."

"I know," Andy tells me. "Mom's smoking out as we speak. Now, back to the salmon—you don't like it?"

Hmmm. This will be tricky. It's like she's loaded up the minefield, and is asking me to walk. "I thought your colors were going to be black and silver," I say carefully.

"They were," she sighs. "But my future in-laws thought that was morbid."

"Ask your future in-laws if they've been planning your wedding since you were five," I remind her. "No, they have not. *You've* been planning your wedding since you were five."

Her future in-laws are East Coast rich, and stuffy as hell. There are even a few Kennedys coming to the wedding. Which at least means there will be drinking, so the evening won't be a total loss.

My sister, on the other hand, comes from a frighteningly crazy— wait, I'm not allowed to use that word—*colorful* artistic family. We have four actors, three writers (including our mother), one director of photography, a costume designer (our father), and a producer. And my poor sister with her MBA from Harvard. She always was the white sheep of the family.

Yes, poor Andy. The stork having dropped her down the wrong chimney, Andy chose as corporate a route as she could think of. She was a huge marketing whiz at one of the major studios until she moved in with her boyfriend to become the upper-class snob she always wanted to be. Pretty much overnight, she went from *Ms.* magazine to *Martha Stewart Living.* I don't mind that type of woman, I just worry that my sister can't ignore her roots forever.

"Look, it's your wedding," I tell her. "Tell them it's a Hollywood thing. Black and silver are the 'in' colors right now. Black is the new pink."

"Salmon," Andy reminds me.

"Salmon," I repeat back.

"Can I invite Drew?" she asks. Or should I say blackmails?

Okay, here's a dilemma. I work for Drew Stanton, one of the highest paid movie stars in the world. If he shows up for her wedding, my sister will look oh-so-cool, and this will justify her color choices to her new in-laws. It's total blackmail. Show up with a megastar in tow, or show up preparing to swim upstream.

"Of course. He'd love to come," I say with the insincerity of a sorority sister. Hey, better women than me have pimped their friends. Or, in my case, their bosses.

I jot down on a Post-it note: *Note to self: Make sure Drew is scheduled to be out of town wedding weekend. Book secret weekend rendezvous with Catherine Zeta-Jones type if necessary, or, if desperate, schedule him for some type of plastic surgery.*

"So, would you prefer silver to salmon?" Andy asks, bringing me back to the conversation at hand.

Great. Now I have the dubious honor of choosing between looking like the inside or the outside of a fish. "What about black? You said your colors were going to be silver and black."

"Yes, but the bridesmaids will be wearing black. You're the maid of honor. I'm thinking, if I put you in silver, you'll look special."

What I want to say is, *How is impersonating a big ol' bag of Jiffy Pop going to make me special?* But my cell phone beeps its call-waiting before I have time.

I check the cell's caller ID. This time it really is Drew. "Andy, it's Drew. Do whatever makes you happy. I've gotta go."

"I'm not Mom," she says in disgust.

"I know. Which is why I don't lie to you. I love you. Bye."

I click over. "Hello."

On the other line, I hear Drew scream at the top of his lungs, "Put the fucking teddy bear down!"

I drop the phone, then quickly drop to my knees and grab it from the floor. "Drew, what are you still doing in looping? You were supposed to be out of there by two."

"They had some sort of tape problem. I didn't even start until noon," Drew tells me in a normal voice, then booms, "*Put the fucking teddy bear down!*"

For those of you who have never watched *Entertainment Tonight,* looping is what we call redoing your lines after a movie is completed. Let's say you had a great scene—the take was perfect, one tear fell from your face as you choked up your line, "I will always love you." The director is sure he cast the perfect actor, you can just hear your Academy Awards speech now, all is perfect . . .

And then a gaffer drops a fifty-pound light on his foot, and screams words you never knew existed.

Well, then you keep the take, but go back later to redo the line. It's sort of the opposite of lip syncing. And this is where Drew is right now.

"Why didn't you call me?" I ask. "I would have gone down there."

"I felt like being alone today," Drew says. "No offense."

"None taken," I say cheerfully. The fact that he is at a sound studio looping his last movie with a team of technicians listening to his every breath seems to have been lost on him.

I am Drew's personal assistant, which means I keep track of all of his appointments, and hang around the set with him to get him coffee, snacks, a pretty girl to talk to, whatever. It's more detailed than that—but you get the gist.

Overall, it is a great job. Forget what you've heard on E! If you can find the right person to work for, it's the best job in the world. You get to travel, you make a lot of money, and you get to go to cool parties. Plus, on days like today, while everyone else is stuck in an office in their business suits, you get to be in your own home, in your favorite plaid pajamas, waiting by the phone for your boss to call.

"Hold on, baby," Drew says sweetly. "Put the fucking teddy bear down!" he screams again. This time I wince, but keep my hand firmly planted on the phone. "Sweetie, can I call you back in a couple minutes?" he whispers. "I'm in Vietnam over here."

And he hangs up on me.

I'm not sure if he's referring to his movie, or the fact that he's having a bad day. Either way, I'm back to being left alone in my plaid pajamas. Life is good. I proceed to write the following bit of advice:

Never expect anyone to take care of you financially.

As I said, I am a personal assistant. I work for megasexy, megastar Drew Stanton—voted *People* magazine's "Sexiest Man Alive." Twice. His wife left him last year after cheating on him for two of the three years they were married. Welcome to Hollywood.

I make $1,500 a week, week in and week out, every week of the year, no matter what. When he's shooting a movie, I make $2,000 a week. The downside: the guy's a complete nut.

For example, he once got me out of my warm bed at three in the morning because he wanted me to book him a private charter plane.

To Montana.

In February.

Did I mention it was three o'clock in the fucking morning? And that he actually expected me to come with him?

Why? "Because," as he told me with great sincerity that night, "everyone keeps talking about how it's the place to go when you want to get away from it all. And I need to get away from it all."

When we got there later that morning, Drew took one step out of the plane, realized it was ten below with the wind chill factor, then turned back around to announce, "Let's try Pittsburgh!"

"What on earth for?" I asked.

"If you truly want to get away from it all, you need to go where no one else is going," he reasoned. "I don't know anyone going to Pittsburgh."

So, off we went to Pittsburgh, where we had a very nice lunch, actually.

Then it was on to Cleveland, where we took a tour of the Rock and Roll Hall of Fame, and Drew still complained of the bitter cold.

Finally, we ended up at the Grand Wailea Resort in Maui. For a week. All of my expenses paid. So, you can see why I put up with him.

Oh yeah, I actually like him, too. Not like-like. Just like.

My home phone rings. Vowing once again to get a downstairs phone with a caller ID screen, I pick up my home line. "Mom, I have a job . . ."

"He hasn't called. Has he?" my friend Dawn says sympathetically.

"Thank you for the vote of confidence," I say dryly.

"Oh. Am I wrong?" she asks hopefully.

"No," I'm forced to admit.

"So, kick 'em to the curb. What are you wearing tonight?"

"I'm not sure I'm in a 'going out' mood."

"No. You're not sure you want to go out tonight just in case

Lunkhead calls at the last minute to ask you out. You're going. I have a limo and everything. Listen, I'm in Makeup on a Ja Rule video. Gotta go. I'll pick you up at eight."

And she's off. I hang up. The phone rings again. Please, please, please be David. "Hello."

"What's the word for using your feet as a tool?" my friend Kate asks.

"Prehensile."

"How do you spell that?"

"P-R-E-H-E-N-S-I-L-E."

She pauses. Clearly, she's writing something down. "Thank you. Do you happen to know how the French prime minister pronounces his name?"

Shit. Now see, if she'd asked me to name the two youngest Brady kids, I would have gotten that. "I'm not sure."

Another pause on the other end of the phone. "Please tell me you know the name of the French prime minister," Kate says.

"I know the name of the French prime minister," I confidently say back.

"You're pathetic," Kate says.

"I'll know it by tonight," I counter.

"Oh good, you're going," Kate says brightly, then changes her tone. "Wait, but I guess that means he hasn't called."

"Do you plan to say anything that will make me feel better during this conversation?" I ask.

She thinks about it a moment. "No matter how old you get, I'll always be older."

"And with a boyfriend," I respond. "You'll always be older with a boyfriend."

"He's not my boyfriend. He's my Fwip."

"Fwip" is short for "Friend with Privileges." The term is Kate's way of avoiding the inevitable. Kate has been dating Jack for nine years, since our senior year of college. Dawn set them up one night, they had what Kate thought would be a one night stand, and they've been dating ever since. He is her boyfriend. I don't care what they call each other—they play slumber party four nights a week, and they are the last person the other one speaks to at night.

Which gives me an idea of what to write next:

If you've been dating someone for a year, you know if you want to marry them or not. Fish or cut bait. Either get married, or set them free. And if a man you've dated for a year hasn't proposed— definitely cut bait.

Which is great advice. And the minute I find someone who actually did get engaged in less than a year without getting pregnant, it'll sound even better.

"So what did you do last weekend?" Kate asks.

"I had an incredibly romantic weekend," I say, with a smile in my voice. "On Friday night we went to *La Boheme* . . ."

"Jack and I got drunk and played Trivial Pursuit . . ."

"Then Saturday we went to the beach all day . . ." I continue.

"We painted the living room. Mr. Anal Retentive and Ms. Let's Get This Fucking Thing Over With . . ."

"Followed by almost a week of waiting by the phone." I finish.

You know, she may be able to pull a king and an ace, but I always have the trump card. My cell phone rings the cancan again. "Gotta go."

"See you tonight," Kate says. "First round's on me."

We hang up, and I check the caller ID on my cell phone. I click on. "Mom, this is supposed to be Drew's line."

"I know, sweetie, but we're having a crisis here, and I need your help. Is fifteen thousand dollars a lot for a wedding dress?"

Good Christ. "You're talking to the wrong girl. I think fifteen thousand dollars is a lot for a car."

"Well, Andy saw this wedding gown she thinks is perfect, but it would be a rush order, and it needs to be made with some special kind of silk or they won't be able to bead it right. I don't understand why she can't just wear my old wedding dress, it's still in perfect condition. . . ."

While Mom continues with her run-on sentence, I write the following:

Never subject your daughter to your wedding dress. Styles have changed.

I mean, should leg of mutton sleeves have ever really been in fashion in the first place? Besides, my mother, God love her, was five months pregnant when she got married. My sister is a perfect size two.

Mom apparently is still talking. ". . . and besides that, if we really want to save money, the real trend right now is papier-mâché dresses. They're really hip, you can't tell the difference, and they're only about a hundred dollars each."

Somehow, I do not see my sister in a papier-mâché dress. This is the type of statement I don't think one should ever have to utter aloud. And I don't want my mother to mention it aloud again—as this would increase the chances of yours truly wearing a silver papier-mâché dress.

Mom continues, taking my silence as some form of encouragement. "I just wanted your opinion, and now that I have it, I want you to talk to your sister. Here!"

Andy immediately gets on the phone. She has that same lovely, irritated voice she's had ever since the one-and-a-half-carat ring was placed on her finger. "What?"

I quickly jot down my next words of wisdom:

Don't spend your whole life looking forward to your wedding day.
Don't spend a year's salary paying for your wedding day. It's just a
day. You will spend more time writing a term paper than you will
at your wedding reception.

As I'm writing, Andy spits out at me, "Heeelllloooo? You know, I
can't hold forever. I have a dress to get. The rest of us have lives,
too."

"How much did Mom say they would spend? Answer in letters if
you need to."

"Chocolate," Andy says, speaking in code. Mom must be hover-
ing.

C—the third letter in the alphabet. That means they said
$3,000—max. "Don't speak in code in front of me," my mother
shrieks from the other side of the salon.

"We're not speaking in code. I'm just hungry!" Andy yells back.

"And how much is the dress you want going to cost?" I ask.

"Donuts."

"Well, at least you aren't hungry for eggs. Or jelly beans, for that
matter. Put Mom back on the phone."

She does.

"There's no talking to her!" my mom says in *that tone*. You know
the tone—every mom has one. "She thinks your father and I are
made of money, like it's not enough we're throwing this shindig at
the Bel Air, even though I got to be married at some neon-belled
chapel in Las Vegas . . . but no, *now* we're supposed to spend another fifteen thousand dollars on a dress she'll wear once, twice at
the most, and don't even get me started on the costs of the
bougainvillea."

Bougainvillea. Is that a flower, or some new drink? I wonder to myself. Back to the matter at hand. "Well, when Andy and I went dress
shopping last week, we did see a lovely dress in that very store for

only four thousand dollars. You think you and Dad could pop for that?"

Dead silence. Dead silence is never good with my mother. Well . . . actually, it's good until she talks again.

"How do you know what store we're in?" Mom asks suspiciously. Shit! "Well, I . . ."

"Andy, show me this four thousand dollar dress your sister likes so much!" my mother bellows right into my ear.

There's a beep. "Mom, I have another call. Can you hold?"

"You put your own mother on hold . . ."

I click over. "Hello."

"Do you want to see hell today?" Drew purrs into the phone. He must still be looping. Hard to find a man who purrs, unless you have your mouth around his—But I digress.

"Hold on," I say cheerfully, then click back over and return to my normal voice. "Mom, it's Drew. I'll call you later." I hang up on her. Saved by the beep. I click back to Drew, and try to make my voice as cheerful and sweet as is humanly possible. "Hi. Sorry about that."

"It's okay. Listen, can you find out if Julia Roberts is available?"

"Available for a date, or a movie?"

"Well, both I suppose."

"She's with someone," I tell Drew. I haven't checked lately, but it's probably true.

"Goddamn it!" Drew belts out at me. "Why doesn't anything ever go my way? I'm gonna die alone!"

Apparently the fact that he's a gorgeous gazillionaire doesn't count toward "things going his way." But before I can point that out in an ever so diplomatic fashion, Drew changes the subject. "I have my interview with *People* magazine this weekend, and the house looks like hell. The dining room is this horrible shade of yellow—I agreed to a color called butter. A good butter where I come from is almost white. This isn't butter. This is . . . some shade much worse than butter. Margarine, maybe."

I want to point out that he has twenty-two other rooms in his fourteen-million-dollar Brentwood mansion. But I also want to keep my job. "I'll call the painters and have them fix it."

"Do you think five hundred thousand dollars is a lot for a car?"

You're asking the wrong person, I think to myself. *I think $500,000 is a lot for a dress.* But I would never say that. I like my job.

Drew just reminded me of a good one. I write in my leather book:

Don't ever read People magazine. It will make you feel bad about your own life.

I'm not sure which type of article in *People* bothers me more: the weddings where everyone's happy, or the drug ODs where we're supposed to feel sorry for the forlorn and tormented millionaires. I mean, Matthew Perry was still dealing with a drug addiction when he was making $750,000 a week? Please.

Anyway, before I can answer, Drew says, "You know, I'm just gonna buy it. I mean, if I hate it, I can always give it to my next ex-wife. Call's at seven A.M. Monday, right?"

"Yes, indeed."

"Great. Take the rest of the day off. Love you," he says, then hangs up on me.

My home line rings. With tremendous self-control I wait until the second ring, then pick up with a bright, "Hello."

"I have, like, two seconds to talk," my happily married cousin Jenn says. "You sounded awful on the machine. What's up?"

"Tell me again why it sucks to be married," I say. Usually she's good for that—even if she doesn't mean a word of it.

"Are you waiting by the phone?" Jenn asks knowingly.

"Yes."

"Okay—here's one. I haven't waited by the phone in six years. The love of my life has called me eight times today. Once to tell me he'd be late tonight, and can I somehow convince a three-year-old and a four-year-old to wait for dinner? Once to tell me that my mother-in-law will not be able to take the kids this weekend so he upgraded the hotel room of our romantic getaway to accommodate our lovely offspring, 'Did not' and 'Did too.' Once to tell me the cat—"

I have to interrupt. "At least you have someone who wants to have a romantic weekend with you."

"At least when you go to bed with someone, you don't wake up to a little person between you in wet pajamas," she counters.

"At least you have someone who loved you so much he wanted to create a little person with you."

"Get those handcuffs off your brother right now!" Jenn screams away from the phone.

Jenn returns to her normal voice as she comes back to me. "Sweetie, I love my kids, but having a family is not the only way to guarantee happiness in life. It's a lot of work, it's very draining, and once you start, you can't go back. You lead an amazing, glamorous life. Try to be happy having this time to yourself. It's a luxury. It goes by so fast. And you're going to miss it when it's gone."

God, I hope she's right. I hope there will come a time in my life when I'm so content, I miss being alone sometimes. When I'm actually happy enough to look back on my single years fondly.

"Alex just threw up on the dog," Jenn says, cutting into my thoughts. "Is it okay if I go?"

"Sure," I say. "Love you."

"Love you, too." And she's gone.

I stare at the phone and blow out a big sigh. Maybe she's right, maybe I should be happy with all this free time. Maybe the grass is always greener. Maybe I should appreciate the luxury of getting to do whatever I want, whenever I want, and not needing to ask permission from anyone about my choices. Yeah, I could go to Paris this weekend if I wanted to. Just get my passport and my Visa card and—

The phone rings. I wait until it rings a second time before I pick up.

Maybe I'm a big hypocrite.

"Hey, you waited until the second ring. Good for you," my younger brother Jamie says.

"He still hasn't called," I say. "Why do men say they're going to call, if they're not?"

"Because we tried saying, 'Hey, great lay. Listen, I may call you at two in the morning when I'm drunk and near your place,' but you repeated it to all your friends."

"I didn't sleep with him," I say self-righteously. Though frankly, if I had, I wouldn't admit it to my baby brother. "So what does it mean when a guy says he wants to 'go out' with you, but he's not sure if he wants to date you?"

"It means he wants to sleep with you, but doesn't want a commitment."

"Pig!"

"Me or him?"

"Both."

"Hey, why you wanna kill the messenger?"

"Because you're all pigs."

"See, that's just offensive limited thinking. The dude was honest with you. He said, 'I wanna go out with you, I just don't want to date you.'"

"And that naturally means he wants to sleep with me?"

"Yes," Jamie says definitively. Then he thinks about his statement. "Actually, any man you go on a date with wants to sleep with you."

"Great."

"And any man you say 'hi' to in a bar—"

"You can shut up now," I say calmly.

"Frankly, any man you've ever made eye contact with who's not gay—"

"I'm hanging up on you now," I tell him.

And I do.

I spend the next five minutes relieved that no one calls, and debating what to write next:

This may be sexist, but . . . when dating, always remember, the treasure doesn't do the hunting.

I paid my therapist $100 an hour to be told the treasure doesn't do the hunting. Sounds great in theory. But how do you feel like a treasure when men have been making you feel bad for more than ten years?

The Dave thing is a perfect example.

You know, if he'd called me Monday, he would have freaked me out.

But on Tuesday I missed him. He crept into my mind between my coffee and my fudgsicle.

And on Tuesday night, I asked my friends about him. And on Wednesday morning, I told my Mom about this nice guy I met.

On Wednesday night I had a date with someone else. And as he plied me with Merlot, and charmed me with his sardonic wit, I thought about how Dave looked when he napped on my couch after a long day at the beach. And I wondered if he liked red wine or white. And if he really wanted girls more than boys, like he told me on our date when we talked about kids.

By Thursday, I wanted another magical weekend. But the thing about magic is if you know the trick, it's not magic anymore. I wondered why he didn't like me so much, and what was so wrong with me that he didn't call.

Let's see, there was that thing where he asked my age, and I wouldn't tell him. No, it must have been when I said that I hated high school, but he was the captain of the football team. No, I mentioned an ex. That must have been it. No, it must have been because he thought I was fat.

Oh please, Dave, call me right now, and I'll fall in love with you. Just be the one nice guy I'm allowed to fall in love with, and it'll be okay and I won't be hurt, and everything will be the way I thought it would be growing up. All I want is the one phone call. Please, let someone I like actually like me back, even if I don't deserve him. Please?

I stare at the phone. Pick it up. Listen for the dial tone. Damn, still there.

It's Friday, and I could have fallen in love. By tomorrow, I'll remember that I have a life to attend to, that magical weekends don't really happen, that there are no nice guys in the world, and these final words of wisdom:

When men say they'll call you, what they usually mean is "goodbye."

Two

Don't smoke.

I write in my notebook as I light up a Marlboro. Well, it is good advice. Unfortunately for me, those Ben & Jerry's calories don't just burn up themselves.

Some people tell me I look a little like Charlize Theron. Granted, these people are mostly in bars, and are trying to get me into bed, but I'm taking the compliment anyway. In reality, I'm a few inches shorter and a few pounds heavier. I suspect Ms. Theron gets her body through working out. I get mine from Marlboros. A girl has a choice when she eats like I do: take up smoking or jogging. I am not a jogger. And I do plan to lose those ten pounds sooner or later, but I don't believe in New Years' resolutions, so it'll probably be later.

I mean, let's face it: we tend to lose those last ten pounds when we're in love. You can go to Weight Watchers all you want, when you're happily in love and having sex all the time, those pounds just melt off—don't they?

I think the other reason people compare me to Charlize is because that's my first name—and up until her I never knew anyone else who had it. My friends call me Charlie. My family calls me Charlie. Dave should really think about calling me—ever.

Anyway, right now I'm standing in front of my house, shivering, and stomping my feet up and down for warmth as I wait for Dawn to pick me up. I jot down in my notebook:

Repeat this mantra when down about men: "I don't need a lover, just several really close friends."

Dave never called. It's eight o'clock. I waited by the phone, filled with false hope, until about 7:58.

I see a black limo pulling up, and quickly stub out my cigarette. Despite how cold I am, I wait for the chauffeur to get out and open the door for me. When I step in, Dawn is draped across the long seat with a glass of champagne in her hand. She looks stunning in a dark red Versace dress with a slit up the side. I hate her. How am I going to get a man tonight with *that* sitting right next to me?

Dawn and I met at a dorm party my first week of college. We immediately became best friends and, with Kate, lived together from our sophomore through senior years.

The first time I saw Dawn, she had a glass of Merlot in one hand and a cigarette in the other. And somehow everything she said matched that personality exactly. Dawn is gorgeous. She is the product of three interracial marriages—something that could only happen in L.A. Her paternal grandfather is Japanese, her paternal grandmother is black, her maternal grandfather is Hispanic, and her maternal grandmother is Jewish. Which means she's the most exotic-looking woman ever to grace her temple—both her Buddhist temple and her Jewish temple. And her Catholic church. And the Baptist one down the street. She considers herself "mostly Jewish" but says, "When I die, God'll sort it all out." She celebrates Christmas, Chanukah, Kwanzaa, Easter, Passover, Halloween, Cinco de Mayo, Mardi Gras, Dia de las Muertas, and the Chinese New Year (I never figured that one out).

Her job: MAW—model/actress/whatever. Only she actually works (most MAWs have an extra W at the end—waitress). When she walks into a room, every head turns: the women, to call her a "skinnybitch," the men, to get themselves into trouble with their girlfriends later. She has dark hair, flawless cappuccino skin, and a mouth that could shame a sailor. But I love her. She's fun, she's actually very nice when you get over her whole "I'm so over you" attitude, and she gets me into the best clubs and parties. This is what I need right now.

Dawn pours me a glass of champagne as I climb in. "Sweetie, we've talked about the eyeliner."

I'd been in the car less than five seconds. Ever feel like you're totally not cool even around your own friends?

"Please don't start," I say. "What looks good on you looks totally unnatural on me."

She hands me my champagne, then pulls an eyeliner out of her purse. "Look up."

I look up out of habit. Dawn has been redoing my makeup since college. She draws black eyeliner on my lower lid. "Whose limo is this?" I ask her while staring at the limo ceiling.

"Steve's. He was the director on the music video I did today. I promised to be in a video for Justin Timberlake in exchange for it, so it's really a work thing."

"You're going to be in a Justin Timberlake video?" I say, sounding way too impressed.

"He wants to go ethnic again, if you can believe that. Look down."

I do. "Are you dating him?"

"Timberlake? Isn't he gay?"

"Steve," I say.

"Hmm . . . define 'date.'"

"Are you sleeping with him?"

"Mmmmm . . . not yet. I can't decide. I think he's the type who would want to cuddle afterwards, and spend the weekend. I can't have a man all in my business, you know?"

"Yeah, I understand. You give a guy like that the least bit of encouragement and then what do you have? A husband, babies . . . happiness."

Dawn puts away the liner. "You look fabulous. Give me your phone."

"No," I say, as Dawn grabs my purse, yanks out my phone, and turns it off.

"Hey!" I protest. "What if Drew calls?"

She pops my phone into her purse. "You're not waiting for Drew, you're waiting for Lunkhead. And his deadline for seeing you this weekend just passed."

I know she's right. I shouldn't get all dressed up—with perfect eyeliner to boot—just to wait by the phone. Nonetheless . . . "I have to be available for Drew twenty-four-seven. It's my job."

"Fine." Dawn pulls out her Web-enabled cell phone, or, as I like to call it, the "Great, now we can wait by the phone, and wait by our e-mail" thingamajig.

"What's his number?" she asks.

"You know his number," I say, crossing my arms and sighing loudly.

"I do?"

"He gave it to you at his birthday party last year. Remember? He programmed it in himself."

Confused, Dawn goes through her address book. She finds it: his home number, cell number, and e-mail address. "Huh," she says, surprised.

Now I ask you, if a guy gave you his home number, cell number, and e-mail address, wouldn't it *occur* to you he might be interested?

It didn't occur to her. Drew spent three months asking me about her. I spent three months trying to get her to call him, saying things like I *think* it's *possible* he *might* like her, and Dawn spent three months saying, "Don't be silly."

As Dawn calls, I open my notebook and write:

If a man gives you three different ways to get in touch with him, he's interested in you. This is not rocket science. Don't play dumb.

"Hi, Drew. This is Dawn Fraiche. I'm a friend of . . . Well, that's *uncanny*! How on earth did you remember me?"

I let my face fall into my hands.

Dawn continues talking to my boss. "Uh-huh. Uh-huh . . . Well, aren't you sweet? . . . No. Listen, I'm about to go into a canyon, but I just want you to know Charlie's having problems with her phone, so if you need to call her, can you call my cell phone instead . . . ? Fabulous. The number's 323-555-8642."

"*No*, what?" I whisper to her.

She covers her phone. "What?"

"You said no to him. What were you saying no to?"

Dawn waves me off with her hand and returns to her conversation.

"I'm afraid I can't," she says into the phone. "Charlie and I are having a Girls' Night Out. Maybe some other time. . . ."

Dawn makes staticky sounds, then yells, "I'm losing you! Bye!" and clicks off her phone. "He wants you to know some friends of his are taking him to Maui for the weekend, so he probably won't be calling, and he'll see you on the set first thing Monday morning."

"What did you say no to?" I ask, trying not to sound panicked.

"Oh, that was weird. He asked if I wanted to fly out and spend the weekend with him and his friends. Isn't that bizarre?"

Clueless. Absolutely clueless.

Before I have a chance to answer, we pull up to Kate's office building. Kate is standing in front in a green Armani business suit, holding a large black leather briefcase, and talking to someone on her cell phone. One can only assume it's Jack.

"Look, the girls are here. I gotta go . . . Yeah, me too. Bye." Kate slams her phone shut, and gets into the limo. She mutters to herself, "The things we put up with for sex on tap . . ."

As Dawn pours her a glass of champagne, Kate falls into a seat across from us, and gives an exhausted sigh. "From now on, do not use the F word, the C word, the B word, or the R word in my company."

The R word. Dawn and I exchange confused glances. I know I will regret this, but I cannot help myself: "What's the R word?" I ask Kate.

"Relationship."

Fair enough, I think. Very Rulesish not to use the R word.

Now Dawn can't help herself. "Wait, then the B word would be . . . ?"

"Boyfriend," Kate says.

Well, now I'm just confused. "Okay, so then the C word would be . . . ?"

"Commitment."

I nod and smile. Just got it. "Which would make the F word . . ." and we all say together, "Future."

"Honestly, Kate, why don't you just marry the poor guy?" Dawn asks.

"I'm not even going to dignify that with a response," Kate says as she throws her phone into her purse, pulls a little black dress from her briefcase, and takes off her jacket.

Dawn knew it was a loaded question. Since their senior year in college, Jack and Kate have not been planning their wedding, they've been planning their breakup. But, as Kate once pointed out, you have to really commit to a breakup for it to take. It takes as much of a commitment to break up as to move in together. You have to say to yourself, "I really don't want to spend the rest of my life with this person. And I'm willing to put in the time and energy necessary to make sure that doesn't happen."

Trying to change the subject, I smile proudly and say, "Dominique de Villepin."

"What?" Kate says as she unbuttons her blouse.

"The French prime minister. It's Dominique de Villepin."

"I thought it was Jacques Chirac," Dawn says.

Kate pulls off her blouse, wearing nothing on top but a red velvet bra. "No, he's the president, not the prime minister."

"Oh, that's right, they have both," Dawn says. "Victoria's Secret?"

"La Perla," Kate says, pulling her black dress over her head. "Charlie, you've sounded miserable all week. And you can't be this upset just because Fuckface didn't call. What's really going on?"

"I'm fine," I insist.

I get one "Shyeah!" and one "Aw, hell no!" You can guess who said what.

"Okay, so maybe I'm a little bummed out," I force myself to admit.

"Why? It's not the thirty thing, is it?" Dawn asks as she pops a piece of nicotine gum into her mouth, then hands me a piece.

I take the gum square. Even though I have no intentions of quitting smoking, I would like to quit for tonight. Orange. It tastes like Bayer aspirin for children. Which actually does taste better than a Marlboro, but the last thing I need is to get addicted to nicotine gum *and* cigarettes.

In response to her question, I mutter, "Maybe. I mean, my little sister's getting married in four weeks, and I'm now a walking cliché."

"Please. She's marrying a CPA who lives in Stevenson Ranch. Are we really jealous?" Dawn says in her "we're so over them" tone.

"Yes, because . . . Wait, do you even know where Stevenson Ranch is?" I ask Dawn. Stevenson Ranch is a fairly new community located way the hell out at the edge of the county. It's very white bread. I can't imagine Dawn has even heard of it, much less formed an opinion about it.

"Not exactly," she admits. "But it sounds too white. So what's the real problem?"

Silence. She knows me. Yes, I am jealous my sister is getting married before me. But I live in a city where absolutely no one gets married before they're thirty. So why do I feel so desperate?

After a few more agonizing moments, I finally spit out, "I've never read *War and Peace*."

Dawn and Kate exchange a bewildered look. They have not a clue what I'm babbling about.

"And I don't speak Spanish," I continue. "I live in Los Angeles, and I don't speak Spanish. Took Latin in school like an idiot and now here I am speaking *nada*."

Silence. Dawn takes another sip of her champagne to stall for time. Kate slithers out of her Armani pants, and pulls her dress down over her waist.

After several pensive moments, Dawn finally gives me a complicated solution to my complicated problem. "So go read *War and Peace*."

"But get the Rosemary Edmonds translation," Kate says, spritzing herself with a bottle of Chanel No. 5. "Most of the other translations are downright archaic."

"No, you guys aren't getting it. I'm going to be thirty next month, and I've never done any of the things I thought I was going to grow up to do. It's too depressing. I'm supposed to have a fabulous career, a fabulous husband, and three children by now. I don't have any of those things."

Silence fills the car. None of us have any of those things. We aren't married. We didn't buy the fabulous home with the white picket fence. We didn't write the great American novel, or star in the great American sitcom, or do anything that will put us in the White House later in life. None of us have ever been to a PTA meeting, and we have no guarantees we ever will.

It's no wonder they can't think of anything to say to me. Who could? What possible solution is there to my life to make it more fulfilled?

Dawn scrunches her lips toward one ear. "Have you gotten laid lately? That usually helps."

"No," I say. "I had the most amazing third date with Dave, and I withheld, and he said he was going to call me and it's been a week and he still hasn't and I'm going to need a lot of drinks tonight."

As I end my sentence abruptly to take a gulp of my champagne, I suddenly have the horrific realization that I'm starting to sound like my mother. Ewwwww . . .

"Why don't you call him?" Kate asks.

"Uh-uh. I've got the Post-It on the phone."

Aaah—the infamous Post-It. What girl hasn't at some point stuck a Post-It on every phone in her house saying, "Don't call him!" Or the longer, "If he wanted to talk to you, he'd call. Go do something constructive!" In college, Kate, Dawn, and I once had three Post-Its stuck on the same phone. Assorted colors—so we didn't accidentally rip off our roommate's Post-It once we called our guy anyway.

"That is such outdated thinking," Kate insists. "The guy hasn't done anything wrong, you had a good time, just call him." She sips her champagne. "Oh, wow!" she says to Dawn, "you got the Grande Dame."

"No," I say right back. "Then he'll accept the date, and I'll sleep with him just to make myself feel more desirable in his mind, and he won't call for the fifth date, and I'll be wallowing in self-pity for another week."

"I don't know. Getting some might boost your ego if you think about it the right way," Dawn says thoughtfully. "I mean, there's something to be said for the virtues of a fuckbuddy." She gives Kate a meaningful stare. "Of course, you're not actually supposed to date them for nine years."

Later I would write:

Women are not capable of having "fuckbuddies." It's a concept men came up with. Don't buy the hype.

"So not true. Works in theory—not in practice," I insist.

"Because inevitably you date the guy anyway, and no matter how hard you try, you get stuck with him," Kate reminds us.

Dawn rolls her eyes. "Did Jack have the nerve to propose to you again?"

"When we started dating, I made my boundaries very clear," Kate insists. Her cell phone rings. She pulls it out of her purse, then turns it off.

I glance at Dawn, who says to Kate, "If you don't answer, he's just going to call seventeen times. And he'll leave seventeen messages, all marked 'urgent,' and you'll feel incredibly guilty by the time you get all the messages. So why not just call him back now, so we can all have a fun night."

"Because we had a fight last night. And he's trying to get me to come over so we can make up. And, if I do that, I'm going go miss Girls' Night, and I don't want to do that."

I glance at Dawn again. Kate has a point. Although I adore Jack—he's one of the nicest guys I've ever met—he does seem to always find a reason for Kate not to go out with us.

Even though I think I know the answer, I ask Kate, "So, what did you guys fight about?"

"My inability to make a commitment," Kate says, staring at her phone.

Um . . . okay. "Is this you saying that, or Jack saying that?" I ask.

"Our marriage counselor."

"But you're not married," Dawn points out.

"I know that."

"And yet you're seeing a marriage counselor?" Dawn asks.

"I am well aware of the irony," Kate snaps at her.

Dawn puts her palms out in a show of surrender. "All respect."

Kate shakes her head. "I've been through this with him a million times. Relationships don't work. When we started dating, he was committed to that. Now he's talking exclusivity, and it's like he never heard me. I am a human being. I have feelings and emotions and dreams and using someone for sex was a part of that. I can't believe he would trick me like this."

Dawn begins shaking her head. It's just so unbelievable. We sip our champagne in silence.

Eventually, Kate sighs, and turns her phone back on. It's still ringing. She picks up. "Look, I'm out with the girls tonight. You can't keep making me feel guilty for . . . I know. I love you, too . . . No, I'm not. It's just . . . yeah . . ."

Kate looks toward us apologetically. "Okay, maybe for an hour," she says into the phone. "But that's it. . . . I love you, too. Bye."

Kate clicks her phone shut, then pleads to us with her eyes. "I'm sorry. Would you guys hate me if I went over there, just for an hour?"

We say "Fine" and "No problem." I mean, why state the obvious? That we won't be seeing her for the rest of the night.

"Thanks. You're the best. I'll be back by eleven."

We drop Kate off at Jack's. She blows us each a kiss, and leaves in her best lingerie and sexiest black dress. But they're going to break up. Really.

Dawn and my eyes follow her out. The chauffeur closes the door, and Dawn turns back to me. "Okay, so back to your problems with men."

"Do you know that I read that the same hormone that is secreted when a woman is breast-feeding her child is also secreted when she has an orgasm?" I say out of the blue.

"That's sick."

"It's called oxytocin. The hormone is secreted during breast feeding to help her bond with her baby, to make her biologically fall in love with her baby. Only it is also secreted during an orgasm, biologically forcing us to fall in love with the man who just gave us said orgasm."

Dawn looks like she's genuinely worried about me. "Promise me the next time you wander into the self-help section, you'll call me. I'll come get you. No questions asked. No guilt trips. We'll just be proud of you for getting out before it got ugly."

"Seriously, it's why we wait by the phone, pining over a man, secretly convinced that he must be in love with us as much as we are with him, because how could we have shared such an intimacy if he didn't give a shit!" I blurt out.

I lower my voice. "It explains why I don't know a single woman who hasn't been shattered by dating. Men can actually go get laid, and make themselves feel better. If we do it, we feel worse. Bottom line."

"Very un–Gloria Steinem," Dawn deadpans.

"You know, she finally got married?"

"No! What is she, like, a hundred?"

I begin my tirade again: "Anyway, that's why we get so attached. It's the damned hormone. And I, for one, am going back to chocolate."

"Chocolate gives you orgasms?" Dawn asks, incredulous at my knowledge of biological trivia.

"No. Chocolate has phenylethylamine—the chemical secreted when you're in love."

It's rare to see someone not have any facial expression whatsoever. Sadly, I did it to my friend. "You're right. You're going to need a lot of drinks tonight," she says.

Three

If the hot spot you would like to frequent has a velvet rope—go somewhere else. You're not paying $12 for a martini for the privilege of having a Gold's Gym reject making minimum wage decide if you're cool or not.

This is actually one of the aspects of L.A. I like best. Other than movie premieres—which are all publicity stunts anyway—we don't do velvet ropes here. There was never a Studio 54 in Los Angeles because if an Angeleno had to wait for more than ten minutes in line to get a drink, he would just go down the street to another club.

Anyway, we arrive at a nightclub located in the penthouse of a skyscraper. It is one of L.A.'s current hot spots, complete with current sitcom stars buying drinks for current *Sports Illustrated* supermodels. Despite being a size 6, I am the fattest girl in the room.

The theme to the bar is an underwater fantasy, so everything in the large room is blue and sparkly. A sparkly blue marble bar, sparkly blue cocktail tables, women behind glass windows dressed as mermaids. And the bar is known for its signature blue martinis, which were recently featured on *Entertainment Tonight*.

Don't eat blue food.

Personally, I think it looks like people are drinking 2000 Flushes, but what do I know?

Dawn and I do a trip around the bar to check out the hot guys. Maybe it's the Veuve Clicquot Grand Dame talking, but I'm happy, and the guys here are *so* cute. Besides, I'm not going to sleep with any of them and secrete the dangerous hormone, so I can look all I want.

Off to the side is a dead ringer for Ben Affleck. Upon closer inspection, it *is* Ben Affleck. Since he's about three leagues out of my league, I move on.

Dawn and I sit at a small, glittery turquoise table and order a bottle of Malbec. Actually, I order a Merlot, but Dawn corrects me by telling the waiter, "No, we'll have a Malbec. Something in the fifty dollar range."

As the waiter leaves, I can't help myself. "What the hell was that about?"

"Merlot is over. Malbec is the next Merlot."

"Are you serious?" I ask a little too loudly.

"Oh, please, can we keep *that* look on our face for the rest of the night, so that no one talks to us," Dawn chastises me.

"I like the old Merlot."

"Please. You'd still be wearing leggings if it weren't for me. The nineties are over."

I pull a tampon out of my purse, and throw it at her. Clearly a woman this bitchy must be on the rag. Missing my insult entirely, Dawn slips it into her purse. (Okay, I guess she *is* on the rag.) Our waiter comes back with the bottle of Malbec, and two glasses interlocked in his fingers. "Compliments of the gentleman at the bar," he informs us.

I would sarcastically say, "That narrows it down," but you can't miss the guy at the bar—a smoldering dark-haired god who smiles ever so seductively as he raises his Tidy Bowl martini to us. Must be for Dawn.

Dawn smiles and waves to him as the waiter pours for us. "Who's that?" I ask, fake-smiling at the man like a Pan Am stewardess.

"Sean Brown. Writes action movies," Dawn says, smiling back and waving. "He wrote that one I was in, *Last Patriot*."

As Sean begins to walk over to us, I see that another good-looking man is with him: blond hair, hazel eyes, not-gonna-kick-him-out-of-bed-for-eating-crackers body. Why is it good-looking men always travel in packs? "I didn't know writers looked like that," I say under my breath as I take my first sip of Malbec.

"They don't. He used to be an actor," Dawn whispers, then gets up, and with great flourish, kisses him hello. "Sean, you gorgeous man, when did you get back in town?"

"Just last week," Sean says, then turns to the man with him. "This is my friend Tom Conroy. He's also a writer."

"Dawn Fraiche," Dawn says as she shakes Tom's hand, "and this is my friend Charlie."

Tom stares at me and smiles. It's a penetrating stare. One that can only make me think of, well, penetrating. Or at the very least, a probing tongue.

"Hi," he croons. I swear, he actually croons.

I can't help but smile. He is *so* cute. But I like Dave, I accidentally remind myself.

But I'm not supposed to like Dave, so I can think this man's cute.

Man—why do I even need a man? I'm so busy mindfucking myself—who needs sex?

"Marty Wolf is over there," Sean tells Dawn as he points to a balding middle-aged guy with a ponytail. "He's a brilliant new director. You guys are going to love each other. Do you mind if I steal her for a few minutes?" he asks me, already whisking my friend away.

"No problem," I say to the air—as they are already halfway across the room by then.

Tom stands by my table awkwardly for a few seconds. "So, are you an actress, too?" he asks me.

"Do I look like an actress?" I say, not bothering to hide the irritation in my voice. "Wait, don't answer that."

"Why?"

"Because if you say yes it'll sound like a line, and if you say no I'll be offended."

He smiles, waves his hand toward my table, and asks, "May I?"

I nod and smile.

Tom sits next to me. "So, I guess you've heard a lot of lines in your time."

What the hell is that supposed to mean? I think, but I don't want to come off angry. Instead, I say diplomatically, "What the hell is that supposed to mean?"

"Nothing. You were just saying that if I said you were an actress, it would sound like a line, so I figured you've heard a lot of them." Tom takes a handful of mixed nuts from a glow-in-the-dark blue bowl on our table. I get the feeling he's actually nervous.

Which I guess is a good thing.

"What's the worst line you've ever heard?" he asks.

"You wanna fool around at my place? It's only a block from here," I respond immediately.

Mr. Conroy nearly chokes on his nuts. "Excuse me?"

"That's the worst line I've heard," I say, smiling to myself for managing to trick him like that, and taking a sip of my drink. "Of course, it only works at fraternity parties."

Tom laughs. Okay, he gets me. I'm starting to like him. "What's the worst line you've ever heard?" I ask him.

"Are you an actress?" He smiles, and I notice how gorgeous his eyes are.

"Touché." I smile back. We clink our glasses together.

"So what do you do?" Tom asks, eating a few more nuts.

I hate that question. It's like the grown-up version of "What's your major?"

"I'm an assistant," I say, not bothering to give out any more information. The last thing I want to do is talk about Drew all night. Oh, who am I kidding, the last thing I want to do is talk about myself all night—but Drew comes in a really close second.

"Interesting," he says, although I notice he's so interested, he asks me nothing more about it. "Are you seeing anyone?"

"No," I blurt out a little too quickly. "No," I say again, reconsidering. Am I seeing Dave? I mean, he hasn't called. But, then again, if a girl asked him that question tonight, I would hope he would say yes.

"You don't sound too sure of yourself," Tom says.

"Find me a woman in this bar who is sure of herself, and I'll get the next round."

He points to Dawn, and I end up buying the next round.

When it comes to finding a man in a bar, remember: the odds are good but the goods are odd.

The evening had started out on such a promising note. But several hours, and I'll admit a few bottles of Malbec, later—goddamn it! the guy got annoying.

As I said, it started out well. He let me know he was thirty-two, had been engaged once, she broke it off. He was from Manhattan, lived in a two-bedroom condo in Brentwood, and wanted to settle down in the next few years. He liked romantic comedies (yeah, I know, they all say that) and loved anything Terry Gilliam had ever done.

It had sounded so promising—until the red flags started.

"So, what do you want to do besides be an assistant?" Tom asked, leaning in as though he was going to kiss me.

"What do you mean?" I asked back. He hadn't asked me about my job all night.

He popped a peanut into his mouth. "Come on, this is L.A. No one is what they want to be unless they're a famous director or something. Are you really a writer?"

"I'm really an assistant," I say. I'm not annoyed yet—but I do see the red flag warning me not to go anywhere near the water.

"Good. Because, and I've had a lot to drink here, so I can be honest with you, I can't be with a writer. I can't take the competition."

Oh, one of those. "You must have gone to an all boys' school," I say dryly.

He doesn't get the insult. "You know what I hate is when a woman wins an Academy Award, and her husband lies to the press and says he's proud of her. It's such bullshit."

I choke on my drink. "Excuse me?"

"Don't get me wrong—I love women's lib. I don't want my wife to be a kept woman. But let's face it, we men want to be the stars in the relationship. So when a woman wins an Academy Award, there is no man out there who can really feel anything but total jealousy. That's just how we were biologically built. We need to be the one going out and killing the bull. Know what I mean?"

I am about to really let him have it when I hear "Last call." It is one-thirty—which is last call here in California. Saved by the bell. I decide to follow my dad's advice, which I put in my book later:

Never start a fight with a drunk. Verbal or otherwise.

The waiter asks us if we would each like one more drink, and Tom responds with an enthusiastic "Yes," before I can say "No."

I am soooo making sure he picks up the check. Asshole!

"So, would you and Dawn like to go get some dinner?" Tom asks.

"Um . . . you know, I have an early morning. See, my sister's get-ting married in a few weeks and . . ."

Before I can finish my excuse, Dawn and Sean walk up to us. "Limo's here. We have to dash," Dawn tells me.

"We just ordered one more drink," Tom says.

The waiter arrives with two final glasses of wine, and the check. He places my drink in front of me, and the check and a drink in front of Tom. While Tom pulls out his Gold AmEx, Dawn picks up his drink.

"Thanks, sweetie," she says, and downs it in one gulp. Tom doesn't even blink.

After she finishes the wine, Dawn sways backward. "Oh my God," she says. She nearly falls from exhaustion, but Sean steadies her. "Are you all right?" he asks.

"Oh," Dawn says, fluttering her eyes while she puts her hand on her forehead. "I'm feeling a little light-headed. I'm afraid I went for a ten-mile run today, and I haven't had much to eat since then. I think maybe the wine just got to me," she lies.

Tallulah Bankhead would be jealous.

"Would you like me to get you some dinner?" Sean asks, con-cerned.

"Oh, you're a love. Could I take a raincheck?" she says, then her knees give out and she stumbles into Sean's arms. "God, this is so embarrassing."

"No, don't worry about it. Would you like to do something to-morrow?" Sean asks.

"I'd love to. Call me in the morning. For now, I think I better have Charlie get me home."

I get up and, with Dawn on my arm, make my way out.

"How did you know I needed an out?" I ask.

"I didn't. I just didn't want to go home with Sean tonight, and you shouldn't be going home with some guy just because you're up-set about Dave." I am still propping her up as we get into the eleva-tor. "Besides, always leave them wanting more."

We get into the elevator, and the moment the door closes, Dawn stands up straight, back to her usual, glorious self.

As we walk out the door, and toward the limo, a good-looking guy says hi to me, and I turn around to talk to him.

"Honey, we are *not* doing the sidewalk sale," Dawn says as she pulls me by the arm away from my new crush and over to the car. She pulls out my phone.

"You've missed six calls," Dawn tells me, looking at my phone.

"Good," I say, smiling. "I'm glad you took the phone away. A mother would have cramped my style this evening."

"They're all from the 323 area code," Dawn says, reading my list of incoming phone calls.

"Gimme that!" I grab my phone and check the list. All six from Dave. I quickly dial *99, to retrieve my messages. He left three.

"Hi, it's Dave. Look, I know this is really short notice, but I've been invited to this party tonight by the guy who just produced Mel Gibson's latest movie. It's a little businessy, but it should be fun. Call me if you want to go. I'm on my cell. 323-555-6742. Beep."

The mechanized voice enlightens me: 8:02 P.M.

Damn it!

Message 2: "Okay, I'm pathetic," a slightly drunken Dave con-fesses. "I'm here at the party, and all I can think about is you, and what an idiot I am that I didn't call you sooner. If I had, you'd be sharing an exquisite Merlot with me. . . . I saw this thing at Costco for forty-eight bucks. Wait, was that crass that I said that? Anyway, maybe you'd be wearing that little black dress I loved so much, and we'd be talking about Billy Wilder movies, and instead you're prob-ably out with some fabulous guy who knows to call more than an hour before a party. And you probably never want to talk to me again. . . ." Is he flirting? Was that flirting? "Call me at 323 . . ." *Beep.*

"11:02 P.M.," the mechanized voice informs me. "Third new message."

"Hi. Me again. The machine cut me off, which I probably deserved. Anyway, my number's 323-555-6742. Call me."

As we walk up to the limo, Dawn gives me the evil eye. "Don't."

"I wasn't even thinking about it," I assure her.

"Yes, you were. But don't. It's a booty call."

"It's not a booty call if he started calling me at eight o'clock."

As the limo driver opens the door for us, Dawn begins her lecture. "Don't tell me, let me guess. He called to ask you out, then when you didn't call him back, he called again to apologize for not calling you sooner."

"Yes," I say as we settle into the car. "And tomorrow I'll call him back."

"Sure you will," my best friend retorts.

And she's right. I'm not home two minutes before I madly dial his cell phone. It only rings once.

"Hello?" Dave slurs into the phone.

For a moment, I am silent. What am I doing, calling a guy I barely know at two-thirty in the morning?

"Charlie? Please tell me it's Charlie," Dave says excitedly.

"Hi," I stammer. "Where are you?"

"Canter's Deli. I'm with a couple of buddies. Come meet us."

"Are you already eating?" I ask, a touch of irritation creeping into my voice.

"Yeah, but that's okay. Come meet us." Man, is his voice sexy. Well, I suppose I could just drive over for a minute. . . .

"No. I better not drive. I've been drinking," I say stoically.

"Me too!" he says, like that's a total coincidence. "Look, gimme your address again."

"I don't think you should be driving, either."

"She's in Silverlake," I hear him tell a friend at the table. "Yes, you *are* driving me . . . ," he yells to his friend. "Because she's the most luminous woman I've ever seen, and it took me six hours to finally get her on the phone, and I'm not getting off the phone until I see her." Dave then gets back to me. "You will stay on the phone with me until my friend drives me over there, right?"

Damn! Did I mention he looks like Tom Cruise? Shit! Shit! What to say? I wish Jamie was here to advise. . . .

"Wait! I've got it on my palm pilot. Here it is! 1912 Silverwood. Okay—I'll see you in twenty minutes!" And he hangs up.

I can't help myself. It doesn't matter what the guy looks like, he can't just invite himself over at three A.M. I call right back.

"Hello?" Dave answers.

"How do you know I'm home right now? How do you know I'm not with some other guy?" I say, maybe a little too belligerently.

"Oh," he says, disappointedly. "Are you with some other guy?"

"No."

"So you're at home?"

"I didn't say that."

The next time he speaks he sounds genuinely hurt. "Well, why did you call me if you didn't want to see me?"

I stare up at the ceiling. How do I get myself into such things? "Be here in twenty minutes, or don't come at all."

I hang up and race to the bathroom to brush my teeth. I then head to my closet, throwing off my evening clothes as I paw through my lingerie drawer. Silk pajamas—no. Ripped T-shirt— definitely not. Ah—a red lace teddy. Perfect. I put it on, then throw a white terry-cloth robe over it. This way, it'll look like I was going to bed, but just happen to be wearing something sexy once in bed. I run over to my book of advice:

If a man calls you at three a.m., he is giving you what we in the 00s called a "booty call." He wants only one thing—do not give it to him. Have some self-respect.

Well, it is good advice.

Twenty minutes later, my doorbell rings. I have brushed my teeth, gargled Listerine, changed my sheets, sprayed Chanel No. 5 on my sheets, sprayed Chanel No. 5 on my neck for good measure, and reapplied my lipstick.

Okay, so I didn't listen to my own advice. Like I'm the first woman in the world who's ever done that.

Four

The heart has a mind of its own.

The following morning, I wake up, and a feeling of love washes over me. Ah, if I thought about it for a few moments—this really could be the guy I'm with forever. Dare I even think . . . no, not yet. With a smile as big as a hippo's, I roll over and put my head on Dave's chest. I look at him, beaming. . . .

It's then that I realize it's over.

He's awake. He's tense. I feel like if he could chew his arm off. . . .

"Good morning," he says, his words catching in his throat.

Translation: "I need to get the fuck out of here."

"Good morning," I say, then I kiss him. It was worth a shot. His lips actually purse. There's an awkward silence that lasts, oh, about half a year.

I finally abort our pregnant pause. "You want to go get some breakfast?" I ask sweetly.

Translation: "Please don't make me feel horrible about what I did last night."

"No. I should get going," he says awkwardly, getting up to leave.

"Something I said?" I joke. I can't help myself. I just can't wait by the phone for another week, second-guessing every detail of last night.

Dave forces a smile as he puts on his underwear. "No. Not at all. You're great. You're amazing, in fact."

"So, naturally, you're leaving," I say, clutching the sheets to keep them over my naked chest as I sit up.

Dave sighs, then sits back down on the bed. "Are you seeing anyone right now?"

I thought I was seeing him. Silly me. But I'm smart enough to know not to enlighten him with that bit of obvious information. "Um . . . there might be a few other guys sniffing around."

"What a relief," he practically belts out. "I mean, I figured you were seeing a bunch of men—a woman who looks like you. Truth is, there's this girl I've been seeing for a bit. She's not my girlfriend, or at least I haven't started calling her my girlfriend yet, but I'm feeling really guilty right now—so I guess she is."

As Dave continues his monologue, and proceeds to get dressed, I stay firmly entrenched in all my covers. There's no way he's seeing me naked again. I'm humiliated enough.

I won't even finish the story. Every modern woman has lived through it. Let's just move on.

There will never be peace in the Middle East.

Well, not the most creative thing I could write, but I'm right, aren't I? I'm sitting at a Beverly Hills wedding salon, waiting for my sister to arrive to put me in something hideous. I don't want to write another anti-wedding comment in my book of advice because, let's face it, women love weddings. We love everything about them. We love the cake, the champagne, the being the center of attention, all the gifts. We love that we can make our nearest and dearest look like a giant cupcake, and not feel the least bit guilty about it.

That said, I've just been dumped. I feel bitter.

No one's here yet, so I open one of the bridal magazines to make myself feel worse. Here's an article that says, "A surprising trend in the South: one out of five brides opts for a wedding with fewer than 100 in attendance." What surprises me is that the other four have more than that. The article then informs me that one of the most popular wedding themes is Cinderella. Yeah—'cuz it worked out for Princess Diana so nicely. I flip through the pages to an article entitled: "The Best Dresses Right Now: Princess Gowns, Outrageous Ruffles"—those must be for the bridesmaids and not the bride— "and One Marvelous Mini!" I turn to the page with the minidress. Yikes! Who would the bride be wearing this for? Is she planning to pick someone up at her own wedding?

Next article: "Tiaras for Springtime!" I would think you would have to be pretty ballsy to wear a tiara, unless your first name happens to be preceded by the title "Princess."

On the next page are some invitations with teddy bears on them. I pull out my notebook and write:

If you are publicly declaring yourself an adult, and old enough to get married, try to avoid teddy bears and cartoon characters for your wedding invitations.

"You look like shit." I look up, and there's my brother Jamie.

"I was up until six this morning," I inform him. "Then I got dumped around eight. What are you doing here?"

"Mom said I had to come so we could take Andy to lunch for her twenty-ninth birthday. Sorry about the dumping. First time?"

"No. I'm happy to report I've been dumped before. Thanks for asking," I say, slamming the magazine shut.

"I meant did you sleep with him for the first time?" Jamie asks.

"That's none of your business."

"Oooh, first time. Ouch," Jamie says, rubbing my shoulder sympathetically.

"How would you know that? I didn't say that!"

My brother Jamie is six years younger than me, five younger than our sister. My parents call him the "oops" baby, but I suspect he was the second choice in that old "save the marriage" adage: new house, new baby, new kitchen. He is the light of my life, which I mean in as unsick and un–Angelina Jolie a way as possible.

Having a little brother is like getting information from the enemy camp. When he was the tender age of five, he explained to me that Bill Gardner must have a crush on me, or he wouldn't call me every day to stay silent on the phone.

"Was he drunk?" Jamie asks knowingly.

I sigh. "Yes."

"Were you?"

Yes, I was, but I'm sure as hell not going to admit it. "I'm not sure I like where this conversation's going."

"Dopamine," Jamie says. "That's your problem."

I open the magazine again and pretend to read. Jamie says nothing further. Damn. Finally I close the magazine. "Okay, I'll bite. What's dopamine?"

"It's the chemical your body makes when you're drunk. It makes you happy," Jamie informs me.

"I thought that was oxytocin."

"No, that just makes you all unnecessarily attached to us. Dopamine makes you happy. The problem is, if you've had too much to drink, the following morning, you wake up depressed, because your body's out of dopamine. That's why you should never sleep with a man the first time when he's drunk. If you do, the next morning he wakes up depressed, and he associates you with his depression. Which, to answer your next question, is why all of us say we'll call you, then never do."

I furrow my brow, and stare at him incredulously. "Where do you come up with this stuff?"

"*Cosmopolitan* magazine," Jamie says proudly. "And I have a lot of ex-girlfriends, and if I didn't listen to them and all their theories, they wouldn't still call me at two A.M. when they need some . . . uh . . . someone to listen to them."

"God, a two A.M. booty call. You long for those things when you're married," my cousin Jenn says, waddling up to us. I'm not being insulting—Jenn is six months pregnant, and that pregnant woman waddle is just starting to take.

I stand corrected on not knowing anyone who got engaged in less than a year. Jenn met her husband—get this—at a wedding. On Valentine's Day. He proposed on their fifth date.

She told him to get serious—she was still in her Residency. (Yes, she's a doctor, besides. Couldn't you just puke?) She "didn't have time" for a relationship. Besides, Rob was an English professor—what could they possibly have in common?

Everything. Jenn actually found a man who liked watching *Mad About You* reruns at two A.M. And could use the word *casuist* in a sentence, and not sound like Diane Chambers from *Cheers*.

Rob proposed every day until their six-month anniversary, when she finally said yes.

They were married, to the day, one year after they met.

They've been happily married ever since, and now have a four-year-old, Alex; a three-year-old, Sean; and another one on the way.

Jamie kisses Jenn on the cheek. "You look great."

Jenn gives him a kiss back. "Please. I've put on thirty pounds already. But thank you." She turns to me. "Have you heard the latest? Black is out, she's back to putting us in orange."

"Salmon," I correct her.

"Yeah, I looked that up. It turns out it's orange."

Jenn was one of those rare brides who picked nice bridesmaids' dresses for Andy and me that we could actually wear again. They were velvet, dark purple—gorgeous. So, for some odd reason, when she became Andy's bridesmaid she thought it would be quid pro quo.

Silly rabbit.

"Like it's not bad enough I'm going to have to be rolled down the aisle—now I have to look like I'm swimming upstream."

"Actually, since you've already spawned, I think you're swimming downstream now," I joke.

"I'm going to get even. I swear I will," Jenn assures me. "Mark my words—I'm a pregnant cranky woman with insomnia—I have time to plot my revenge."

"Charlie has to wear silver," Jamie informs her.

Jenn turns to me with an "Oh my God" look of disgust just as my sister rushes in.

"I'm sorry I'm late," Andy says, breathless. "I've just had the most hideous fight with Hunter." Yes—Hunter. That's her fiancé's real name. We were so relieved to find out his last name wasn't Green. "He's just being horrible. And on my birthday, too!"

Jamie and I exchange glances. None of us want to know, but we can't help but ask.

Sigh. I guess I'll take the bomb. "What happened?"

"I asked him to come today, and do you know what he said?" Andy's voice is getting high enough to rival Minnie Mouse, and she looks like she's about to burst into tears.

"I'm sure whatever you want will be fine," Jamie says.

"I'm sure whatever you want will be fine!" Andy says at the same time, although in a much more frantic tone. "Like this wedding isn't important to him at all." She pulls out a tissue and dabs her eyes.

"Well . . . ," I begin, trying to calm her down. "You should see that as a compliment. It means he trusts your taste."

"And that's just the beginning!" Andy nearly screams at me. "Do you know what he did when I took him to register last night?!"

"What's 'register' mean?" Jamie leans in to ask Jenn.

"It's when you pick out a bunch of presents you want people to buy for you," Jenn tells him.

"Cool! You mean like a letter to Santa Claus?" Jamie asks, beaming as he turns to Andy. "Can you register for an Xbox?"

"No!" she exclaims, then turns to me. "Anyway, we were looking at linens, and he picks this revolting maroon duvet . . ."

Jamie looks at me questioningly. "Blanket," I tell him.

". . . that just screams, 'Hi, I'm a bachelor, and I don't want to get married.' So naturally, I'm appalled and I tell him so. Only I don't want to be rude, so I just say, 'Honey, I don't think there's a dust ruffle to match that.' And he actually says to me—"

"What's a dust ruffle, and why do you need one?" Jamie asks.

For this, Andy slaps him on the arm. "That's exactly what he said."

"I was just asking," Jamie tells her, then looks over to me inquisitively.

"It's something you put on the bed that hangs over the space underneath the bed," I enlighten him.

"Oh. So, like, you can hide your dirty clothes under there?" Jamie asks.

Andy's eyes widen. "If you're in a fraternity, yes! For most people it's to keep dust bunnies out from under your bed."

"But if they're under your bed, and no one can see them, who cares?" Jamie asks.

Andy slaps his arm again. Jamie rolls his eyes, but takes it like a man. Or should I say, a little brother who knows her wrath could be so much worse.

"Anyway, Hunter's taken no interest in anything about the wedding. It's like it's become all my job."

"Didn't you quit your job just to—" Before I even finish the sentence, I know I'm toast.

"Whose side are you on?!" Andy screeches at me. I can tell from her body language, she's thinking about swatting me, too. But I'll hit back, and a bride and maid of honor rolling around on the floor of the bridal salon pulling each other's hair out would be tacky.

"Sweetie, calm down," Jenn says. "Let me explain how this works. If men were interested in planning weddings, there'd be subscriptions to *Modern Groom* magazine. There aren't. You do the math."

Andy is about to slap her on the arm, but Jenn puts up her dukes. "Look, I have no shame in my condition. I'll sit on you."

Andy sighs heavily, then pulls a folded magazine page from her purse. "Look at this. It's how to deal with various types of groom personalities." Andy unfolds the paper and gives it to Jamie to read. Then she looks at me. "I'm thinking of calling it off."

Knowing she does not mean that for a second, I provide the reassurance that she needs in her moment of insecurity and crisis. "And give up the one-and-a-half-carat ring?"

"If he really loved me, he'd show interest in the thing I was interested in," Andy says, then points to the article Jamie's reading. "Look at this one: 'The "Take Charge" Groom.' This is a man who is so excited about his wedding, he is planning every detail, to the exclusion of his lovely bride."

"This is a man who hasn't come out yet," my brother says.

To which my father yells from the doorway, "Will you guys stop it with that! I'm not gay!" I look over, and there are my parents. My father is holding a big silver wrapped box, which I'm going to guess is Andy's first wedding gift.

He hands it to her as I ask, "What are you doing here?"

"Your mom wanted to get a man's opinion of what you're wearing. Plus, she offered to buy me lunch afterwards."

Andy opens the present. It's a maroon dust ruffle. My father beams. "I found it at Bloomingdales! Now you don't have to fight about it anymore!"

Andy bursts into tears. The day went downhill from there. Which led me to my final word of advice for my descendant:

If heredity is real—we're both screwed.

Five

No one should have to wake up if the small hand is still on the left side of the clock.

I awaken at four A.M. Monday morning (the right side of the clock—which is even worse) to start my day. Bleary-eyed, I slam down the button on my alarm clock, then pick up the phone to call Drew.

He answers on the first ring with a frantic, "I'm up!"

"Good," I say, suppressing a yawn and lighting a cigarette. "The P.A. is going to pick you up at four-forty precisely."

"Got it. Call me back in fifteen minutes," he orders, yawning, then hangs up on me.

I hang up the phone, putter over to my shower, quickly do the morning washing routine, then walk back to the phone and dial him at 4:20.

"I'm up!"

"I gave you five extra minutes," I tell Drew.

"Christ, I need water."

"Are you hung over?" I ask as I rub moisturizer into my face.

"No," he says indignantly. "Maybe. What's it mean when a woman says she's not looking for a relationship?"

"It means, 'Talk me into it.'"

"Damn, that's what I thought. So much for a port in Maui."

I light another cigarette, and jot down in my book:

There's no such thing as free sex. Eventually you pay for it.

A woman pays for it differently than a man—we wait by the phone, and fill ourselves with self-loathing—but it's still a universal.

"Which P.A.'s picking me up?" Drew asks, cutting into my thoughts.

"Madison, I think."

"Is that a guy or a girl?"

"Guy."

"Then five more minutes," Drew says, and hangs up.

Three calls later, and we're all on our way to Stage 8 of the 20th Century Fox lot.

I love being on sets. It's like being at Disneyland. There's something about walking into an old haunted house, or a Park Avenue walkup, or a Christmas village—complete with snow and glittery ice—that reminds me of the sense of magic and wonder I had as a kid.

On this particular set, for the movie *In My Heart,* there's fake snow and glitter everywhere. It's a romantic comedy, and the stage is decorated to look like Christmas in an East Coast sea village.

As I walk on the set, I am dusted with glitter—literally. It rains down from above.

"Sorry Charlie!" I hear one of the art department guys yell.

"No problem, George. Good morning!" I say brightly as I step over some wide cables and head to Craft Service to pick up my morning coffee.

This is where I see Jordan Dumaurier sipping a coffee with several of the crew guys.

There's no such thing as a perfect man.

Jordan is perfect. Have you ever seen a young Parker Stevenson in old *Hardy Boys* reruns? Jordan looks so much like him, that on the first day of the shoot, several girls on set checked the call sheet to make sure his last name wasn't Stevenson. (This is Hollywood. You never know. I remember years ago telling this actor named Ty that he was a dead ringer for Tyrone Power. Turns out Ty's full name was Tyrone Power Jr. Oops.)

Anyway, Jordan's last name was Dumaurier—no relation to anyone famous. Jordan Dumaurier. Hmm. Charlize Dumaurier. A bit "character from *All My Children*," but you know, it's a sacrifice I'm willing to make.

Jordan's the film's still photographer, which means he takes pictures of the actors during rehearsals. Those pictures are then used for press kits and the DVD box. It also means he has lots of time to talk throughout the day. Which is what he is doing at this very moment.

"Man—you're wrong! Magic Johnson is the best player of all time," Jordan says as I pour myself a cup of coffee, eavesdropping on their conversation.

"Dude," Keenan, a beefy grip, argues, "wrong MJ—Michael Jordan. Five MVPs and six championship rings. And if he hadn't taken time off to play baseball, he'd have eight rings instead of six."

I sneak over to them with my coffee. I stare at the ground and try to remember how to breathe. It's stupid, I know, but every time I get around this guy, I feel like a geeky little teenager with braces and bad skin.

"You're both wrong. What about Wilt?" Jeff, the focus puller, vehemently disagrees. "One hundred points in a single game. He *averaged* fifty points a game one year." Jeff turns to me. "Help me out here, Charlie."

Reminds me to write in my book:

Most women have no interest in sports. Don't apologize for it.

"Um . . . ," I say, looking down at my shoes nervously. Damn it! Say something witty, something really clever. . . .

"Charlie's got my back on this," Jordan says brightly. "She knows Magic could've led the league in scoring if he'd wanted to. He made everybody on the team better. Plus, Magic played against better competition. How many rings did Michael win before Magic and Bird retired? Just one. And Wilt only won two his whole career." I look up timidly to see he's smiling the most gorgeous smile, and looking *right at me*. (Yikes!) "That's what you were going to say, right?"

"Uh . . . I think Johnson was quite good," I say weakly.

"Charlie! How can you agree with him?" Keenan lays into me. "Michael never had big-time players around him in the early days. He wasn't just a big scorer, either—Rookie of the Year, Defensive Player of the Year, thirteen All-Star games—and he was still a star at age forty."

Okay, when guys start quoting sports statistics, all I hear is "Blah-blah-blah, blah-blah-blah, blah." But to point that out right now might not be clever and cute, so instead I nearly whisper, "Well, you make a valid point, too."

"Check back in five years and you'll all be wrong." I hear Drew next to me as he puts his arm around my shoulder. "Check back in five years and, one word, LeBron."

There's a round of "Hey Drew"s and "How's it going?"s.

"Splendid," Drew tells them. "Had a sweet weekend in Maui *and* this really hot girl called me from out of the blue. I'm thinking of taking her to the wrap party next week."

Uh-oh. "What girl?" I ask nervously, hoping to God it's not Dawn.

"Cool," Keenan says. "Is she J. Lo hot or Britney hot?"

"She's 'makes Halle Berry look like Hattie McDaniel' hot."

Shit.

We get one "cool" from Jordan, a "sweet" from Jeff, and a "daaammmnnn," from Keenan, followed by an appreciative high-five for Drew.

"Thanks," Drew says as he high-fives Keenan. "I've got to get to Makeup. But Jordan, I have a question for you. I'm having a little dinner party this Thursday night after work. Are you available as a photographer for some candids?"

I can tell from the look on Jordan's face that he thinks the question is a bit odd, but he's not about to say no to the film's star. "Yeah, sure."

"Great. It's at my house, seven o'clock. There will be an hors d'oeuvres hour, followed by a three-course meal—should be over around midnight. A thousand dollars enough?"

Jordan's eyes nearly bug out. "Are you kidding? That's great."

My eyes, on the other hand, have narrowed into suspicious little slits. I stare at Drew as he leads me away, yelling over his shoulder to Jordan, "Charlie will give you the address. Dress up a little—I want you to be a guest as well, so the other guests feel relaxed enough for pictures."

When we're far enough away, I say under my breath, "What dinner party? I don't have anything scheduled for you."

"Yeah, I'm gonna need you to arrange a dinner party for me," Drew says cheerfully. "Come with me to my trailer."

We get to Drew's trailer, and Drew walks in ahead of me. As I enter, a palm frond smacks me in the face.

"Careful," Drew warns me a second too late.

I instinctively grab my face to check for blood, then step into Drew's trailer, newly decorated to look like a native Hawaiian hut from the 1800s.

"Aloha," Drew says, smiling wide as he puts a purple pikake lei over my head, and kisses me on the cheek. "Do you like what I've done with the trailer? Pretty cool, huh?"

I put my hands on my hips and look around. The walls are adorned with palm fronds and flowers, grass mats cover the floors, old koa wood rocking chairs replace his plush purple couches, and slack-key guitar music is being piped in from God knows where.

"It's very . . . striking," I say delicately. "What did you do with your old couches?"

Drew opens a small refrigerator and hands me a premade Mai Tai. "I moved them to my house. Why? Do you want them?"

"Yes," I say immediately. They are $10,000 dark purple velvet couches that he had made when he found out his chakras were purple, and decided to redo his trailer all in purple in order to have his surroundings be more in harmony with his chakra. That would be two weeks ago. If it weren't for Drew's constant quest for spiritual fulfillment (always accompanied by a frenzy of redecorating), I wouldn't have any furniture in my house. That's another benefit of working for a movie star—all the free castoffs.

Drew turns on some electric tiki torches and little plastic tiki dancers that remind me of the Brady Bunch visiting Hawaii. He stretches his arms out wide, basking in his new surroundings. "Oh, I love the feeling you get when you're in Hawaii. It's so spiritual!"

Light-up dancers are spiritual?

"I'm thinking of becoming a kahuna," Drew says, handing me a bowl of macadamia nuts.

"A what?" I ask.

"A kahuna. It's sort of like a high priest in Hawaii." He pops a nut into his mouth, grabs a Mai Tai for himself, then sits on one of the rocking chairs. "I've decided when I'm finished with the film, I'm going to move to Hawaii and study the religion of its people."

"Which is what?" I ask, taking the rickety old rocking chair across from him.

Drew looks confused. "Which is what—what?"

"The religion of the Hawaiian people—the one you want to study. What's it called?"

Drew considers that for a moment. "I'm not really sure. I suppose that will be my first question on my journey to self-enlightenment.

"Now." Drew's face suddenly turns serious. "We need to talk."

Nothing good has ever come from a conversation that begins with, "We need to talk." And, frankly, what it really means is, "You need to listen."

Drew continues, "I met with a fortune teller in Maui, who was brilliant by the way, and we need to spend more time together."

Uh-oh.

"We already spend sixty hours a week together," I calmly point out.

"Yes. But that's as employer and employee. We need to start hanging out as friends."

I've never been so scared in my life. Is there such a thing as friendly harassment?

"Starting with Thursday," Drew continues. "I'd like you to be a guest at my dinner party. Of course, I'd also like you to organize the party. Now, we'll need a cheese course—I read somewhere that this year everyone's doing cheese."

I open my work notebook (not to be confused with my advice notebook) and jot down "cheese course" as I remind him, "You're not allowed to have cheese."

"I'm not?" he asks, sounding genuinely surprised.

"No. Your doctor told you to cut down on your meat, and to cut out bacon and cheese entirely."

Drew looks at me like this is the first he's heard of it. "Why?"

"Because your cholesterol's two-twenty."

"Well, isn't there a pill or something I can take for that?" he asks.

The question must be rhetorical, because before I can answer, he gets up from the rocking chair and begins pacing around the trailer like a caged jaguar. I can hear the grass mats crunching underneath him. "Get Phil to cater, and have him include Brie. I love Brie."

I write down "Brie" in my notebook. "What if Phil isn't available on such short notice?" I ask, hoping this will dissuade him enough to cancel the evening.

"Then get the sous chef he had—what's his name?"

"Dante?"

Drew jerks his head toward me and stops mid-pace. "Dante? Seriously? Greek?"

"No. Upstate New York white bread, but with hippie parents."

"Dante." Drew stands lost in thought for a moment. "What do you think of the name Dante Stanton?"

"I think your mother would kill you."

"I don't mean for me. I meant if I ever had a son."

"I think you'll have enough to fight about with your son without adding his name to the list."

"Olives!" Drew points to me accusingly, and I recoil, startled. He begins pacing again. "Greeks do the best olives! Let's have an olive platter."

I puff out my cheeks, and breathe out slowly, trying to relax as I write down "Olive platter." This has red flags all over it. "What do you want for the main course?"

"I don't know. What's Dawn's favorite food?"

"Martinis," I say sarcastically.

Drew stops again. "You know, I'm picking up a negative vibe here."

I put down my pen. "I'm sorry. It's just . . . I'm not sure if Dawn is available Thursday night."

"Oh, she is. I called her, and actually it's the only night she's available this week. So I booked her."

Rats.

Drew pulls out a piece of paper from his pocket. "As a matter of fact . . . she said there was some reason for you to be the guest of honor." He reads the scrap of paper. "Yeah, here it is! Turns out you're turning thirty next week." He says it like, "Wow—did you know fourteen percent of Americans go to McDonalds on any given day?"

He stuffs the paper back in his pocket. "Do you think I should get you a cake?"

What I want to say is, "I think you should get me a Valium the size of a donut." But instead, I sit in a stunned stupor.

Drew points to me and says—in a tone I swear to God is exactly like my mother's—"You know, you're not getting any younger. It's time we found you a man."

That shocks me out of my silence. I stand up. "I hear George Clooney's looking for a new assistant. Been nice working for you."

Before I can get to the door, Drew takes my arm and spins me back around. "Look, I'm not getting any younger, either. I'll be thirty-three in a few months, and what have I got to show for it? One divorce, a broken engagement, and a mother who calls me once a week to let me know if she doesn't get grandchildren soon, I'm out of her will."

I look at him, confused. "Didn't you buy her her house?"

"Not the point." Drew pulls me back to my rocking chair, kneels down next to me like he's going to propose, and puts both his hands over mine. "When I was in Maui, I was on a beautiful balcony by myself, watching this gorgeous sunset, and all I could think about was what Dawn would think of the sunset."

He turns his eyes away from me, as though he's embarrassed by this new vulnerability I'm seeing. "Don't you want someone to come home to? Don't you want to find someone who knows everything about you—even the stuff you wish to God weren't true—and loves you anyway? Isn't there someone you want seeing your sunset?"

He looks like he's about to cry. I glare at him. "That's a speech from your last movie," I say accusingly.

Drew stands up, and his voice immediately changes back to normal. "Well, of course it is. But why is it such good dialogue?" He gestures emphatically with clenched fingers. "Because it resonates. . . ." He looks around his trailer. "I think I need some wooden carvings. Maybe of Pele. She's the fire goddess, you know. That would make the room more authentic, don't you think?"

Drew walks around the trailer, and continues to monologue about authentic Hawaiian replicas. I tune him out, instead thinking about what he just said about finding someone (the fact that a writer wrote it for him notwithstanding).

The dinner is a really bad idea. And when Drew has really bad ideas, I'm the one whose job it is to bring him back to reality. To keep his life in order. To keep him grounded: get him to his appointments, meetings, and dinners in time for . . . what? For him to go home to an empty house?

For me to go home to an empty house?

I heave out a big sigh. "Dawn's favorite meal is coq au vin."

Drew turns to me, smiles wide, and kisses me on the cheek. "Chicken it is. I'm going to invite Doug Adler—he's a manager who's been after me to sign with him. He's single, and I think you two might hit it off. I've also invited Jordan for obvious reasons. And then there's this yoga instructor . . . a little crunchy granola, but a nice guy—"

"Whoa, whoa, whoa," I interrupt. "What do you mean you asked Jordan 'for obvious reasons'?"

"Oh, come on! You look at him the way I look at a Krispy Kreme. And, frankly, the only reason I'm speechless in front of a Krispy Kreme is because I've already got it in my mouth. Whereas you haven't had Jordan—"

"Please stop," I say immediately. "If you love me, you won't finish that thought."

Drew's lips purse, and his eyes get wide. "I do love you. Just because I'd rather say things like that onscreen than to a real person doesn't mean I don't feel it."

That's the best compliment Drew's ever given me—and I have no response. Saying "I love you, too," to your boss sounds disingenuine.

But Drew waits for me to say it anyway.

"And you love me, too . . . ," he says with a "repeat after me" tone.

"And I love you, too," I say awkwardly.

He gives me a self-satisfied smile. "Good. By the way, just in case things go well, I need you to go to the pharmacy to pick up some Viagra for me. I had the doctor leave it under your name."

For a second there, I thought we were going to have a warm, fuzzy moment. Silly me. "Drew, isn't it bad enough I had to pick up that rash cream for you under my name?"

Drew looks at me blankly, not following.

I continue. "I'm not really comfortable with the pharmacist thinking I have a sex problem."

"As long as you're out, why don't you buy yourself a new dress for the party," Drew says, pulling several $100 bills out of his wallet and handing them to me.

I immediately grab them. "A pleasure doing business with you."

Drew puts his wallet back into his pocket, and turns his back to me, suddenly concentrating on his script.

This would be my cue to leave.

As I turn to go, he almost whispers, "I also realized in Maui that you are one of the nicest, most genuine people I know, and you deserve to be happy."

He doesn't say anything else, and his back is still to me.

"Thank you," I say quietly, then leave him to his work.

Should I have stayed and pointed out that paying some guy $1,000 to be my pseudo-date for the evening probably wouldn't make me happy? Of course I should have!

But I thought about a quote I would later put in my book of advice:

Insanity: doing the same thing over and over again and expecting different results.—Albert Einstein

I mean, what I'd been doing so far hadn't given me a soul mate. Why not try something new?

Besides, I can't remember the last time a man was so determined to make me happy, even if it was for his own selfish reasons.

Six

A hostess should always have a glass of something fabulous on hand to serve to her guests.

I'm paraphrasing Colin Cowie. I'm not sure I'm always the best hostess, but I have to say, I love the sentiment.

If you don't know who Colin Cowie is—he is L.A.'s host extraordinaire! Imagine Martha Stewart being gracious, instead of condescending. Which reminds me:

If you ever want a good laugh, go find some old TV shows from a woman named Martha Stewart. She used to teach women in the 21st century such useless wastes of time as making your own wrapping paper, gluing seashells onto tissue boxes, and how to fold fitted sheets.

I hated her before the insider trading. I mean, why not just roll the fitted sheet in a ball and throw it in your linen closet like everyone else? And do you ever wonder who's actually making aluminum foil Christmas ornaments using "thirty-six-gauge aluminum foil" and "tin snips," then giving the ornament "a tarnished finish" with the use of extrafine steel wool and something called aluminum blackener?

But I digress.

Monday morning, about an hour after Drew and I talked, Dawn called to tell him that Colin Cowie's catering company was my absolute favorite, and suddenly, Dante the Greek was out, and Colin's people were in.

Then Drew took it upon himself to plan the whole event. I didn't have to lift a finger. He invited the guests, planned the menu, even had his dining room painted—again. I am actually getting to show up tonight as a guest. A real guest.

It's Thursday night, and I am dressed in a brand-new sparkly black dress (slightly above the knee, so as to be sexy, yet not trashy), black seamed stockings (I read it makes a man run his eyes up your leg) and FM pumps (just in case they don't get the other two, more subtle, messages).

As I drive over to Brentwood on this cool, drizzly Los Angeles night, I feel glamorous, sexy, and hopeful. There is nothing that could bring down my mood.

Except the phone ringing.

I make the mistake of putting on my headset and taking the call. "Hello."

"Put the scanner gun down, and no one gets hurt!" Andy yells into the phone.

"Hi, Andy."

"Sorry. *Someone* was trying to sneak a set of barbecue tongs onto our registry," she says accusingly.

"The nerve of some guys. Finally showing interest in the registry," I respond sarcastically. "The man should be shot."

"Will you just go over to linens and look at fingertip towels?" Andy says in irritation.

"Andy, as much as I'd like to listen to you argue with your beloved, I'm about to go into a canyon. . . ."

"Okay, this'll just take a second. I've decided on your shoes. I opted for the ones we looked at that looked like a tap shoe, only with a chunky wedge heel instead of the thin one, and also the two-inch strap across the top now has a fabric peony."

"A what?"

"It's a kind of flower."

I cringe. "I suppose one that can be dyed to match the silver dress?"

"Absolutely! And they'll do it for free, so you only pay the two hundred sixty dollars plus tax."

"Two hundred sixty dollars for a pair of dyed-to-match shoes I'll never wear again?!" I scream into my headset.

"They're Italian silk satin."

"They're the ugliest things I've ever seen."

"That's because you haven't met the groom's mother yet," Andy whispers to me.

"Andy!" I scream. Then I inhale—one, two, three—and exhale—one, two, three. "Andy," I say, determined to sound calm if it kills me, "I love you. But I do not have two hundred sixty dollars to spend on a pair of shoes."

"What about those Stuart Weitzman shoes you bought for three hundred dollars?"

"That doesn't count. I was using Drew's credit card, which he said I could after the camel incident, so it wasn't my money. And besides . . ."

I stop at a red light, and don't finish my sentence. I don't have a "besides." This is her wedding. She's only going to do this once (or "twice at the most" as her wedding coordinator keeps reminding us), and how I act on this occasion could be held against me for many moons to come.

"Fine," I sigh, "but I draw the line at the faux fur stole."

"I totally agree," Andy assures me. "We decided on real fur."

"Dyed to match?" I ask through gritted teeth, my hands clenching the steering wheel. The guy in the SUV to my right, who had pulled around me to speed past when the light turns green, takes one look at my face and lets his car drift backward.

"Of course," Andy says. "I mean, what animal rights crazy is gonna throw a paint ball at you in the middle of the Hotel Bel Air?"

I decide not to point out that a big paint splotch in the middle of my dress might be an improvement. Instead I say, "Buy the shoes, buy the stole. I'll pay you back. I'm at Drew's now. I gotta go."

"Did he get his invitation yet?" Andy asks.

"Did I get my invitation yet?" I ask, irritated.

"Of course not. I know you're coming. The first round went to people who might be busy."

Before I can verbally take offense, Andy yells, "We're not getting Emeril—we're getting All Clad! Drop that paella pan this instant!" to Hunter, then a quick "Gotta-go-love-you-bye," to me.

I pull up to the iron gate of Drew's house and buzz the intercom. A man's voice with a British accent answers, "Good evening. How may I be of service?"

"Hi. This is Charlie Edwards. I'm here for the dinner party," I yell into the intercom like I'm ordering a double double at In-N-Out at two in the morning.

"Excellent. Mr. Stanton has been expecting you."

The black gate slowly slides open, and I drive through the gate, down a gray stone driveway, and into a circle filled with cars all more expensive than my Toyota Prius (and all owned by Drew).

Later I would write in my notebook:

Never judge someone by the car they drive.

But actually, I'm totally intimidated in this mini parking lot of luxury vehicles, so I park and get out of my car as quickly as possible, so no one can guess which one is mine.

Drew's mansion is sort of a Mediterranean villa surrounded by an enchanted forest of rose bushes, Hawaiian orchids, and trees. I walk up the gray slate footpath, now dotted with candles leading up to the doorway.

I push the doorbell, and hear the melody of "Play that Funky Music White Boy," but in a doorbell tune.

A butler, who I do not recognize, answers. "Good evening," he says as he opens the door for me to enter. "May I take your coat?"

"Yes, thank you," I say, as though having this level of exceptional service is the norm for me. "I'm sorry. I don't think we've met. I'm Charlie, Drew's assistant. I don't think I've seen you here before."

"I'm only here for the evening," the butler tells me in the queen's English as he takes my coat. "I actually work for Master Puffy D, Master Stanton's neighbor. I'm on loan, so to speak."

"I love your accent," I say.

"And I yours, madam. My name is Jeeves, and I'm at your service."

While Jeeves (seriously?) puts my coat in the hall closet, I look around the front entry. Drew's house looks magical tonight, even more so than usual. The lights have been dimmed, candles flicker everywhere around me, and Sarah McLachlan's CD *Fumbling Towards Ecstasy* lilts in the background.

"Mr. Stanton requests that you make yourself comfortable in the drawing room," Jeeves informs me.

Jeeves leads me to Drew's "drawing room" (what the rest of the world would call his living room).

I walk into the drawing room, and it's decorated even more exquisitely than the front hallway. A roaring fire crackles in the fireplace, and there are so many candles here, I feel like I'm at church (but in a good way). There's a fully stocked bar in the corner, complete with a bartender. Perfect.

Drew bounds in, looking positively stunning in a dark blue suit he had made at Saville Row last year, and waving a large ivory card in front of me.

"It came!" he yells excitedly, thrusting my sister's wedding invitation in my face. I grab it and look—teddy bears. Is she out of her fucking tree?

"Which tuxedo do you think I should wear?" Drew asks, beaming. "The Armani, the Gucci, or the Turnbull and Asser?"

"What's the one you had made when we went to England?" I ask, staring at the invitation and discovering that Hunter's middle name is Thompson (Thompson?).

"Turnbull and Asser," Drew says.

"Yeah, that one," I say distractedly, running my finger lightly over the invitation. They actually paid to have the teddy bears engraved. Good grief. "And wear those cufflinks you had made when we were there, too."

Drew's face lights up even more. "Ooohhh, you mean the diamond ones from Deakin and Francis. I love those. Remind me that we need to get back to London soon, and do some shopping."

Suddenly he furrows his brow and taps his index finger to his chin to give his "thinking face." "Wait, do you think I might look too flashy? I don't want to come off as too Hollywood."

"Don't be ridiculous," I say, still focused on the invitation, and wondering how Andy found salmon-colored sparkly ink. "Everyone's supposed to wear a tux. Besides, the Turnbull one makes you look hot."

Drew smiles, visibly surprised. "You think I'll look hot?"

"Huh?" I say, as I look up from the invitation. "What? Yeah. Definitely."

What I didn't tell him was the universal truth:

All men under forty look hot in tuxedos. All men over forty look distinguished.

The bartender hands us each a Christofle martini glass filled with chilled vodka with what looks like flecks of gold floating throughout. It looks like a snow globe souvenir of California during the gold rush.

"Try this," Drew says proudly. "It's the new drink: the Academy Award martini!"

I'm dubious, but I take a sip. The metal tastes . . . weird. I peer into the glass and squint my eyes. "What is this floating in my drink?"

"Edible gold leaf," Drew tells me. "I read about it in a magazine. The guy I bought it from says if you drink too much your poop can turn gold."

Drew makes this last statement with such joie de vive, I'm not sure how to respond. But before I can anything, I'm saved by the bell.

The doorbell rings and, within seconds, Bachelor #1 enters the drawing room. He is gorgeous: dark hair, smoldering dark eyes, and a perfectly chiseled body that can only come from working out actually being your career.

Drew's face lights up when he sees him.

"Chris!" he says brightly, walking up to him, doing the shaking of the hand with the half hug thing, then leading him to me. "Charlie, I'd like you to meet—"

"Hi, Chris," I interrupt, kissing Chris on the check. "How have you been?"

"Good, good," he says, smiling to show off his bright white teeth. "You? Your mother still making you crazy?"

"You have no idea," I say, then turn to Drew. "Drew, Chris is my mother's, um, gentleman friend."

"Part-time gentleman friend," Chris corrects me.

"Chris is my mother's whatever," I say. Which is true. When my mother first started dating this twenty-nine-year-old, we asked her what we should call him: boyfriend, friend, "Dad," pool boy? Mom said "whatever," and the name stuck.

Oh, another one for my book:

The difference between a middle-aged man and a middle-aged woman is that when a woman dates someone thirty years younger than her, at least she knows she looks like an idiot.

Okay, my mother doesn't, but most women would.

Chris and I talk for a few moments when the doorbell rings again. Jordan enters the drawing room, looking perfect in a gray suit, red silk tie, and a camera hanging around his neck. As I am about to say "hi," he flashes his camera to take my picture. I blink my eyes a few times, trying to clear up the green square filling my vision, as Jordan walks up to me.

"You look gorgeous," he says, taking my arm and kissing me on the cheek.

He kissed me! I think. Okay, just the cheek, but still . . . *and* he said I looked gorgeous.

"Thank you. You're not so bad yourself," I say.

Inwardly, I cringe at my lame response. You're not so bad yourself? What am I—Mae West?

Jordan smiles, blushes a little, and turns away. "I clean up okay. Look, since you're the only person I know here tonight, do you mind if I hang out with you when I'm not working?"

Is he serious?

"Oh sure," I stammer. "No problem. You can count on me. Maybe we can sit together at dinner . . ."

As I continue to babble, Jordan looks past me and his jaw nearly drops. I turn to see who or what he's looking at.

Behind a married couple coming in, I see Dawn, wearing a gold beaded bias cut dress with one slit up the leg to show off her perfect calf and thigh (and, frankly, her recent bikini wax, but maybe I'm being bitter).

"Charlie!" she yells to me, her face beaming. "Have I got gossip for you!"

I start to make my way toward her, only to be pushed out of the way by Drew.

"Dawn, you look stunning," he says, kissing her hand lightly.

It's a good thing men don't have tails, or this lovesick puppy would be wagging his so fast, it would look like a helicopter.

"Can I get you a drink? We have ice-cold martinis at the bar," Drew says as he takes Dawn's hand and begins to lead her to the bar.

"That would be lovely," Dawn says, then mouths to me, "Gossip."

"Great," Drew says, then yanks her toward the bar so fast it looks like her neck is going to snap backward. As they pass us, she turns to me, stretches her arms out wide, and mouths, "Huge."

I cock my head as Jordan takes a picture of Drew dragging poor Dawn to the bar.

Then he turns to me. "She's cute. What's her story?"

No! No! No!!! "Her story is she's a spectator sport," I say cattily. "Fun to watch, but if you try to go out on the field, there's going to be blood and broken bones all over the place."

It came out sounding harsh, but it's the truth, actually.

"That's a shame," Jordan says. "I have a friend who would have loved her."

Two more couples come in, both married. One couple I recognize—Gigi and Nick. She's a producer, and he's a stay-at-home dad. The other couple I don't recognize, but I assume they're married, since they both wear wedding rings, and seem to have no problem separating from each other long enough to mingle with the other guests.

This is usually a sign of an older, more secure couple. I hate it when I'm at a party talking to a guy, just chitchatting, only to have his ferocious young wife angrily introduce herself to me as "Mrs. Jones—Frank's wife" and verbally piss around her territory to let me know he's taken.

Dawn walks up to Jordan and me, sans Drew. "Hi, I'm Dawn. You must be Jordan." I glare at her. How would she know that if I hadn't told her all about him?

"I must be," he says, a little confused. "I'm surprised Drew has talked about me."

Dawn looks at me as I shake my head ever so slightly in disapproval.

"Um . . . okay," she says, putting her hand on my back and steering me away. "Listen, do you mind if I steal my girl for a minute?"

At that moment, Drew bounds up to us, a martini in each hand. "Dawn, I told you it would only take them a minute to make a martini without gold leaf. Why did you leave me?"

"Well, sweetie, I just assumed that you would want to go greet your other guests. I didn't want to get in the way."

"What other . . ."

Dawn points to the two other couples, and Drew frowns. "Oh. Right." He hands her a plain martini, and Jordan a gold one. "Promise me you won't move from this spot."

"I promise," she assures him.

Drew rushes away from us to greet his other guests. The three of us stare in his direction. He's so hyped up, I would swear he was on cocaine if I didn't know for a fact that he never touches the stuff. ("Kills my pot buzz," he insists.)

Dawn gently pushes Jordan toward Drew and the other guests. "Wouldn't it be divine if you got some snaps of the guests arriving. You know, before they're all drunk and bleary eyed?"

"Oh, yeah," Jordan says, snapping to attention. "Charlie, can you watch my drink?"

"Sure. It would be my honor."

"Thanks," he says, smiling that perfect smile, handing me his martini, and walking away.

"I'll be right here," I continue stupidly. "We're not going anywhere. Don't let your martini get warm. Umph . . ."

Dawn puts her hand over my mouth. "What's our rule?"

If you can't say something intelligent to a cute guy, shut the hell up!

"Correct," Dawn says, taking her hand off my mouth. She takes a sip of her martini. "Okay, now I have big news, but it's totally on the D.L."

I look at her blankly. "The what?"

"The D.L. You know, the downlow?"

I continue to look at her blankly. Dawn bites her inner cheek. "You know, sometimes I'm amazed you've ever had a black friend. The downlow: it means it's a secret!"

"Ooohhh . . ." My face lights up. "Is it about Justin Timberlake being gay?"

"No, it's about someone we know . . . So he's definitely gay?" Dawn asks, totally losing interest in her own gossip.

"I have no idea. You worked with him. So what's the gossip?"

Dawn looks around the room to make sure no one's listening. "Guess what I did all day?" Dawn says in that *I know something you don't know* singsongy tone. "You will never guess."

"Discovered the secret to cold fusion," I deadpan.

"I went engagement-ring shopping."

I stare at Dawn, in shock. She smiles and nods her head. I immediately leave her in a huff to give Drew a piece of my mind. "Oh, for God's sake. He's met you once, and talked to you on the phone twice. Drew!" Dawn flips me back around. "Not for me. For Kate. I went with Jack."

"Jack?"

"He's gonna propose tonight," she beams. "Like, for real. He got a room at the Hotel Bel Air, and he's going to take her there for drinks tonight, pop the question with a Tiffany's one-and-a-quarter-carat diamond solitaire, set in platinum, then retire for the evening in the room to celebrate. Isn't that romantic?"

"Wow," I say, stunned.

"Do you think she'll ask me to be the maid of honor?" Dawn asks.

"If she loves *me,* she will," I retort.

"What do you mean?"

"Have you been paying any attention to the hell I've been going through being my sister's maid of honor?"

"That's different. Your sister's nuts."

"Oh, yeah. And Kate's the pillar of sanity," I say sarcastically.

Drew appears, seemingly out of nowhere, with a good-looking man by his side. "Charlie, Dawn, I'd like you to meet Doug Adler. Doug is a manager over at Grovner, Caraway and Reese."

Doug's good-looking, but not in a "works too hard at it" kind of way. He's about six-foot-two, with wavy dark hair and green eyes. And he has good taste in suits, wearing a navy blue wool Brooks Brothers.

"Nice to meet you," we girls say.

"Charlie is my assistant—a real girl Friday. And Dawn . . . ," Drew nearly swoons, starstruck. "What can I say about Dawn? Other than her drink is empty. Will you two excuse us?"

He pulls Dawn away from me for the second time in less than five minutes, and I now have time to get better acquainted with Bachelor #2.

"So, have you known Drew very long?" Doug asks.

"About three years. You?"

"We met recently. I'm trying to convince him to become a client." Jeeves the butler silently hands him a gold martini, which he takes. "So, Drew tells me you live in Silverlake. Do you like it there?"

I hate small talk. Over the next ten minutes, I had to abridge my life down to I'm the oldest of three, never been married, no kids, and never been to Australia (the answer to a loaded question designed for him to go on and on about camping in the outback. Yawn.)

The entire time I was keenly aware that Jordan hadn't come back for his drink (though he did wave to me a few times while he walked around the room, taking everyone's picture).

"And what do you like to do for fun?" Doug asks.

I've had enough of this. Time to take the mask off. "Well, I like to wallow in self-pity while watching old *Mary Tyler Moore* reruns and eating Krispy Kremes hand over fist," I say, then gulp the last of my martini. "You?"

Doug smiles, genuinely amused. "Well, on Valentine's Day I like to wear all black, chain-smoke cigarettes, and watch *Casablanca* backwards."

Cute and funny.

But I still couldn't help mentally keeping track of where Jordan was at all times.

Once all the guests had arrived, Jeeves announced that we were to adjourn to the dining room.

Drew had redone his entire dining room—and not just for the *People* magazine shoot. The walls were now painted a dramatic red (Dawn's favorite color), and the whole room looked magical in gold and red.

The lights were dimmed to highlight the red and gold candles on and around the table. All different kinds of candles surrounded us: ruby red, square candles, gold pillar candles of assorted heights, votive candles in deep red cut crystal.

Drew's mahogany table was draped in a dark red silk tablecloth, which matched his new gold and red formal china, and gold flatware. Dark red roses floated in crystal centerpiece bowls, along with floating red and gold candles. Low square red and gold candles surrounded the bowls, flooding us with candlelight. Everything was low enough on the table that you could actually see all the guests while seated. (I hate it when the hostess has a gorgeous flower centerpiece so high I spend most of the meal craning my neck to look around it at the person seated across from me.)

Dinner was set for twelve. As we walked in and saw our place cards written in gold calligraphy, I was thrilled to discover that Drew had seated me at one head of the table, with Jordan to my right and Doug to my left. Drew sat at the other head of the table, with Dawn on his left and one of the married women on his right.

We began our meal with a cheese course. Along with Drew's triple crème Brie, they served a Saint André, which is another triple crème cheese that we learned came from the Rovergue zone of south-central France, a Reblochon, a Morbier, Parmigiano-Reggano, and a Gorgonzola, along with an assortment of olives, breads, figs, and cornichons (which are little pickles).

The caterers served the cheese course with a Domaine Ott Rosé from France. Contrary to what I thought of when I thought of rosé—which would be pink wine in a box on a kitchen counter somewhere—this wine was slightly sweet, and absolutely decadent.

Next came the salad course, Drew's favorite type of salad, called a "Flower of Endive." Basically, it's a circle of endive leaves standing up like a tulip, and tied together with an edible ribbon of a blanched leek. When the host announces it's time to let the flower "bloom," everyone unties their leek, and the endive leaves "blossom" into a salad of watercress, baby frisée lettuce, blue cheese, and pine nuts with a Dijon mustard dressing. The chef paired it with a Napa Valley chardonnay, which was also delicious.

During the first few courses, I had little time to see or speak with Jordan—he was too busy running around the table taking pictures.

But I did have a chance to get to know Doug better, and I liked what I saw.

"So what made you become a manager?" I ask. I sneak a glimpse of Drew putting his arm around Dawn's shoulder as Jordan takes a picture of them.

"Oh, I was a wimp," Doug says humbly. "I wanted to be a screenwriter, but I was terrible. Then I dabbled in acting, but I hated the auditions. So now I just send my clients to the auditions, and take ten percent."

"You were a screenwriter?" I say, knowing that's usually good for five minutes of small talk. "So what kind of stuff do you write?"

"Bad romantic comedies. But I don't want to talk about that. Everyone in town has a half-written screenplay. My fourteen-year-old neighbor has a half-written screenplay. Let's talk about books. What's your favorite book?"

He's buzzed—so maybe he's genuinely asking me that. But it sure sounds like a stupid first date question to me. "Hmm," I stall, "I guess it would have to be anything not written by Kafka."

"Could you be more specific?" he says, finishing his glass of chardonnay, then filling his and my glasses back up.

"*A Connecticut Yankee in King Arthur's Court,*" I finally decide.

"Why?" he asks, tilting his head, and looking genuinely interested.

"Because it made me laugh when I was twelve, and it made me cry when I was twenty. And that's a great book."

Jordan flashes his camera, catching me leaning in seductively toward Doug. Damn, didn't see him watching. I immediately turn to him. "Jordan, come sit with us. You've barely touched your wine or your salad."

"That's because I'm working," Jordan says, smiling at me pleasantly.

Doug smiles to Jordan. "When a beautiful woman asks you to join her, you should oblige."

Jordan gives Doug a weird look, like he's not sure if he's being challenged or not. Finally, he shrugs. "Okay," he says cheerfully. He sits down, puts down his camera, and picks up his glass. "Here's to beautiful women."

Doug raises his glass, and so do I.

"No, dear," Doug says, gently taking my hand and putting it down. "You don't toast yourself."

I smile awkwardly, happy to receive the compliment, but not sure how to take it in front of Jordan.

"So what were we talking about?" Jordan asks.

"Favorite books," Doug says. "Do you have one?"

"One? Kind of hard to narrow it down to one. But I guess it would have to be *Auntie Mame.*"

"Isn't that a movie?" Doug asks, slightly derisively.

"It is," Jordan says with a smile, either not noticing the veiled insult, or choosing to ignore it. "It's based on the book by Patrick Dennis."

The caterers begin clearing our salad plates. "Hmmm . . . ," Doug says with a patronizing tone. "Personally, I prefer the classics: *A Tale of Two Cities,* or *Plato's Republic.*"

"That's more of a play, don't you think?" Jordan asks innocently.

"It's philosophy," Doug counters.

"It's a dialogue written by Plato using Socrates and himself as the two main characters. That's a play, not a book. And if we're going to choose a favorite philosophy thinly disguised as a play, I'd have to go with Sartre's *No Exit.*"

Jordan turns to me. "Do you know the play?"

"Sure. That's the one where three people spend eternity with each other in the same room. Forever. Right?" I say, looking over to Doug to make sure he doesn't think I'm taking sides.

Jordan's face lights up. "Yes! And because they're in hell, they're totally mismatched to be in a room together." He takes a sip of wine and looks right at Doug. "Happens all the time."

I'm not quite sure how I got in the middle of this, but it is making me uncomfortable.

"So, Charlie, if you were in hell, who would you be stuck in eternity with?" Jordan asks.

Right now, my answer would be him and Doug. But instead I say, "My mother and her mother."

"You don't like your grandmother?" Jordan asks, surprised.

"No, I don't like my mother when she's around my grandmother. It's not pretty."

"Mine would be Adolf Hitler and Saddam Hussein," Doug chimes in.

Before Jordan can nail Doug with a response, and let's face it, Doug threw one right down the middle for him, Drew suddenly appears, putting his arms around Jordan and me, smiling like the gracious host that he is. "Now I don't believe I'm hearing Socrates and Sartre being discussed on this side of the table. Clearly, none of you have had enough wine."

As he cheerfully refills Jordan's glass, he says, "Now on our side of the table, we're talking about sex toys and the chicken dance. I'm pro."

Both men laugh, and the situation is defused. Drew pats Jordan on the shoulder a few times. "You've taken some great shots. Now remember, you're also my guest here. Have some wine and relax."

He walks back to Dawn, who waves to me. I wave back.

For the next hour, things go swimmingly. The three of us were soon onto a new topic: Sports. I had no idea who they were talking about (something about field goals being out of bounds, but only in Sacramento?), but I did appreciate Jordan smiling and nodding his head in appreciation while he listened to Doug's theories about . . .

I'm pretty sure it was basketball. Or maybe they switched to football at one point. Does New York have a Knicks *and* a Giants?

The main course was the best coq au vin I've ever eaten, served with French bread, and a Beaulieu Vineyards George De Latour private reserve cabernet. I have to say, kudos to Colin Cowie's people for taking all of Drew's seemingly unmatching ideas and serving the best meal I'd had in I don't know how long. By the time we were finished with the chicken, I was pleasantly stuffed, a little buzzed, and feeling hopeful for my dating future—be it with Bachelor #2 or Bachelor #3.

It was then that my promising evening came screeching to a halt.

Jeeves and the caterers came out carrying silver trays of Baccarat flutes, and magnums of Dom Pérignon. So far, so good.

But after the drinks are poured, Drew stands up and taps his glass with his dessert fork. "Ladies and gentlemen: although the purpose of this evening was to bring together some of my favorite people so they could meet, we also have a wonderful reason to celebrate."

He walks over to me with his glass and raises it. "My assistant Charlie . . . and, oh hell, why not just say it? One of my closest friends . . ."

Since when? I think.

". . . is celebrating a milestone this weekend. She's turning thirty."

I can see the headlines now: "Crazed Assistant Stabs Movie Star Twelve Times with Butter Knife Before Taking Her Own Life with Dessert Fork."

"And gentleman, believe it or not, she's still available." Drew takes a quick conspiratorial look around the room to the single men while the rest of the guests laugh, and I force a smile, cringing inside.

"So let's raise our glasses to the most beautiful woman I know"— he pounds his fist onto his chest twice—"on the inside. To Charlie!"

Everyone raises their glasses. "To Charlie!"

And out of the kitchen comes . . . a wedding cake.

Is it technically a wedding cake? Maybe not. But it has three layers, the bottom layer a large square, shaped like a white-and-silver-striped package, the middle layer a bit smaller, square shaped, with red frosting polka dots on a silver rolled fondant, and the top tier looks like a square-shaped gold package, complete with a big bow of gold frosting.

"You like it?" Drew asks, beaming with pride, then whispers to me, "I got it from the same baker who's doing your sister's wedding."

"It's very . . . memorable," I say, horrified.

He smiles as he continues to whisper. "See, this way the guests subconsciously associate you with weddings."

"That's very sly," I say, wishing the earth would swallow me up whole.

"And the piece de resistance," Drew says aloud to his guests as the caterer starts putting birthday candles all over the monstrous creation. "Thirty-one candles! Thirty, plus one for good luck."

People should quit putting an extra candle on a woman's birthday cake when she turns ten.

As Drew begins lighting the sea of candles, I quickly scan the room for a fire extinguisher.

Everyone begins singing "Happy Birthday," and I want to run from the dining room screaming, but I'm afraid that might draw attention to myself.

Jordan starts taking pictures, knowing in his heart how much I will want to remember this moment for eternity.

After everyone finishes singing, Drew says brightly, "Okay, make a wish."

This is always tricky. On the one hand, what girl doesn't secretly want to wish to find her dream man in the next year? On the other hand, if I thought it would work, what I would really wish for right now is to be on my couch, alone, eating a pint of Häagen-Dazs and watching old *Sex and the City* reruns.

I opt for the first wish anyway, reasoning that I have a shot at finding my dream man this year, but no chance in hell of being teleported to my couch right now. I inhale a deep breath, and blow out all the candles.

Everyone applauds.

"Jordan," Drew says, handing him a cake knife, "Would you like to help Charlie cut the cake?"

Oh, Jesus.

Jordan looks up from his camera and asks, "Shouldn't I be taking pictures of this?"

"I'll help Charlie!" Doug says, jumping out of his seat.

Doug stands behind me, puts his right hand over mine, and we cut the bottom layer of the cake, as Jordan takes our picture.

Groan.

Thank God it's chocolate. A fine dark chocolate cake with chocolate mousse filling. We cut the first piece, and send it down the table to Dawn.

"The middle layer is white cake, with a cream cheese filling," Drew says as the caterer whisks the cake away (thankfully making it disappear into the kitchen so that it can be cut and served properly). "Who wants what?" Drew asks.

I end up eating a slice of each. Hey—I've had quite the evening, and no cigarettes. (Because God forbid whoever is interested in me find out that I smoke.) I deserve a treat.

Dessert goes by relatively quickly, and soon people are collecting their coats and purses from Jeeves, and saying their good-byes.

I take that as my excuse to bail.

I grab my purse and coat, and prepare to say good-bye.

But before I can, Drew comes over to me, waving his hands and shaking his head. "No, no, no. Wait," he says, "The night's young. Where are you going so soon?"

"It's getting late," I remind him, "and we both have an early day tomorrow."

"Can't you stay for one more drink?"

"I don't think I should. I've had a lot to drink tonight."

I am interrupted by the caterer, who hands me a white cake box. I look down at it, confused, then look up at the caterer questioningly.

"It's the top of your wedding cake, ma'am," he says, smiling.

"Birthday cake," I correct him, maybe a little too vociferously.

"Maybe you can put it in the freezer for a year, and take it out on your thirtieth birthday's first anniversary," a voice behind me jokes.

I turn around, and there's Jordan, laughing. I can tell he's not making fun of me, he's making fun of the cake, and I start laughing, too. Really laughing. It's the first time tonight I've felt relaxed enough to truly laugh.

"I've never understood that 'freezing the top of your wedding cake' tradition. First of all, who wants to eat year-old cake?" I say, still smiling from his joke.

Jordan laughs. "That. And I know myself well enough to know that if the cake's any good, it won't make it through the first night anyway. I'd be eating it in the limo on the way to the honeymoon suite." He turns to Drew. "Thanks so much for the job. I think you'll be very happy with the pictures."

"I'm sure I will be," Drew says. "Should I write you a check now?"

"No. Let's wait until Monday, when I can show you what I've got." Jordan turns back to me. "And now, fair lady, I bid you a humble adieu." He bows, and kisses my hand lightly. It's so cute!

"Would you like to stay for one more drink?" Drew asks him. "I have a fifty-year-old scotch that's supposed to be excellent."

Jordan smiles. "Tempting. Maybe another time. I want to get into my darkroom and get to work."

He shakes Drew's hand, and I watch him leave, wishing he would have stayed. Wishing I was some other person—someone enticing enough to make him want to stay. Someone prettier, thinner, smarter, someone who didn't smoke. . . .

Smoke! Damn! Now I want a cigarette.

Dawn walks up to us, carrying her wrap and her purse. "Thank you for the lovely evening," she says to Drew, and kisses him lightly on the cheek. "We should do this again sometime."

"Okay!" he says, excitedly. "How about tomorrow night?"

"I'm afraid I have a night shoot," Dawn tells him.

"Saturday?"

"Girls' Night," we both say simultaneously.

"Who's having Girls' Night?" Doug asks, coming up behind me.

"We are," I say quickly, hoping to dissuade Drew from joining us. "Our friend Kate is getting engaged, and we hope to celebrate with her that night."

"Or alternately," Dawn adds, "comfort her when she breaks up with her boyfriend for having the nerve to propose."

Drew and Doug exchange a confused look. Neither Dawn nor I bother to explain further. (If we did, it would take so long to explain Kate's relationship that it would be Saturday night before we even left Drew's house.)

"Well," says Doug, taking my hand in his and swinging it playfully, "I'm sure she'll want to spend the later part of the night with her fiancé. How about if Drew and I meet you then?"

A date! He's asking me on a date! Ooohh, just the thought of it is making me happy and excited. I look over at Dawn, grinning from ear to ear.

She shakes her head "no" ever so slightly. I purse my lips and frown back at her.

Rats. No date for Charlie.

"I don't think Saturday's a good fit," Dawn says diplomatically. "I mean, what could be more boring than listening to a bunch of women talk about weddings?"

"Don't be silly," Drew says, cheerfully oblivious to the subtle hint that he's not wanted. "If you start to get boring, I'll tell you to change the subject." He puts his arm around Dawn. "Now, where should we go?"

Dawn darts her eyes at me, hoping I'll be more blunt with Drew. (As if.)

Drew uses our silence as an invitation to plan our evening. "We could hit Joseph's, but that's kind of over. That new place near Miyagi's has a VIP room that's pretty cool. Oh! What about that place in Hollywood with the aquarium?"

Dawn starts to interrupt. "Maybe we could see each other sometime next week . . ."

Drew ignores her completely. "Blue, no. Kafka's, too snooty."

Dawn looks to me for advice on how to handle him. I shrug. Finally, she relents. "Broncing Bill's."

"No," Drew says, shooting down her idea. "I don't like the food there."

"Neither do I," Dawn agrees. "But that's where we're going."

"The tourist bar?" Doug asks, surprised and a little patronizing.

I flush in embarrassment for about half a second, before Dawn retorts, "No, not the tourist bar. The 'I already go to the trendy clubs on Tuesday and Thursday nights, and I want to wear jeans and drink bourbon' bar."

Nice comeback. Man, I wish I could be like Dawn. She could out-attitude J. Lo.

Or Barbara Streisand.

Or Puff Daddy.

Doug smiles. I can tell from the look on his face—point taken.

"I can't wait," Drew says, then asks Dawn, "Can I walk you to your car?"

Yeah, I think. *Because the walk out to his gated driveway can be so dangerous this time of night.*

But she says yes, and they walk out together, leaving Doug and me to our lonesome.

Doug offers to see me to my car, too, and what with it being so dangerous and all, I let him.

We get out to my car, and I am relieved to see Dawn's car parked so far away, she and Drew can't see us.

"I had a really good time tonight," Doug says.

"Me too," I agree.

He puts his hands in his pockets, and I fiddle with my car keys, and stare at my cake box.

We continue that awkward "Is he going to kiss me, or should I just get into my car?" moment for a few more seconds before he says, "Maybe I could take you to a Lakers game some night."

"That sounds like fun!" I say brightly, although honestly I have no idea what I said during the course of the evening that makes him think I would find it the least bit enjoyable.

Doug smiles, "Okay. We'll talk about it more Saturday."

And then he leans in and kisses me. His lips are so soft, and he's close enough that I can smell his cologne (Lagerfeld? Calvin Klein? Something with vanilla—because he smells like a giant chocolate chip cookie.)

He pulls away, and smiles. "See you Saturday."

Seven

Don't go out with a man just because he looks good on paper.
You're not kissing paper.

On my way home, I check my messages. Five on my cell phone.
I hit *86. The first one's from Kate. "Oh shit, you're not there, either," I hear her say, and I can tell she's been crying. "Can you call
me back when you get this? It's kind of important."

Knowing Jack was proposing tonight, I don't even bother to listen to the other four messages. I immediately call Kate at home.

She picks up on the first ring, sniffling. "Hello?"

"Hi, it's me. What happened?"

Kate begins crying aloud. She's crying so hard, she can barely get
the words out. "Jack and I broke up."

I don't say anything. I want to ask a million questions about how
it happened, but I can't even think of where to begin.

Kate stops crying long enough to say, "He proposed tonight."
Then she starts crying again. "Shit, shit, shit."

I can hear her grab a Kleenex. "Charlie, what's wrong with me?
Why don't I want to marry him?"

I stop at a red light, grab my pack of cigarettes, and hit the pack twice to pop one out. "I don't know. Why don't you want to marry him?"

There's a long silence on the other end of the phone. I can hear Kate taking deep breaths to calm herself. "Because he's not the one," she says sadly. "He never was. He was almost the right one. We almost fit. It's just never been quite . . . I don't know. It's just . . . we don't quite fit. God, I'm such a screwup."

"You're not a screwup," I insist.

"I am. I threw away a perfectly good man because I can't commit. God, Dawn's gonna hate me."

"Dawn's not going to hate you," I say as I light up my cigarette.

"Yes, she is. She helped Jack pick out the ring. She set us up, for God's sake. She loves him. Hell, I love him. Charlie, what's wrong with me?"

"Nothing's wrong with you," I assure her. "As a matter of fact, I'm gonna tell you something in confidence. But I don't want you repeating it to Jack, or holding it against me, if you two end up getting back together."

"We're not getting back together," Kate insists. I'm silent, still waiting for my promise. "But, okay, even if we did, which we won't, I won't hold it against you."

"All right," I say. "This is the healthiest I've heard you in years."

"Come again?" Kate says.

"Well, let's face it, you're not stupid. You knew there were a lot of things wrong in the relationship, you just chose to ignore them because there were so many good things you didn't want to give up. Now, you're at the point in your life where you're strong enough to give up the good stuff. You're strong enough to expect more from your life. I'm proud of you for that. Most women aren't that strong. They're so terrifiied of being alone that they stay with the wrong guy, rather than risk loneliness waiting for the right guy."

There's silence on the other end. "Thanks," she says.

More silence. More sniffling. "I'm used to talking to him nine times a day. I don't know how I'm going to get through tomorrow. Hell, I don't even know how I'm going to get through tonight. I know this sounds really stupid, but can you come over? I really can't stand to be alone right now."

"I'm already driving towards you," I say. "I'll be there in ten minutes."

"Thanks. I know I'm being stupid. It's just . . . I don't even know how I'm going to get through tonight. He's my last phone call."

"You're not being stupid. You're being human." My phone beeps. "That's me. Can I get it?" I ask.

"Okay," Kate says.

"I'm not leaving. Stay on the phone. And, remember, I'm proud of you."

"Thanks," Kate says.

I click over. "Hello?"

"Jack left me a bunch of messages," Dawn says. "They broke up."

"I know. I have her on the other line. She's afraid you're going to be pissed at her."

"What? Why?" Dawn says incredulously.

"She thinks because you set them up, you're gonna hate her."

"Well, that's ridiculous," Dawn says. "Tell her I'm driving over there. She shouldn't be alone right now."

"I'm on my way there, too. Can you pick up some snacks?" I ask.

"Sure. Booze, too?"

Never drink when you're depressed.

"No. That's the last thing she needs right now," I say.

We say our good-byes and hang up, and I go back to Kate to tell her we're coming over.

• • •

Dawn and I were up with Kate until about three in the morning. She couldn't sleep, and who could blame her? It's hard to give up your college boyfriend anytime, but to do it at thirty? Now that takes guts.

I was proud of Kate, because she followed a tenet of advice some people spend their whole lives terrified to follow:

Don't ever be afraid to be alone.

Eight

Some days are a total waste of makeup.

Friday, bleary-eyed, I spent most of the day on set looking for Jordan (who, it turns out, wasn't even called in that day), trying not to answer too many personal questions about Dawn from Drew, and trying to dodge my family's phone calls, a series of cat-and-mouse that began after the following exchange with my parents at six *fucking* A.M. in the morning:

My phone rings, and I make the mistake of answering, assuming that if anyone is going to call me this early in the morning, either someone's pregnant, or someone died. Or it's Drew.

I pick up the phone and answer "Hello," while straining to unglue my eyes and read the clock.

"Did I wake you?" my father says cheerfully.

"Huh?" I grab the clock. 5:58. No, not even six. "Dad, what's wrong? Is Mom okay?"

"She's fine. Are you still asleep?" he asks in astonishment, like everyone else in L.A. has already had their morning jog and breakfast, and I'm being lazy.

"Yeah, I'm still asleep. It's not even six o'clock."

"What are you going to do? Waste the whole day in bed?"

This is a question I'm sure originated in the Midwest—where he's from. It's right up there with those golden oldies, "Cold enough for you?" and "The cold builds character." "Dad, I'd only be wasting my whole day if my day were expected to end at nine in the morning with Regis and Kelly. What's wrong?"

"Nothing's wrong. What makes you think anything is wrong? How did your date go?"

I sit up in my bed, and look for my cigarettes. "It wasn't a date. It was just a few guys Drew thought about setting me up with. One of them was Chris. You know, Mom's Chris?"

"He's not there, is he?" my dad asks, slightly panicked.

"No!" I practically yell back, as I pull a cigarette from the pack. "I'm pretty sure there's some rule about that."

"Thou shalt not covet thy mother's irritatingly young and stupid boyfriend?"

"Something like that," I say, finding my matches, and lighting up. "Be nice to Mom. He's not *that* stupid."

"He thought Napoleon was a dessert," Dad says in disgust.

"Napoleon is a dessert, Dad."

"Not when it's marching on to Waterloo," Dad points out. "Is someone else with you?"

I take a drag from my cigarette. "Okay, in the first place, that's a rude question. In the second place, I'm not going to dignify that question with a response, and in the third place . . . you don't want to know."

"So, in other words, no."

Damn. "No," I am forced to admit.

"Has that guy David called?"

"No," I say, upset with myself for ever mentioning David to my mom, knowing full well:

Anything you tell one parent goes to the other parent. Withhold information accordingly.

"Well, you'll find someone," Dad assures me. "In the meantime, I just called because I needed to vent."

I rue the day my mother ever gave my father *Men Are from Mars, Women Are from Venus*. It's disconcerting to have a middle-aged man use expressions like, "I need to vent" and "I am going into my cave emotionally right now. Don't follow me."

"Okay, Dad, what's up?" I ask calmly, knowing from the book that I should force myself to listen, validate his emotional feelings, and not to try to fix the problem.

"Your sister invited that horrible Mr. Wharton."

"Dad, she had to invite Grandpa. He's Mom's father."

"He's an asshole."

"Yes, he is. But you have to be nice to him."

"Why?"

"Because I said so, that's why," I say in the exact tone he used to give me when I was a little girl.

"I'm afraid I'm going to need a better reason," Dad says, and I hear him turn on the early morning news. "And frankly, right now you're hurting my feelings."

"I'm sorry," I say, not even vaguely sorry. "How about because you love your daughter, and because you're not the parent who causes drama."

"Sure. Take his side," my father says.

"Will you take a hit of pot and calm the fuck down?!" I hear my mother chide from another room.

"I'm not smoking any more of that stuff. I don't trust your dealer," my father yells back.

I'm afraid to ask. And yet it's like looking at a car accident, or a really bad date at the next table—you just can't help but want to know a little more. . . . "Why?" I ask.

"Why what?" my father asks back.

"Why don't you trust Mom's dope dealer?"

"Oh. Well, I went and got one of those drug tests, you know the kind that companies use to test employees before they hire them, because I wanted to know how long the pot stayed in your system, you know in case I go scuba diving—"

"I didn't know you had ever been scuba diving," I interrupt.

"I haven't. But I'm planning a midlife crisis, and I think scuba diving should be a part of it. You know, pristine beaches, cute little girls in their bikinis, poker. . . ."

Before I can ask what poker has to do with scuba diving, he continues, "So I take this drug test. And what does it tell me but that I've tested positive for PCP!"

I gasp. You got to hand it to my Dad—it takes a lot to get me to gasp in this family.

"So," he continues, "it turns out, your mother's dealer had 'accidentally' laced her lid with PCP! Well, I told him a thing or two! Let me tell you, that seventy-eight-year-old woman from Venice, your mother's old pot dealer, sure, she may have been a silly little grandmother who put stickers on her bags, and insisted you eat her brownies, which were dubious. And she may have bored you with picture after picture of her grandchildren, but you can be sure the marijuana you got from her was clean!"

"Well then, why don't you just go back to her?" I ask, wondering how I ended up in this conversation.

"She died," Dad says, like she did it just to inconvenience him. "I mean, what has the world come to when you can't even trust your pot dealer?"

Mom picks up the other line, and asks accusingly, "Who are you on the phone with? You should never talk about drugs on a portable phone."

Ah, the words of wisdom you get from your elders. It's precious, really.

"The DEA," my father says. "They're coming to get you."

"It's me, Mom," I say.

"Hello, dear," Mom says. "Ed, don't you have to get ready for work?" Mom asks my father.

I can actually hear him roll his eyes. "Fine. I love you, Charlie."

"Me too, Dad. Good night."

After he hangs up, my mom whispers, "Give me a minute to get to another room. We have to talk."

Happy. Happy. Joy. Joy.

Thirty seconds later, I can hear the waterfall from the outdoor pool, so I know Mom is outside.

"I need to talk to you about your sister," Mom whispers urgently. "You need to have a talk with her. I told her that even though your father and I are paying for this entire wedding, she is entitled to invite whomever she wants."

Which, of course, in Mom language, really translates to "Run every name by me. I'm not paying two hundred dollars for a dinner for someone I can't stand."

". . . only now she's invited that bitch Julia!"

I sigh aloud. "Mom, she's Dad's sister."

"Don't defend her!" Mom practically shouts, then begins loudly whispering, "She wishes you were dead."

I sigh heavily into the phone to subtly hint to my mother that I am tired of repeating the same tired point over and over again. "No. When Dad told her you were pregnant, and you guys weren't married, she said she wished you'd have a miscarriage. Now, while that is a horrible thing to say, it is not the same thing as wishing I were dead now."

"Do you secretly hate me?" my mother asks accusingly. "Is this some reverse Oedipal thing where you want to marry your father and kill your mother, and that's why you never take my side?"

Why is it mothers always have to go to the Electra complex?

"Mom, in the first place, no offense to you, but if I met Dad thirty years ago, I would have thought he was gay. So, no, I do not secretly want to marry Dad. And in the second place, it's been thirty years since Julia said—"

"You make that sound like a long time ago," my mother says.

Instead of pointing out the obvious:

Don't hold a grudge for thirty years. While you're home stewing, the other guy's out dancing.

I instead try to diffuse the situation by changing the subject. "Mom, what are you doing up this early?"

I ask this because my mother has never been out of bed before the crack of noon. Except when she's working. And she's a writer so, like I said, crack of noon.

"I haven't been to bed yet," my mother tells me, and I hear her inhaling from her pot pipe. "Chris and I had a long conversation last night. Apparently, your boss tried to set you up with him last night, and it got him quite freaked out. We're thinking of taking our relationship to the next level."

He didn't seem freaked out at the party. But then again, he's a yoga instructor, so maybe you can't tell. However, speaking of freaked out, which I now am, I ask, "What next level?"

My mother sighs audibly. "Well . . . your father and I have decided to live together . . ."

My parents are divorced, but they're living together. Swell.

Mom continues, "You know, because it looks like he and Jeannine are over, and you know, he'll need some mothering right now, and I'm such an earth mother . . ."

"Right," I say halfheartedly.

I finish my cigarette, get out of bed, walk to my dresser, and open my cake box, where about a third of the cake still sits. (I guess the top layer of my wedding cake wouldn't make it to the second day, either.) I take a fingerful as my mother continues.

"So I tell Chris that your father will be living here, and he's okay with it, but asks if he can move in, too. And I say, I just don't know, two men under the same roof, and me with a cleaning lady only once a week, and he says . . ."

Blah, blah, blah, she talks . . . something about Mrs. Robinson . . . blah, blah, blah. I can't concentrate. I am too busy loving this cake! The top layer is this buttery yellow cake, which I don't normally like, but it is sinful, and has this nice chocolate chip filling with vanilla.

"So, what do you think?" Mom asks.

Shit! She does that to me every time! And now I've got to bs my way through the rest of this conversation.

Fortunately, she's been my mother for a really long time, so I know how to do that. I smile to myself, so proud am I of my next line: "Well, Mom, in your heart you know the answer. I think it's time you quit asking everyone else's opinion, and just do what you know is right."

She's silent. I've really hit home with my logic. "Of course," she says. "Of course you're right."

Yay! Home run! I should have been a therapist.

"Would you carry the baby?" she asks earnestly.

Huh? Wait, stay calm, think back on what she was talking about, something about Mrs. Robinson. . . .

"You weren't listening to a thing I said, were you?" Mom asks dryly.

I look down at my hardwood floors sheepishly. "I heard the part about two men and only one cleaning lady."

My Dad yells, "Jacquie, go to bed!" and I am saved.

"I have to go," Mom says. "Your father's calling me to bed. God— never thought I'd be saying that again. I love you. We'll talk later."

She hangs up. I hang up and finish off my cake.

I pick up again to call Drew. It rings three times until I hear Drew yell, "I'm up!"

"Wakey, wakey," I say.

"Five more minutes."

"Okay, but only five. It's already after six, and . . ." He's already hung up. "And why am I talking to myself?" I say out loud for no reason.

I call Kate to make sure she's okay; she lies and says she is. Then I take a quick shower, then I call Drew back.

"I'm up!"

"Your driver will be there in less than ten minutes. Did you kiss her?" I ask, lighting up another cigarette.

"Yeah, but it was one of those quick pecks on the lips. Very Hollywood," he tells me.

"Better luck Saturday," I say.

"I hope so," he says. "Promise me you'll get her good and liquored up."

"Only if you promise me you'll get Doug good and liquored up."

"Deal," he says, then hangs up.

Well, at least it's Friday.

On the way to work, my phone rings, and I see from the caller ID it's my sister Andy.

I pick up anyway, adjusting my headset so I now look like someone who talks to herself in the car.

"Hi, Andy," I say, suppressing a yawn.

"I hate our family. They're a bunch of nutcases," Andy says, nearly in tears.

"What, *now*? You're just figuring that out *now*?" I ask.

"I don't know why we're going to play Mendelsohn's wedding march when I walk down the aisle. Why don't I just have the theme to the *Addams Family*?"

That's a good question, actually.

"Dad says he's not coming to the rehearsal dinner if Grandpa comes," Andy continues, "and Mom says if she sees Julia she's going to punch her lights out. Can you talk to them? *Please?*"

"All right. I'll talk to them. Go have a normal day, and try not to think about it," I say, trying to sound reassuring.

We talk for another minute, and I hang up just as I get to the studio.

Today they are shooting the big finale. You know, where the guy gets the girl, and everything's a happy ending. Which reminds me: I pull out my notebook and scratch down:

Make sure most of the movies you see have happy endings.

Yeah—I know. I'm such a commoner. I don't care. Life can be depressing enough without paying ten bucks to see even more sadness. I mean, let's be honest, how many times have you seen *Citizen Kane*? How many times have you seen *When Harry Met Sally*?

So, you see my point.

Do you still rent movies in the 22nd century? If so, rent When Harry Met Sally, Auntie Mame, *and* His Girl Friday. *You can then rent* Fight Club (*which is an awesome movie, but depressing*), *but you must follow it up with a Cary Grant comedy such as* Mr. Blandings Builds His Dreamhouse *or* I Was a Male War Bride. *Enjoy!*

About time I start giving the girl some practical advice.

I walk around the set, and think of the scene they're shooting to-day. Drew plays a detective who has to bring a beautiful fugitive (played by his costar, the gorgeous Heather Crowe), across the country for her trial. It's a screwball romantic comedy, with a really happy ending.

As the other members of the crew begin pulling cables, setting up cameras, and lighting the set, I walk over to the fake jail cell. For some reason, even though I got a nice kiss from Doug last night, I'm still thinking of Jordan. Not that he'd give me the time of day. But I imagine myself as the beautiful convict, handcuffed to Jordan, the tough but sweet detective, and he kisses me through the cell, and . . .

Mmmmm, I sigh to myself, dreaming of that kiss. See, this is why we go to movies. If you ever kissed someone handcuffed to you in real life, it would be kinky.

I turn around and head over to Craft Service to get cappuccinos. At seven o'clock exactly, I open the door to Drew's trailer—and nearly choke on all the smoke billowing out. It looks like Spicoli's van in *Fast Times at Ridgemont High*. I sniff. Nope, not marijuana. More like flowers.

Bracing myself, I walk in to see Drew has redecorated his trailer again, this time in an Indian motif. His new couches are done in jewel-toned silks of dark red and dark green, with delicate gold embroidery sewn in geometric patterns throughout. Candles and incense burn everywhere (hence the smoke), and sitar music is piped in from . . . I still can't find any speakers.

I look around at the newest decorations—elephant heads. Not the whole elephant, mind you. Just the head. An elephant head on a human body, sitting in meditation position. An elephant head with six human arms and legs. Five elephant heads on eight arms and legs. An elephant on a giant . . . rat?! I move closer to a pewter elephant incense burner to get a better look.

"Ganesh," Drew says to me.

I turn around to see Drew lying on his new couch, making some sort of guttural noise. I'm not sure if he's chanting, or trying to sound a mating call to a female elephant. Please God, let it be chanting. "Excuse me?" I say.

"Ganesh," he repeats.

"Gesundheit," I respond.

Drew opens his eyes, and sits up. He starts talking to me like a three-year-old describing the latest episode of *Blue's Clues*. "I was watching the most amazing program last night after you went home. It was all about Ganesh, the Hindu god of India. The more I heard about it, the more I realized, I'm destined to be Hindu."

I furrow my brow. "What happened to becoming a kahuna?" I ask.

Drew waves his hand at me as if to say *pshaw*. "That wasn't for me. It turns out you have to do years of intense studying to become a kahuna. I'm not a student, I'm a movie star. But this . . . you're born into it. So I've decided I must have been born a Hindu, I just didn't know it since I was born in Rhode Island."

I try to keep from visibly shaking my head. "Drew, the Hindu religion is very complicated, you can't just . . ."

Drew jumps up from the couch and hands me what looks a stone elephant doing yoga. "This is Ganesh," he says, as though he's introducing me to his new puppy.

"Nice to meet you, Ganesh," I say sarcastically.

Drew looks at me with complete sincerity. "According to the host of this program, the world is not created in the way we Westerners think of when we think of the word *creation*. It exists, but does not exist. It is only a relative reality, an illusion that we think of as truth, but that might not be truth. We are the product of Maya—the power of illusion."

He stares at me, eyes wide open, slowly bobbing his head up and down, like he's just told me the meaning of life. I look back at him, nonplussed. "Okeydokey. Well, it's good you have a hobby. You want to go over your weekend schedule?"

I can tell from the way he's looking at me, that wasn't the response he was going for. But he shrugs and says, "Yeah, okay. Whatever."

I hand him his cappuccino, and go over his schedule for the weekend.

I stare at a printout of his schedule, and take a sip of my cappuccino. "All right. We start with an eight A.M. jog with your trainer—"

"Whoa. Way too early," Drew states emphatically as he sips his cappuccino. "Cancel that."

"Followed by free weights at nine . . . ," I continue.

"Cancel that," Drew says, nodding.

"Then yoga with Chris at ten . . ."

"Cancel that, but tell him it has nothing to do with him rejecting you last night." Drew takes another sip of his cappuccino, and scrunches up his lips in disgust. "Does this have sugar in it?"

"No. Equal," I say. "Which brings us to your eleven o'clock appointment with your nutritionist . . ."

"Yeah. Cancel that. That guy's diet is too strict. Find me someone who allows sugar in my coffee, bacon for breakfast, and a nice glass of scotch at night."

I sigh. "Okay, here's the thing. You specifically told me to force you to stay on this diet until you lost, and I quote, 'these goddamn eight pounds.'"

"Yeah, I know. So you'll get rid of him?" Drew asks, switching cappuccinos with me (mine has sugar in it).

I shake my head. "You said that no matter what you told me, that I absolutely, positively had to make sure you went to this appointment, or you would fire me."

Drew rolls his eyes. "Look, sweetie, I love you. But if I wanted a woman to hold me to everything I said, I'd still be married."

"So you're sure you want me to cancel the appointment?" I ask.

"I'm sure," Drew promises me.

"Fine." I make a note on my pad, but the truth is, I cancelled the appointment last week. "Therapy from twelve to two . . ."

"Oh, good." Drew says, pulling out a pen and writing it down. "I can talk about Dawn."

"Hospital visit for Make a Wish at three . . ."

"Got it."

"And then you have a meeting at five with some guy named Robert Browne from *Maxim* magazine. Your publicist arranged it."

"Oh, shit!" Drew yells. "Blow Me!"

I look over my notes. "Is he some interviewer? I don't have him on my computer."

"No, he's one of the editors. I totally forgot. I need you to write my 'Blow Me' list."

I stare at him blankly. He returns my stare with an expectant smile. After several moments of confusion, I finally manage to stammer out, "To say that I am disturbed by the sound of that really is an understatement."

"It's for *Maxim* magazine," Drew informs me. "They're having celebrities write a 'Blow Me List,' which is basically a list of things that make you want to say, 'Blow Me.' I need you to write it for me."

"Why can't you write it?" I ask.

"I'm not very good at hating things. My life is so charmed," Drew says with not the least bit of irony in his voice. "But you're always complaining about something. And you're so much funnier than I am."

I blink at him several times. He just keeps smiling at me. "Don't we know a writer who can do this?" I finally manage to ask.

"No. I'm supposed to write it," Drew insists. "Which means you have to write it."

Okay, how do I say no without getting fired? I have to be tactful and diplomatic. Let him know how much I treasure my job, and how important it is to me. "Are you out of your fucking tree?!" I blurt out.

"Oh, come on," Drew says, waving me off. "Look, to show my appreciation, I'll get you a limo for your Girls' Night tomorrow."

"The night that you invited yourself to?!" I whine. I'm trying not to whine, but I can't help it. When I get upset, I sound like Minnie Mouse, just like my sister.

"And I'll pay you a thousand dollars, cash," he offers.

"How many words do you need it to be?" I answer immediately. Hey, I'm not stupid.

"No word count—just a top ten list," Drew says. He wins. He always wins.

"Write me fifteen or so, and I'll pick my favorites."

Dying is easy. Comedy is hard.

I hate Drew for this. I spend the next four hours in Drew's director's chair, on set, coming up with a "Blow Me" list.

1. Men who don't call.

I cross that off.

1. Sixteen-year-olds trying to sell you wrinkle cream at Bloomingdales.

I cross that off.

1. Hillary Clinton.

Maybe.

And, as I'm thinking about people who don't call, the phone rings (or I should say vibrates, as we're on the set, and no cell phones, pagers, or anything with sound is allowed on a set).

I see it's Andy, so I run off the set and call her right back.

As I walk onto the set of the exterior of a Manhattan street, Andy picks up. "Hello?"

"Hey, it's me. What's up?"

"Mom and Dad just faxed Hunter and me a seating chart for our wedding."

Uh-oh. I wince. "Did you ask them to do that?"

"Are you upset your younger sister's getting married before you?" Andy asks me back.

Ouch. "Well," I begin, preparing to give an upbeat answer, when Andy interrupts, "I'm just asking, since apparently it's 'Ask a stupid question' day!"

Double ouch. As I pass the fake Zabars, I remind her, "You know, I'm one of the only people on your side here. You should be nice to me."

"I'm sorry, I just can't believe everyone's making this so awful for me. This is supposed to be the happiest day of my life, and instead I just want to get it over with. Do you know Hunter's mother just added fifty more guests to our list, and Hunter won't tell her no? And now I get this stupid seating chart . . ."

"How bad is it?" I ask warily.

"Well, Dad wrote the name 'your dumb-ass grandfather' on the seating chart with a big arrow pointing to the top of the page, pointing to the word *Canada*. . . ."

I rub my right palm into my right eye, feeling a headache coming on. "Where did Mom put Julia?"

"Next to an arrow at the bottom of the page, pointing to the words *six feet under*. Look, are you busy tonight? I really need you to come to Mom's house so we can sort everything out."

"I guess I can do that," I tell her, only because I can't think of a good excuse not to. "But if you're going to ask them for more money for more guests, wouldn't you rather do it without an audience?"

"Are you okay turning thirty without a boyfriend, or is your career enough to sustain you into old age?" she counters.

"Will seven o'clock be okay?" I ask immediately, dreading whatever her next "stupid question" would be.

"Divine. I'll see you then. Love you. Bye," Andy says, and clicks off.

"Love you, too," I say, and head back to the set.

I hate her. I really do.

Nine

Everything happens for a reason.

I'm not quite sure what possible reason the universe could have for me to write a "Blow Me" list. But, nonetheless, two hours later, Drew and I are back in his trailer, going over it.

As he sits on his new silk couch, sipping his seventh cup of coffee of the day, I read from my clipboard. "Okay," I begin. "Number one. Sylvester Stallone, Ben Affleck, and any other actor who's won an Academy Award for writing."

"I can't say that," Drew says, shaking his head.

"Why?"

"I like Ben. Besides, what if I decide to write a screenplay someday? Then no one at the Academy would vote for me."

A screenplay?! He can't even write a "Blow Me" list! But instead of pointing out the obvious, I scratch it out, and we move on. "Number one. Anyone who calls you 'Sir.'"

"Why would I hate that?" Drew asks.

"Because it implies you're old," I say.

"No, it doesn't. It implies the person respects me."

"Because you're old," I counter. But I see his point, and cross it off. "Somehow, it works better as people who call me 'ma'am,'" I tell him. "All right. Number one. Martha Stewart."

"Oh. I can't write that."

This is getting tiresome. "Why not?" I ask, clearly irritated.

"Because a few years ago I made kegel on her show, and I don't want to offend her."

"Kugel," I correct him.

"Excuse me?"

"You made kugel on her show. Kegel is . . ." I'm so not explaining this to my boss. Although, if he did make Martha Stewart kegel, *that* is a show I would want to see. But I cross her off the list. "Never mind. Number one. Roger Moore, George Lazenby, Timothy Dalton, and Pierce Brosnan, or anyone else not Sean Connery, playing James Bond."

"I can't say that," Drew says, taking a sip of his coffee (now with two sugars).

I roll my eyes. "Now what?"

"Pierce is a good guy," Drew says emphatically. "I don't want to hurt his feelings."

"I agree. Pierce is a good guy. But I doubt he's reading *Maxim*, and even if he is, if he has any kind of a sense of humor, he'll think it's funny."

Drew furrows his brow, and shrugs. "Okay. That's one, I guess."

"Good." I put a star by that one. "Number two. Britney Spears."

"Oh." Drew looks up, and smiles appreciatively. "I like that one."

It was a safe bet. No straight man I know will admit to liking Britney Spears. And yet they all loved that kiss.

"Good. Number three. Fat-free ice cream."

"Fat-free what?" Drew says, jerking back his head.

"Ice cream," I repeat.

"You're making that up," he accuses me. "Isn't that a contradiction in terms?"

"No, I'm not. And yes, it is," I tell him.

"Well, is it any good?" Drew asks.

"Of course not," I practically spit out. Apparently, it is stupid question day after all.

"Okay, you can put that one down," he says.

"Good. Three down, only seven to go. Number four. People who have been to a *Star Trek* convention more recently than they've been out on a date."

"Good. I hate those people," Drew says.

My phone interrupts us. Drew looks at it expectantly. "Is it Dawn?" he asks.

I check the caller ID. "Yeah."

"Answer it!" he demands, and jumps up from the couch, suddenly a nervous wreck.

I do. "Hello."

"Are you alone?" Dawn asks.

"Ask her about me," Drew whispers.

I silently wave him off. "Yeah. What's up?"

"What do you think of Drew? Be honest."

Shit. I can't tell her what I really think of Drew with him sitting right next to me.

Drew whispers, "Is she asking about me?"

I jab my index finger at him harshly, and put it up to my lips to pantomime *Sssshhh*. "Why do you ask?" I say nonchalantly into the phone. "Do you like him?"

"Yeah, I think I do. He's called me every night this week, and we talk for hours. I haven't met a guy like that in a while. And he's sent me flowers every day this week, which normally would creep me out. But, I don't know, for some reason, I think it's kinda cool."

"Drew did that?" I ask, audibly floored. I never thought of him as a "talk for hours" kind of guy. Unless he's talking about himself, of course.

Drew hands me a note he's just scribbled: *If we get married, I'll make sure she makes you the maid of honor.*

Threats will get you nowhere, I write back, just as Dawn says, "Yeah. At first, I thought he was a bit overbearing, but now I like him. He's really quite sweet." She pauses for a second. "And you're sure he's not there?" she asks suspiciously.

"No," I lie, while scribbling down, *She likes you.*

There's silence on the other end. "Oh, my God. You are truly the worst liar I've ever met. He's sitting right there next to you listening to every word I say, isn't he?"

"No," I say, as weakly as a kitten. "Actually, he's standing in front of me, sort of towering over me."

"Put him on," Dawn says.

I hand the phone to Drew. "She wants to talk to you."

Drew takes the phone cautiously. "Hello?" His voice immediately softens. "Hey, baby. Did you have a good time last night? . . . Yeah. Me too. . . ."

He covers the phone. "Get out," he says matter-of-factly.

As I grab my coffee and head out the door, I hear Drew say, "Oh, just working on that 'Blow Me' list I told you about. . . ."

Great. He told everyone in the world about this list but me.

"I'd love some ideas!" Drew says as he takes a pen and writes, *Michael Jackson . . . Al Sharpton . . . any white person who celebrates Kwanzaa . . .*"

As I stand outside Drew's trailer waiting for him to get off the phone, I contemplate their new relationship. Maybe he's not the self-centered twit I always think he is. Maybe he's actually a nice guy who wants to find a soul mate. Who's just like the rest of us: just trying to figure out where he fits in the world, like everyone else. Sweet, insecure . . .

"Charlie! I'm off the phone! Blow me!" Drew yells as he swings open his trailer door.

Or not.

Several crew members turn around as I shake my head, and walk back into his trailer.

When I walk back in, Drew's grinning at me like a lovesick high school girl. "She likes me! She really likes me!"

"I know," I say, a bit patronizingly, as I walk back over to the couch and have a seat.

"She sure is a sweetie," Drew says. "Can I buy her jewelry yet?"

"Too soon. Now, back to the list."

"Right." Drew hands me his list of Dawn's suggestions. "I can't use any of these, can I?"

"No," I say, taking Dawn's list, crumpling it into a ball, and throwing it into the new elephant trash can. "Number five . . ."

"Anyone who confuses me with Tom Cruise," Drew says, finishing my sentence.

Yeah, that would be my number five, I think sarcastically. I mean, what man wouldn't hate that? I know the last thing I would want to say to my date, even more than, "I got herpes from my last boyfriend" would be, "You sure look a lot like Tom Cruise." It would be like someone telling me I look like Heidi Klum. "Okay, I can write that," I say slowly, giving him time to reconsider.

He doesn't. "And people who say they love all my movies, and then name films I'm not in."

"Great," I say, writing down numbers five and six (hey, even if they're stupid, at least I'm two closer to being done). "Any others?"

"Nope. That's it," Drew says, downing the rest of his coffee.

"Number seven. Hillary Clinton."

"I can't say that," Drew says, reaching over to take my coffee.

I let my shoulders slump, and drop my chin into my "Oh, for God's sake" look. "You can't stand Hillary Clinton."

"Yeah. But what if she runs for president? I want to be invited to the White House again."

I cross Hillary's name off my list, then cross another name off. Drew glances at my pad. "Who was that?"

"Dick Cheney. Same principle. Okay, what about supermodels who weigh one hundred pounds, even with their fake boobs?"

"Why would I hate them?" Drew asks.

Clueless. Absolutely clueless. "Because all women do!" I retort.

"But Dawn's one hundred pounds," Drew tells me. "And aren't you about a hundred pounds?"

I burst out laughing. I can't believe how dumb men are. "Dawn's almost a hundred and thirty pounds, and she works out everyday. I'm . . . Well, let's just say, more than a hundred pounds."

"Really?" Drew says in utter amazement. You'd think I had just told him that yes, the moon really was made of cheese. "Well, I guess it's okay then."

"Women around the country will adore you," I say dryly. "Number eight. Women who wear tiaras at their wedding instead of veils."

Drew looks at me blankly. I scratch it out. "We'll just change it to women who don't know anything about sports. Number nine, autobiographies written by celebrities who are under thirty."

Drew nods appreciatively.

"And number ten . . . stupid top ten lists."

Drew smiles, and gives me an appreciative round of applause. "Your limo will arrive promptly at seven o'clock tomorrow evening."

"Thank you," I say.

We hear a knock on the door. "Mr. Stanton," I hear Madison, our P.A., say through the door. "Your new elephant is here. Her trainer wants to know where to put her."

"That reminds me," Drew says to me, "I'm gonna need you to find someone to redo my backyard. I bought an elephant."

I peek through the curtain to see a huge elephant being led by her trainer to Drew's trailer.

I let my head fall into my hands.

Ten

Our family isn't crazy, they're colorful.

At seven o'clock, I pull up to my mother's house in Beverly Hills. The second I get out of the car, I hear gunfire.

I race up the walkway to the front door, use my old key, and burst inside.

"Mom!" I scream from the front hallway.

I hear crying from the guest room downstairs. I run over, and there's my mother's "whatever," Chris, collapsed in a corner, sobbing.

"My God, what happened?" I ask, racing up to him.

Chris tries to speak, "Your . . . your . . ." He continues sobbing. He tries to talk, but he's crying so hard, he can't catch his breath to get more than a word out.

"Chris, you've got to calm down," I say, feeling myself starting to shake. "What happened?"

"Your . . . mother . . . ," he manages to squeak out.

"What about Mom?" I say, terrified. "Chris, what happened to her?"

"She . . . she's gone," he says, then howls like a wolf, and falls into my lap.

Oh my God. My mother. What the hell's happened? My mommy.

The first love of my life. The only woman who ever truly loved me unconditionally. Who had total faith in me. Who said I could do whatever I wanted in my life, as long as I tried my best, worked hard, and took chances when I needed to.

Sure, she criticized. But that was only because she loved me so much, and wanted the best for me. And sure, she may have called me every frigging day of my life, but that was only because she cared, and she missed me.

And how did I reward her for giving me all that love? By being bitchy, getting annoyed, wishing she would love me less. And now? Now that she's gone, I can never take that back. I can never let her know how much she means to me. How much I love her. How much I—

"Darling, I didn't hear your come in," my mother says cheerfully, interrupting my thoughts. I look up, and there she is, standing in the doorway, wearing an apron and wiping her hands with a towel. "Your sister and Hunter are already here."

Once again I hear a loud gunshot. *Bang!* Mom doesn't even flinch.

Instead, she makes a *tssk* sound with her mouth. "By the way, Jeannine sent the divorce papers to your father today. So he's a bit on edge."

Bang! goes another gunshot as I ask, "How on edge?"

"He's shooting air rifles in the backyard."

Bang!

"Don't you worry the gunshots are going to scare the neighbors?" I ask, alarmed.

"We live near the Osbournes. Do you really think anyone gives a crap?" my mother asks in return.

Before I can answer, she sees Chris sobbing on my lap, and sighs. "Chris, sweetie, you're getting Charlie's skirt wet." Mom walks up to him and hands him a pink pill and a small glass of water. "Take another Valium, love, and try to get some sleep."

Chris lifts his head from my lap, lets Mom feed him the pill, then put the glass to his lips. He drinks the water, then falls onto her chest. Mom puts her arm around him like she used to do to me when I was a kid. "Good," she says soothingly. "Now, can you make it upstairs, to my room, and get some sleep?"

He nods, his face buried in her chest.

"Good," she says, then stands up with him. The two walk out of the guest room, me following behind.

I stare in disbelief as I watch the two climb the stairs. "I'll be up in a few hours," Mom tells Chris. "If you can't sleep, there's a Deepak Chopra audiotape on the nightstand, as well as *Sounds of the Rainforest*."

"Okay," Chris says quietly. "I love you."

"Me too, sweetheart," Mom says, then comes back down the stairs to me, acting as though nothing out of the ordinary has happened. "I've made a roast chicken for us . . ."

Bang.

". . . with roasted potatoes, and some asparagus, which I know you're not crazy about, but your father is, and he's had quite the day . . ."

Mom puts her arm around me, and slowly leads me toward the kitchen. I am speechless.

Bang.

"Now I'm not sure how much he'll eat. He's in quite a snit."

We enter the kitchen, and I see Hunter holding the air rifle, my father by his side. Andy is sitting at the kitchen table, her face buried in her hands. A glass of red wine is in front of her.

"Darling, you haven't touched your wine," my mother says to her, sounding like Donna Reed.

Andy lifts her head, glares at my mother for not seeing the complete absurdity of the situation, and drains the wine in one gulp.

"Well," Mother says in a slightly huffy tone, "I hardly think you could detect the hints of cocoa and cherries that way, but I suppose it's your life."

Bang. Hunter shoots a tin can off Mom's back gate. "That is so cool, Ed," Hunter says, pumping the gun, then shooting again.

"Yeah," my dad says, brightening a bit. "The trick is to think about your ex-wife, then pull the trigger. You don't have one of those yet, do you, son?"

Yet?

"No, sir," Hunter says, handing my dad his gun back.

"Good, good," Dad says, taking the gun back. "Sometimes I wonder why anyone bothers to get married. You just end up divorcing them and giving them half your money anyway." Mom hands him a joint. "Thank you, love."

Dad takes a big hit of pot while I calmly take the gun out of his hand and stick it in the broom closet.

"And on the subject of people bothering to get married," I begin, "Let's talk about your daughter."

Mom turns around and her face lights up. "You mean, you're—"

"Nooo," I say, sighing. "Your *other* daughter."

"Right," Mother chimes in. "The subject on the table is seating arrangements."

Hunter and Andy exchange a panicked glance with each other, and I know the extra guest subject has not been broached. "Actually, Mom, I think we need to start with the *number* of guests."

Mom turns to Andy. "We did agree on two hundred, right?"

"Yes!" Andy says immediately. "*We* did agree on two hundred. Emphasis on the *we*."

Mom looks at my Dad, who sits down and takes another hit of pot, ignoring the conversation.

Hunter coughs self-consciously. "Unfortunately, my mother did not agree to two hundred. She has insisted that we invite fifty extra guests, friends of her and my father's."

My mother grabs her chest in horror (she likes to do that), but Hunter quickly adds, "However, I will be more than happy to pick the up the extra costs."

"Not necessary," Dad says immediately.

Andy and I look at each other in shock. We could *not* have just heard that right.

Hunter continues, "You're being very gracious, sir. But I don't want us to get off on the wrong foot. . . ."

"Will there be women your mother's age there?" Dad asks Hunter.

Hunter looks at me like "What the hell is he talking about?" I shrug. I honestly don't know. Finally he says, "Well, yes sir. Many of them—"

"Are any of these women single?" my father interrupts.

"Um . . . some of them are divorced, or widows . . ."

"Then bring them to my tent," Dad says with a determined tone. "I need a woman. And I am too old and fat to be chasing women my daughters' age. If I have to pay ten thousand dollars more to meet women my own age who aren't already in my social circle, so be it."

I must say, that went a lot easier than planned. We all heave a collective sigh. "Okay, then," I say, "on to the subject of seating."

"I want all the single women my age at my table," Dad says. "And don't be shy about letting them know I'm on the market," he says to Hunter.

"No, sir . . . ," Hunter begins.

"Ed," Mom says, "you can't sit with the single women. You have to sit at the bride's parents' table."

"Why?" he asks.

"Because it's tradition," she insists, slightly raising her voice.

"So is the bride being a virgin, but we did away with that years ago. Hell, you and I personally did away with that. . . ."

"Okay, then we won't have a bride's parents' table," Andy says quickly, interrupting him before he can get too graphic. "We will, however, be having siblings, parents, grandparents . . ."

On that note, both my parents wave their arms in the air, yell, "Aaahhh, shit!" and "Goddamn it!" respectively, and walk out of the room, leaving Hunter, Andy, and me by our lonesome.

Thirty seconds of silence pass. Then a minute. The three of us are staring at each other in silence like we're in some sort of high-stakes poker game.

Hunter finally speaks. "Do you think they're coming back?"

"Unfortunately, yes," Andy and I say in unison.

When they do come back, they are carrying a giant purple board with them, with green circles pasted on it, and numbers on each of the tables, from 1 to 20. Dad sets the board down on the kitchen table. "This is the seating plan for the hotel dining room."

"Hold on," Mom says, then goes to a drawer, pulls out five more green circles and a glue stick, and glues the five extra tables onto the board.

Dad points to Table 1, in the center of the room. "You are here," he says to Andy and Hunter. "Now, there are ten people per table, so which eight people do you want joining you?"

Andy and Hunter start debating which eight people they can both stand to be with all night, and we are off!

It only took four more hours, two more crying fits, three pints of Häagen-Dazs, one cancelled engagement, one "Fuck this—we're just going to Vegas!", seventeen "No, they hate each other—you can't put them at the same table"s, twenty-three "She's crazy (he's crazy), we can't have Hunter's family find out how nuts our family is," and seventy-two "Okay, fine"s in a variety of tones, before everything was sorted out and they let me go home.

Oh yeah, and one "I love you. I would not have gotten through this tonight without you."

Andy probably said one of those to Hunter later on, but the one she said to me made the whole night worth it.

Eleven

Never judge people by who they date—your own sex life is confusing enough without trying to figure out everyone else's.

I say that because right now I'm a little confused about my sex life. Or lack thereof.

I mean, I have a date tomorrow with Doug, who's a really good-looking guy, and also a good kisser, and who seems nice, available, and interested.

But I miss Jordan.

Isn't that stupid? I've barely talked to him for four months on the set, and after one night seated next to him at a party, I miss him.

And, despite having not slept much last night, I can't sleep.

I open a bottle of Blackstone Merlot, and pour myself a glass as I look at the call sheet, which is the list of everyone on the crew, their jobs, phone numbers, cell phone numbers, and sometimes their e-mail addresses.

There it is: Jordan1313. Hmm. Maybe I'll write him a quick thank-you e-mail for coming to my birthday party. Just to say hi.

Be yourself. Don't try to impress anyone. You're enough on your own.

I spend the next forty-five minutes and two glasses of wine composing my quick "thank-you" e-mail. I type, I erase. Type, erase. Finally, I just get online and send what I have.

My computer tells me "You have mail." Yay! I love that sentence! I cheerfully look at my mail list. Mom: no, Dad: no, advertisement for porno, printable coupons for diapers(!). Oh, here's one from Kate. Time-stamped less than fifteen minutes ago.

To: AngelCharlie
From: KissMeKate

Sorry I didn't call you back. Jack's been calling all day, and I guess this breakup might take a while. Can't wait to see you tomorrow night. First drink's on me.

BTW, do you happen to know the Minority Whip's name in the Senate? I'm spacing.

Sometimes I think she writes stuff like that just to make me feel stupid, and look it up.

I start to write, *Do you happen to know the only person not to get fired from WJM on the last episode of the Mary Tyler Moore show?* as my response, just as I receive an IM (instant message) from Jordan1313.

Jordan1313: Are you online?

I stare at the message. No one ever instant-messages me. It's one of those things that they always advertise on the commercials, that you can instant-message and talk to each other online, but I never actually do it. I just pick up the phone and call people.

Besides, Jordan can't be home on a Friday night.

AngelCharlie: Jordan?

Jordan1313: In the flesh. What are you doing home on a Friday night?

Well, that's a good question. How do I respond?

AngelCharlie: Just recovering from the week. You?
Jordan1313: Celebrating! I didn't have to work today, so I took the whole day off. I went to the museum, then the beach. Kicked back some beers with my boys at Gladstone's, then headed to St. Nick's. It was great! I'm wasted!

Museum? A guy who goes to the museum on his own? Without being dragged? And he's drunk? Is God just messing with me right now? Gorgeous, cultured, drunk, and alone? I'm practically licking my lips.

AngelCharlie: What are you wearing?

I type, only half jokingly, then hit SEND.
God—did I just write that? I would never say something like that in person. But somehow, in the anonymity of the Internet, it doesn't seem like I'm really talking to *him.*

Jordan1313: Swim fins, a tutu, and a ten-gallon hat. You?

So much for Internet flirting being easier than real flirting. Apparently, I'm just as lame at it.

AngelCharlie: A tub of jello and a smile on my face. Hold on while I get another glass of wine.
Jordan1313: Excellent. I'll go get a beer.

I run into the kitchen to pour myself another glass of wine. Decide to grab the rest of the bottle and bring it with me.

This is good—I have just set up that I, too, am drunk, which is sort of like the lame girl's mating call. I can now say whatever I want, and if I'm embarrassed in the morning, I blame it on the booze.

Although I adhere to an important rule:

Always take responsibility for your actions.

I mean, I just can't stand people who get wildly drunk, do and say stupid things, then claim they can't remember anything in the morning so they don't have to deal with whatever fallout has occurred. I can't even tell you the number of asshole men who have—

> Jordan1313: I'm back. Did you miss me?
> AngleCharlie: With every fiber of my being. I don't know how I got through it.

This is so cool! I can totally be myself around him. If I can't see him, I can't walk into walls, or stare at the ground, or chew on my cuticles while my eyes dart nervously around the room to focus on anything but him and his amazingly blue eyes.

> Jordan1313: Can I ask you a confidential question? Drew's not gay, is he?

Or I could just make a fool of myself in front of a gay man. God, please don't let him be gay.

> AngelCharlie: No. Why?

I type, bracing myself for the answer.

Jordan1313: Well, I got this kind of weird vibe from him at
the end of the night. He was very insistent that I join him after
the party for a drink.
AngelCharlie: LOL! ☺ No, that was for me. Drew was trying
to play matchmaker.

That was written in a jokey way, right? Like, "Oh, that airhead
Drew—trying to set people up who would never have any interest
in each other."

Jordan1313: You're kidding! I didn't even know you were
available. Wait a minute—how can you be available?
AngelCharlie: Yeah. That's one of those questions a girl
loves to answer—what the hell's wrong with you that you're
still single?
Jordan1313: I didn't mean it that way. I'm single.
AngelCharlie: That's different. When a guy is single, he's
"available." Or if he's over thirty, he's "a catch." When a
woman's single, she's "looking." And if she's over thirty, she
"has baggage."
Jordan1313: Just so long as you're not bitter. ;)
AngelCharlie: I may be having some issues about turning
thirty.

I light up a cigarette. I'm not sure why I wrote that. It just felt right.

Jordan1313: Yeah. Like what?
AngelCharlie: Like my younger sister's getting married in
two weeks, and I'm not, and what the hell's wrong with me,

and why don't I have someone, and where are my 2.3 kids and a dog?

Jordan1313: Thank God you said dog. If you had said cat, I'd have to break it off with you immediately.

AngelCharlie: If I had said cat, I would have destined myself to stay single. If I had said cats, plural, I would have destined myself to being the crazy cat woman every kid in the neighborhood is afraid of. Have you turned thirty yet?

Jordan1313: Yeah. A few months ago. I had my own crisis. I broke up with my fiancée.

AngelCharlie: Yikes! I have no response to that.

Jordan1313: Unfortunately, neither did she. Well, other than screaming and crying and throwing things.

AngelCharlie: What made you decide to break it off?

He doesn't type back an answer. For a while. And I try to figure out how to take back the question. Damn, things were going so well. Why did I open my mouth?

Jordan1313: Incompatibility.

He finally writes back.

AngelCharlie: I'm sorry. It's none of my business. We can talk about something else.

Jordan1313: No. I'm glad that you asked. Truth be told, none of my friends have asked much. Guys sort of don't talk about these things. And now I don't have a girl to talk to about it, as my old best friend, her name was Janet, is now my sworn enemy.

AngelCharlie: You can talk to me about it.

Yeah, I know the rule:

Never ask a guy about his old girlfriends.

But it seems to me that maybe he needs a friend right now more than a love interest. And, it's strange, but right now, I want to know everything about him. And ex-fiancées are a part of that.

> Jordan1313: That's really sweet. Really. But I don't feel like talking about it right now. I'm drunk, I'm happy, and I'm talking to a cute girl. Why would I want to bring myself down?

He called me cute! I did not imagine it. I have it in writing. Cute. Is there any way to save these conversations for posterity? Nooo, that would be creepy.

> AngelCharlie: Okay.
> Jordan1313: But I really appreciate it. You're the only person except my mother and my sister who's asked for any details.

He gets along with his mother *and* his sister? Why is it men always get along with their mothers, but women don't? Universal mystery.

> AngelCharlie: No problem. If you ever do want to talk, my number's on the call sheet.

It's a subtle way to drop the hint. I'm careful so as not to be so desperate that I say, "And my cell phone number, and my address . . ."

Jordan1313: Thanks, I might. But let's change the subject. What wild thing are you doing on your birthday?

AngelCharlie: I'm almost too embarrassed to say. Dinner with my family. Fortunately, afterwards my friends are taking me out for a late night "I can't possibly be related to these people" drink.

Jordan1313: That sounds like fun.

I type "Maybe you could join us," and then hit SEND. But nothing happens.

I madly press the SEND button over and over again. Nothing.

Suddenly, I hear a robotic voice tell me, "Your session has ended. Thank you. Good-bye."

Noooooooooooooooooooooooooooo!!!!!!!!!!!!!!!!!!!!!!!!!

My home phone rings. Okay, stay calm. Maybe it's Jordan calling me. After all, I did just say my number was on the call sheet. Maybe he doesn't know I only have one phone line, and that my Internet access is connected to it.

I read the caller ID: Private caller. I pick up, and answer flirtatiously, "Hello?"

"Is there any way I can give money to the Brentwood Police Department without it looking like a bribe?" Drew asks.

I don't like the sound of that. "Drew, why didn't you call me on my cell?"

"I tried. But your phone went straight to voice mail. So, do they have, like, a policeman's ball or something?"

"What did you do?" I ask accusingly.

"I didn't do anything!" Drew says defensively. "But Cindy might be having some issues with her new home."

I'm just going assume Cindy is the new elephant. "What happened?"

"Well . . . first of all, did you know that female elephants can *roar*? Actually, it's kind of a combination of a roar and a cry. Kind of like how a puppy cries the first night you bring her home, and she realizes she can't sleep with you . . . mixed with a jackhammer."

I am speechless. Utterly speechless. But I have to say something. "I thought we agreed that Cindy . . . is that her name?"

"Yeah. It's short for Cinderellaphant."

"Very witty. I thought we agreed that Cindy was going to stay with her trainer until we got all those pesky little things like zoning laws worked out."

"Yeah, but then I started thinking about how nice it would be to come home to the pitter-patter of big feet, and, I don't know, I just had to take her home."

I hear a deafening roar on the other end of the phone. Then I hear Drew yell, "Daddy will be right out, sweetie!" He returns to his normal voice. "Anyway, Cindy's very upset, and I tried to let her into the house, so she'd calm down, but she didn't fit. Then the neighbors called the cops, and they were so nice about the whole thing, but they did tell me that it would be in my best interest to find Cindy a new home. Now. So, long story short . . ."

Too late.

". . . I need you to come over and call whoever it is that takes refugee elephants and tell them to come get Cindy."

Goddamn it! I have got to look for a new line of work. I mean, doctors should be on call. I understand that, they save lives. But no one should be called in the middle of the night to deal with a home-sick elephant.

Before I leave, I quickly get back online and try to IM Jordan.

AngelCharlie: I'm back. Did you miss me?

I wait. Nothing.

AngelCharlie: Hello?

I see "You Have Mail" lighting up my mailbox. I click on. A note from Jordan. I download it onto my hard drive, so I can save it for our future grandchildren.

Jordan1313: Hey, it's me. Where did you go? I guess I should be going to bed anyway. Thanks for the chat. See you Monday.
xoxo
Jordan

I spend the rest of the evening helping move Cindy to a zoo, and debating what Jordan's "xoxo" means.

Twelve

You gotta fight for your right to party.—Beastie Boys.

I spent most of Saturday checking my e-mail every twenty minutes to see if Jordan had written back. Last night, I sent him a quick note explaining that I had been bumped offline, that I was sorry, and that I would love to talk with him again sometime via e-mail.

The e-mail was light, flirty, and only a few sentences.

It only took me an hour and a half to write.

Jordan hadn't written back as of 6:52 P.M., but I checked the status of the e-mail I had sent him, and it turned out he hadn't checked his e-mail all day. So, really, his lack of response was no reflection on me.

That night, the last Saturday night of my twenties, the limo took Kate, Dawn, and me out to a fairly trendy Western bar on Sunset Boulevard. Yes, that's right—a Western bar. There's a mechanical bull and everything.

At the risk of sounding like a Hollywood snob, never go to a bar that's been featured on *E!* and *Sex and the City,* unless it's (A) Monday afternoon, when there's still parking available, or (B) you have the uncontrollable urge to talk to pasty-looking tourists who are here because they "heard Madonna hangs out here" or want to know "what Jennifer Lopez is really like."

Now that I've done my official "oh, I'm too hip for the room" spiel, I've got to admit . . . I love the place. They serve a margarita the size of a trough, and they have the hottest straight bartenders in the city (male and female). The bartenders not only look good, they'll do shots with you occasionally, which doesn't make you feel nearly so stupid late in the evening. And did I mention the mechanical bull?

We enter the bar, a Universal Studios version of a tavern from the wild, wild West. A man who looks like Brad Pitt's younger brother yells to us from behind the bar, "Ladies, what can I get ya?" It's still early, so we snag seats at the bar, and introduce ourselves to "Bob." He recognizes Dawn (yeah—what else is new?), and gives her a big hug that seems genuine. I order a margarita, Dawn a Long Island Iced Tea, and Kate a daiquiri. "All right." Bob flashes a smile at us, then goes to make our drinks.

Bob reappears with shotglasses of murky green liquid which he calls "an apple martini," then beams, "on the house, ladies. Who's drinking with me?" He puts four shots of the green goop down on the bar. We each take a shot, and Bob takes the fourth.

Bob lifts his glass. "Who wants to get drunk tonight?"

We yell, "We do!"

"Who wants to get laid tonight?"

We yell, "We do!"

"Who wants to get me tonight?"

We laugh, then down our shots. It's going to be a night to regret. I love nights like this!

Once we have our drinks, Kate starts scanning the room. "Okay, so how does this whole meet market thing work? Is it like college? Do the men walk up to us, or can we walk up to them?"

"It's a hideous process of degradation designed to make us go running back to our apartments screaming for our self-help books," Dawn says.

"Which, of course, we would never admit to owning in a place like this," I say.

"I'm serious, guys," Kate nearly whines. "I haven't been out there in almost a decade. Just go over a few quick rules."

So we do:

Don't talk to new guys after one A.M. *If he hasn't made the move before then, he's out.*

Don't go for the cutest guy in the room. If he says he doesn't have a girlfriend, he's lying. Or gay.

And finally:

Advice is like a sandwich. If you know someone is hungry, you can offer them a sandwich. They may even ask for a sandwich. But if you put the sandwich in front of them, and they don't eat it, there's nothing you can do. You can't force someone to eat a sandwich.

I say this because, within one minute—one minute!—a gorgeous man is waving to Kate from across the room.

Kate smiles and waves back.

Dawn pushes down Kate's hand. "What did we just tell you about the cutest guy in the room?"

"But I know him. That's Mike. He's one of the other hosts at the station."

Dawn and I stare at the gorgeous man across the bar. "That is *not* a face for radio," Dawn says, and I shake my head up and down in agreement.

Kate hops off her bar seat. "You guys are so silly. It's just Mike," she says, then leaves us.

We watch as she gives the blond Adonis a hug. "She's in here two

minutes, and does better than we do in two years," I say, only half
jokingly.

"I can only take solace in the fact that, on the inside, she's shattered and heartbroken right now," Dawn says sarcastically.

We watch Mike smile, and kiss Kate on the cheek. "Right," I
concur.

"Can I buy you ladies a drink?" Drew says from behind me.

"I'm afraid we're waiting for someone," Dawn answers, staring
right at him, her voice dripping with irritation.

"Dawn!" I exclaim, and quickly turn around to apologize for my
friend's rudeness. Standing before me is a new, less improved version of Drew. He looks awful. "What did you do . . . to your face?" I
ask gently, trying not to sound too horrified.

"You like it?" Drew says proudly. "I had Vic do it."

Vic is Drew's makeup artist, and he has made Drew up to look like
he has a large, broken nose and a double chin. Drew doesn't look
bad, he just kind of looks . . . normal. But for Drew, that's awful.
Dawn squints her eyes, and juts her chin forward, trying to get a better look at him. "It is you. Why the hell did you do that to yourself?"

"Well, I figure this way, we can do whatever we want tonight, and
no one will care. No one will ask for my autograph, no one will try
to buy me a drink, or try to get some personal information out of me
that they can sell to the National Enquirer, no one will hit on me . . ."

"You got that right," Dawn exclaims, looking disgusted. "You go
wash yourself up, boy."

"No," Drew insists. "I want to be a normal person tonight. This
way I can be."

Bob the bartender comes up to Drew, now sitting in Kate's seat,
and asks him, "Can I get you anything?"

"Yes. Get me a shot of Maker's Mark followed by a Sam Adams
chaser."

Bob stares at Drew quizzically. "Have I served you before?"

Drew fidgets in his seat nervously. "I don't think so."

Bob tilts his head, thinking, "You look really familiar. Did we audition together?" He snaps his fingers and smiles. "That's where I know you. You auditioned for the Budweiser ad, didn't you?"

Drew immediately covers himself. "Wow. I did. You have a great memory."

"Sure. You're the guy who kind of looks like Drew Stanton. What's your name again?"

"Ken," Drew says, putting out his hand for a handshake.

Bob shakes his hand. "Ken. I never forget a face. Hey, you know my friend said he saw Drew Stanton a few weeks ago over at Revolver."

"I've never been . . ." Drew starts to say, but stops himself. "Isn't that a gay bar?"

"Oh, yeah. I'm pretty sure he's gay. I heard he broke up Tom Cruise and Nicole Kidman."

Before Drew can refute that statement, one of the women bartenders says, "That's not true!" in a tone to let Bob know she thinks that's the stupidest thing she's ever heard. "My friend Cheryl says he's quietly been dating Bruce Willis for about a year."

"Bruce Willis?!" Drew snaps his head around to her, as I whisper, "Don't go there. No one knows who you are. Remember?"

Drew turns to me and whispers back indignantly, "If I were gay, I could do a hell of a lot better than Bruce Willis."

Dawn bursts out laughing. "I like you," she says to Drew. "You crack me up."

Drew smiles, and all is forgiven with the bartenders.

"Let me get you that drink, Ken," Bob says. "Do you want to start a tab?"

"I do," says Doug, joining us. "It's all on me tonight. I'd like a Bass, please."

As Doug puts down his credit card, I suddenly remember how

handsome he is. His hair is looking a little less gelled tonight, and he's in jeans and a nice T-shirt. And those eyes—they look like clear emeralds.

As Bob hands Doug his beer, I say, "Weren't you guys supposed to be coming later this evening?"

"What can I say?" Doug says, shrugging sheepishly. "When I see something I want, I have a problem waiting for it."

So charming. I sigh. I want to kiss him hello. I am suddenly remembering that kiss Thursday night. It was a nice kiss. His lips slowly parting, not too much tongue right off the bat, him smelling like a cookie . . .

"Are you going to ride the bull tonight?" Doug asks, jolting me out of my daydream.

"Excuse me?" I've never heard it put quite that way before.

Doug jerks his head toward the mechanical bull. "Nothing sexier than a woman riding a bucking bull," he says seductively.

"Baby, if you think that, we got to get you to some strip clubs," Dawn says in her "I'm so over you" voice, and takes a sip of her Long Island Iced Tea.

I laugh a little too loud in front of Doug, then turn to Dawn and mutter under my breath, "Knock it off."

She mutters back, "I'm sorry, but why doesn't he just open with 'I'm looking for a slut with skills?'"

"Back o-off . . . ," I say in a quiet, lilting voice.

Doug laughs and says, "No, she's right. That line might have been a little weak."

Dawn raises her glass to him, they toast, and a truce has been forged. Doug turns to me. "So what's your best line?"

I think for a minute, and smile. "Hi, I'm Charlie. Do you want to go outside and make out?"

Doug laughs, and Drew stares at me. "Have you ever said that to a guy?"

"No," I admit. "But it's still my best line." I turn to Doug. "What's your best line?"

Doug takes a moment to think about it. "Well, it has to be said a little while into the evening . . . But I think it has to be, 'So, Charlie, what are we going to name our children?'"

I roll my eyes and smile. "How drunk does the girl have to be for that to work?"

Doug chuckles. "Oh, she not only has to be wasted out of her mind, but we have to be at a wedding." He looks over at Drew. "What about you, Drew?"

"It's Ken," Drew reminds him. "Drew's evil twin brother with the double chin."

"Sorry . . . Ken," Doug corrects himself.

Drew looks over at Dawn, clearly debating whether he really wants to give her his best line. He smiles. "Hi. I'm Drew Stanton."

Dawn and I both groan in disgust as Drew defends himself. "Hey, I'm telling you, nine times out of ten, it works. Women have an image of me that has nothing to do with who I really am, and whether they like me or not has nothing to do with who I really am. I might as well use it to my advantage."

Dawn and I groan again.

"And I'll tell you something else—I am just like every other guy out there. You want us or you don't want us based on what you imagine us to be. It has nothing to do with who we really are. At least not at first."

I have to say, that gives both Dawn and me pause. He's right. I mean, how many first dates have we all gone on hoping we've found our Prince Charming? Assuming he'll be nice to us, assuming he wants a relationship. Hell, just assuming he doesn't have some girlfriend he's cheating on that night. It really has nothing to do with the guy du jour. It has nothing to do with a real relationship that might be forged in the future. It's all about what's going on in our heads at that moment.

Knowing this, I vow to forget about Jordan, and focus all of my attention on the man who has shown interest in me. In the man who wanted a date with me. In the man who kissed me.

Drew stares at his beer mug, tapping the rim of it nervously. "So . . . Dawn . . . what's your best opening line?"

Dawn doesn't miss a beat. As Drew takes a sip of his beer, she looks him right in the eye with her most seductive look and says, "Honey, I'd like to ride you like a Harley on a bad stretch of road."

Drew chokes on his drink, nearly spitting it on her, and she gives him a self-satisfied smile.

Our next few hours were a haze of drinking, bull riding, and more drinking. Kate quietly sat in a corner, lovingly staring into Mike's eyes all night. The rest of us were not so quiet.

Knowing that I had a limo for the night, the boys quickly switched from beer to well drinks, downing giant glasses of drinks with names like "Texas Tea." And all of us were doing complimentary shots with the bartenders all night. The drinks seemed to have loosened both men up. (Or maybe it loosened Dawn and me up. Does it really matter?)

Doug made me laugh all night. Now that he was rip-roaring drunk, he wasn't nearly as pretentious as he had been during the dinner party.

Right now, Drew is in line to ride the bull, and Dawn is with him to cheer him on. Doug and I are "guarding their seats," sneaking some kisses, and talking.

"You really are cute tonight," Doug says, leaning in to me like he's going to kiss me.

"You're pretty cute yourself," I say, blushing and returning the compliment.

Doug comes back with, "Not as cute as you."

Isn't it truly amazing what passes for conversation when the two people involved are still at that *Oh my God, our knees are almost touching!* phase? Soon, we'll graduate to "You hang up first . . . no, you . . . no, you . . ."

Doug leans in for a kiss and the two of us start making out like teenagers. He breaks from the kiss just long enough to say, "You are the best kisser."

"Only because I have such a good partner."

Yes—it's a marriage of the minds at this stage. Doug begins nibbling my ear, and I'm so turned on, I'm pretty much ready to jump him right here and now, and give everyone a show on this bar.

Suddenly next to me, I hear, "Doug?"

Startled, I jerk my head back and whip it around to a fifty-something man in jeans, looking a little out of place. Doug turns to him and, smooth as silk, shakes his hand. "Jeff. Good to see you. What brings you here?"

The older gentleman sighs. "Oh, my girlfriend wanted to come, and I can't say no to her. We're actually leaving soon, but I wanted to stop by and say hi."

"Well it's good to see you out of the office," Doug says, a little too slickly, then introduces me. "This is my girlfriend Charlie."

"How do you do?" I say, not responding at all to the girlfriend comment.

"Jeff Caraway."

"Oh," I say pleasantly, recognizing the name immediately.

"Jeff owns the company I work for," Doug says, although he really didn't need to tell me that. Jeff Caraway is one of the biggest behind-the-scenes names in Hollywood.

"Charlie works for Drew Stanton," Doug says.

"Oh, I know Drew," Caraway says, although I have a feeling "know" is a relative term. "Good guy." Caraway pats Doug twice on the shoulder, and says, "I should get back to my lady. Nice to meet you, Charlie."

"You, too," I say politely.

Caraway walks back to "his lady," a little embryo of a thing, and Doug turns to me, embarrassed.

"Girlfriend, huh?" I say flirtatiously.

He shrugs. "What, you don't think so?"

"Well . . ." I smile, and actually blush. "I don't know . . . ," I say, my voice trailing off.

I look to the ground, then look away. I can't actually face him, because then that would be admitting I'm into him. (I can just hear my mother in my head sarcastically saying, "God forbid he should know that.")

And if I look into his eyes, all I will want to do is kiss him.

So I do.

And I'm interrupted again.

"Charlie," I hear Kate say in an apologetic tone.

I quickly stop kissing Doug to see Kate holding hands with Mike. "We're gonna take off."

"You're what? No, no, no . . ."

Could I have been more subtle?

Kate yawns. "Look, you guys are having a great time, and I don't want to spoil it, but I'm exhausted, and I need to go to sleep. Mike's offered to give me a ride home."

I'll just bet he has.

"Will you excuse us for a moment?" I ask Mike and Doug, then grab Kate's hand and pull her out of their hearing range. "What are you doing?"

"Going home."

"Alone?" I ask.

"No. Wasn't that the whole point of the evening?" Kate asks back.

"No. The point was to have a night of female bonding with your friends."

"Which is why you're making out with a guy right now, instead of talking to me?" Kate asks sarcastically.

I look over her shoulder at the two men. "You make a good point. I'm a shitty friend. Let me grab Dawn, we'll say good-bye to the guys, and I'll take you home."

Kate laughs. "Why? So we can all leave the men we like in the name of female bonding?"

"Yeaaahhh . . . ," I say in a tone of "ddduuuuhhhh . . ."

Then I think about it. "Well, that does sound kind of stupid when you say it like that," I say to Kate.

Kate kisses me on the cheek. "Don't worry about me. I'll be fine. I'll call you tomorrow."

And she walks back to Mike, takes his hand, and walks out the door.

Is it just me, or does she seem to be taking this whole breakup thing too well?

Thirteen

Don't drink and drive.

Limos are the best thing ever! At two o'clock in the morning, Drew, Doug, Dawn, and I piled into the limo, and debated what to do next.

"I vote for Canter's!" I say, referring to the famous old deli on Fairfax.

"Why?" says Drew.

"Because they have food there," I point out.

Dawn has already pulled a bottle of champagne from the cooler in the back, and as she pops the cork, Doug pulls out glasses. "I say we go to my place," Doug says, then looks at me and winks. "I have food there, too."

"You're a guy who works sixty hours a week," I say. "How do I know you really have food there?"

Doug smiles as he hands me a glass of champagne. "I happen to be a very good cook. Name a dish—I'll make it."

I look up to the ceiling and pucker up my lips, thinking. Finally I come up with, "A triple decker ham and swiss, on rye, mustard only, no mayo."

Dawn rolls her eyes, and hands Drew a glass of champagne. "You're just saying that because you want to go to Canter's."

I smile at her, as Drew gives another suggestion, "Caviar—beluga. Toast points. Cold potatoes. And a dollop of crème fraiche." We all stare at Drew. "My house. It's all set up in the fridge."

I look at Doug, and he's got that, *God, I want to kiss you so much right now* look on his face.

So I bail on the Canter's idea. "All right," I tell Drew. "But you two go. I think I'm going to take Doug up on that cooking for me idea."

I dip my chin down, bite my lip slightly, and give Doug my best innocent girl look.

Well, as innocent as a girl can look who's almost thirty, wasted, and going to a man's apartment at two A.M.

Dawn opens her eyes wide and stares at me. I'm not sure if it's disapproval of me going home with Doug, or of me leaving her with Drew. "Charlie, why don't you come with us?"

Drew takes the moment to put his arm around Dawn and nuzzle her neck. "What? Don't you trust me alone with you?"

And I could have sworn I saw Dawn fidget like a schoolgirl with a huge crush on the captain of the football team. "Of course," she says to Drew, smiling and turning her head toward him as he nuzzles her neck. "It's just that I don't want to be rude."

"*They're* dumping *us.* We're not dumping them," Drew points out. "Besides, I promise to be a gentleman."

Dawn squints her eyes at him suspiciously. He smiles. "Seriously," he says. "I have three guest rooms, and you can wear a pair of my pajamas. I just don't want to say good night yet."

Weird. I can tell he's telling the truth. They're not going to do anything tonight. Drew, who could pretty much have sex with any woman he wants tonight, wants to not have sex with Dawn.

I've got to admit, there's a little part of me that's jealous of that.

Don't do anything in your life just to get someone else's approval.
Yours is the only one that matters.

By the time we drop Drew and Dawn off twenty minutes later, I am determined not to sleep with Doug tonight. I don't care how great he is—I am going to feel terrible about myself tomorrow morning if I do sleep with him.

Doug and I wave good-bye to Drew and Dawn, Dawn makes plans with me for tomorrow night, and the driver closes our door.

The second the door is closed, Doug leans over to me and whispers, "I missed you." And he gives me the most dreamy kiss. I mean, dreamy—that is the only way to describe it. He is a wonderful kisser. We kiss until we hear the driver open and close his door, and then wait until he lowers the partition.

"Where to, ma'am?"

"Uh . . ." I shrug, looking at Doug for directions.

"100 Ocean Avenue," Doug tells him. "But first we need to make a stop. Can you take us to the Ralph's on Bundy and Wilshire?"

We kiss until we get to the grocery store, which is only a few minutes away. He tried to move his hand over my bra once, but I maneuvered his hand away expertly, and he didn't push it.

When we get into the Ralph's, I feel a wave of nostalgia. "Hey, this is the Ralph's Dawn, Kate, and I went to when we went to UCLA."

"You and Dawn have been friends for that long?" Doug asked, surprised.

"Oh, yeah. We were roommates in college," I say, then sigh. "So many moons ago." I take a moment to stroll down memory lane before I turn to him. "We used to have these pig-out nights during finals week. We'd get frozen pizza, potato chips, ice cream, whipped cream, Hershey's syrup, and Oreos. Then we'd each get a candy bar for the drive home, so we didn't have to wait until we got home to start eating."

Doug smiles at me, grabs my waist, and pretends he's going to tickle me. "That is the cutest thing I've ever heard. Let's get all those things."

"Really?" I say, scrunching up my face and smiling. "You don't think that's silly?"

"Of course it's silly. That's why we have to do it." Doug takes my hand, and we walk hand in hand down the aisles, getting our pig-out food.

We're at Doug's place about twenty minutes later, a beautiful two-bedroom condominium located on the sixth floor of a building in Santa Monica. He has a view of the ocean from almost every room.

The place is a little too bachelory—if this were the eighties, he'd have a Nagel painting up. The carpet is bright white, the couches are bright white. No three-year-old's grape jelly–stained hands have been in here. And, not to get too graphic, but it doesn't seem like any bachelorette who might be out of Tampax has been here, either. I mean, the place is white, white, white.

As we unload groceries onto the white marble countertops, I start thinking about the future. I know, I shouldn't. But I'm not talking *wedding day* future—just *what would it be like to have him be my last call of the night?* immediate future. And *what would it be like to have his tongue in my . . .*

Bad Charlie. I mentally roll up a newspaper and swat myself on the nose.

Doug pulls out a pizza pan as I pull out a frozen Red Baron pepperoni pizza. "I still can't believe you wanted to get the vegetable lovers one," I tease him. "What kind of a wuss are you?"

Doug puts some aluminum foil over the pan. "Hey, I was doing that for you. I figured a woman with your figure has to eat a lot of vegetables."

"Hey! I think you've got your new best line," I joke as I put the pizza on the aluminum foil. Doug laughs and gives me a quick peck on the lips. "Let me put this other stuff away. Would you like some Merlot with your pizza?"

"Merlot? A man after my own heart. Yes, yes, a thousand times yes."

"Great." He pulls a corkscrew out of the kitchen drawer and prepares the bottle. "Wine will be ready in a moment. Pig-out food will be ready soon, too."

I walk over to his living room window to check out his view.

Then I walk out to the balcony and look at the stunning view of the ocean. It sparkles in the moonlight. And despite how high up we are, I can hear waves crashing down below. In the silence of a three A.M. city, all I can hear are waves. I don't remember the last time I was so at peace with the world.

As embarrassed as I am to admit this, I start imagining what it would be like to live here, to have that sense of serenity around me all the time. Man, to have coffee in the mornings on the balcony, smelling the sea air, or reading a good book in the living room, just occasionally glancing up at that gorgeous view. Or getting up at dawn and jogging on the beach. Okay, wait, scratch that one—or making love listening to the ocean waves as you—

Stop it, Charlie! Put that out of your mind. You're not supposed to be thinking about sex yet.

Doug comes up behind me, donuts his arm around my waist, and kisses my neck. "It's a beautiful view, isn't it?"

"It's stunning," I agree. "Where I live, the best view I get is of all the dogs at the dog park across the street."

"That's a good view, too," Doug says, turning me around and handing me a glass of wine. "Now, this is a '91 Merlot. A client gave it to me, so if it sucks, we'll pour it down the drain and start over."

I take a sip, and it is true ambrosia. (Of course, after how many drinks I've had tonight, the $1.99 Charles Shaw Merlot from Trader Joe's might be true ambrosia—but still.) Doug takes my hand and leads me back into the kitchen. "You know what that goes well with?" He pulls out the bag of Double Stuff Oreos.

"Now see," I say jokingly. "Why people bother with caviar and toast points, I'll never know."

Doug takes his glass of wine and hands me a cookie. "You want to see the rest of the house?"

"Sure," I say, taking the Oreo.

I pop the cookie into my mouth as the house tour begins.

"Well, you've seen the gorgeous balcony . . . which I like, but I'm afraid of heights, so I don't go out there much. Here's my office . . . ," Doug says, bringing me into a very utilitarian room with a black leather chair in front of a three-thousand-dollar laptop computer (I know this only because I recently picked one up for Drew) on a chrome-and-glass desk. I look at his bookshelf. *Plato's Republic* is there, along with the complete works of Charles Dickens, Shakespeare, a few Stephen King books for good measure, et cetera.

"It's nice," I say politely.

"Okay, it's boring. We're moving on," Doug says, taking my arm gently and moving me out of the office. We pass a washer and dryer. "Laundry room," he gestures to the right, then, gesturing to the left, "bathroom . . ."

Ooooh, a Jacuzzi tub. I love those! But I better not say that—sends the wrong message. I notice it's clean. Too clean. I'm going to guess he had a maid come in today. To impress me, maybe?

"And, in front of us, the master bedroom." Doug gently takes my hand and leads me in. It's right out of *Architectural Digest*. The room is so exquisite, I'm afraid to step inside. It's a confection of white: white plushy carpet, the kind that makes your toes happy; a (made) king-sized bed with a white bedspread; light teak dressers and nightstands; white lamps.

"You made the bed," I observe.

"No, I didn't," Doug admits. "I had a maid come in today. You

know, just in case I was having important company over later." He
grins sheepishly, and I am hooked.

"Optimistic," I flirt.

I lean in to kiss him. We quickly begin a mad frenzy of kissing.
Doug tries to pull me onto the bed, which is awkward because . . .
"Hold on. Merlot on white!" I yell, trying to get my glass to a nightstand before it stains. He quickly takes my glass and his, puts them
on the nightstand, and we continue our mad frenzy.

Always leave them wanting more.

Okay—the pizza might have burned. I wasn't that hungry anyway.

Fourteen

No matter how you feel, or what you've done, take comfort in knowing that someone, somewhere, has been in the same position you're in, and has felt all the same feelings you are feeling right now.

I wake up the next morning very proud of myself for not having sex with Doug yet. Okay, so most of his clothes are off. Mine aren't. And, no, I'm not being a bit Monica Lewinsky about definitions here—no sex of any kind.

Kissing, though. Lots and lots of kissing.

I love making out with a new guy. I love how the kissing is its own reward, how there's still so much to look forward to. It's not a prelude, like "Okay, ten minutes of this, then the clothes are off, fifteen more minutes, then five (five?), then he's off to bed, and I'm off to the kitchen for a chocolate Pop-Tart, and maybe a rerun of some old show on Nick at Nite."

And you're still so excited to be kissing each other. You're still at that phase where you can't believe he's even interested in you.

Ahhh, this is the best part.

I'm smiling as I wake up, and instinctively roll over onto his chest and into his arm. Ooooh, I fit well here. Some guys, you don't fit so well. They're too tall, or too short, or way too into their own space. But Doug is perfect. He smells perfect. He fits perfect.

Right now, he is perfect.

That lasts about two seconds.

Doug opens his eyes, smiles, and whispers, "Morning."

I whisper back, "Good morning," and kiss him. He pulls me on top of him, we neck for a while, and I debate my "no sex" rule.

Then the phone rings. I hear his answering machine go off. "Hi, this is Doug. I'm not able to come to the phone right now, please leave a message." Beep.

"Hi, Doug, it's your assistant, John. Look, I'm sorry to bother you so early . . ."

Doug nearly throws me off of him, and grabs the phone. "John, what's up?" he says calmly, all business. "Uh-huh . . . Uh-huh . . . Okay, patch him through to me. . . . Hello, Mr. Rocco? This is Will Madrid's manager. I want you to know that Will will *never read your script!*"

I jump at how loud Doug has just screamed. I flinch backward unconsciously as Doug continues to scream at the top of his lungs.

"No actor of mine reads unless I say so! You should never have given him that script directly! Everything goes through me!"

As the person on the other end of the phone defends himself, I start looking around for my stuff—just in case I need to make a quick escape.

"No!" Doug screams, leaping from the bed. "He's not smart enough to know what to read and what not to read! That's why he employs me! That's why he has a manager! And I'll tell you something—you will never have Will in your movie! You cannot use his name, you cannot even say he's seen the material! Your movie is over!"

Doug slams down the phone, making me jump for the second

time in thirty seconds. Doug turns to me, gives me a tender hug, and softens his voice. "I'm sorry, sweetie. Business."

Be wary of people who say "It's just business" as their excuse for unethical behavior.

I stare at Doug, not quite sure how to respond to the Dr. Jekyll/Mr. Hyde outburst. "Don't you think you were a little harsh to that guy on the phone?" I ask gently.

"No," Doug says softly, pulling me closer to him. "You have to understand, I'm the bad cop for these actors. They want to be the good guys—someone asks them to read a script, they say yes. It's my job to then tell the person no."

"Yeah, but you could have done it a little more gently," I point out, trying not to sound too appalled by his behavior.

"If I had done it gently, he might have gone back to Will. The point was to get him to leave my client alone." Doug lifts my chin and puts his lips to mine. "Now, what can I make you for breakfast?"

I smile, trying to get back into the mood. "Some eggs would be nice."

"There's this great little breakfast place down the street," he suggests. "Why don't I take you there?"

His phone rings again, and inside I'm already wincing. Doug picks up on the first ring, carrying his phone over to his walk-in closet and ignoring me completely. "Yeah? . . . put him on. Hi, it's Doug . . . No, that's *not* acceptable! We've already discussed this."

And the volcano explodes again. "You know, you are really wasting my time here! Why the *fuck* would you call me on a Sunday morning to insult my client with that kind of an offer?!"

By this point, I've already grabbed my things and started to head out the bedroom door, because I know, by heart, one of the golden rules of dating:

On your first date, see how he treats the waiter. That's how he'll be
treating you in six months.

Okay, so in this case it's people who want to work with him and
his clients. Same rule applies.

Doug hasn't even noticed me. He's too busy screaming, "You
know, sometimes I wonder how incompetents like you can even get
a job!" Suddenly he covers the phone and runs after me, his voice
returning to normal. "Sweetie, what's wrong?"

"I'm . . ." What am I? I'm speechless, I'm appalled . . . "I'm gonna
go. I'm feeling a bit . . ."

Doug yells into his phone, "I'm on another call! Can you fucking
hold, you piece of shit!" Then he puts his arm around me tenderly,
and rubs my arm. "What's the matter honey, are you hung over?"

"Yes!" I say emphatically. "Very. And I'd really like to just get
home and rest, if that's okay with you."

"Sweetie, I can take care of you . . . ," Doug says, sounding like a
mother hen.

Okay, think. What would Dawn say in this situation? "You know,
clearly you have work to do, and I have a lot of errands to run today,
so why don't we just see each other later in the week?"

Oh my God. I've become a guy. I'm actually telling someone I
plan to see him again just to make a clean getaway. But my hand is
now on the front door, and it just might work.

Doug looks confused. "Well, okay. How about Wednesday?"

"That's great," I say, "I'll call you." Then I give him a quick peck
on the cheek, and race out his front door.

"Let me at least drive you home . . ." Doug yells down the hall after me.

"Not necessary. I've got my cell phone with me. I'll just call a
cab," I yell back as I scurry to his elevator, and get the hell out of
Dodge.

Fifteen

When I get home, the disaster of Doug is still lingering in my head. So I decide to use it to good advantage by coming up with another bit of dating advice:

Never throw good money after bad. And when it comes to dating, never throw good time after bad. Cut your losses! Dump the bastard.

The rest of the day went by pretty uneventfully. First I called Kate to see how the rest of her night went.

"Oh, it was so nice," she says blissfully. "We kissed all night. He's so wonderful."

"You didn't sleep with him, did you?" I ask, worried.

"Not that it's any of your business, but no," Kate answers, sounding irked with me.

"Good. Did he get your number?"

"I know him through work. He already has my number," Kate points out, now sounding really irritated with me.

"Okay," I say. This is awkward, because I already know where this relationship is going, and she doesn't.

"Don't give me that tone," Kate says.

"I'm sorry. I didn't mean to give a tone," I say carefully. "I hope everything works out."

"Me too. Anyway, I've got some work I have to catch up on. I'll see you tonight," Kate says, and hangs up.

I forgot one other bit of advice I should have given her last night:

You won't meet your future husband at a bar.

But I suppose this is a lesson most of us have to learn through trial and error.

Next, I call Drew to ask him how his night went, to tell him what happened with Doug, and to let him know in no uncertain terms that he will *never* (okay, I didn't scream it, but I wanted to) sign with this asshole manager. Then I call Dawn to see how her night went.

Both of them said that they had a good time, but neither would give me details. I hate that. I spend much of the day obsessing over what happened between them that neither of them would tell me about it.

I checked my e-mail several times throughout the day for a note from Jordan—but nothing. Rats!

That night, the night before my thirtieth birthday, Dawn and Kate came over with champagne and pizza, to celebrate the last night of my twenties (and, after my second to last night going so badly, I say, "Good riddance!").

And to create "mate maps" for ourselves.

"What the hell is a mate map, and why am I wasting my time doing it?" Dawn says, holding a glass of champagne as she and I stare at three 2' × 3' rectangles of white posterboard on my coffee table.

Kate sits on my couch flipping open a bunch of magazines. "Don't sound so negative. It's a really good idea. This woman I interviewed on my radio show wrote a whole book on mate maps. It is *the* confirmed way to find the man of your dreams."

"Is this woman married?" I ask as I light a cigarette and take a seat on my sofa.

Kate looks up from her magazines, irked. "You needn't be a chicken to find a good egg."

"No, all you really need is to find enough chickens to buy your stupid book," Dawn says, flopping into the overstuffed chair across from us.

Kate glares at her, then chooses to ignore the barb. "Now, we each take a piece of blank posterboard, and think about the qualities we really want in our future mate. You know, things like 'blond hair' or 'solid build.' "

Kate hands us each an old issue of *Cosmopolitan* as she continues, "We go through these magazines for ideas, and cut out anything that appeals to us. So, like, if we want him to have blue eyes, we cut out a picture of blue eyes, and glue it to the board. If we want an athlete, we cut out a picture of a basketball or a football, and glue that onto our board. The idea is, at the end of a few hours, you have a collage that represents the perfect man for you. The theory is, if you dream of him, he will come. And, with a little luck, in more ways than one."

Dawn flips through her *Cosmo,* then looks at me. "Do you have any issues of *Fortune* magazine?"

I throw Dawn a back issue of *Fortune,* and she takes her scissors to begin.

"Oh, I almost forgot," Kate says, handing us each a thick Magic Marker. "If you can't find the quality you want in a glueable form, you can also use a pen, and write down words like *committed* and *good-hearted* in thick, black Magic Marker."

So the three of us took our Magic Markers, magazines, and big white pieces of posterboard, and set about to create our perfect men.

Two hours and a magnum of Veuve Clicquot later, we were ready to read our mate maps.

I stare at my mate map, hidden from my friends, as Kate begins, "Okay, let's start with an easy one. Hair color?"

"I go with brown or black," I say.

"Blond," Kate lets us know. "Definitely blond."

"I don't care," Dawn says, "as long as he didn't cry watching *Beaches*."

Kate glares at Dawn. "Political party?"

"Democrat," I read from my board.

"Republican," Kate reads.

"Or *Love Story*. I hated that movie," Dawn mutters to herself. " 'Love is never having to say you're sorry.' What a crock. Love is constantly saying you're sorry, even when you know damn well you're right."

"Are you gonna take this seriously or not?" Kate asks.

"I am very serious," Dawn says, opening another bottle of champagne. "A guy who cries at movies is gonna let me know how he's feeling every minute of the day, and I don't need that kind of aggravation in my life."

I light another cigarette. "I know just what you mean. In the seventies, we told men we wanted them to tell us exactly how they felt, and what they really thought. What were we thinking? Shut up already! *CSI* is on."

"Dawn, pick a hair color and a political party, or you can't play anymore," Kate insists.

Dawn rolls her eyes, pours herself another glass of champagne, then looks at her posterboard pensively. "Anyone who is a member of the Cocktail Party."

Kate gives up, and moves on to the next question. "Commitment?"

"Yes!" all three of us say in unison.

Kate points to the symbol on her posterboard. "See, I glued it right there."

I cock my head. "I don't really think a prison cell should be your symbol for commitment."

"Schyeah," Dawn says sarcastically, "girlfriend doesn't have any issues there."

"Don't hate," retorts Kate.

Dawn puts up her index finger. "Okay, you are way too white to be saying that."

"Job?" I ask, trying to change the subject. "I don't care as long as he's happy."

"Political investigator, or rock 'n' roll legend," Kate reads.

"Political? . . . Isn't that what Mike does?" I ask Kate.

"Coincidentally, yes," Kate admits.

"Mike, the fair-haired Republican," Dawn adds.

"Hey, it's not my fault Mike looks so good on paper," Kate acknowledges. Her cell phone rings.

"Don't pick up!" Dawn and I say in unison.

Kate reads her caller ID. "I won't. It's not Mike. It's Jack." She throws her cell phone down on my coffee table. As she stares at it, she asks, "If a guy says he'll call you, how many days does he usually wait?"

Uh-oh. "Well," I begin cautiously, "it depends on the guy. . . ."

"Don't call him," Dawn says definitively to Kate.

Kate furrows her brow. "I wasn't going to call him," she says dismissively.

"Good. Because if he doesn't call you, it means he's not interested."

"Thanks for the vote of confidence," Kate says dryly.

"And don't believe him when he runs into you at a club in three months and says he 'lost your number,'" Dawn continues.

Kate squints her eyes, observing her. "Have you got any more dating tips for me?" she asks sarcastically.

"Always," Dawn says, smirking. She knows she's being made fun of. She doesn't care. She gives her advice cheerfully, without the slightest hint of malice. "One. Your future husband ain't at a club. Two. Your future boyfriend ain't at a club. Three. If he doesn't call you within twelve hours of the first time you kissed—Next! Forget he ever existed. Have your own private little *Spotless Mind* memory erase, then move on."

Kate laughs, shaking her head. "Wow. I hope I never get that cynical."

Dawn smiles a genuine smile. "Me too," she says sweetly, then leans over to give Kate a kiss on the cheek. "Your lack of cynicism is one of my favorite things about you."

Which is a really sweet thing to say, and probably even true.

But, sadly, the rules that Dawn gave were definitely true.

Sixteen

When you get really depressed at how unfair the world is, remember: half the planet didn't get a clean drink of water today.

Normally, I am comforted by that statement. Really. I know I'm lucky to live where I do, have the friends I have, and the job, and all that. But right now, all I can focus on are the things I don't have, instead of the things I do.

After the girls go home, I race to my computer to see if Jordan is online. He isn't. I pour myself another glass of champagne, and hang around the Internet for about a half hour (my new version of waiting by the phone). Then I give up for the night.

I decide to lie in bed with the rest of the Veuve Clicquot and watch a *Behind the Music* episode about Destiny's Child. Beyoncé has just told us that they were not the overnight sensation everyone keeps saying they were. "We paid our dues," she lets us know. She was nineteen at the time. Time for some more words of wisdom:

No one can ever say they've "paid their dues" at the age of nineteen, unless they've just won the gold medal in women's gymnastics.

It's a little after midnight, and I can't sleep. I flip through the channels on the TV, and I see the following statistic: ninety percent of teenagers lie to their parents. All I can think is, "Until they turn twenty-one, at which time the number jumps up to one hundred percent."

Lie to your parents. They so rarely want the truth anyway.

I mean, really, when your mom asks, "So, have you fallen in love lately?" does she really want to hear, "No, but I am sleeping with a guy who's been divorced twice, and won't buy me dinner."

I flip the channel. There's the inaugural address from the president of Peru. Thank God for satellite TV—I might have missed this.

Flip. *Blue's Clues.* At 12:15. Are there a lot of kids up at 12:15 dying to find out how to make chartreuse out of green and yellow?

Flip. The original *Family Feud* from the 1970s. "Name something a man picks up on his way to a date." Oddly, condom is not the number one answer. I wait to see all the answers pop up. No condom. Ah, those glorious seventies, when the only thing you had to worry about getting was pregnant.

Flip. An old *Friends* rerun. Jennifer Aniston as Rachel is upset because she's just met Ross's new girlfriend, Julie.

I turn off my TV and stare at my book of wisdom, ready to cry. I remind myself again that I am very lucky to live where I do, have the job that I have, and friends that I love. But tonight, here in my bedroom, all by myself, I'm ready to burst into tears. I'm thirty. Thirty years old. Who'd have thought the last ten years would have gone so fast? I'm officially old. And, let's face it, I'm never going to be Jennifer Aniston. I'm never going to be as beautiful, or as rich, or as famous. Hell, why stop there? I'm never going to be as smart as

Albert Einstein, or as great a writer as Tolstoy, as historically important as John F. Kennedy . . .

I was supposed to be married by now. My sister will be married
when she's thirty. Hell, she'll have a kid. I'm never going to get married. I'm never going to have kids.

I have a lot of things in this world—I know I shouldn't be depressed. There are people in this world who have never had a hot
soapy shower or a pint of ice cream. I've had both tonight.

But I can't help it. There comes a moment in your life when you
realize that no matter how hard you try, you're never going to be
fluent in Spanish. Or go on that African safari you've read about
since you were a kid. Or be as excited as you used to be about
catching fireflies. I keep trying to find my answer to life—and it gets
more elusive the older I get.

I always thought that by this point in my life I'd be married to a
wonderful man, with a four-year-old named Samantha, a two-year-
old named Ben, and a third one on the way. And a dog—I always
wanted a dog.

The phone rings. If it's Dave, I'm going to invite him over—so I
can kill him in his sleep. I pick up. "Hello."

"I need you to come over," Drew says urgently.

Not tonight. I really can't deal with this tonight. "Drew, it's after
midnight. I'm tired and I'm drunk. Whatever it is, I am sure it will
keep until morning."

"Actually, it won't. You need to come now."

He's being awfully cryptic. "Is there a dead woman in your bed?"
I ask.

"No."

"Did you adopt a hippo that the neighbors are complaining
about?"

"Of course not."

"Then it'll keep until tomorrow. I'm really upset right now, I'm too drunk to drive, and you really do not want to push me tonight."

Drew's silent for a while. "Clearly . . . I have done something to upset you," he says calmly. "And . . . obviously I am remorseful of this, and need to make it up to you."

Well, that's more like it. "Yes, you do," I say, totally sure of myself.

"And what can I do that will show you how sorry I am for whatever I have done to wrong you?" Drew asks.

"You can let me stay home tonight," I say, proud of myself for standing up to him and his silly demands.

"Yeah, okay, that's not gonna happen," Drew says, his voice changing back immediately. "So let's say I take you to London next month, and we take you shopping. Meanwhile, you come here now."

"I'm not . . . you can't just . . . . Oh, hell."

Thirty minutes later, a cab brings me to Drew's place. I press the intercom to his gate, but he doesn't answer. Hmm. I press the code to let myself in. As the cab pulls up to Drew's front door, I see there are no lights on downstairs. The place looks deserted. Looks kind of spooky. I pull out my cell, and call Drew.

"Yo," he answers.

"I'm out front."

"Okay, pay the cabbie. And don't come in until you see he's driven off. I'm in the bathroom."

I have no idea what to make of this, but I hang up, pay the cab driver, and watch him leave. Once his taillights disappear from the road, I let myself into Drew's home. "Hello?" I yell from the front door.

"I'm up here!" Drew yells from upstairs. "Come on up! I'm in the master bath!"

I start to walk up the stairs, feeling a little creeped out. He's being awfully cryptic. "Are you dressed?" I yell to him as I climb the top step, then move down the hall toward his bedroom and the master bath.

"Not exactly!" Drew yells to me.

I get to the doorway of his bedroom, and stop. No blood—that's probably a good sign. I return to my normal voice. "Do you need me to find some guy to help you get dressed?"

"No," Drew says, panicked. "No guys. No one but you."

I take a deep breath to brace myself, then walk into Drew's bathroom. I would say I recoil in horror, but frankly nothing I see surprises me.

There's Drew, in nothing but a pair of silk boxer shorts, and his arm stuck down the toilet. We exchange glances.

"I can explain," Drew says.

I walk in and quickly examine my surroundings. Drew has redone his whole bathroom to match his trailer. The walls are a deep blue, the towels look rich and exotic. And there are candles, incense, and elephants everywhere. "You don't need to explain," I say. "My truth is just an illusion. I think my movie star boss has his hand stuck in a toilet, but really I'm a frustrated housewife from Sheboygan who wants to break out of Wisconsin and become a porn star."

"Just get me out," Drew demands.

I walk over to Drew, and donut my arms around his naked waist. "All right, at the count of three, I'm going to pull you—one, two, three . . . Ugh!" We both pull, but to no avail. "Okay, try again. One, two, three . . . Ugh!" My palms must be sweaty, because my hands slip off his stomach and I fall to the ground. "Let me call a plumber."

"No! No plumbers!" Drew practically barks at me. "I can't have this in *Star* magazine. I can just see the headline: 'Sexiest Man Alive's Secret Flushed Out.'"

He has a point. "Okay," I say, standing up and walking over to the toilet to look inside. "Why don't you tell me what happened, and we'll figure this out together?"

"I was decorating my bathroom to be more in line with my spiritual beliefs. I had the room painted, got new towels, and I got all these cool Ganeshes. So, I'm putting them around my bathroom, when one fell down the toilet. I tried to reach in and grab it, only I forgot that I was wearing my Rolex, and I guess it got caught on something, because now I'm stuck."

Yeah, it could happen to anyone. I look inside the toilet. "Well, maybe if we flush, the water pressure will sort of push your arm out."

"I can't do that."

"Why not?"

"I'm not flushing God down the toilet! What would that do to my karma?"

I try to give him the best *you are such an idiot* look I can muster, but he just stares at me blankly. Finally, I look around for bubble bath. "Hold on," I say, then grab some L'Occitane Lavender from his tub and pour it into the bowl. Drew looks into the bowl, curious. "What's this going to do?"

I put my hand in the toilet bowl, and start soaping up what I can of his arm. "Hopefully, it's going to make your arm, and the pipe, slippery enough that we can pull you out."

Half a bottle later, I get back behind him, and donut my arms around him again. "Okay, one, two, three . . . Ugh!" Drew comes out flying, landing on top of me. Yup, naked sexy guy on top of me—backward. This is exactly how I wanted to start my thirtieth birthday.

Drew stands up and washes himself off. "Fabulous. Can I get you a glass of Cristal?"

I sit on the bath mat in a stupor thinking, *How exactly did I get here?* "Yeah. I suppose."

Drew looks at his toilet bowl. "Your arm's smaller. Would you mind retrieving my Ganesh?"

I would say I stared daggers at him, and told him what I thought of that request, but I'd be lying. I just put my hand down the toilet, grabbed the little red elephant, and threw it to him.

Two minutes later, we are downstairs in Drew's well-appointed kitchen. Drew has put on a bathrobe and is pulling a bottle of Cristal champagne from his refrigerator while I pull some champagne flutes from his cupboard. I want to burst into tears. I don't think my life could get any lower than having to retrieve something from a toilet.

"You okay?" Drew asks as he pours the champagne. "You look . . . weird."

That came out of nowhere. I'm jarred by the question. I thought I was doing better at covering up my depression. "I'm fine," I lie. "Just a little tired."

"Oh," Drew says. "Cheers." He clinks his glass with mine.

"Yeah," I say sadly. "Happy birthday to me."

"Your birthday's today?" Drew asks, genuinely surprised.

"Yes. You threw me a party, remember?"

"Well, yeah. But I didn't know it was today. That's why you're all bummed out? Just because it's your birthday?"

"Kind of," I say, shrugging and taking a sip of my champagne. "It's complicated and boring, and I don't want to talk about it."

"I tell you about stuff that's complicated and boring all the time."

"Yes. But you pay me to listen to you," I half joke.

"Hmm," Drew says. Then he walks over to my purse and hands it to me. "That'll be one dollar."

I smile at him, touched by the sentiment. Oh hell, I'm drunk. What could it hurt to just tell the truth?

In vino veritas—*in wine there is truth.*

I pull my wallet from my purse, pull out a dollar . . . then let him have it. "I don't want to turn thirty in six hours. Which, by the way, is when I'm officially thirty. I'm not ready to be old yet. Just eight years ago, I was in college, and I could do anything I wanted. I hate that I've already made choices. And I hate that even with all I've learned over the years, I still wait by the phone, and still feel bad when men don't call me."

"God," Drew says, looking genuinely pained for me. "That must be painful."

"What? Getting old?" I ask. I put my wallet back in my purse, then pull out a pack of cigarettes. I offer Drew one.

"No. Waiting by the phone," Drew says, taking a cigarette from me. "Do women still do that?"

My God! For an Academy Award–nominated actor, he sure can be dense. "Yes, we wait by the phone!" I bark, taking out a cigarette and putting it up to my lips. "Jesus, men can be stupid. No offense."

"None taken. I can be incredibly stupid," Drew says, grabbing a silver lighter from the counter and lighting my cigarette. "I hate being the asshole who doesn't call. I mean, I always mean to call again."

"So why don't you?" I ask, maybe a little too angrily.

Drew lights his cigarette. Takes a long puff before he speaks. "Well, I can have a good time on a date no matter what. I mean, I've been on dates when it's been like talking to a brick wall. But I can have fun at a tax audit, so I usually have fun anyway."

He continues, "But I know women, and after a few dates they start thinking about the future. Which means I have to start thinking about the future. And, usually, the girl is great, or I wouldn't have dated her at all. But she's not the one. So if she's thinking about the future, I better not keep her hopes up by going out with her again. I don't want to hurt her. But then, I'm stuck. What do I do now? Call her and say, 'Hi, I don't think we should see each other anymore because I don't want a commitment'? The girl would either think I was conceited, nuts, or a complete jerk."

I take another sip of champagne, and think about that. He's right. If anyone ever called me to tell me he didn't want to give me something I hadn't even asked for, I'd think he was a complete asshole, and I'd repeat what he said to all my friends as a dating war story. "I guess you're right," I say more brightly than I expected. "I never thought about it that way."

"Who's this guy you've been waiting by the phone for? Jordan? Doug?"

"No. A guy named Dave."

"How many dates did you have?"

"Three. Well, four." Hey—if you have sex with him, that should count as a date.

"Then he didn't think anything was wrong with you," Drew assures me, then takes another drag from his cigarette. "And you didn't do anything wrong, if you're worried about that."

I was. "I'm also never going to be Jennifer Aniston," I tell him.

Drew looks at me, confused. "Why would you want to be?"

The "duh" is definitely in my voice as I answer, "Because she's beautiful, and successful, and she can buy whatever she wants, and go wherever she feels like going. And people will still remember her in a hundred years, so she's immortal. And she still gets great jobs, even though she never has to work again. And I'll bet *she* doesn't wait by the phone."

Drew is silent, thinking. Shit! I shouldn't have said she never has to work again. Why was I so desperate for a friend that I made the mistake of talking to my boss?

"You ever read *TV Guide*?" Drew asks me, interrupting my thoughts.

"I think *read* is a very figurative term. Why?"

"Years ago, they did this issue honoring the fifty greatest TV stars of all time."

"And Jennifer Aniston wasn't in it, and therefore I should feel better?" I say, sighing.

"No, she wasn't," Drew says, "but that's not where I'm going with this. I saved the issue because on the cover were the greats: Mary Tyler Moore, Bill Cosby, Carroll O'Connor. And inside were Johnny Carson and Carol Burnett and a bunch of others I've been honored to meet over the years. And you know what all these stars had in common?"

"Money beyond their wildest dreams?" I ask, irritated and now getting even more depressed.

"No."

"Fame and success beyond their wildest dreams?" I ask. God, how is this supposed to be cheering me up?

Drew shakes his head. "Uh-uh."

"Then I don't know, and this is making me feel worse, because there's not one thing I can say about my life—"

"They've all lost a child," Drew says somberly.

I stand there in stunned silence. Drew continues, "And I'll bet every one of them would have given up all their money and success to have their kid back. I'll bet they'd have given up every fucking thing in the world to hug their baby again."

I didn't know what to say. Drew went on, "And that's not including people like Oprah Winfrey, who was molested as a child, Roseanne Barr, who gave up a child for adoption, Lucille Ball divorcing her husband, the one great love of her life, after he had slept with half the women in Hollywood. Hell—how many divorces do you think came to those fifty people?"

Drew went on, "Don't be jealous of anyone. I guarantee you, if everyone walked into a room, and dumped their problems onto the floor, when they saw what everyone else's problems were, they'd be scrambling to get their own problems back before someone else got to them first."

I thought about what he said. Pretty profound for Drew. I cocked my head at him. "That's last line's from a movie, isn't it?"

"Okay, yes. But the rest of it was me."

Drew and I talked until dawn that night. I guess I could be sad that the one man in my life I can talk to until dawn is my boss. But I'll tell you, I sure felt a lot better. And the following morning, I had another bon mot for my book of advice:

A good long talk can cure almost anything.

Seventeen

Life begins at 30.

God, if this is the beginning of the rest of my life, I'm so screwed.

Later that morning, bleary eyed and a bit hungover, I took a cab to my car, then headed over to the set. While en route in my car, my cell phone rings. I check the caller ID. It's my mother. I put on my headset and pick up anyway.

"Hello, Mom."

"Happy birthday, sweetie," she says brightly.

"Thank you. Happy birthday to you, too," I say back. For some reason, when someone says "happy birthday" to me, it's like "Merry Christmas" or "Happy New Year." I always feel like I should respond, "To you, too."

"I want to warn you about your father's gift so you don't go all ballistic when you get it at dinner tonight," Mom says.

"Oka-ay," I say cautiously.

"I mean, your father loves you. He would never mean to hurt your feelings."

My father's gifts never hurt my feelings—they're just weird. Last year he gave me a blowtorch. Apparently it's to make crème brûlée without having to put it in an ice bath in your oven. I don't make crème brûlée, and I use my oven for storage.

The year before that he got me surfing lessons. Me, with my horrible, debilitating fear of sharks. (It goes well with my fear of snakes and fear of commitment.)

"I'm sure whatever he gave me is fine," I say. My cell phone beeps. "Mom, hold on a sec. . . ." I click on. "Hello."

"Hi, it's Dad. I just wanted to give you a heads up on your mother's gift. It was bought with the best of intentions."

The road to hell was paved with the best of intentions.

I'm paraphrasing—but you get the point.

"Dad, I'm on the other line. Let me call you right back," I say, then click back to Mom. "All right, I'm back."

"He got you an appointment with Ramone at Frederic Fekkai," my mother says, her tone expressing outrage.

"The hair salon?" I ask, confused.

"One and the same," Mom says, now getting angry. "I told him you didn't want to change your hair color, but he insisted. He said with how gray your hair is getting . . ."

"Whoa, whoa . . . Whoa!" I sputter out.

"I know. How insulting, right? I mean, it's not *your* fault you got that early gray gene of his. It's from his side of the family, you know. . . ."

"I am not going gray!" I belt out as I slam on my brakes to allow a Lincoln Navigator to cut me off.

"Honey, please, I'm your mother. I love you, but don't you think we all know why you've chosen to be a blonde these past few years?"

I swear, she's chiding me. "I chose to be a blonde because I felt like doing something different with my hair!"

"Sweetie, you shouldn't be embarrassed by it. Valerie Bertinelli turned gray at twenty-seven, and look at how successful she turned out," my mother informs me. "She used to be blonde, but now she's back to that beautiful dark hair she had when she was on *One Day at a Time*."

I'm speechless. It's just too early. "Mom, I'm almost at the studio. I gotta go."

"Okay. Have fun on your special day," Mom says cheerfully. "Oh, and when your father calls and tries to warn you about the present I got you, tell him that I am totally right, that it's for your own good, and that at least my gift was well thought out."

Never give someone a present that's "for their own good."

"Dad's not going to call," I insist as my phone beeps again. Speak of the devil.

"At least I got you something practical. And it's something you would never buy for yourself," Mom says, then clicks off before I can say good-bye.

I click back to my dad. "Whatever Mom got me, I'm sure she meant well . . ."

"She got you Botox injections."

"Excuse me?" I say, slamming on my brakes to let a Ford Expedition cut me off.

"From her dermatologist. You know, for that wrinkle in between your eyes from scowling at her all these years? This'll get rid of that in time for your sister's wedding."

Botox, for anyone living in a cave, is the poison botulinum toxin (yeah, as in *botulism*), diluted and put in a vial, then injected into your forehead to make your wrinkles go away. I look at my forehead in my rearview mirror. I'll be damned! I do have a wrinkle between my brows. And, now that I'm looking at it, one big horizontal line across my forehead. Happy birthday to me. "Oh. My. God. I do have a wrinkle between my brows."

"It's hardly noticeable," Dad assures me.

"Yeah," I say bitterly, "so unnoticeable, my mother wants to poison me to get rid of it."

"You sound upset," Dad says.

Nothing gets by him. "Yeah, well, this day is sucking already, and it's not even eight o'clock. Shit!" I slam on my brakes as a Mercedes SUV cuts me off.

"Are you upset about turning thirty?" Dad asks.

"Yes . . . No . . . I don't know. I don't want to talk about it," I say, changing lanes and making a right turn into the studio lot.

"I would give my left ball to be thirty again," Dad tells me.

"Charming," I say dryly as I ease past the guard gate and wave to the guards who I see every morning. "Do you know by the time John Lennon was my age, the Beatles had already broken up?"

"Cheer up," Dad says. "When John Lennon was my age, he'd already been dead for more than ten years."

No matter who you are, and what's going on in your life, there's always someone out there worse off than you.

"That's a good way to look at it, I suppose," I say (because, frankly, I have no comeback to that). As I park my car, I see the P.A.'s car pull up, with a comatose Drew inside. "Dad, Drew's here. I gotta go."

"Loveyoubye," Dad says in one word, and hangs up.

I get out of my car just as Drew gets out of the P.A.'s car, wearing dark glasses, and looking like death warmed over. Actually no, not even warmed over. Just death. I'm starting to feel guilty for keeping him up so late.

"Good morning," I say. "How was your night?"

He yawns. "I stayed up all night with a girl, and I didn't even get any."

"That's a shame," I say, playing along. "Was she cute?"

He covers his mouth as he yawns again, this time rather loudly. "Very. But if I ever hit on her, she'd sue my ass. Can you go to Craft Service and get me a venti cappuccino?"

"You mean a large," I remind him as we walk to the Makeup trailers. "Ventis are from Starbucks."

He rubs his red eyes. "Sweetie, no disrespect, but I don't mean a large. I mean an extra, extra large. I mean, have them take the biggest container they can find, hose it down, then fill it with coffee. I want a trough of coffee, if they have it."

"I'll see what I can do," I say, chuckling.

I head over to Craft Service, which is the caterer for the morning food and the snacks throughout the day, and see that they have a cake set out for me—a big Costco birthday cake with "Happy 30th Charlie!" written on it.

Well, this day's just getting better and better.

From behind me, someone puts his hands over my eyes.

"Guess who?" Jordan's voice demands.

"Hmmm . . . ," I say. "Helen Gurley Brown."

"Taller," he says, keeping his hands over my eyes.

"Heidi Klum?" I guess.

"No. But if you know Heidi Klum, I'd like an introduction."

"Kobe LeBron."

Jordan takes down his hands. "Who?"

I turn around. "Now you know how I feel whenever you name professional athletes. How are you doing?"

For some reason, as I talk to him this morning, I can't believe how calm I am. This is Jordan. *The* Jordan. And I'm talking to him like he's a normal person.

"I'm good," Jordan says. "I just got your e-mail this morning. I'm sorry you got bumped offline. I should have waited for you to come back, but I was tired."

The middle-aged man from the Craft Service truck yells, "Next!"

I turn to him. "Good morning, Juan. Can you get me a regular cappuccino, and a huge one for Drew?"

"Of course," Juan says happily. "Nonfat milk, no sugar."

"Thanks," I say brightly, then turn back to Jordan. "So, what did you do with your weekend?"

I try to keep the question light and breezy. What I really wanted to say was "Where the hell were you?"

"I went up north," Jordan says as he pours himself a regular coffee from a huge urn on one of the tables. "It was a spur-of-the-moment idea."

"Did you have fun?" I ask, still lightheartedly. I want to grill him for details, but I don't want to look too interested.

Jordan gives a weird look that I can't decipher, and says, "Not really. It was okay, I guess."

I don't know what that means, so I don't respond.

Jordan takes a sip from his Styrofoam cup and says, "Anyway, can you follow me over to my gear? I want to give Drew the proofs from his party."

"Sure," I say, taking my two cappuccinos and following Jordan over to his gear of cameras, tripods, lights and lenses, and various packs of film. Jordan pulls out a large white envelope and a medium-sized box wrapped in light purple paper.

"Happy birthday!" he says, handing me the purple box.

"Oh my God!" I say, beyond excited. "You shouldn't have!"

"Open it."

I rip off the paper voraciously. It's a beautiful, antique silver frame. Inside is an 8"×10" black-and-white photo of Dawn and me from the party. She's saying something that's making me laugh, and neither of us knows our picture is being taken, so we are totally at ease, and totally ourselves.

It's an amazing picture. He's somehow managed to capture a real moment in my life. You know how, with most pictures, you smile your stewardess smile for the camera, no matter how you're feeling inside? Well, this picture isn't like that at all. We're both just being ourselves—this is just how we are when no one's looking. And he's somehow managed to capture the spirit of Dawn and our friendship in one split-second shot.

"This is the best present I've gotten in I don't know how long," I say. And I mean it.

"It's just a little something," Jordan says, shrugging. "I love how the shot turned out. You're both so amazingly photogenic."

I'm amazingly photogenic? I think in disbelief. Me? I have hated almost every picture I've ever been in. But this one I love. "It's really wonderful. I know just where I'm going to put it—on my fireplace mantle in the living room," I say as I give Jordan a big hug.

He hugs me back, and man does it feel wonderful! We stay in the hug for a few seconds too long (well, define "too long"). He rubs my back lightly, and I feel like I could spend the rest of my life in those arms.

Finally, suddenly feeling a little nervous and self-conscious, I break from the hug. "Drew's in Makeup. Do you want to follow me?"

"Sure."

We walk over to the Makeup trailer, and open the door to the smell of lotions, powders, and hair spray, combined with lots of coffee.

Vic, Drew's makeup artist, an effeminate black man in his early thirties, rubs concealer under Drew's eyes.

Drew tells him, "I'm sorry, you have your work cut out for you today. I know I look like crap."

"Honey, if I can make Barbra Streisand look good, you know I'll have no problem with you."

"Thanks," Drew says, and puts his hand out to Jordan. "Hey man, how's it going?"

"Good," Jordan says, and they do the new handshake. "The pictures from your party turned out great."

He hands Drew the white envelope. Drew opens it and pulls out the proof sheets as Jordan says, "I didn't know which ones to blow up for you. I figured you would want to choose your favorites, then tell me which sizes you need."

"These are excellent!" says Drew. "I particularly like the ones of Dawn."

Thanks, I think sarcastically.

Drew scans through the sheets pretty quickly. When he gets to the last sheet, he pulls it up close to his face and scrutinizes a particular shot. "Oh, I like this one of Dawn and Charlie."

Drew hands me the sheet, and points to the shot. "Charlie, look at this one. You look amazing! Jordan, doesn't Charlie look amazing?!"

I'm not sure I like the tone of shock that comes with the question (which, to me, sort of sounded like, "Can you believe such a Quasimodo could look normal?"), but I did like Jordan's answer. "She was the most beautiful woman at the party."

I think I am starting to swoon. What does swooning feel like?

"Yes, she was," Drew confirms, lying through his teeth. "And, can you believe it . . . she's still single."

"Drew . . . ," I say under my breath.

"I mean, Jordan, don't you just wonder how it's possible that some man hasn't just snatched this woman up?"

"I know I do," Vic agrees, brushing powder over Drew's nose. "Beautiful woman like that. I'm telling you, straight men are just ignorant."

"We are," Drew agrees vehemently.

"Drew . . . ," I say, still under my breath, but starting to let a little anger creep into my voice.

Drew ignores me, choosing to address Jordan. "I ask you, how can a man chance letting a woman like this get away? I'm telling you, it's a mystery, wrapped in a conundrum, cloaked in a riddle . . ."

"Oh honey, it is a mystery wrapped in bacon," Vic says, "because that girl is so delicious, if I were a straight man, I'd eat her up. Know what I'm saying?" He snaps once in the air. "Oka-ay?"

Drew snaps in the air in agreement. "Oka-ay!"

"Okay . . . ," I interrupt, wanting to bitchslap both of them. "So, Jordan has to leave now, and go to work," I say pointedly to Drew. "And you'll pick out some pictures later, right?"

"Oh," Drew says, looking at the pictures again and spouting off a list. "I can pick them now. One of each, in a four-by-six. Anything with Dawn or Charlie in it, give me doubles. I want the one of Dawn and me alone in a five-by-seven, and can you make a five-by-seven of the one of Dawn and Charlie?"

I got to hand it to him—the man knows what he wants.

"Charlie, can you give him a check for fifteen hundred dollars?" Drew says to me, then turns to Jordan. "The extra five hundred will cover prints, right?"

Honestly, some people don't even vaguely live in the real world.

"That is more than enough," Jordan says, and shakes Drew's hand. "If you ever need me for a party again . . ."

"Oh, I might," Drew says immediately, looking at me. "I think Charlie mentioned something about having Magic Johnson over for dinner. . . ."

"Good-bye, Drew," I say sternly, pushing Jordan out the door.

Drew yells after us. "Of course, Charlie would know! She's at all my parties!"

The door closes, and we walk over to Drew's trailer, so I can cut a check for Jordan.

The rest of the day I didn't get to spend on set. Instead, I had to drive out to Drew's cabin at Lake Arrowhead, two and a half hours away, to deal with a pipe that had burst over the weekend. Yeah— tell me I don't lead a glamorous life working in show business.

There's a story of a janitor who works in the circus, cleaning up the animal poop. When he complains to his friend about cleaning up poop all day, the friend suggests he quit. "What," the janitor says, horrified, "and give up show business?"

Anyway, by the time I get back, it is seven o'clock, and they have just wrapped for the day. I look around for Jordan briefly, but he is gone, so I make my way over to Drew's trailer.

Drew is out cold on a brand-new white couch. When I open the door, he bursts up into a sitting position. "I'm up!"

"It's just me," I say, throwing my stuff down on a white table and falling into a white chair. His trailer is now done in all white: white couches, white carpet, chairs, tables, lamps, walls. Everything's white, white, white. "What happened to all the Ganeshes?" I ask.

Drew sits up. "I talked to a psychic on the phone today. She said the toilet thing was a sign. I need to be in harmony with my chakras. Hence, nothing but neutrals."

I won't even ask. "I just saw Madison. He's ready to drive you home."

"Wait. I have something for you," Drew says eagerly, then walks over to his new white desk and pulls out a small, purplish brown box wrapped with a copper-colored string bow. "Happy birthday."

I take it, and read the top of the box. In gold lettering are the words BURKE WILLIAMS, BEYOND THE SPA.

I pull off the bow and open the box. Inside is a cream-colored card stating that this certificate entitles Charlize Edwards to a "Stress Therapy Day" compliments of Drew Stanton.

I stare at it and try to come up with an appropriate response.

When someone presents you with a gift, no matter how strange, do not respond with "Huh?" "Yikes!" or "What the hell is it?"

I'd been hinting for lots of things I'll never buy for myself: a pair of Jimmy Choo shoes, a Prada bag, dinner at The Palm. Burke Williams is one of the hottest day spas in L.A. Anyone who even vaguely knows me knows that I've never been to a spa, I have no desire to go to a spa, and that I think they are a waste of . . . I read further: he spent over $500 on this!

You will always know people who have more dollars than sense.

As I continue to stare at the gift in silence, Drew looks at me and smiles, proud of himself. "You love it, don't you?" he says confidently. "Dawn helped me pick it out. You get a private herbal bath, a full massage, something called an Emilee's Intrigue—which includes another massage, a Hunter's Retreat, and an Ultimate Facial—complete with foot massage. And I've included all the tips, too, so it's totally free!"

All I can think is, *Dear God, I work for Niles Crane.* I feel like a mother who's just been given crayons for her birthday from her three-year-old. I glue a smile onto my face and look him right in the eyes. "I love it."

"I knew you would!" Drew exclaims proudly. "Well, actually, I asked Dawn, and she said you would."

"Did Dawn happen to say *why* I would love it?" I ask.

"Yeah. She said you needed to do something about those clogged pores if you wanted to capture Jordan's attention."

"I don't have clogged pores," I say, bristling.

"She said you'd say that," Drew tells me, "and that I'm supposed to tell you that you've had clogged pores since the day she met you. And not to get all huffy."

Lovely.

"And she also says, and I am to quote her exactly, 'And don't be acting like this is some dumb-ass gift because, girl, you ain't never been to a spa, so don't be saying you don't like something you haven't even tried.'"

I look at Drew—the classically trained actor—and I am immediately suspicious. "She said 'ain't even tried,' didn't she?"

"Yes. But I didn't think I could pull that off," Drew admits. "Anyway, Dawn's coming with me to the wrap party Friday night. You guys should go Friday afternoon, before the party. You can have the day off."

"What do you mean 'we guys'?" I ask.

"Well, I didn't want you to go alone, so I got her a 'Stress Therapy Day,' too."

Yeah, because I'm really going to want to be around her right now.

Drew hands me the spa's "menu" of the services provided. I must say, it does sound rather indulgent. There's a steam room and a Jacuzzi, too. And I do like Jacuzzis. Maybe it won't be so bad.

"What's an Emilee's Intrigue?" I ask, reading the menu.

"Spelled with two *e*'s. It's this thing where they cover you with eucalyptus leaves, wrap you in hot towels, and immerse you in steam."

What am I? A tamale?

"It's supposed to get rid of all the toxins in your body," Drew continues. "Then they give you a full-body massage afterwards."

I continue reading. "And then I get another body massage?"

"You can never have too many massages."

Well—can't argue with him there.

"Dawn says that spa days for women are necessary, the way golf is for men," Drew tells me.

"Dawn also says, 'So many men, so few who can afford us,'" I remind him.

"Well, she's right," Drew agrees. "Besides, when was the last time you had people putting all their energy into trying to make your day perfect?"

Hmm . . . Good point.

And I suppose I can always hint for a Prada bag at Christmas.

Eighteen

Parents should not make mistakes. They do anyway. Love them anyway.

This will be the only time I ever utter the following words: Dinner with my family that night was uneventful. I mean, the presents I got were indeed disasters, but I had been warned ahead of time, so it wasn't so bad. And I suppose Frederik Fekkai beats Supercuts.

Kate and Dawn then gave me the birthday present of letting me cancel on our after-dinner drinks, so I could pass out that night.

I spent the next two days off the set, doing all those boring things you hear about celebrity assistants doing: picking up dry cleaning, going to business managers and lawyers and picking up financial papers, meeting the cable guy at Drew's house, meeting the plumber at Drew's house, setting up appointments with Drew's dentist, shrink, and psychic (don't ask).

Thursday, I spent the whole day at gyms, interviewing personal trainers for Drew. Each one was supposed to give me a "sample session" of what Drew could expect on a given day. That meant that I was theoretically supposed to work out five different times that day.

Uh, yeah.

No matter how successful you are, no one can work out for you.

Now, you would think that would be the kind of advice you would never have to give a person. But maybe my great-grandniece will be an ultrasuccessful mega moviestar, in which case she might also be an idiot who pays her assistant to go through five personal training sessions in one day.

I came up with a few more bits of advice for my journal during those few days:

Chase your dreams daily. I'm not just talking about the big dreams, obviously if you want to be a great baseball player, or ballerina, or artist you must work at it every day. I mean, chase the little dreams. If you dream of having an ice cream cone one day, go out and get one. If you dream of going to the beach another day, jump into your car and go.

Spend a night listening to the bartender's problems.

There is nothing more painful in life than to be invisible. Try never to make anyone in your life feel that way.

Embrace all cultures.

If the Coffee Bean/Tea Leaf still exists in 2100 and whatever—go get an ice blended mocha. They are ambrosia—the gods drank these on Mount Olympus.

Get your hands on the DVD (or whatever technology is the 22nd-century equivalent) of a TV show from the 1970s called The Mary Tyler Moore Show. *It describes not only how single girls felt during the 1970s, but also how we felt in the 2000s.*

Buy real estate. They're not making any more land.

No one likes to be judged. If you're going to advise someone, do it without judgment.

All mothers should read that one.

Never scold someone. Making someone feel bad about themselves shouldn't make you feel better about yourself.

All heads of security on game-show sets, not to mention self-important assistant producers on soap operas, should read that one.

Don't do something just because everyone else is doing it.

I started to write, *If everyone else jumped off the Brooklyn Bridge . . .* but then I stopped myself, because it's not the same. If everyone else was carrying their stuff in a Kate Spade bag, I'd have one in a second. As a matter of fact, I do.

But it's usually good advice.

I spent the evenings checking my e-mail and seeing if Jordan was online, but he never was.

That Thursday evening, while I was online, my sister forwarded me an e-mail honoring Erma Bombeck, who wrote a list called "If I Had to Live My Life Over" after she found out she had terminal cancer.

Don't worry about who doesn't like you, who has more, or who's doing what.—Erma Bombeck

It struck me for some reason, so I decided to pass it on.

I was just about to get offline when I got an IM:

Jordan1313: Charlie? So what are you doing home alone on a Thursday night?

He called! Well, sort of.

AngelCharlie: Who said I'm alone? I'm kidding. It's so good to hear from you. I've missed you this week.

Which is true.

Jordan1313: Yeah, me too. Debating basketball hasn't been nearly as much fun without you. ☺ What have you been doing with your days?
AngelCharlie: Well, today I worked out with five different trainers at five different gyms.
Jordan1313: Wow! I knew you had to work out to get a body like that, but I didn't know it was that excruciating.

A body like that? Is he kidding?! He's flirting. That's not my imagination—he's flirting.

AngelCharlie: Speaking of Wow's—Wow, that's quite a line. You don't get a body like this through exercise. You get it through indiscriminate eating. Anyway, I was just interviewing personal trainers for Drew. I didn't manage to do the whole five hours.
Jordan1313: How many did you do?
AngelCharlie: I did most of the first session, and most of the second session. When the third session's trainer saw me come in with an In-N-Out burger in one hand, and a chocolate shake in the other, the guy knew this was a desk interview.

Jordan1313: LOL. I didn't see you the rest of Monday. Did you have a good birthday?

AngelCharlie: It was wonderful.

You don't always have to lie through your teeth. Sometimes, you can lie with your fingers tap, tap, tapping away. If I said it was fine, instead of wonderful, it might look like I'm being negative or pessimistic. If I mentioned my crazy family, it might scare him away (God knows there are days when they scare me away). So I decide to keep my responses upbeat, positive, and light.

Not that I'm overthinking this—I'm not.

AngelCharlie: I love your present. I put the picture up on my mantle. You have amazing talent.

He doesn't write for a while. I can't tell if he's checking other e-mail or Web sites, or if I somehow wrote the wrong thing. I look at what I wrote. I don't think I said anything bad.

Jordan1313: Thank you.

He finally writes,

Jordan1313: So, since we wrapped today, do you have to work tomorrow?

AngelCharlie: No, Drew gave me the day off.

Jordan1313: Cool. Do you want to go to the beach with me before the party?

Shit, shit, shit. Now I take a while to write.

AngelCharlie: I'm afraid I can't. Drew got me this spa day for my birthday, and it's tomorrow. I'm really sorry. Can I take a rain check?

Jordan1313: Spa day, huh? My mom loves those.

Great. Now I'm reminding him of his mother.

Jordan1313: It was just a couple of crew guys hanging at the beach before the big wrap party. No big deal. But, of course, the scenery would be more beautiful with you in a bathing suit.

That is definitely flirting.

Jordan1313: I'm gonna go grab a beer. Can you hold on?

And *that* is definitely flirting.

AngelCharlie: Of course. I could use a glass of wine myself.

Jordan1313: Now, no getting cut off.

AngelCharlie: If I do, wait for me.

I run downstairs, open a bottle of Clos du Bois Merlot, pour myself a glass, and happily take the glass and the bottle back upstairs with me.

When I get back Jordan is writing:

Jordan1313: Doo, dee, doo, doo, dee, doo . . . such a girl . . . you make me wait for you . . .

AngelCharlie: What was I gone for? A minute?

Jordan1313: Hey, if you thought that was only a minute, you'd think I was a genius in bed.

Oh. My. God.

AngelCharlie: I would, huh?

Jordan1313: I'm sorry. I'm getting flirty, aren't I? You can just ignore me.

AngelCharlie: I can't imagine being able to ignore you. So what are you wearing?

Jordan1313: Tonight, I've moved on to a bridesmaid's dress and flip-flops.

AngelCharlie: I hate you.

Jordan1313: Why?

AngelCharlie: Well, for one thing, you've killed any chances I've had of flirting. And, for another thing, you've just reminded me of being a maid of honor at a wedding in two weeks.

Jordan1313: Wow. Maid of honor. I was a maid of honor once.

I wait a moment before I type.

AngelCharlie: I have no response to that. You've rendered me speechless.

Jordan1313: Proving again that you would think I'm great in bed—it being so easy to render you speechless. No, I was a male maid of honor for my sister's wedding. I got to wear a tuxedo.

AngelCharlie: Well, then you managed to avoid the worst part of being a bridesmaid—the outfit.

Jordan1313: God, for me the worst part was how crazed my sister got. Has your friend called you in hysterics and made you come over to see how one bridesmaid's dyed-to-match shoes are half a shade lighter than the other bride-maid's dyed-to-match shoes?

AngelCharlie: SOL (Smiled out loud.) I know you're telling the truth about being a maid of honor. You've just used the words "dyed-to-match shoes" in a sentence.

Jordan1313: Wait—this'll really impress you. Teal. Puce. Fuchsia.

AngelCharlie: SOL. But you're a photographer. You could have know those colors anyway.

Jordan1313: Hmmm . . .

I wait. I assume he's typing something. After about thirty seconds this pops up . . .

Jordan1313: Registry (a word that goes with the sentence, "What the hell was she thinking? Moss-colored plates?") Seating chart (which goes with, "You can't put those two any-where near each other. They had a fight in 1952.") Response card (which goes well with, "Oh my God, they're bringing their children. The kids aren't on the invitation." and "He's bringing a date. The invitation specifically didn't say 'plus one'.")

AngelCharlie: LOL. You really were a maid of honor. I'm gonna guess your mother made the plates comment.

Jordan1313: Yeah. My sister and mom don't have the best relationship. It's not bad, they just always seem to be picking at each other.

AngelCharlie: What a shock. You've just described every woman and her mother I've ever met. It's my sister's wedding, too. A little over two weeks from now, so I would say the crazi-ness has started, but it started when she announced her en-gagement six weeks ago.

Jordan1313: Well, at least you get it over with in two months. Mine took over a year. And, I got to tell you, the brother has to remain calm no matter what. So, what are you wearing?

Hmmmm . . .

AngelCharlie: A red velvet teddy and high-heeled pumps. ☺
Jordan1313: I meant to the wedding. But . . . Ouch.
AngelCharlie: Why ouch? What's wrong with it?
Jordan1313: No, no—ouch. It's a guy expression. It means I've got a visual that will sustain me until tomorrow night's party. How about . . . Damn!

I can't think of anything to write. I just stare at the screen. Finally I decide:

You miss 100% of the shots you don't take.—Wayne Gretzky

AngelCharlie: I'm tired of typing. Do you want to just pick up the phone, and call me?

I hit SEND and nothing happens. I click my mouse to send again. Nothing. I start rapid-fire tapping when I hear, "Your session has ended. Thank you. Good-bye." Then my phone starts ringing.

It's one o'clock in the morning. The fact that about five people could be calling me right now kills me.

I race to the phone, hoping against hope it's Jordan. "Hello?"

"I just had the biggest fight with my mother."

About five people could be calling me with that news.

"What happened?" I ask Drew, sighing inwardly, and not even bothering to ask why he didn't call on my cell phone.

"One of the women from the bridge club told her I was gay."

"Well, that's ridiculous," I say, bringing the phone back to my computer, and staring at the screen. I told Jordan to wait for me if I got cut off. I wonder if he will. "Everyone in Hollywood is rumored to be gay. Did you tell her that?"

"I did. But she said that Clara, that's the woman from the bridge game, says her daughter's friend slept with me. Her daughter's *male* friend."

"It's always a friend of a friend. Tell her to get names."

"It won't work. Then she starts in on me about why don't I have a girlfriend? Why am I so pretty? Why did I get that plastic surgery on my nose five years ago? Why did I coincidentally choose a woman who cheated on me after less than a year?"

This is going to be a while. I walk over to my leather work bag, pull out the crew list of phone numbers, and get Jordan's number. "You do have a girlfriend," I remind him as I pull out my cell phone. "Dawn."

"Dawn's not my girlfriend," Drew insists. "Not yet, anyway."

I dial Jordan's number. "Well, your mom doesn't have to know that," I point out. "She lives in Arizona. When are the two of them going to run into each other?"

Jordan's phone rings and rings. No answering machine picks up. Which means he's still online waiting for me, and that his phone won't cut him off. Damn it!

"Tomorrow," Drew says.

"Excuse me?" I say, redialing Jordan's number.

"My parents are driving in from Phoenix for the wrap party. Dawn's meeting them tomorrow."

Ring, ring, ring. Damn, damn, damn. "Did you tell me about this?" I ask nervously. "Because I don't have it on your schedule."

"I'm telling you now," Drew says. "Mom announced it to me

while we were on the phone. She says that we're obviously not close anymore, or I would have been comfortable enough to tell her I'm gay."

What is it about mothers? I think.

"I think I need a Valium," Drew says. "Did I ever have a prescription for Valium?"

"No," I say, hanging up my cell phone after two more tries to Jordan.

"What about a prescription for Klonopin? I've been reading good things about that."

"That's for panic attacks," I say.

"So?"

"So, you don't have panic attacks."

"Well, I need something." Drew thinks for a moment. "What about Prozac?"

"You can't drink with it."

"Paxil?"

"You've already been on it," I remind him. "You didn't like the side effects."

"What side effects?" Drew asks.

I pause for a moment, trying to figure out how to say this tactfully. "The . . . um . . . sexual side effects."

"Oh yeah. Right." I hear him turn on his television. "Turn on Channel 208."

I walk over to my remote, turn on my television, and flip to Channel 208. It looks like a golf game. I stare at it. "What are we watching?" I ask.

"Golf."

That's it. He says nothing else. I stare at the game, confused. "Why is everyone dressed weird?"

"They're not," Drew says. "This is a game from the 1970s."

He keeps giving me answers like they won't lead to more questions. "Well, if this game is from the 1970s, don't you already know how it ends?"

"Well, *of course* I know how it ends. That's why it's on ESPN Classic."

Again—like it won't lead to another question. "But if you already know how it ends . . ."

"Haven't you ever seen *Romeo and Juliet*?" Drew asks.

"Yeah . . ."

"Well, you knew how that ended," Drew points out.

We watch the golf game for the next five minutes, while I continue to try to call Jordan (both his home and cell numbers) from my cell phone, to no avail.

"Now *that* is a beautiful shot," Drew says appreciatively. "What about Seroquel?"

"It'll put you to sleep for twenty-four hours, and you'll miss the wrap party."

"Krispy Kreme?"

"As far as I know, those are still available over the counter."

"Excellent. Bring me a dozen—three chocolate, with the sprinkles, three of the classic glazed, and six of whatever you're having."

"You know what would be even more fun? Why don't you call Dawn, and ask her to bring you donuts? I'm sure she'd love to see you," I say, hoping to get back to my conversation with Jordan.

"I can't do that!" Drew insists. "Then I'd have to tell her why I'm upset, which means I'd have to admit that my parents are coming tomorrow because my mother's crazy. I can't have her knowing how screwed up my family is. I'm still at the point in our relationship where everything has to be light, fun, and romantic."

Do I sound like that? My God, I sound like that. It sounds so bad when you hear it out loud.

I sigh out loud. "Drew, it's getting late, and I'm in my pajamas . . ."

"How much do I pay you a week?" Drew asks, clueless.

I make the mistake of thinking this is a genuine question. "Right now? Two thousand dollars a week."

"And, do you think if I'm paying someone two thousand dollars a week, I even want to *hear* the sentence, 'It's getting late'?"

I sigh, "All right, but you're paying me back for the donuts."

"Ah, I love you," Drew says happily. "I swear, if you weren't already spoken for, I'd snap you up in an instant."

I don't even know what that means. But before I can ask, he interrupts my thoughts with, "Okay, I need to go get high, so I have the munchies when you get here. Bye."

And he hangs up on me.

When we get off the phone, I race online, but Jordan is off. He sent me an e-mail:

> I waited for fifteen minutes, but you didn't come back. I guess I'll see you tomorrow night.
>
> xoxo
>
> Jordan

Damn it!

I try his phone again, and get his machine: "Hi, this is Jordan. I'm not able to come to the phone right now. Please leave a message." Beep.

"Hi, it's Charlie," I begin, then can't think of what to say. "I'm really sorry. I got a call from . . ." I can't say Drew. That's the type of thing that gets rumors started. "A friend. And, uh, she . . ."—I lie, knowing that if he got a call, I'd rather hear it was from a he—"she was pretty upset so I couldn't get off."

I wait for him to pick up, but he doesn't.

"Anyway, I'm really sorry . . . I guess I'll see you tomorrow night," I say, then slowly put down the phone.

Life is not fair.

Alas, why is it never not fair to my advantage?

Nineteen

You should never have a job that you hate so much you think "Thank God it's Friday" every week of your life.

I write in my journal Friday, around eleven in the morning.

I spent the night at Drew's house, in one of his superplush guest rooms. I don't know why I hate going to his house in the middle of the night. It's like a hotel there. My room was decorated exactly to look like a suite where he once stayed at the Four Seasons.

We talked about his parents at great length that night, and I said I'd tell Dawn about meeting them tonight at the wrap party. (To "soften her up," as I told Drew.) That was more for Dawn than Drew. If she had to have a "Meet the Parents" freak-out, I'm sure she'd rather have it around me than around Drew.

So much is going on at this wrap party tonight. Tonight—the last night I will ever definitely see Jordan. God, I'm tensing up just thinking about it.

But the spa day will help. I need to pull out all the stops. I need to be gorgeous and enticing. I need a facial. I need my skin exfoliated and buffed to a glow. I need a massage, so I can feel relaxed and confident tonight. I need . . .

Frankly, I need a drink. I'm not looking forward to this spa day at all. I feel ridiculous. But I'm trying to be upbeat for it.

I meet Dawn at the Virgin Megacenter on Sunset and Laurel Canyon promptly at ten o'clock. Actually, I just had to get a latte from the Buzz coffeehouse in the plaza, so it was 10:02, but there's no way she would ever know, because she's always late. Dawn, of course, is nowhere to be found. I call her cell phone, and get the machine.

"Hi, this is Dawn. I'm not home right now. You know what to do." Beep. "Hi, it's me. I'm sure we said ten, but I figured just in case you overslept, I should check in." The elevator door opens, and a gorgeous black girl steps out. "Never mind. I think I see you."

I click my phone shut, and walk right up to . . . Tyra Banks. Damn it! They don't even look alike, other than the damn perfect bodies. "Sorry," I say as I make an immediate right, going toward Wolfgang Puck's restaurant.

"Charlie?" Tyra asks. I turn around, surprised. I met Tyra last year for all of an hour at some party Drew was throwing. How the hell did she remember me?

"Hey, you. I didn't recognize you at first," I stumble. Has anyone ever said that to her? "How are you?"

We give each other a hug. (In L.A., anyone you've ever met gets a hug at the very least. And if they're a member of the opposite sex, they usually get a kiss as well.) "I'm good," she says. "Working a lot. Has your love life gotten any better since we last spoke?"

Good Christ—I have no idea who I was even dating/obsessing about we when last spoke. "No, it didn't," I say remorsefully. "But I'm hanging in there. How's yours?"

"It's good. I heard about Drew's latest breakup. Can you send him my sympathies?"

"I will," I say.

The elevator door opens, and Dawn walks out. She's looking perfect, as usual, in a low-rise sweat suit, and carrying a big black bag. She stops in her tracks when she sees Tyra. Dawn looks so stunned that I wonder from the look on her face if they dated the same guy.

"Uh, Tyra, this is my friend Dawn," I say awkwardly.

"Hi. Have we met before?" Tyra says brightly, extending her hand.

"I think so," says Dawn, looking pained as she takes the supermodel's hand. "I think we met at the MTV awards last year at one of the afterparties."

"Right. Good to see you again," Tyra says, then turns to me. "I'm in a bit of a rush. Will you say hello to Drew for me?"

"Of course," I say, forcing a smile and worrying about Dawn. Why does she look so upset?

Tyra kisses me on the cheek. "It was great seeing you." And she's off.

Dawn and my eyes follow Tyra as she disappears into the Virgin record store across the way.

"I know her stylist, and those boobs are actually real," Dawn tells me in disgust.

"So?"

"So?!" Dawn nearly shrieks. "So it's, like, just totally unfair that a woman can even look like that—much less that she pretty much succeeds at anything she tries."

I've never known Dawn to be jealous of anyone's looks, or anyone's success. As we make our way to the lobby of Burke Williams, it occurs to me for the first time that Dawn may be insecure about her own beauty and success. Dawn never seems insecure about anything. When the Lord deals you four aces, it's hard not to be grateful.

Fortunately, I come armed with newfound, sage advice. "You know a friend of mine once said that if everyone walked into a room, and dumped their problems on the floor, when they saw what everyone else's problems were, they'd be scrambling to get their own problems back before someone else got to them first."

"What the hell is that supposed to mean?" Dawn snaps.

"It means you shouldn't be jealous of anyone else. You don't know what kinds of insecurities and issues they have to deal with every day."

"Oh, for God's sake! You're gonna tell me not to be jealous of a woman who doesn't have to clean her own toilet. Grow up. And stop taking those fortune cookies so seriously," Dawn says, opening the spa door for me. "Add 'in bed' to the end of the sentence, and be done with it."

We enter the lobby, and the man at the front counter cheerfully says, "Welcome to Burke Williams. I'm George. What can we do for you today?"

Dawn answers before I can open my mouth. "I'm Dawn Fraiche. I should be scheduled for a milk bath, a Japanese shiatsu massage, then a Savannah's Surrender"—a what????—"then an Ultimate Facial. My friend here has the Stress Therapy Day, but she'll have the Fango Mud bath, and she doesn't want the Ultimate Facial, she wants the Nourishing Facial."

"I do?" I ask.

"Of course you do," Dawn says to me confidently.

"Why?" I ask.

"Why what?" Dawn turns to look at me as though it's just occurred to her I'm even here.

"Why don't I want the Ultimate Facial?"

"Because they massage your feet, which you hate. Oh, that reminds me . . ." She turns back to George. "Did Drew Stanton call you with his credit card number?"

"Yes, ma'am," George says brightly. "This morning."

"Great. We'll be needing pedicures as well. Just charge it to his card," Dawn says. "Oh, and do you know if Kate Lopez scheduled a massage?"

"Let me check," George says, then taps his keyboard a few times. "Yes, she called this morning. She's scheduled for three o'clock."

"Kate's coming?" I ask Dawn.

"Yeah. She's meeting us here at two-thirty, after her show. Apparently, she talked to Mike this morning."

"How'd it go?"

"She wouldn't say. All she said was, 'Men are fuckwits. I need a massage, and some quality girl time.'"

"Amen to that," George says, and nods in appreciation.

"Okay," Dawn says to him in her "black girl fabulous" voice, and they high five.

Then she turns to me. "I almost forgot." She pulls a wrapped birthday gift from her big black bag, and hands it to me. "This is from Kate and me. Happy birthday."

"Yay," I say happily, and tear open the paper. Inside is a shoebox with the Jimmy Choo logo.

"You didn't," I say, beyond excited.

"We did," Dawn says, clearly proud of herself. "Size seven. The ones you were looking at last month."

I pull them out, and they are stunning—open-toed high heels with rhinestones on the straps.

"Those are so cool!" George exclaims.

"Aren't they?!" I agree, taking off my shoes right there in the lobby to put on my new Jimmy Choos.

"That's why we need the pedicures," Dawn says, admiring the shoes. "When I told Drew about them, he insisted we add pedicures to our day."

I put them on, and they fit perfectly. They are truly the coolest shoes I've ever owned. "I love them."

"I knew you would," Dawn says. "I have to be honest, though—I had to wear them on a video shoot. The wardrobe person gave them to me for half off at the end of the day."

"Jimmy Choos half off are still twice what I spend on your birthdays," I say happily, taking them off to put my tennis shoes back on. "These are going to be perfect for tonight."

"Together with your black silk skirt . . . ," Dawn says.

"I'm not sure about that skirt," I say quietly, knowing I've already lost this battle. "It's kind of tight on me. . . ."

"And that red wraparound top," she continues, deliberately ignoring my "too tight" comment. "You will look divine."

George finishes typing on his computer. "Okay, your herbal baths are at eleven, and the rest of your treatments begin at the top of every hour at noon, one, three, and four. Please go to the quiet room five minutes before your treatments begin, and your therapist will come for you."

"Thank you," we both say.

"We encourage you to spend the next hour enjoying our facilities. We have a whirlpool, sauna, and steam room, and you're welcome to use any of those for as long as you like. Would you like someone to lead you in, and give you a tour?" George asks us.

"No," Dawn says, opening the double doors to the spa. "I've been here before. I can show her around."

"Great!" George says, and hands us two keys with little ropes on them. "Here are your keys. Lockers forty-six and forty-seven."

We walk through a hallway, and the sounds are hushed. There is a fountain up ahead of us, gurgling soothingly while quiet music plays in the background. The hallway is kind of cold, but the atmosphere is relaxing.

"I think that's called the waiting room," Dawn whispers. "It's the only place where both men and women are allowed."

We turn left and head to our lockers.

"That's the quiet room," Dawn says, pointing to a bunch of over-stuffed leather chairs. "You go there right before your appointments and read magazines."

I am starting to feel cold, but then Dawn opens the door to the women's locker room, and a whoosh of moist heat envelopes me.

The large locker room is painted in a soothing tone of beige. We walk to the locker area and find our lockers. I open number 46. Inside is a beige robe and plastic slippers.

"The steam room is right there," Dawn says, pointing behind us. "Sauna's next to that."

We both take off our clothes and put on our robes.

I feel weird being here. I'm not sure why. Maybe it's being naked in front of all these women with perfect bodies. I feel like I should have a swimsuit on or something.

And there are "assistants" all over the place: girls who are cleaning up, handing patrons towels, stuff like that. I'm an assistant. I feel like a fraud letting these girls wait on me.

"The Jacuzzi's over there," Dawn says, pointing. "I say that's where we start."

We head over to the Jacuzzi area, which has two Jacuzzis surrounded by beige cement urns filled with washcloths in ice, and dry beige towels. The walls are painted to look . . . I don't know, Greek, maybe? Paintings of cracks and urns. Maybe Italian.

It would help if I had ever been to Greece or Italy.

Dawn puts her robe on a hook, so I follow suit. One of the Jacuzzis has two women already lounging in it, so we jump into the other one.

I sink into the Jacuzzi, lean my head back onto a folded towel, and try to relax. After a minute or so, I have to say, I'm starting to feel better.

"So," I say to Dawn as I sink farther into the water to let the bubbles jet against my neck. "Did you know Drew's parents were coming to the party tonight?"

Dawn's eyes are closed as she talks. "Yeah. He called me this morning."

"You okay with that?" I ask.

She shrugs and opens her eyes. "I don't like meeting parents. Actually, I'm okay with it once they get to know me. But I hate that first moment of 'Oh my God, she's black.' They never say anything, so it's just this look of shock followed by not bringing it up for ages.'"

I roll my eyes. "They're not going to think that," I insist. I've heard this argument from Dawn a thousand times, and I think it's ridiculous.

"Yes, they are," Dawn assures me. "But that's okay. Most people get past it fairly quickly."

I want to say more, but she closes her eyes again, and I know the subject is closed.

One of the women in the other Jacuzzi yells *Ssshhh,* so we decide to be quiet for a while.

Which gives me some time to obsess about Jordan.

I checked my e-mail from Drew's house this morning, and he hadn't sent anything else since last night. Nor had he received my apology e-mail yet.

Rats! I could be on the beach with him today, and instead . . .

"Grab me a washcloth, will you?" Dawn says.

I take a washcloth from the ice urn, hand one to her, take another for myself, and put it on my forehead. Aaaaahhhhh . . . This is pretty relaxing.

Maybe I could get used to this.

We spend the next forty-five minutes in and out of the Jacuzzi, and frankly I could have gone home happy just with that.

But then our official spa day begins. We go into a room with a large bathtub on each side. I get into the tub on the left, and Dawn the tub on the right, as two women run the water for us.

My woman asks if the temperature's good. I say yes, and she smiles, and pours some sort of mud mix (I don't know what they call it) into my tub. She swirls it around in the tub, and I get in.

Once again, I feel weird. I'm really not comfortable with people waiting on me. But I do like my bath; it's warm and smells heavenly.

The women leave, and dim the lights. I close my eyes, relax, and sink farther into the tub.

"Bet you never thought you'd be taking a bath with me," jokes Dawn.

I laugh. "Yeah, well, you've met my parents, so I guess we've moved to the next level."

Dawn giggles a little. "You've met them. Are Drew's parents as nutty as yours?"

"I'd like to think no parents are as nutty as mine. You know, you could see this as quid pro quo—you meet his parents, he's got to meet yours."

"Yeah," Dawn says dubiously, "that would work if I had told them about us."

"You haven't told your parents about Drew?!" I say, maybe a little too loudly.

"Ssshhhh," Dawn says, lowering her voice. "We don't want to be shushed again."

"But why not?" I ask.

"Because we've only been dating a week?" Dawn says in a sarcastic "answering in the form of a question" tone.

"Yeah, but . . ." I grasp for something else to say. "I don't know. I just thought you guys were really clicking."

"Oh, we are," Dawn says, closing her eyes and relaxing her neck against a bath pillow. "But, you know, I'm not sure where this is going. And, until I do know, I don't want it around my old neighborhood that I'm dating a movie star."

"I guess . . . ," I say, wondering why that would be such a bad thing.

We're both silent for a few minutes, just enjoying our warm baths. Actually, that's not true. I'm not enjoying the bath right now. I'm worried that if Dawn's not telling anyone about Drew, she's not serious about him, and he's going to get hurt. I know Dawn, and I love her more than anything. But she can sometimes go through men faster than I go through bottles of shampoo.

Or donuts.

Well, okay, nobody goes through men as fast I go through donuts, but shampoo. Definitely shampoo.

I finally decide to broach the subject again. "But you do like him, right?"

"Hmm?" Dawn says, opening her eyes again. I think I woke her up. "Yeah, I like him a lot. He's a good person. And really sweet, and adorably cute. It's just, you know, there are issues."

I shouldn't ask. I should just let it go. It's none of my damn business. "What kind of issues?"

"Hey, come on, every time I've ever seen Drew, there are women throwing themselves at him. Who needs that kind of aggravation? Besides, he's your boss."

"Yeah, but . . ." I can't think of a comeback. "I mean, I understand, it is a pain that women are always all over him. But, you know, you can't really blame *him* for what they're doing. And, as for him being my boss . . . I mean, you guys are already an item, right? So, you know, that train has left the station."

Dawn gives me this look like, *Yeah, I guess you're right.* But I know she doesn't completely believe me.

I decide to let it drop, and relax in my tub to obsess over Jordan.

At five minutes before noon, the two of us head to the "quiet room" and I sit in a big leather chair and pick up a woman's magazine while I wait for my massage.

I look at the cover, where a beautiful twenty-something has had her teeth whitened via computer, her body stretched via computer, and the flyaways in her hair airbrushed away.

I think even I would look good if you ran me through a computer.

Anyway, on the cover is an article that tells me, "Yes! You can finally change your body!" which is diagonal from the article stating, "Sorry supermodels—men on why they love us as is."

I put down the magazine, shut my eyes, and try not to obsess over Jordan.

"Charlize," a woman says from the doorway, and I can tell everyone's looking around for Charlize Theron. Nope—just me. I get up in my robe and follow the woman through a hallway.

An older, tiny Asian gentleman says, "Charlize?" and I am already dreading saying I had no preference between a man or a woman therapist. I should have said, "I don't care if it's a man or a woman—but not a Yoda."

The gentleman brings me to a room with lilting Asian music like you sometimes hear in yoga class. (Yes, I've been to a yoga class. Once.) He asks me to disrobe, lie on the massage table, and put the sheet over me. Then he leaves.

I throw off my robe and climb under the sheet. The man comes back in, and begins my massage.

Ouch! It hurts like hell. But it's a good "ouch," and after my last few days of no sleep, I fall asleep immediately.

He wakes me at some point and asks me to turn over, under the sheet. I do, and he begins rubbing the tops of my legs.

Aaaahhhh . . . And, within a minute, I'm out cold again.

The masseur wakes me again to tell me the massage is over. As far as I can tell, my massage lasted three minutes, and I slept the rest of the time. But I must say, I feel so much better. I feel energized— ready to take on the world.

Well, ready to take on Jordan, anyway.

The man leaves for a moment to let me put my robe back on in privacy. Then he comes back and leads me back to the quiet room, where I am to wait for my next session—something called an Emilee's Intrigue.

I don't see Dawn, so I get back into my chair, feeling beyond wonderful, and pick up another woman's magazine. There's an article called "Orgasm Do's and Don'ts: Make Him Go Wild For You."

I just can't motivate myself to read it. I'm so relaxed right now, it seems like too much work.

A middle-aged woman with a British accent calls my name, and it's off to my Emilee's Intrigue.

Once again, the therapist leaves the room to allow me to disrobe in privacy. Only this time, I get on my tummy and don't bother to pull the sheet up.

She comes back in and, in her British accent, cheerfully asks, "Have you had an Emilee's Intrigue before?"

"No," I admit. "Actually, until today, I had never even been to a spa."

"It's pretty fantastic, isn't it?" she says. "I gave my mum a spa day as a gift recently. She thought it was silly at first, but ended up loving it. Now, what I'm going to do is give you a massage, but I'm going to combine it with heated rocks placed on pressure points around your body. . . ."

"Oh, I already read about it in your menu," I say. "It sounds great."

I get yet another massage, only this time there is heat involved, and man, I'm feeling so wonderful.

I'll admit, when we moved on to putting eucalyptus leaves all over me, I felt silly. But then the steam from the hot towels hit, my sinuses cleared up immediately, and when she started massaging my scalp, I fell asleep again.

Aaaaahhhhhhhhhh . . .

A little over an hour later, I went back to the locker room, where I had forty-five minutes to wait for my next session, the "Hunter's Retreat."

I don't remember having felt this relaxed and happy in my whole life. I'm telling you, my mother could be here with me, and I'd still be relaxed.

Okay, maybe not. I mean, they don't do miracles.

I decide to slip into the steam room, which also smells like eucalyptus—I think. Well, it smells good, anyway.

I lay a towel down on the wooden bench, and lie down on top of it.

Dawn walks in about a minute later and lies down on the bench across from me. Neither of us say a word. All is peaceful in the universe.

Until a minute later, when a woman in a towel swings open the door and yells, "Men are assholes!"

I look over at Kate as she storms in. "How did you know we were in here?"

"I didn't. I've been walking from room to room, making that statement," Kate says, taking her towel off and laying it on a free wooden bench. "And not one woman disagreed with me. As a matter of fact, several women told me if I couldn't find you guys, I was welcome to join them and commiserate."

Dawn squints to see Kate through the steam. "Did you make it through your show okay?"

Kate lies down on the towel. "I did better than okay. I opened my show with a new political topic: Male politicians: How are these fuckwits still in power? You should have seen the boards lighting up with callers."

"Won't you get into trouble with the FCC for saying fuckwit?" I ask.

"No," Kate assures me. "I bleeped myself so it came out 'beep' wit. But I notice none of the women needed a cue card."

Dawn nods. "I take it the Mike conversation did not go well."

"Oh, not only did he spend the entire week not calling me, *and* avoiding me in the halls at work, but when I finally went to see him in his office today, he actually tried to hide under his desk."

"Final verdict?" I ask.

Kate lowers her voice to sound like a man, "Hey, we had some laughs. Let's not make it into a big thing."

"Sorry," I say.

"What makes it worse is, while I'm out thinking about that asshole, a perfectly nice guy is calling me every day, trying to convince me to marry him." She sighs. "I'm telling you, I have sworn off men. That's it. From now on, I'm just going to focus on my friends and my career."

Famous last words.

The three of us spend the next half hour in a three-way debate about why anyone dates. Although, I guess it's not really a debate if everyone is "con."

Then we head to the quiet room, where I pick up a financial magazine. "Are you ready for retirement?" it asks me.

I don't want to stress myself out, so I put the magazine back down.

Ignorance isn't really bliss. But some days, it's just easier.

A girl calls me for my Hunter's Retreat.

I go back down the hallway with a new therapist named Patricia, who leads me to one of the "wet rooms," which sounds a lot raunchier than it actually is.

I walk into the wet room, which is a large, white, tiled room that looks like a giant shower, except there are bouquets of flowers everywhere.

I hang my robe, slide onto a big waterproof massage table, and prepare to be exfoliated.

The huge showerhead turns on above me, and the water is perfect. As the shower cascades down on me, I become even more relaxed, if that's possible.

"Is this your first trip to the spa?" Patricia asks as she scrubs some sort of granular stuff on my back.

"Yes," I say, hardly able to breathe as she scrubs me down. We don't say anything more. The whole thing is so relaxing, and everything smells so good, I think I fall asleep for a few moments.

Patricia has me turn over, and we do the whole thing again.

Patricia finishes scrubbing, then rinses me. Next she cleans me with—I'm not sure what. It feels kind of funny, like cotton balls in baby oil. "What are you using now?" I ask.

"Wheat stalks. Soaked in essential oils," Patricia tells me. As relaxed as I am, I can't help but wonder who the first person was to be standing in the middle of a wheat field thinking to himself, "You know, we could soak these in lavender oil and sell them in New York City and Los Angeles. There's gold in these here amber fields!"

But the stalks smell good, and as I am being cleansed, I go back to thinking about Jordan.

I'm wondering what he would think of a place like this. Would he make fun of it? Most men do. Then again, I did until earlier today. Does he even like baths? Or is he more of a shower guy?

Damn it! I haven't even kissed him yet, and I'm in the middle of this luxurious and decadent experience, wondering what someone else would think of it. What's wrong with me?

As I force myself to put Jordan out of my mind, I am rinsed again. Then Patricia asks me to dry off. I do. In the final part of the treatment, she massages oil all over me. It sounds weird, but nothing could be more soothing. I am ready to sleep for twelve hours.

When I emerge from the wet room, I head back to the ladies' locker room. I ask a spa attendant if they have any coffee. Relaxed is one thing—but I'm so sleepy I could pass out for a fourth time. She tells me that they only have herbal tea and water with cucumbers in it. Cucumbers?

No matter. Back in the ladies' locker room, I grab a towel and head for the steam room again.

When I get in, I can't see a thing. "Dawn," I try to whisper.

"Goddess in the corner," she whispers back jokingly. The wall of steam begins to clear, and I see we're the only two in here. I put a towel down, and lie down on the bench below her.

"How are you feeling?" she asks.

"So good, I'd like to see about moving in here."

I can hear the smile in her voice. "I knew you'd like it. You make fun of me, but I know you pretty well."

"Oka-ay . . . ," I admit. "You were right."

"It's just like that time in college when you said you didn't like chocolate fudge Pop-Tarts."

"Oh, was I ever that young?" I ask nostalgically. "Where's Kate?"

"She's at the front desk, trying to schedule a facial," Dawn says. "So give me the latest dish on Jordan before she gets back and chastises you for ever allowing someone with a Y chromosome to enter your thoughts."

"Okay, but promise not to tell Drew," I say.

"Why would I tell Drew?"

"You just have to promise. He doesn't fall under the mate rule yet."

The "mate rule" is a rule that we made up in college that basically states that when you tell someone a secret, they are absolutely, positively not allowed to tell anyone other than their mate. The theory is that (1) you're supposed to tell your mate everything, and (2) he's a guy, so he won't care most of the time anyway.

But this way, you do get to spill the secret to one person. And, let's face it, most of the time we told our boyfriends anyway, so there was no point in feeling guilty about it.

"Once I meet his parents, does he count as a mate?" Dawn asks.

"No!" I say vehemently. "Although maybe once he meets your parents."

"You know full well that could take years," Dawn says, crossing her arms in frustration.

"That's what I'm counting on," I say. "Which is why this is a real secret. No telling Drew."

"Okay, fine."

I let her in on every detail of the online conversation, followed by the instant message conversation from the week before, and how Drew interrupted both times.

Dawn got the gist of my dilemma, and we talked for so long, we ended up walking over to get the pedicures together, babbling the whole time about what to do about Jordan. Then we talked through the pedicures, only taking a break to discuss what shade of red polish I should choose to match the red wraparound blouse I was going to wear tonight. (Guess who chose the red polish? Well, in my defense, sometimes Dawn does know what's best for me.)

By the time we were done, we decided that Jordan was absolutely flirting, and that I had to make my move tonight.

My spa day ended about an hour and a half later, after an amazing facial that consisted of four layers of stuff spread on my face, and something called "extracting," which is basically getting all the gunk out of my pores. It was painful, but I have to say, I positively glowed after the facial was done.

I didn't want to leave—I mean, I really didn't want to leave.

But I only had a few hours to get ready for the party, and I was so relaxed, I was going to need yet another nap when I got home.

I decided I would ask Drew for the same present for Christmas.

And my birthday next year.

And Groundhog Day.

And I had a new bit of advice for my great-grandniece:

Money can't buy happiness. But it sure can rent it for a while.

Twenty

Every action has a consequence.

And, damn it, tonight I am going to take action!

I spend over two hours getting ready. I try on at least five differ-ent outfits, then start putting different tops with different skirts. I can't decide if I want my look to be short, tight, and slutty; or long, flowing, and dignified.

Until Dawn calls. "Hello?"

"Don't make me come over there and make you change into the red top and black skirt," she threatens without preamble.

So I wear the red top and black skirt—frankly, because then I can blame her if I don't get any type of positive response from it.

After that, it was another hour of makeup and phone calls, where I actually called Dawn to ask if I should wear the "plum" eyeshadow with the shadow called "spun sugar," or go for "lilac" instead.

Eventually I look in the mirror and decide that I look okay (which doesn't sound good, but for me, on a scale of 1 to 10, that's a 45). Then I take my car keys and head out the door, determined to change my life.

Okay, well, at least my dating life.

Okay, at least for tonight.

The wrap party is in an elegant hotel in Marina Del Rey, a beach city just south of Santa Monica. Unfortunately, I was one of the first people to arrive: not only no Jordan, but no Drew, or Dawn either. Not even a Keenan.

I walk around admiring the ballroom, which is decorated all in white, I'm not sure why. But it looks dreamy—white tablecloths, white chairs, white Christmas lights drizzled throughout the room. Even the bar is done all in white.

And, speaking of the bar, did I mention all the drinks were comped? So I head to the bar by my lonesome, order a Merlot, and walk out to the lanai to gaze at the view.

The hotel has an amazing view of the harbor, with all the local boats bobbing in the light breeze. It's a bit nippy out, but the lanai has heat lamps over all the tables, so I make my way over to the table with the best view, sit down, and contemplate what's next.

I am starting to feel nauseated. You know that feeling they call *butterflies in your stomach,* when you know you're about to see the person you really like, and you can't help but feel sick? I guess it's called butterflies in your stomach, because if you said a guy made you physically ill, that might be construed as a negative.

But that's what I am feeling. It probably doesn't help that I haven't eaten all day, but I wanted to look thin for this outfit.

The second I see the waiter with the silver tray of shrimp the size of a baby's foot, I abandon thin for yummy.

"Shrimp?" he asks. I take four, each on a toothpick, and down them like a woman from a deserted island. The waiter strolls away from me, over to a couple by the fence. I stop the poor waiter on his way back inside, and grab four more.

As I hastily stuff my face, I hear from behind me, "You really do get a body like that through indiscriminate eating."

Oh, hell.

I turn around, and there's Jordan, looking gorgeous in a burgundy jacket and tie and black pants. He's grinning from ear to ear.

Shit, shit, shit.

"Well, this is embarrassing," I say through a mouth bursting with shrimp. "I'm sorry. I haven't eaten all day. I'm famished."

"Hey, nothing sexier than a woman who has a voracious appetite."

I'm not sure if that's a line or not. And I don't care. He just said "nothing sexier."

I unceremoniously pop the last of the shrimp into my mouth. "Well, then I guess you're going to worship me."

I can't believe I am feeling this at ease with him. The butterflies have magically gone away. I'm just really happy to see him.

"I already worship you," Jordan says, sitting down. He looks at me lasciviously. "And if we were online, I'd make a joke about being on my knees worshipping you."

I crinkle my nose up, in on the joke. "But since you're not, you won't."

"No. Then it wouldn't look real," he says, then scoots his chair a little closer to me. "So what happened to you last night? I waited, just like you told me."

"I'm sorry, a friend called me, and——"

Before I can finish my thought, I hear a loud, "There you are, Jordan. Perfect table!" followed by several crew members walking over with their wives and girlfriends. We are immediately at a table full of very loud partygoers.

Rats.

"So," I ask Jordan, trying to act like I'm actually happy to have all the new company (as if!), "Was this the group I missed today?"

"In the flesh," Keenan says. "Have you met my new bride, Constance?"

"I haven't," I say, and immediately begin talking to the woman on my right for the next twenty minutes or so.

I had no choice. The second this group showed up, Jordan went from "flirty, interested guy" to "totally not interested, just one of the crew" guys who hangs out with his buddies. So, I just talked to the other women at the table for the next hour, making sure it looked like Jordan and I were just friends, and that I wasn't interested in anyone at the party.

During that next hour, Jordan somehow managed to end up on the other side of the table from me. It wasn't his fault. He went to get drinks for everyone, and when he returned, someone had taken his seat next to me. I didn't want to be bitchy, and say, "Sorry, this seat's taken," but when Jordan came back, I could have sworn he looked disappointed.

Finally, I just threw caution to the wind, and left the table. "I'm going to go look for Drew," I announced to my tablemates.

There were mild protests (I notice not from Jordan), but I insisted I was working tonight, then I made my way inside.

And good thing I did. Jordan was right behind me. "Do you mind having some company?" he said, catching up to me.

"Not at all," I say. Aaahhh—my plan worked. I thought if I could separate myself from the herd, he might start the hunt again.

Pink's "Get the Party Started" is playing, and people have begun getting on the dance floor. "Would you like to dance?" I ask him.

He tenses up his shoulders and puts his hands in his pockets. "I'm not much of a dancer."

I let it go. "No problem. Maybe after another drink or two."

"Speaking of which, I need another beer. Can I get you something?" he asks.

"I would love a Merlot," I say, and walk with him to the bar.

"So," Jordan begins, "this friend of yours—was she okay?"

"Yeah," I say awkwardly, still not wanting him to know it was Drew. "Just my sister. Some wedding-day jitters, that's all."

"Oh," he says, and I can't read his expression. I'm not sure if he believes me or not. "Well, one of these days, we should switch to DSL, so neither of us gets bumped offline by a phone call, and we can talk longer."

I smile. "I would like that."

He smiles, and we have an awkward couple of seconds. I think maybe he's going to kiss me, but instead he turns to the bartender to order a Sam Adams for himself and a Merlot for me.

"Make that two Merlots," I hear Dawn say to the bartender from behind me, "and I think it would be easier on all of us if you just handed over the bottle."

Jordan and I turn around to see Dawn, looking stunning as ever in a dark green cocktail dress. "Have you met them yet?" I ask, referring to Drew's parents.

"Yes. They're out parking the car. Drew told them it was valet, but no, his father wants to find a space on the street. 'No point in your company paying for us to park. It's just a waste of money,'" Dawn says, imitating Drew's dad perfectly. Then she turns to Jordan and puts out her hand. "Hi, I'm Dawn. Jordan, isn't it?"

She says it like, 'I'm not sure if we've met,' and Jordan knows she's lying. But he bows and kisses her hand. "Charmed. You are looking lovely tonight."

Dawn looks at me and winks. "Love this one. Keep this one."

When Dawn sees Drew and his parents walk in, her whole body deflates. "Oh God, round two."

"They're really nice," I insist. "They're just a little small-town, that's all."

"Do I look small-town?" Dawn asks me.

"No," I admit.

She turns to Jordan. "When *you* see me, is there anything about my appearance, my attitude, or my demeanor, that says small town?"

"I would have to say no," Jordan admits.

The bartender sets down our drinks, along with a full bottle of Merlot. Dawn throws down a five-dollar tip, takes her glass of wine, and thrusts the bottle at me. "Take this, bring it to a table where I can get at it, and keep 'em coming all night." Then she gulps half her glass of wine and turns to face her accusers. "Damn—why can't we meet parents on the wedding day? Then you only have to do it once."

Jordan and I watch her cross the room toward Drew and his parents.

"Is she always this nervous?" Jordan asks. "She seemed so cool and confident at the dinner party. Almost conceited."

As I watch Drew's parents light up when Dawn gets to them, I smile. "Under that confident woman is a pretty insecure little girl," I say, thinking I've just described every woman I've ever met.

Jordan picks up his beer between two fingers, laces the wine bottle between another two fingers, then takes me by the hand and leads me to an indoor table. "Well, I guess we better stay close by. You know, I don't get why women are so afraid to meet the parents."

He puts the wine and beer down on the table, and pulls out a chair for me(!). "I mean, you should meet my mom," he continues. "She's got to be the easiest person in the world to get along with."

"Really?" I ask, pretending to be interested, although what I really want to say is a bitchy, "Yeah, easy for you to say, you're not the one who risks a woman hating you and referring to you as 'that slut my son is sleeping with.'"

"Oh, sure," Jordan assures me. "You'd love her. You both like spa days, and you both like beautiful shoes. I'm sure you'd have a lot to talk about."

My face immediately lights up, and I pull my legs out from under the table. "Don't you love these? They're Jimmy Choo. Dawn and my friend Kate got them for me for my birthday!"

"They make your legs look amazing," Jordan says in a tone that is getting me nervous and breathless.

A waitress walks up with a silver tray of plastic squirt guns and plastic handcuffs. "Would you like a souvenir from the movie?" she asks.

"Hmm," I say, grabbing a pair of handcuffs. "I may want to use these later."

I give my Groucho Marx eyebrow raise, and take a squirt gun as well.

"Would you like one too, sir?" the waitress asks Jordan.

"No, I'll pass," Jordan says.

"When people start squirting you later, you might want ammunition," I point out, so he reluctantly takes the plastic props.

We have an awkward few moments of silence again. More like a minute or two, which when you've got a crush on a guy is the equivalent to a month and a half. Jordan looks deep in thought. I wave to a few people, say hi to a few people. He does the same.

Think, girl. Think of something witty to say.

Finally, I take my plastic handcuffs and try to put them on him. He pulls back—but in a playful way. "Hey, lady!"

"What?" I say, smiling.

"You don't know me well enough to be doing that," Jordan jokes.

"Oh, I'm sorry. Let's see. I know your favorite book is *Auntie Mame*—which I've read since the dinner, and I have to say, I loved it. And that you have a married sister. What else should I know about you?"

"You read *Auntie Mame* just because I recommended it?" Jordan says, surprised.

I shrug. "Yeah . . . ," I say, not sure if this is a good thing or a bad thing. "I read a lot of books."

"I'm flattered," he says, taking a sip of beer. "Now I wish I had read something you liked."

"Well, you've been reading our instant messages. I like those a lot," I say.

We stare into each other's eyes. The DJ slows down the music, switching to an oldie, "Save the Best for Last" by Vanessa Williams.

"Would you like to dance?" Jordan asks me.

"I would love to."

He takes me by the hand and brings me to the middle of the dance floor. He takes my right hand in his left, puts his right hand around my waist(!), and leads me around the floor.

I'm in heaven. Never has a dance gone by so quickly, and yet gone on forever. Oh, and does he smell good! What is that? Lagerfeld? Chanel for Men? Old Spice? Who cares—I just want to stay in this moment forever.

The song ends, and Jordan stares into my eyes. This is it—the first kiss. That magical, delicious . . . why is he staring past me—what's going on?

I turn around, and Drew is at our table, madly waving at us to come over.

I swear, I'm going to go over to that man's house one night, and smother him with a pillow.

The next three hours were fine. I mean . . . they were fine. I shouldn't complain. I got to see people I'm not going to be seeing anymore who I've been working with for months. I got to help Dawn get through the "Meet the Parents" night. I got to see Drew's parents, who really are a nice couple.

But I did not get to have one more romantic moment with Jordan. I mean, really, how can you have a romantic moment when squirt-gun fights are breaking out all over the ballroom?

Around midnight, Drew's parents say they're tired, and the four of them decide to go home.

Jordan and I say good-bye to them, I make promises to call everyone tomorrow, and they leave.

Thank goodness.

Now's the time. Without giving myself a moment to chicken out, I say to Jordan, "Do you want to take our drinks outside, and look at the view?"

"That sounds great," Jordan says, taking me by the hand and walking me outside. We walk to the fence overlooking the water, and sip our drinks in silence. A full moon shines over the harbor, reflecting off the black water and making everything sparkle. It's so romantic. I wish I had the nerve to just lean over and kiss him.

But I don't.

But this is the last time I may ever see him—so I have to do something.

"So—who on the crew would you sleep with?" I blurt out.

Think before you speak.

Jordan nearly chokes on his beer. "Excuse me?"

"You know how Keenan does that pool among the guys about who on the crew you would most want to sleep with. Who did you choose?"

He smiles, and takes another sip of beer. "Did you talk to Keenan?"

"No. Why?"

Jordan glances over at the party inside. He takes my hand again, and silently leads me around the corner, behind some trees. Then he takes the plastic handcuffs, and puts one around my wrist. I move my drink to my other hand.

This can't be happening! This gorgeous, stunning, spectacular man might kiss me! No, I gotta be wrong.

"I thought we didn't know each other well enough," I say stupidly.

Jordan smiles, puts the other cuff on his hand, and stares into my eyes. "Now we do."

We both pause, cuffed together, waiting for the kiss. Maybe I'm supposed to lean in.

"This must be one of those awkward silences you always read about," I say, looking down nervously at my shoes.

Jordan smiles even wider, and leans in to kiss me. As his lips touch mine, I feel like sparks hit my mouth—my lips get all tingly. Then the rest of me starts to get tingly.

We kiss for a minute, five minutes, an hour, who knows? Oh, this is one of those times when it's great to be single. Every time we stop kissing, if only to take a moment to breathe, I grin from ear to ear, looking like an idiot.

After a while, I ask him, "Do you want to go back to my house and have a drink?"

"I would love that," he says. "Is it nearby?"

"No. Actually, it's in Silverlake. About thirty minutes from here, in no traffic," I stammer. Shit—why did I even say anything? Now, he's going to think I mean "spend the night," which I don't.

I mean, I don't think I do.

No, I don't. I definitely don't.

"That sounds great," Jordan says, uncuffing our hands and finishing off his beer. "Meet me in the parking lot in ten minutes. I'll follow you in my car."

Hmm, maybe I do mean spend the night.

Sometimes, when you're single, it's good to make your married friends jealous.

Okay, I may let him spend the night, but I am not going to sleep with him! Just kiss. For eight or nine hours. Now that would truly be perfect. No over-the-sweater action, no letting his hand rub my stomach (because then, you know, if he moves his hand up, you're sweeping your hand over his in such a way as to sweep his hand back down, but if he goes too far down, then you're really toast). No kissing of the neck or ears—well, maybe a little.

I cannot believe I have turned thirty, and I am still having mental battles with myself over men and sex.

I also cannot believe how much I want to get this guy back to my place!

We each make a hasty, separate exit from the party, then meet up in the parking lot ten minutes later, excitedly kissing before we reach our cars, then making out at my car for a good twenty minutes.

And Jordan follows my car back to my place.

As I fumble for my house keys, I warn him, "The place is a mess. I didn't know I was having company."

He stands behind me, rubbing my shoulders seductively. "Well, we could keep the lights out, so I don't see the mess."

I smile, turn around, and kiss him again. This is so great!

I put the key in the lock, do not turn on the light, and when we get inside, I pull Jordan down on the couch, so we can continue making out.

He tries to undo my top, but I swoop my hands over his, and gently push him away. He stops kissing me, and sits up. "Is it okay if I take off my jacket? I'm kind of hot."

God, yes, you are, I want to say. But I'm not that drunk. "Sure," I say, and stand up from the couch. "Can I get you that drink?" I ask, suddenly nervous, and wanting to cool down the room a bit.

"Um, sure," he says, I think a bit confused as to why I suddenly stopped kissing him.

I make my way to the kitchen, and turn on a light. I am so nervous. I don't want to go too far tonight. I want Jordan to call me again. I like him. I don't want to blow it (no pun intended).

Jordan comes into the kitchen, looking around. "This is a really nice place. Do you have roommates?"

"Nope," I say, pulling out a bottle of Stag's Leap. "It's just me. Merlot okay?"

"Yeah, that's great," he says, still looking around the room. "How many bedrooms?"

"Three," I say nervously, rummaging around in the cupboard for a few decent wineglasses. Why is it we only give people decent wineglasses when they get married? Shouldn't we be giving them to the single people who are still trying to impress potential mates?

I manage to scrounge up some Crate and Barrel wineglasses. "I actually bought the place last year," I say, putting a wine opener into the bottle. "I think I bought at the wrong time. They say the market's going to go down."

What am I babbling about? I'm supposed to tone down the mood, not kill it.

Jordan looks around. "It's a nice place. I love old houses. Built in the 1920s, right?"

"Yeah," I say, surprised, as I open the bottle and pour his wine. "1925. How did you know that?"

"I grew up in L.A., We moved to Orange County when I was twelve, but I still consider this home. I love these older places."

"Really? I grew up in L.A., too!" I say in that, "Oh my God, I love pizza, too" first date tone as I hand him his glass. "I grew up in Beverly Hills. You?"

He chuckles as he takes his glass. "We weren't so well off. Just a little house in Burbank. But it was nice. Built in the 1930s. The schools were good. . . ." He shakes his head. "God, the schools were good . . . could I be sounding any stupider right now? I'm never good at the in-between-kissing conversation. I think I better shut up."

He puts down his glass, takes me in his arms, and French-kisses me again, making my knees lock.

"So," he asks after we come up for air, "can I get a house tour?"

"Maybe soon," I say, flirting. "Why don't we have our wine in the living room first?"

"Okay," he says, picking up his glass in one hand and taking my hand with the other.

I take my wine and follow him.

But instead of leading me back to the living room, he pulls me upstairs. "I thought we were waiting for that house tour," I remind him.

"We are. You can show me the backyard in the morning."

I open my mouth to protest, but he turns to me and sticks his tongue in my mouth before I can say anything. Oh well, so we end up in the bedroom. The important thing is—no sex tonight.

I'm serious.

We put the wineglasses down on the nightstand, and continue kissing on my bed. The phone rings. I let the answering machine pick up.

"Hi, it's me," my voice comes on the machine. "Do it now." BEEP.

"Hi, it's your father. I know you're not at home, but I just wanted to wish you good luck with that guy Jordan tonight. I hope he takes your mind off that jerk David."

Jordan abruptly stops kissing me, and turns to look at the machine. I want to shrivel up into my comforter.

"Remember," my father continues, "we men are easy. We just want to know which chair is ours—you know what I'm saying? Oh yeah, and I'm not sure I'll be able to live with your mother much longer. Call me in the morning."

He hangs up, and Jordan stares at the machine. "Do you need to call him back?"

"No," I say, a pit forming in my stomach. "Why?"

"Your father just said he might leave your mother."

"No, no. They're divorced. But they're living together, and she's making him nuts."

"Your parents are divorced, but they're living together?" Jordan asks, justifiably confused.

"Yeah," I say, sighing, then forcing a smile. "They're very . . . interesting."

What I meant to say was crazy, but you know what they say:

When you marry a man, you marry his family.

Or when you marry a woman.

Or, in my case, when you're vaguely thinking about dating a woman, at least to the point where you're in her bed.

The phone rings again. At this point, I'm in a quandary: if I turn down the machine, it will look like I'm hiding something. If I don't, well, there might be something I need to hide. I begin kissing Jordan again, in the hopes he will ignore my father.

"Hi, it's me. Do it now." *BEEP.*

"Hey, baby, it's me, Dave," Dave purrs into the phone. "I miss you so much."

Fuck.

I jump up and turn down the machine. Jordan sits up. "You have anything you want to tell me about?"

"No," I say a little too quickly. "I'm just . . . embarrassed, that's all." I'm watching my machine to see that the message is continuing.

Jordan looks at the now-silent machine. "I take it Dave is an exboyfriend."

I have no idea how to answer that one. "Ex-shag" sounds trampy. "Well . . . kind of . . . yes."

Okay, that sounded bad. But letting Jordan think I'm some guy's booty call is even worse.

Jordan scratches his neck self-consciously. "An ex-boyfriend who still calls you at one in the morning?"

"It looks worse than it is," I say weakly.

The machine stops, and the phone rings again.

I don't pick up. *Ring. Ring. Ring.*

The silence between Jordan and me is deafening.

"You know," Jordan says softly, "maybe I should go."

"No!" I insist, then try to kiss him again. "Stay. I want you to stay."

"It's . . . a little weird. Can't you see that?" he asks. He's being so soft and sweet. I wish I could say or do something to make him like me again.

"But . . . I like you," I say.

And it's out there. And Jordan says nothing for several moments. Just stares at my hardwood floors—debating.

"You know what?" Jordan finally begins. "I like you, too. But this isn't the right time. You've got some baggage right now, and frankly I may have a little baggage in my own life right now, too. Maybe we should wait until we're both on solid ground. This is going to sound like a really un-guy thing to say, but I'm really not into one-night stands."

"Neither am I," I insist, although at this moment even I'm not buying it. "Look, Dave's gone. I promise. I really like you. I think you're gorgeous and you're funny and you're nice and this was just bad timing, that's all."

Jordan stands up and hugs me. Damn it, and it's the "Let's just be friends" hug. "I should go anyway. Are you gonna be okay?"

"Yeah," I say, confused. "Why wouldn't I be?"

"I don't know," he says with a shrug.

Jordan gently takes my hand, and walks down to my door with

me. He kisses me on the cheek, then tells me to "call him when things settle down."

The moment he leaves, I am terribly sad, and I almost go look up his cell number on the crew list just to call him and make him come back.

But I don't.

Instead I spend the next few hours alone. And definitely not okay.

Twenty-one

In five hundred years, none of this will matter.

"I feel like a dead shark," I say to Jenn the next day as we peruse the third floor at Bloomingdale's, searching for wedding presents for Andy and Hunter.

"I could go for some sushi," Jenn replies. "I could go for sushi, I could go for a caffeinated coffee, a martini . . . Hell, I could go for some alfalfa sprouts at this point. But I can't. I'm pregnant."

She reads the printed registry in front of her, then lifts up a particular crystal champagne flute. She looks at the price tag on the bottom, and shakes her head. "Two hundred fifty dollars for a pair of crystal champagne glasses in the middle of earthquake territory. Another victory for marketing."

"I didn't mean I felt like *eating* shark, I meant I felt *like* a dead shark," I say. Then I think about what she just said. "Since when can't you eat alfalfa sprouts?"

"Since there's some bacteria that grows on some of them that's very bad for little fetuses," Jenn tells me as we walk over to the formal china.

"Huh. And sushi's bad because . . . ?"

"Some parasite, or maybe it's a bacteria, too. Who knows? With the way the doctors talk nowadays, it's amazing any of us came out alive. You know, my mom has a picture of your mother, nine months pregnant, with a cigarette in one hand, and balancing a martini glass on her belly. And you turned out fine."

Instead of debating that dubious point, I glance down at my sister's registry. "My sister registered for a one-hundred-and-sixty-dollar brownie pan."

"What's wrong with that?"

"She doesn't cook."

"Neither do I, but I have this pan," Jenn says. "I mean, I used to cook." Jenn looks up in the air nostalgically, reliving a cherished memory. "Oh, I used to make great stuff . . . homemade brownies, coq au vin, haricots verts, fettucine Alfredo, three different types of fondue. . . . You name it, I could make it. Now I've learned that ravioli comes in ten different varieties—and God bless Chef Boyardee for that."

I sigh. "Well, I do cook, and no one's handing me a hundred-and-sixty-dollar brownie pan. It's so unfair—not only do I not have a soul mate, I don't even have a gold brownie pan. I don't get two-hundred-and-fifty-dollar champagne flutes, or a . . ." I read from the list and knit my brows together. "What's a dutch oven?"

"It's a large pot. I think it's also called a stock pot. Used for pot roasts and beef stews."

"The one she's registered for is two hundred and seventy dollars."

"Well, then don't buy it," Jenn says, a tone of irritation creeping into her voice. "God, I hate women who use weddings and babies as excuses to try and rob their friends blind. Do you know I had to go to a baby shower of my husband's friend's wife—not even someone I knew—and she was only registered at Bellini, and only for things one hundred dollars and above."

I look at Jenn blankly. She enlightens me. "It's a store where they sell you cribs for twelve *hundred* dollars that you can get at Toys "R"

Us for a hundred and fifty. And every woman in Brentwood seems to shop there."

"See, I would have guessed it was yet another food you couldn't eat."

"Very funny. We have to sit."

We walk over to a chair next to the wall of china plates. I have to admit, as much as I'm dying to have a baby, seeing my poor cousin sprawled out like this does make me take pause about the whole pregnancy thing.

"Has the morning sickness stopped?" I ask.

"Well, no. But it has stalled out a bit," Jenn says, rubbing her legs. "Of course, now I'm on to heartburn that could kill a goat."

Eww. "And that's better?" I ask, disbelievingly.

"Oh, much." Jenn pulls out a pack of Tums from her purse, and pops two in her mouth. "Back to you. You feel like a dead shark."

"Yeah. Like in the Woody Allen movie."

"I don't know what you're talking about. I haven't watched a film of his since he married his daughter."

"She's not his daughter. She's his stepdaughter," I point out.

"You're right. That's so much more normal," Jenn says dryly. "Anyway, if I can explain Bellini, you can explain the dead shark."

"It's from *Annie Hall*. See, a shark has to keep moving forward, or it dies. Lately, I'm not moving forward."

"Sweetie, don't feel that way," Jenn says, and pats my hand lightly. "Jordan's going to want to see you again. His ego got bruised last night, that's all. Wait online for him tonight, talk to him via the Internet, and make sure Drew doesn't call you in the middle of the night and cut you off. That should patch things up."

My jaw drops for a second, and I look at her in a mild panic. "You don't think Jordan thought that was Dave calling me in the middle of the night those two times, do you?"

Jenn gives me a patronizing look, like that was the first thing that popped into her mind, and how can I be so stupid? "I would say that's a safe bet."

I notice Jenn's sons Alex and Sean bound up the escalator, their father chasing behind them.

Sean just turned three. He is the cutest thing ever, and makes me want a child so much my heart hurts. He runs up to his mother, slams into her, then climbs into her lap. "Mommy, Mommy . . . Dad says we can get ice cream, but only if you say it's okay. Please, please pleeeeaaasssseeee . . ."

Alex, four, is also the cutest thing ever, and was the first one to make me want a child so bad it made my heart hurt.

But together, they make me vow never to have kids.

Alex races over to Jenn, and tries to push Sean out of her lap so he can get on. "Move!" he yells to his brother as Jenn's husband Rob tries to pry him away from Jenn.

"No!" Sean screams. "I was here first!"

"Well, I called it!" Alex screams back, now trying to hit him.

People are starting to stare.

"There's plenty of room in my lap for both of you," Jenn says in a ridiculously calm voice, as she moves Sean to her left leg and pulls Alex onto her right.

In the exact same tone of voice, she smiles and says to her husband, "I told you not to bring them up here."

"I know," Rob says. "But they wanted ice cream."

"Okay, sweetie," Jenn says to him, a crack forming in her wall of calm. "Look around. China shop. Two bulls. China shop . . ."

"I know," Rob says, now in an equally *we are not going to have a fight in front of the kids* calm voice, "but if I said ice cream was okay, and then we went to dinner in an hour, you would have been pissed."

"Daddy said pissed!" Alex says, giggling hysterically.

Jenn gives each of her boys a kiss, then gently pushes them off her lap. "Okay, you can each have one scoop of ice cream. But you have to be really good for Daddy, and you have to calmly walk outside, using your inside voice, and not touching anything."

"Yay!" they both scream in glee.

"Inside voices," Jenn reminds them quietly and calmly. "Now, each of you hold Daddy's hand, and Mommy will see you in an hour."

Rob leans down for a kiss. "I'm sorry," he says sweetly.

"It's okay," Jenn says, although her tone tells me she's barely keeping it together.

"I love you," he says, and rubs her belly lightly.

She smiles like a schoolgirl, and kisses him on the nose. "I love you, too," she says, and all is well in the kingdom again.

Until they leave. "That's what you're racing towards?" Jenn asks, then blows out a sigh of exhaustion. "Never having a moment to yourself? Quietly fighting with your husband about stuff you never used to fight about? Having two boys throw themselves into your pregnant lap? The total exhaustion that comes from pregnancy? And let's not forget never spending money on yourself ever again without guilt."

She's crabby, so I'm not going to say it to her now.

But yes, that's exactly what I'm racing toward.

Twenty-two

None of us like to walk away from a game when we're losing.

Jordan didn't call me all week, and neither did Dave. I spent a week replaying the whole night in my head—what else could I have said to make him stay? What could I have done differently? I wrote him an e-mail, then rewrote it, then deleted it and started over again three times, still never sending it.

I was online waiting for him every night.

I thought about calling him, but that's pathetic, right?

The following Friday, Kate, Dawn, Andy, and I boarded a Southwest flight out of Burbank, and headed for Las Vegas, for Andy's bachelorette party. There, we were to meet eight of Andy's friends at the Mandalay Bay Resort and Casino, a massive gold hotel at the south end of the Strip.

Our little foursome landed at two-thirty on Friday afternoon, and took a shuttle over to baggage claim (yes, the airport is that big). After getting our bags and waiting in the ridiculously long taxi line outside the airport terminal, we made it to the Strip, and into Mandalay Bay.

Mandalay Bay is sort of an ornate version of Polynesian meets French colonial meets a South Seas island. I swear the place smells like coconuts. This is a good thing. I immediately relax the second I enter the enormous marble lobby.

We wait in the check-in line, and Andy and I go first. As we approach the check-in counter, a pleasant woman with the nametag SUSAN smiles warmly, and says, "Hi. Welcome to Mandalay Bay. Are you checking in?"

"Yes," says Andy. "Andy Edwards and Charlie Edwards. We should have a room with two double beds."

"Great. Can I see some ID please?" Susan asks as she types our names into her computer. "I see we have you upgraded to a junior suite, compliments of Mr. Stanton. Will that be satisfactory?"

Andy and I exchange a look.

"*Drew* Stanton?" I ask, suspiciously.

Susan types some more. "Yes, he's already checked in," she tells me, then gives me his room number. "You're listed as his guests, along with Dawn Johnson and Kate Lopez, who have the room adjacent to yours."

I hear Dawn at the check-in counter next to us. "Charlie, get your butt over here!"

I smile politely to my sister and walk over to Dawn and Kate.

"This is Girls' Weekend," Kate says to me accusingly.

"Don't look at me. I didn't invite him."

"Well, I certainly didn't invite him," Dawn snaps. "Why would anyone want the man they're dating to be with them at a bachelorette party?"

"I don't know. But I also don't know what we can do about it at this point," I say to Dawn.

"Guys, over here!" I hear Drew yell, and the three of us look across the lobby to see Drew, waving excitedly like a moron.

"Go talk to him," Kate says, pushing me in his direction.

As I walk up to Drew, he gives me a great big hug, picks me up, and twirls me around. "I am so excited. I haven't been here in ages."

"Ummm . . . about that. What are you doing here?" I ask, treading lightly.

"Well, it was a spur-of-the-moment kind of thing. You know, the movie's over, I'm bored, Dawn and you are gone, so I call Jordan . . ."

"Jordan?!" I practically shout.

"Yeah, he's over there," Drew says, cocking his head behind him. I look over his shoulder, and see Jordan in the casino, playing slots.

No, no, no, no, no . . .

"I knew you were bummed out about the wrap party, and him not calling you, so I called him, and we got to talking—" Drew says.

"How did you know that?" I interrupt to ask.

"Dawn told me," Drew answers back innocently. "Anyway, we got to talking, and he tells me he's just out of a five-year relationship, which is tricky. But, mostly, he thinks you're in love with this guy named Dave. So I told him, she's so not in love with him—he's an asshole. And then he said—"

"Wait," I interrupt. "When did I tell you about Dave?"

"Remember—the night of your thirtieth birthday. You were talking about hating to wait by the phone."

Shit. I knew that night would come back to haunt me. "Why can't you use your special powers for good instead of evil?" I ask Drew.

A middle-aged couple walks past us nervously, getting a good look at Drew. "We love your movies," the woman says timidly to him.

Drew turns to her and flashes that award-winning smile. "Well, thank you so much," he says, as though no one's ever complimented his work before. "What's your name?"

"Kathy," the woman says, her voice cracking. "This is my husband, Bill."

Drew puts out his hand. "Drew Stanton. Good to meet you."

We spend the next minute with him signing autographs, taking pictures, and ignoring me. I'm finally ready to turn around and leave him in a huff, when the couple leaves.

Drew turns back to me. "Anyway, Jordan and I start talking about Vegas, and I tell him where you're staying, and he says if you gamble there you get free stuff—"

"Comps." I sigh.

"Yeah, that's what he called them!" Drew says, pointing to me in recognition. "So I call Mandalay Bay—"

"*You* called?" I just have this image of him saying, "Hi, this is Drew Stanton—famous movie star–sex god extraordinaire, and I'd like to learn about this thing you call comps." I was sure they would have hung up on him.

I wish I could hang up on him.

"What?" Drew says, clearly insulted. "Are you saying I am incapable of making a phone call?"

"Drew, you can't make a cup of coffee."

"I can't make a *decent* cup of coffee. I've certainly learned that you can take a teaspoon of Yuban instant, and put it in a cup with water, and if you want espresso you add a tablespoon of instant—"

"What the hell are you doing here?" Dawn snaps from behind me.

"Darling!" Drew says, taking her hand and kissing it. "You know, I'm pretty sure one of the guys here offered to introduce me to a hooker, but I said, 'No,' I wanted you."

Dawn looks at him blankly. Turns to me. "Make him go away."

"Do you know how to play baccarat?" he asks her, oblivious to her ire.

"Of course," she responds.

"Good. Because I told them I'd bet a million dollars over the course of this weekend," Drew says, then turns to me. "Do you know they gave me all three of our rooms just for doing that?"

Before I can respond with, "Are you out of your fucking tree?"

Drew turns back to Dawn. "But I've only been playing blackjack, and it's taking too long. I won, though," he says cheerfully, pulling out some thousand-dollar chips from his pocket.

Andy and Kate come over to us. Andy hands me a plastic card room key and my driver's license. "Okay, they sent a valet to take our luggage up to our rooms. Everything's comped this weekend. Drew, you're amazing," Andy says. She looks at his hand, and sees the chips. "Wow. I've never actually seen that color chip up close."

"Yeah, I got a few more." Drew pulls a handful out of his pocket, and holds out his palm to show her his winnings.

"Can I see one?" Andy asks.

"Sure," he says, handing her a thousand-dollar chip like it's nothing. "You can have one if you want. I got a bunch."

I can tell Andy doesn't know if she should accept it or not. She stares at the little chip in the palm of her hand.

I don't have such issues. I mean, he just ruined my weekend. "Can I have one?" I ask.

Drew gives me one. Sweet.

"What about me?" Kate asks.

"You're the one who just broke up with her fiancé, only to get blown off by some guy at work, right?" he asks.

Kate glares at Dawn.

Dawn shrugs. "What?" she says innocently. "Mate rule."

Kate rolls her eyes at Dawn, then admits to Drew, "Yeah, that's me."

"Good," Drew says, smiling. "Then you deserve two." He hands Kate two $1,000 chips. "God, I wish my fiancée had broken off our engagement."

Kate's face lights up as she stares at the chips. She turns to Dawn. "This is the *best* boyfriend you've ever had!"

Dawn sighs and crosses her arms. "Yes, he's a great boyfriend. But it's Girls' Weekend. He can't be here. He has a penis."

"Thank you," Drew says proudly.

"For what?"

"For noticing."

Dawn shakes her head, astounded at his obliviousness. He puts his arm around her and kisses her forehead. Then he gives his best "act cute" face, and offers her a chip.

Dawn smiles, despite herself. "You're a very hard man to resist."

He smiles, pleased with himself.

Then Dawn sees Jordan at the slot machines. "Please tell me you didn't bring Fuckface with you."

"He's not a fuckface," I say.

"Who? Jordan?" Drew says merrily. "He's my dog!"

Jordan turns around, sees me, and waves. He's smiling. I smile back, and wave a small wave—sort of a Princess Diana, hand barely moving, dignified wave.

Oh, he's so cute.

"He's not your dog," Dawn reprimands Drew. "You are way to white to be saying that."

Andy turns to Drew. "Can I order room service?" We all turn to her. She glances at each of us, confused at the attention. "The woman at the front desk told me everything was comped. Does that mean I can order room service?"

Drew smiles. He's in. "You can have whatever you want, my love. Whatever they don't comp, I'll cover. I just want you to be happy."

Never trust a man who says, "I just want you to be happy." What he really means is "I just want you to be happy—so I can get whatever it is that will make me happy."

"I think I'll get an omelet," Andy says, beaming.

Yup, that's my sister. Bought off by an $8.95 breakfast item. "So, do you want to come out with us tonight?" Andy asks Drew.

"No!" Kate, Dawn, and I answer simultaneously, before he has a chance to get a word in edgewise.

Drew scratches his ear self-consciously. "Actually, I think since it's a Girls' Weekend kind of thing, we should let you go solo tonight."

Whew.

"But do you think I could borrow Dawn for a little while? I need her help," Drew says, lightly grasping Dawn's hand.

"Of course," Andy says, a little disappointed. "But if you change your mind, we'll all be at Red Square at six o'clock, having martinis at the ice bar. I'd love to buy you a drink."

Drew looks to me for approval. I nod ever so slightly.

He smiles. "I'd like that," Drew says to Andy. "I'll see you at six."

Then he turns to Dawn. "Okay, we have a date with a baccarat table. Guys, we'll see you later."

Drew and Dawn disappear into the casino. Kate heads up to her room. I ask Andy to go meet the valet up in our suite, and to order me a filet mignon from room service.

Then, butterflies floating around in my stomach, I make my way over to Jordan at the slot machines.

"Hey," I say awkwardly as I stand beside him like a self-conscious idiot. "You winning?"

"Hey. How are you doing?" Jordan asks, just as awkwardly, then kisses me on the cheek. "Nah, I'm out about twenty bucks so far. But I got a free drink out of it." He holds up a bottle of Corona. "You?"

"So far, I'm up a thousand dollars, and I haven't gambled yet."

Jordan looks at me quizzically. "Drew was winning," I tell him. "He gave me a thousand-dollar chip."

Jordan nods. "Oh." Then, after a moment, "He told me he was the one who called you and interrupted our e-mail chat. How come you didn't tell me it was him?"

I shrug. "I have this confidentiality agreement I signed with him when I started working for him. Bosses calling you in the middle of the night . . . that can sound a lot worse than it is."

A waitress quickly marches over to me, her pencil poised over her notepad. "Can I get you anything?" she asks me.

"Um . . ." I look over to Jordan to see if he would like the company.

"The Coronas are pretty good," he says, so I order one of those.

Once the waitress is gone, I take a twenty-dollar bill out of my pocket and slip it into the machine next to Jordan's. For the next minute or so, we both play slots. There's dead silence, save the *ding-ding-ding* of the slots. I pull the handle, he just presses the button.

Ding-ding-ding.

By the time the waitress comes back with my drink, we're both down about ten dollars. After she hands me the drink, Jordan hands her a four-quarter tip.

When she leaves, we finally start talking again.

"Drew's a hard guy to say no to," Jordan says clumsily, desperately trying to get the conversation going.

"To quote Jeremy Irons in *Reversal of Fortune*—'You have no idea,'" I joke.

"You know, we got a suite with a dining room in it?" Jordan said. "And the living room is bigger than my living room at home."

"I doubt my room is as grand. But it is free—he got my sister and me comped."

Now it's time for the other awkward part of the conversation. But I might as well get it out there. "Drew did explain that I'm here for a bachelorette party, right?"

"Yeah. You and your friend Dawn, your sister, a bunch of other girls. No men allowed." Jordan presses the button again. *Ding-ding-ding.* "Speaking of, how's Dave?"

"I wouldn't know," I say decisively, then take a sip of my beer for courage. "He's an ex. I don't see him anymore, and I'm not the type to stay friends with exes who call me at one in the morning."

Jordan smiles and takes a sip of his beer. He presses the button. Seven. Seven. Seven.

"Oh my God!" I scream. "You just won!"

"Yeah," he says quietly, still smiling. "Looks like my luck may be changing."

Twenty-three

What happens in Vegas stays in Vegas.

I spend about ten more minutes with Jordan (and, after losing my twenty dollars, vow not to gamble anymore this weekend), then make my way up to our junior suite.

Junior is a misnomer. The room is huge, and truly fabulous. It makes me think of the word *romp*—as in, one should *romp around* this suite while staying in it. Our view is spectacular, with floor-to-ceiling windows overlooking the Strip. Our beds are so big and so comfortable, I wonder whether the hotel realizes it is encouraging its patrons to never leave the bed long enough to gamble in the casino.

The all-marble pink bathroom has a Jacuzzi tub the size of an Esther Williams pool, a toilet with its own room, and its own phone. (Um, exactly who absolutely needs to take a phone call when they're using the facilities?) And the pink marble floor is so shiny and slick, Andy and I decide to take off our shoes and skate around on it in our socks like little girls at an ice-skating rink.

I am already having a wonderful time.

When room service comes, the server sets up our food in front of the windows, giving us a view of a pyramid, a medieval castle, the New York skyline, and the Eiffel Tower.

Then he pops the cork of a bottle of Dom Pérignon. I look at Andy, surprised. "Why did you order champagne?" I ask as the server hands Andy a full glass.

Andy stares out at the magnificent view, sips her champagne, and sighs. Her mood has suddenly changed from frolicky to fickle. I chalk this up to pregnancy hormones.

"Are you sure you want to drink that?" I ask as the server hands me a full glass, then puts the bottle in a silver ice bucket next to our table.

"It's my bachelorette party. I'm supposed to drink it," Andy says with a touch of bitterness.

"But what about the . . ." I look down at her tummy, then back up to her face, as if this is some code the server won't figure out.

"Oh my God!" Andy yells out. "I'm not pregnant! Jesus, you plan a wedding in less than three months, and everyone jumps to the same conclusion."

I continue to look at her, dubious. "Do I look pregnant?" she asks, irritated.

"No," I answer immediately, knowing the universal truth.

It is rude to ask a woman if she is pregnant. But it is a death wish to answer "yes" if a woman asks, "Do I look pregnant?"

As Andy signs for the food, she practically spits out at me, "I just want to have a good time, and not think about the wedding for a while. Is that okay?"

"Um . . . yeah." I say, still a bit taken aback. "Um . . . congratulations."

"On what?"

"Not being pregnant," I lamely attempt to joke. "Puts you ahead of Mom and Dad. And now you can drink at your wedding."

Andy glares at me. Maybe she's just glaring, and not at me, but it hurts just the same. I hate fighting with my sister.

The server leaves, and the two of us begin to eat our food in silence. Several minutes pass, and all I can hear are the forks clinking against the plates.

I decide to tread carefully in these dangerous waters. "I know maybe I haven't been as happy for you as I should be," I say tentatively. "I'm sorry. I guess I'm just a little jealous."

"Thank you," she says, finishing her glass of champagne and pouring herself another. "It's not you, it's me. I'm just mad at Hunter."

"Men aren't very into weddings."

"It's not that," she says, and I know to be quiet and let her talk. "It's that the only reason I'm having this fucking bachelorette party is because he's out with his boys this weekend having a bachelor party."

Again, I am tempted to speak. To try to say something comforting, maybe give a good bit of advice. But I learned long ago:

When a friend is in pain, usually all you need to do is shut up and listen.

The hard part about that, of course, is training yourself to shut up.

"Do you know who Shaquille O'Neal is?" Andy asks me.

"Some Irish guy?" I guess. "I think Kate's mentioned him. Is he the mayor of Boston, maybe?"

Andy looks stunned.

"I'm kidding," I say. "He's a basketball player."

"And he's an asshole," Andy informs me.

"Oh," I say, not sure where this is going. "Is he throwing Hunter's bachelor party?"

Andy sighs out loud. "No! A couple of years ago, when he was on the Lakers, they were playing in the playoffs. After one of his games, he's being interviewed, and he keeps calling one of the opposing team members *she*. *She* did this, and *she* played like that. It was supposed to be this huge insult, and he thought he was being so damned clever, you could see it by the way he was smiling. And at some point, since none of the reporters were laughing, he said, 'And you heard me right, I said *she*.' Like that was the most clever insult someone could come up with—to call an opponent a woman. That is the worst thing someone could be called—a woman.

"Now, mind you, if this same fuckhead had called the man 'white' as an insult, it would have been a top story on the news that night, or at least on ESPN. That's what happened with that Rocker guy in Atlanta when he made those racist comments about New York. Everyone demanded apologies. But not one reporter, not even one of the women, asked for an apology from O'Neal. Not one."

I nod, listening. Andy continues, "So apparently, in this day and age, it's not okay to be racist, but it is okay to be sexist. It's not okay to degrade blacks or Hispanics, but it's perfectly acceptable to degrade women. Yeah, we've come a long way, baby."

Bile could be coming from Andy's mouth, she's so angry. But I must be missing something. "Okay, so the guy's an ignorant ball player. What's that got to do with you?"

Andy's lips purse as she stares out the window. She takes another sip of champagne. "Every woman I talked with thought Shaquille O'Neal's actions were disgusting. And yet not one man I talked with did. They all cited 'tradition.' Men traditionally insult their opponents by calling them women. It's appalling, it's disgusting, but hey, they've been doing it for years, so how can we girls get so upset?"

Andy downs the rest of her champagne. "And now I'm faced with the next insulting, degrading tradition: the bachelor party. Where future grooms routinely watch women strip for them, dance for them, and maybe even have sex with them, because these poor guys have, quote, 'only got a few more nights of freedom.'"

Shutting up isn't too hard now—because I honestly don't know what to say. She has a valid point. I have heard of some pretty crazy bachelor parties, and it is weird that no woman ever puts her foot down to say, "Oh, hell no!"

But I also wonder why Andy's marrying a man she doesn't trust.

Twenty-four

*If such a thing as a bachelor party still exists in your lifetime, and
your fiancé is such a dolt that he insists on having one, let him. But
have your bachelorette party the same weekend.*

That afternoon, Dawn, Kate, Andy, and I trudged our way
through the pyramids of Egypt, the streets of New York, and Le
Boulevard de Paris. And we even got to play with a lion cub at the
MGM Grand!

I had a good time, but there was one trend that worried me.
Andy had the "wandering eye," so to speak, and seemed to be flirting with an awful lot of guys.

I mean, on the one hand, everyone flirts, particularly at a bachelorette weekend. There's no harm in it. But, on the other hand,
something was off. I couldn't put my finger on it, but my sister
wasn't acting like herself.

Late that afternoon, we dressed up in our sexiest togs (and, in my
case, my awesome Jimmy Choo sparkle shoes) and headed down to
Red Square, a bar in Mandalay Bay with a Russian theme, known
for having over one hundred different kinds of vodka, not to mention a bar made of ice.

Yes—real ice—they have a freezer within the bar that keeps the ice block frozen, so you can set your drink on it. It's like a skating rink for martinis. It's my favorite place in Vegas.

As our group of ten women take up all the available chairs at the bar, the bartender, a good-looking man wearing a black turtleneck, black pants, and the nametag CHRIS, walks up to us. "Ladies, what can I get for you this evening?"

"I want a Red Square martini," my we-all-thought-she-was-pregnant sister says to the bartender.

"What?" her friend Jody, a beautiful redhead who'd be even prettier if she didn't talk so much, turns to look at Andy in shock. "You want a *what*?!"

"A Red Square martini," Andy says innocently. "They have these blue cheese–stuffed olives in them . . ." Her voice trails off as she looks around. All of her friends are staring at her.

"Wouldn't you rather have a nice glass of water?" Jody asks. "Or juice?"

"I'm not pregnant!" Andy shouts, making some of the other customers at the bar turn to stare.

Deciding to make a joke of it, Andy smiles and waves her arms up in the air with a theatrical flourish. "So, everybody drink!"

The girls all laugh in relief, and everyone gets different kinds of martinis, all made with various brands of vodka.

As the girls who are still standing huddle around those of us in chairs, we talk about the wedding, men, babies, the wedding, jobs, the male strip show we're going to see tonight, who of the single women plans to get laid tonight, and the wedding.

"I want to get laid tonight!" Andy announces after her second martini.

"No!" Jody insists. "Hunter can't come tonight."

Andy is much more cheerful now, but she starts up again with her anti–bachelor party rhetoric. "How come none of you guys are saying 'Last weekend of freedom!' I'll bet that's what my future husband's friends are saying."

"Please," Dawn deadpans, "women's lib does not mean imitating men's worst qualities just so we can lower ourselves and be equal to them."

"Besides," I say sternly, "we wouldn't want you to do something you'd regret in the morning."

"And yet, you'll let me get married next weekend," Andy jokes. But it's a bitter joke.

Jill, a blond friend of Andy's, leans into us. "Oh my God, don't look. But I think Drew Stanton is in the lobby."

Every girl looks, although the rest of them with more interest than Kate, Dawn, and me.

Drew, dressed in a light blue button-up shirt and gray pants, but no jacket or tie, walks in with Jordan, looking incredibly hot in a tan shirt and khaki pants. I notice several heads turn to acknowledge Drew and whisper about him, but no one bothers him.

Drew walks right up to Dawn and kisses her on the cheek. "Hello, darling."

She turns to kiss him on the lips, "Hi, sweetie."

Jordan comes up to me, but doesn't kiss me. "Hi," he says awkwardly.

I respond back with a seventh grade, self-conscious, "Hi."

"You look very nice tonight," Jordan says, and I feel like we're in an episode of *The Brady Bunch*. Tonight's episode: Jan's awkward date.

Drew leans into the three of us and whispers to Dawn, "So, is that deal we made still on?"

She kisses him on the cheek and says sweetly, "It is. Now get out."

"Excellent," Drew whispers back. "Ladies," he announces in his grand 'I can project to the back row' theater voice, "finish your drinks. You have two limousines waiting outside to take you wherever you may wish to go. Compliments of yours truly. We would love to meet everyone back here for a drink—say, around one-ish?"

The girls all scream in approval and gulp up their drinks.

Kate looks over at Jordan, asking him the question she knows I want answered. "So, what are you boys up to tonight?"

"I have no idea," Jordan says.

"No asking questions," Drew says, putting his arm around Dawn's waist.

She gives him a kiss on the cheek, then tells us, "The deal is, the guys can do whatever they want tonight, and we can do whatever we want tonight." She turns to Drew and smiles. "Only one rule applies: the women you two came to see get the last dance of the evening."

"I wouldn't have it any other way," Drew says with just a touch of smarm.

I like how she slipped that in—you *two*.

Drew raises one arm and yells, "Tallyho!" and, like a pack of dogs in a foxhunt, all the foxy ladies gulp the rest of their drinks and, with Andy leading the pack, get up to start their hunt for single men.

The five of us follow Andy's friends out. We walk through the massive lobby, and out to the front of the hotel, where indeed, our limousines await us. The first limousine quickly fills up with Andy and six of her already drunken friends. One of Andy's friends opens the top, stands up, and screams, "Whooooooo," like she's in a *Girls Gone Wild* video.

Kate, Dawn, and I cringe. "Let's take the second limo," Kate suggests.

"You read my mind," Dawn agrees.

Jordan and Drew walk us to the limousine. Kate immediately gets in. I, on the other hand, stand there like an idiot, trying to think of something clever to say to Jordan before I leave. Something that will have him thinking about me all evening.

I can't think of a thing.

Drew wraps his arms around Dawn's waist playfully and gives her a big hug. "Now, you be good for me tonight."

Dawn smiles. "All right. But when I'm bad, I'm more fun."

They begin to French-kiss as Jordan and I look on awkwardly. I feel like we're the prom couple driving in the front of the car, while the other prom couple's having sex in the back.

Jordan doesn't even try to kiss me. Instead, we both stare at each other awkwardly while they take forever . . .

And ever . . .

Finally, Kate gets out, pounds on the top of the limousine, and screams, "People are waiting! Off you go! Chop, chop!"

They abruptly stop, and laugh.

"Okay, fine," Drew says. He kisses Dawn once on the hand, then walks toward his limousine ahead of us. "Jordan, kiss Charlie good-bye, so we can get out of here."

Jordan freezes. "Um . . ."

You'd think he was a deer staring at a Mack truck coming at him at fifty-five miles per hour.

Very nice. Since it's never gonna happen, I roll my eyes and get into the car.

Dawn follows, the limousine driver closes the door, and I look through the window to see Jordan still staring at me in contemplation.

"Open the window," Kate orders me.

"No," I insist. "This has gotten embarrassing. And I'm not that desperate."

"Please"—Dawn smirks as she hits the button to open the window—"you are totally that desperate."

I smack her hand off the Down button, and hit the button to

close the window back up. "Yes, I am. But I don't want him to know that."

As the car drives off, I watch Jordan still standing there, his hands in his pockets, watching us go.

I can't help myself. "Driver, stop!" I yell.

We stop. And, with Kate, Dawn, and Andy's friends watching, I roll down the window. "Hey!" I yell to Jordan.

Confused, he jogs up to me. "Yeah?"

"Drew's right. Kiss me good-bye."

Jordan smiles sheepishly, then leans through the window to kiss me. The women in the car cheer, whoop, and applaud.

When we break away, I can't help but feel giddy. "I'll see you at one?"

"I'm counting the minutes," Jordan says, giving me one more kiss, then tapping the roof of the limo twice to alert the driver to go.

And we're off!

We spend the next hour cruising the strip, sipping champagne, and listening to the other girls' problems with men, which included such golden oldies as, "Well, I'm dating this guy who's still technically married . . ."

A man who claims he is "still technically married" is married. Get the hell away from him.

Or the famous "We've been dating for four years, but he says he's still not ready for marriage. What does that mean?" (It means he doesn't want to get married. Or not to you, anyway.)

Or the even more classic, "We had a great time, and he said he'd call me. But that was two weeks ago. Do you think I should call him?" (I won't even dignify that with a response.)

Oh yeah, and there was that one glorious minute where the girls chatted about how gorgeous Jordan was.

Over the course of the next several hours, we did the standard bachelorette party agenda: male strip club, bridal scavenger hunt, and several clubs where Andy, wearing a cheap bridal veil, flirted with every man in the room.

That wouldn't have been so bad. But once we got to Ghostbar, the nightclub on the top floor of the Palms Hotel, things got out of hand.

I had high hopes when I walked in: floor-to-ceiling windows with breathtaking views of Las Vegas, space-age silver furniture, a full bar. But within ten minutes of our group getting in, I saw a good-looking boy (yes, I mean, boy—he looks all of twenty-two) start dancing with Andy, and the two quickly became inseparable.

Uh-oh.

After a while, Andy's new friend takes Andy by the hand, and they both walk up to me. "This is my sister Charlie," Andy drunkenly slurs, nearly falling on me. "And my friends Kate and Dawn. Guys, this is my new friend John."

"Nice to meet you," I say, holding out my left hand for him to shake.

I did this on purpose. That way, he had to break free from Andy's hand to shake mine.

"Nice to meet you," John says, breaking free from Andy just long enough to shake my hand, then taking her hand back. "You have a gorgeous sister."

"Yes, I do," I say. "She's also an engaged sister. Did she mention that?"

"No. But the veil kind of gave it away," John says cheerfully.

Shit. He knows she's taken, and it's a plus to him.

Men who chase married women, or women in a serious relationship, do so to avoid commitment. This is why, when you finally start dating someone after a long dry spell, suddenly the men come out of the woodwork.

Christina Aguilera's "Dirrty" begins playing. "Oh, I love this song!" John says to Andy. "Dance with me!"

And he pulls her away.

A little after midnight, two of Andy's friends had already left the club with men in tow, using the lame excuse that they were "so tired" and "needed to get back to the hotel." I say this excuse is lame only because they were holding hands with guys they had met two hours before, and had already publicly kissed on the dance floor.

I mean, come on, is there a man on earth who's really inviting you to his hotel to "just talk"? I mean, even if that's all that happens, it sure as hell wasn't his idea.

Anyway, the other girls are clearly making their nocturnal plans, so it's time to call it a night. I make my way to the dance floor, where a very smashed Andy is falling all over John and telling him how gorgeous he is.

I peel her off of him ever so gently. "Come on, Cinderella. It's after midnight. We have to go, or you'll turn into a pumpkin."

Andy falls onto my shoulder in a drunken stupor. "Oh, I'm having such a great time. Let's stay a little longer."

"No," I say firmly. "Drew's meeting us at one, remember? We need to leave. Now."

"Oh." Andy's fuzzy little brain takes a second to process this information. Even wasted out of her mind, she knows who's paying for this weekend of bacchanalia, and that he's my boss to boot. She turns to John with sadness in her eyes. "She's right. I'm really sorry. We're meeting friends at Mandalay Bay. I gotta go."

Andy tears herself away from John, takes off her veil, and begrudgingly follows me off the dance floor.

John follows her. He's cheerful, upbeat, and not giving up so easily. "Wait," he says, taking her hand. "Let me come with you."

Andy looks over her shoulder at me, her eyes begging me to let him come with us.

I shake my head no.

"I don't want you to leave your friends," Andy tells John.

"Don't be silly. I'll bring a few of them along. My friend Bob's getting along really well with your friend Deborah."

I turn to follow John's line of sight, and see Bob making out with Deborah.

Yeah—I'd say they're getting along.

"Okay!" Andy says brightly, her face lighting up. "We'll be at Red Square. Do you know where that is?"

"I do," John says, and he's glowing. He looks totally in love, and thrilled to be included in the rest of the night's festivities.

How is it that men are so good at looking totally in love, when really they just want to get laid?

Anyway, I round up what is left of the girls, and we all head back to Red Square in the limousines.

John manages to snag a ride back with us, and was at least gracious enough to talk to Dawn, Kate, and me during the twenty-minute ride back.

"So," John says to Dawn, "I've been meaning to ask you all night—are you an actress?"

Dawn squints her eyes suspiciously. "Why?"

"'Cuz you totally look like this babe on that show *Water Babies*. You know, Mike's girlfriend. The one who dies."

Man, did he ever make points with Dawn. She'll never admit it, but Dawn loves being recognized. "That was me," Dawn says, verbally warming up to him. "But that was over two years ago. How did you ever remember that?"

"Well, you're very . . ." John clears his throat. "Well, you're a very . . . attractive woman."

Dawn smiles at him. "Where are you from again, John?"

"New Orleans. I'm just here for the weekend for my buddy Dan's bachelor party."

I cock my head. "Didn't we meet Dan?" I ask.

"Um . . . yeah," John says, shifting in his seat uncomfortably. "He went back to Mandalay Bay with your friend Jill."

"Goddamn it!" Andy yells suddenly, startling everyone in the limo.

John's voice softens, and he rubs her leg. "What's wrong, darlin'?"

I know exactly what's wrong. She's pissed off that a bachelor is cheating on his future wife at this very moment. And with her friend, no less.

"It's just that . . ." Andy begins angrily, but then changes her tack, her voice softening. "You know what? Nothing." Andy leans her head on John's chest, and he gently strokes her hair.

It's a good thing she had three chaperones there, or that wouldn't have been all he was stroking.

Ten minutes later, we're back at Red Square. There are no chairs available at the bar, but there's a table with a small couch and three chairs on the other side of the room.

We head to that side, and John snags the couch, immediately pulling Andy next to him. We take the chairs, and everyone waits for Andy's other friends to show up.

Which they don't. And neither do John's friends.

Now, obviously, this is a covert action. No one's supposed to come back to see Andy and John, because that would keep them from getting together. John's friends are supposed to pretend they got lost getting back to the bar, and just went back to their hotel rooms.

In addition, John's friends need to play wingman, and keep Andy's friends from showing up by plying them with drinks, a late-night breakfast, gambling, sex—whatever it takes to keep them from showing up to rescue their girl, and keep her from doing something she might regret in the morning. And I guess they succeeded, because none of Andy's other friends show up.

Not that it matters. I've never had a problem being the cock blocker.

The waitress comes and we order a round of drinks. Kate and I stick with champagne, Andy orders a Red Square martini, Dawn gets a dirty martini, and John gets a beer.

"Where is everyone?" Andy asks, standing up to scan the crowd.

John gently pulls her back down to the couch. "I'm sure they'll be here soon," he says flirtatiously, and it's at that point that I'm positive no one else is coming.

John leans in to kiss Andy when Kate asks him point-blank, "So, what are your intentions?"

John stops in midair and turns to Kate, confused. "I'm sorry?"

"Well, you're obviously about to make out with a woman who's getting married next week. Making out with her is going to seriously mess up her head during what should be one of the happiest weeks of her life. I'm just wondering . . . are you going to call her all weekend, then blow her off? Or is tonight a one-night stand?"

Kate asked the question liked the interviewer she is—with not a trace of bitterness or judgment—just a genuine curiosity for the truth.

John and Andy both look at her, stunned.

The waitress walks up with our drinks. As she puts them down, John pulls away from Andy and takes out his wallet to buy the round.

"Put that away. Your money's no good here," I hear from behind me.

"Excuse me . . . sir," John says with utter respect, his eyes wide.

"Drew!" Andy says, slinking back into John's arms. "We've been waiting for you."

I turn around to see Drew, wide awake, almost sprightly. Jordan, on the other hand, is so drunk he can barely stand up.

If you get a man too drunk, the desire for sex goes up—but noth-ing else does.

Drew puts his hand on my shoulder. "Charlie, your boyfriend here is a lot of fun. But he cannot hold his liquor."

"In my defense," Jordan says, leaning on my chair, "most people cannot go through a fifth of Maker's Mark in an hour."

"Come on, that was an appetizer," Drew maintains. "And didn't we have those In-N-Out burgers to sober us up?"

"Followed by shots of Jack Daniel's," Jordan reminds him.

"That was dessert," Drew says, smiling at us all. He looks at the waitress. "Can you get us each that Russian beer you guys carry, and charge everything to my room?"

"Of course," the waitress says with a smile, and leaves.

John stares at Drew, clearly starstruck. If he can remember Dawn from two years ago, I can't even imagine what he's thinking now. Drew puts out his hand to him. "Drew Stanton."

Why is it that famous people always give you their first and last names? Like, if you met Brad Pitt and he said his name was Brad, you'd think, *Gosh, what a coincidence—does he know how much he looks like Brad Pitt?*

John puts out his hand. "John Gerber. It is an honor to meet you, sir. I've seen all your movies."

"You have?" Drew asks excitedly. He takes a seat right between John and Andy, pushing them to opposite sides of the couch. "So, which one is your favorite?"

"Oh, definitely *Marksman,*" John says, taking a sip of his beer and forgetting about Andy completely. "You should have gotten the Academy Award for that. You were robbed."

"I thought the same thing," Drew says, then puts up his index finger in a mock *Sssh.* "What did you think of my Tybalt in *Romeo and Juliet?*"

"The fencing was amazing!" John says, his hands waving around excitedly.

"Thank you. You know I did all the stunts myself. We had this great choreographer—I was fencing for a month. Oh, and the research I did . . . Did you know much of Italy is built in cul-de-sacs?"

"I didn't know that," John says, with the excitement of a college freshman with a crush on the professor.

"Sure. See, that's why Tybalt says he's leaving the city, but then comes back—he gets lost!" Drew turns to Andy to include her in the conversation. She stares at him in shock. I'm sure she's wondering how could he steal her date like this.

The waitress comes with their beers, and hands the bill to Drew to sign.

As Drew autographs the bill, John says to Andy, "I can't believe you know Drew Stanton, and didn't even tell me."

"Why would it have come up?" Andy asks, clearly irritated.

"You know what else I liked?" John says to Drew. "*Timber*. What was it like to work with Catherine Zeta-Jones?"

"She's amazing. Beautiful, funny. Love, love, love her husband."

"Is he as nice as everyone says?" John asks.

"He's better," Drew answers.

"You know, you should have at least been nominated for that one," John says, sounding incredulous that the Academy members could have overlooked such a phenomenal performance by Drew.

"Thank you," Drew says, turning to Andy. "I love this guy! Hey, do you mind if we steal him for a little while?"

Andy looks at him, horrified, but doesn't say anything.

"What are you guys up to?" John asks.

"Yeah, what are we up to?" Jordan asks apprehensively, falling into my lap.

Drew ignores Jordan, focusing on his new buddy John. "The concierge told me about this great strip club that doesn't get hopping until two. Jordan and I are gonna go. Do you want to come along?"

Jordan whispers to me, "He's not really going to make me go out again, is he?"

"Hey, I'm just happy he's not dragging me," I whisper back.

John looks past Drew, over to Andy, who's now leaning back on the couch with her arms crossed, sulking. "I think I better stay here," John says, although in a tone that's full of regret.

"That's a shame," Drew says. "We've got a fully stocked bar in the limo, and I can get us into the VIP room."

Dawn abruptly stands up and drains her drink. "Looks like you men still want to party. Why don't you go with them, John? We girls need to get some sleep."

Andy stares at Dawn, eyes wide, too stunned to speak.

"Well, if Andy doesn't mind," John says, standing up and looking at Andy.

"Why would I mind?" she nearly spits out. "Hey, why hang out with me when you could be getting drunk with a movie star, and getting the VIP treatment from strippers?"

Not missing a beat, Drew kisses Andy on the cheek. "Baby, you're the greatest."

Drew jumps up from the couch and hits Jordan on the arm as he walks out of the bar yelling, "Tallyho!"

Jordan nearly falls off my lap. "I'm really growing to hate him."

He kisses me on the cheek, then drags himself out of the bar, right behind John and Drew.

Kate, Dawn, Andy, and I sit in silence. I take a nervous sip of my drink, and get ready for Andy to start screaming at me about my stupid boss. Instead, she lies down on the couch and says, "I think I'm going to be sick."

Twenty-five

When out for a heavy night of drinking, remember—don't mix grains.

Half an hour later, I am holding up Andy's hair as she pukes her guts out in our bathroom.

"I am never drinking again," she vows, then throws up again.

Eventually, she flushes the toilet and lies down on the cold marble floor.

"Do you want me to help you move to the bed?" I ask.

"No. Just leave me here to die."

"We could put a trash can by your bed in case you need to throw up again," I suggest.

Andy takes a deep breath. "Tempting."

There's a knock at the door. I leave the bathroom as Andy gets sick again.

I cross the suite, and open the door to Drew and Jordan.

Drew bounds in. "What did we miss?"

I look past Jordan. Andy's new buddy John is nowhere in sight.

"Where's John?" I ask Drew as he and Jordan walk in and I close the door.

"He's at the strip club," Drew tells me, walking over to the mini-bar. "We had a bit of an incident."

"What happened?" I asked, concerned.

Drew pulls out a mini bottle of Jack Daniel's. "There was a photographer from *Celebrities Uncensored* across the street, so we bagged the idea."

As Drew opens the Jack Daniel's bottle and takes a swig, I look to Jordan for an explanation. "What did he do?" I ask accusingly.

"Oh, it wasn't so bad," Jordan says, falling into a chair. "Drew didn't want to get out of the limo with sleazy photographer guy there, so instead he called the bouncer over to our window, slipped him a hundred, and asked him if he could take John to the VIP room solo. Then he gave John a thousand dollars in cash, and told him to call his buddies to hang out."

I sigh, and glare at Drew. "So you just left him there? By himself? With no way to get home?"

Drew finishes off the mini Jack. "No way to get home?" he says, sounding like he's talking down to me. "I left the guy with a thousand dollars in a VIP room with a bunch of strippers who think he's friends with Drew Stanton. Getting home is the last thing he wants to do." Drew stands up, puts his arm around my shoulder, and kisses me on the cheek. "I love you, sweetie. But, honestly, you sound like such a girl sometimes."

"Bring him back!" Andy angrily yells from the bathroom. Then she throws up again.

Drew walks into the bathroom doorway. "I can't be seen in a place like that," he says haughtily. "I'm an upstanding citizen in my community."

I give Jordan a weak smile. "Will you excuse me?"

I push past Drew in the doorway as Andy flushes the toilet again. "Do you need anything?"

"I need you to bring John back," Andy says, forcing herself to sit up.

Drew sits next to Andy. His voice becomes calm and soothing, like he's playing a therapist in a film. "So, what's the deal? Are you having issues about settling down, or is this some grudge fuck kind of thing?"

I yank Drew up by his arm. "I can handle this. Why don't you go see Dawn?"

"Aw, she's asleep. Besides," he says cheerfully, "this is real-life drama. I live for drama. I'm an actor."

I put out my arm and point to the doorway. "Out!" I say sternly.

Drew looks at Andy, slumped over the toilet, then back at me. Andy, me.

He slowly stands up to walk out.

But then he grabs my hand and leans into me. "I'll give you another thousand-dollar chip if I can stay," he whispers.

"No," I say quietly, hoping Andy can't hear us.

"Two thousand."

"Drew . . ."

"Two thousand dollars, and you can have next week off to help your sister with her wedding."

I yank Drew out of the bathroom. I'm drunk, I'm worried about my sister, and I'm getting angry. "Now, listen: you are a great boss, and I know you'd like to help, but you cannot put a price on something as private as—"

"Give her three thousand dollars and the week off, and not only can you stay, but I'll tell you why I want to cheat on my fiancé," Andy yells from the bathroom.

"Sold!" Drew says, leaving me to go back to Andy.

I walk in after him and watch as he sits down next to Andy, who falls into his arms.

Jordan walks over to me, hands me a small bottle of Evian water for Andy, and mouths, "I'm gonna go."

I nod as I take the water.

So much for my wild night.

I sit down by the sink, on the cold tile floor, across from Andy and Drew. We're all silent for a while. I listen to Jordan's footsteps as he leaves. When the door clicks shut behind him, I say to Andy, "So, what's up?"

She looks up at me. "You can't tell Mom."

"Schyeah. Like that would ever happen."

Andy puts out her left hand and stares at her one-and-a-half-carat diamond. She smiles the saddest smile I've ever seen. "Hunter slept with his ex-girlfriend."

Drew and I exchange worried glances.

"After you got engaged?" Drew asks.

"No. Before. Right before," Andy says. "Like, the night before. He told me about it the next morning."

Neither Drew nor I say anything for the longest time. I can't stand the silence—it seems to go on forever. I open my mouth to speak, but Drew shakes his head and puts his index finger over his mouth as if to say *Sssshhhh*.

When someone finally does speak, it's Andy. "He came to my apartment at five in the morning, all teary eyed. He told me what happened, and I broke up with him—right then and there. He begged me to take him back, said he'd do anything to make it up to me, blah, blah, blah, and I said marry me, because I won't put up with this bullshit from a boyfriend, and now, here we are, the happy couple."

Whoa. I didn't say that, but whoa! "So, we'll call off the wedding," I say calmly to Andy, like it's no big deal. "No one has to know why. You'll just say things didn't work out."

Andy nods her head slightly, like of course that's the thing to do.

Drew looks at me, then looks back at Andy, and announces, "I don't think she wants to call off the wedding."

"Of course she does!" I insist. "My sister's not a doormat. She's not going to put up with some bastard—"

"He's right," Andy interrupts. "I don't want to call off the wedding. I really want to marry Hunter. I just want this to have never happened."

Well, what the hell am I supposed to say to that?

"Man, I know just how you feel," Drew says, shaking his head. "You're feeling like 'If I'd just been sexier, or prettier, or smarter, this wouldn't have happened. More clever maybe. More successful. Something. If I had just been good enough for him, he wouldn't have wanted anyone else.'"

I can tell from the look on Andy's face, Drew just nailed how she feels *exactly*. She cocks her head at him. "I forgot. Your wife left you for another man, didn't she?"

"Yeah. But she cheated on me with another guy the year before that," Drew tells her. "And, man, I felt like I must be the most pathetic person in the world when I found out."

Andy's eyes begin to water. She wipes a lone tear from her left cheek. "Yeah. And you want to know the really stupid thing? I actually wanted to know all the details. Like somehow, if I knew the when and the where, I could go back and change what happened."

Drew nods. "I did that. Like it had anything to do with me. 'Oh, she did it when I was out of town doing reshoots, if only I had brought her with me . . .'"

" 'If I hadn't insisted on going to bed early that night . . .' " Andy continues.

"If I hadn't sent her to Maui in a five-star hotel bungalow with my best friend, a man who, by all accounts, was a complete dog. I mean, what the hell was I thinking?!" Drew says.

We both stare at Drew. Um . . . okay.

I lean over and give Andy the bottle of water. "I'm sorry. Is there anything I can do to make you feel better?"

Andy shrugs. "Say something to make the hurt go away," she says weakly.

Drew pulls Andy into his arms and gives her a hug. "Aw, sweetie . . . hasn't Hunter said anything to make you feel better?"

"No," Andy says, starting to tear up again. "He tells me how much he loves me, but it doesn't make me feel better. He tells me I'm beautiful, I still feel ugly . . . he tells me how great our future is going to be, and how sorry he is, and how he's going to make it up to me, and I still feel like I'm going to crumple up into a ball and die."

Andy takes some toilet paper and wipes her eyes. I can tell from the way she's breathing that she's doing everything in her power not to cry. "I just wish there was something he could say that would make me feel better. That would make me feel like things are going to be okay."

Drew blows out a big sigh. He lifts Andy's chin and puts her face up to his. They lock eyes, and for a second, I'm sure he's going to kiss her. But, instead, he gives her these words of advice: "If people could unfuck, they'd do it every day."

Andy looks stunned for a few moments. Eventually, she shakes her head. "I'm sorry. I don't know what movie that's from."

"It's not from a movie. It's something my father once told me. And, believe me, it pertains to more than affairs," Drew says. "Look, Hunter came to you. Right afterwards. He knew he'd just made the biggest mistake of his life, and he wanted to fix it. He would do any-thing in the world to make it go away, but he can't. If he could un-fuck, he would."

Andy takes a moment to process that information. She laughs ever so slightly. "You know, for the first time since the engagement, someone has finally said something that makes me feel like maybe there's some hope."

"Good," Drew says, patting her arm. "Let me tell you something else that's going to make you feel better. That horrible feeling you have inside right now? The one that's making you nauseous, that makes you feel so weak you want to crawl into a corner and cry your guts out? It goes away."

Andy takes a deep breath. "You promise?"

Drew smiles. "I guarantee it. And when you're celebrating your fiftieth wedding anniversary with all your kids and grandkids, it'll be nothing more than a speed bump in your relationship. It might not even occur to you to think about it."

Andy smiles and kisses him on the cheek. "Thanks." She looks at me. "Both of you. For listening. I really needed to talk to someone, but I couldn't. And that just made it worse."

"Hey, what's a maid of honor for?" I say.

Andy crawls across the floor and lies on my lap. "I'm really sorry I messed up your night. You can go see Jordan now if you want."

I smile. "Nah, I'll see him tomorrow night. Make him work for it."

Drew left about twenty minutes later. As I walk him to the elevator, I ask him, "That last speech you made, about the speed bump in fifty years, that's from the script you're reading now, isn't it?"

"Yeah," Drew says brightly, stepping into the elevator. "It's great dialogue, isn't it? I'm playing a therapist. I'm telling you, this one has Academy nod written all over it."

I shake my head as the elevator door closes.

A few hours after that, a very hungover Andy called Hunter and asked him to come to Vegas with his boys, including my brother Jamie, and make it a joint bachelor/bachelorette party.

He did. He just got into a group of cars with his buddies in the middle of the night, and drove out to see her.

And when he got to our suite, he looked so happy to see her, I'm pretty sure he had been hoping she'd call all along.

As I watched from my bed, pretending to be asleep, Andy opened the door, and the second she saw him, she burst into tears again.

"I'm sorry, I'm so sorry," she said over and over again, as she sunk into his chest and continued to sob.

"What happened?" Hunter asked softly, rubbing her back.

"I just . . . I just really love you," Andy said, unsuccessfully trying to catch her breath and stop crying.

"Well, I love you, too," Hunter said, hugging her more tightly. "That's why we're getting married."

"No," Andy said softly, breaking apart from him and swallowing her tears. "I mean, I really, really love you. And I want to spend the rest of my life with you. I don't think I realized how much until last night."

Oh shit—now he's going to think she slept with someone.

"I love you, too," Hunter said, smiling and gently wiping the tears from her face. "Why don't you go clean up, and I'll buy you breakfast?"

Andy nodded her head up and down several times, then walked into the bathroom, closed the door, and turned on the shower, as Hunter threw his luggage on her bed.

"She didn't sleep with anyone," I told Hunter, once I knew Andy was out of hearing range.

Hunter turned to me and smiled. "I know."

I sat up, trying to clarify. "I mean, she didn't sleep with anyone, she didn't kiss anyone, she didn't do anything other than get sick in our bathroom all night."

"I know," Hunter said in a completely self-assured, but very sweet tone. "I know my future bride pretty well."

It was at that moment I realized this marriage was going to be just fine.

And I had a new bit of advice for my book:

If people could unfuck, they'd do it every day. This also applies to undating.

Twenty-six

Comparisons are odious.—Sir John Fortescue

Romantically speaking, everyone was having a better Saturday than me. Hunter and Andy were spending the day by the pool, hugging and nuzzling each other like they were the only two people on earth.

Drew and Dawn left the group to take a helicopter ride around the Grand Canyon, presumably where they were hugging and nuzzling each other, and acting like they were the only two people on earth.

The bachelors and bachelorettes from Hunter and Andy's respective groups were hooking up like bunnies. My brother Jamie was probably hooking up with Kate, which I thought was an accident waiting to happen, but I couldn't say anything to dissuade either of them from flirting this morning, so I gave up.

Me? I was spending the day trying to figure out what went wrong with Jordan.

The day started out so promising. At eleven o'clock in the morning, I went to Drew's suite to ask Jordan to breakfast. I glued on my happiest smile and knocked on the door—ready to embark on a romantic adventure!

I had the whole day planned out in my head. I would ask Jordan to breakfast, thereby separating him from the herd, so to speak, and whisk him off to someplace fun—just the two of us. Someplace like the Palatium Buffet at Caesar's Palace, with its all-you-can-eat omelet bar, or maybe the Buffet at the Bellagio.

I would order a glass of champagne and encourage him to do the same (you know, to loosen him up), and we would talk openly and freely, with no reservations, just like we did online.

We would spend hours looking into each other's eyes, and saying such witty bon mots as "Oh my God! I love Italian food, too!" and "You're right! Bruce Willis has been overlooked by the Academy!" as we perused all the attractions that Las Vegas has to offer: the dolphin pool at the Mirage, the tiger cubs at the MGM Grand, maybe ride the roller coaster at New York, New York.

We would talk and laugh all afternoon, and I would occasionally rub his arm, maybe take his hand while we walked through the casino, then ask him to dance while we listened to a middle-aged diva with a Princess Diana haircut sing "Having My Baby."

Oh, it would be silly and fun and perfect, and by the end of the night we would be inseparable.

God has a sense of humor. Don't believe me? Just look at a zebra, and tell me what was going on in his mind that day.

Okay—so back to the door. I stand in front of the door: makeup on, cute miniskirt on, Chanel No. 5 wafting about my neck, legs shaved, smile plastered on my face.

I am ready for my close-up!

I knock on the door, and wait.

No answer.

I knock again.

Damn it! He couldn't have gone to breakfast alone. I look around the hall nervously. Now what?

Finally, being the discreet girl I am, I pound on the door and yell, "Jordan! Are you in there?! It's Charlie!"

"Sorry! Hold on!" I hear from the other side of the door.

Whew.

Jordan opens the door, wearing nothing but a hotel robe, and he looks perfectly dreadful.

I mean, I didn't know people could really turn a shade of green—I always thought that was just an expression. The only pink in his entire face is in his eyes.

I force a smile and pretend nothing is wrong. "Hi."

"Hey," Jordan says, then covers his mouth to burp. "I'm sorry I took so long. I was asleep."

"Oh," I say, at a loss. I stand in the doorway, stupidly waiting for him to let me in.

He doesn't.

I look down the hallway nervously, buying myself some time. Nope, he's really not going to ask me in. Finally I eke out, "I'm sorry I bothered you. I was just going to ask if you wanted to have breakfast with me."

Jordan shakes his head as though trying to clear out the cobwebs. "Hmm? Oh . . . yeah. Breakfast. Okay. Do you want to come in?"

He opens the door for me, and takes a few steps backward as I walk in.

This is a bad idea. "You know what?" I say, taking a quick peek around to see how the other half lives. "You look wiped. Maybe I should come back later."

"No, no. I just need to get changed," Jordan says, taking my arm and gently leading me into the full-size living room area of the suite. "I'm afraid I'm a bit hungover this morning. Food would be good for me. Have a seat. I'll be ready in a minute."

He sits me down on the sectional sofa. "Can I get you anything?"

"No," I say, forcing another smile. I watch as he walks over to the minibar, pulls out a bottle of Evian water, and downs it in one gulp. He looks miserable. He leans on the minibar for support, and rubs his temple.

I wince just watching him. "Can I get *you* anything?" I ask.

"Do you have any aspirin?" Jordan asks, furrowing his brow and rubbing his head.

"No," I say apologetically. "But they probably sell some downstairs."

Jordan nods, then walks silently to his bedroom and closes the door.

Feeling awkward, I take a look around the suite. There's a dining room with a highly polished table for six. The living room could easily fit twenty. And they have an even more magnificent view of the Strip than we have in our room.

Plus two full bedrooms.

I wanna be rich.

Anyway, I look over at Jordan's closed door. Feeling awkward, I yell to him, "Are you sure you don't want me to come back later?"

"No," he yells through the door. "Give me one more minute."

Feeling uncomfortable, I grab a magazine from the coffee table and start leafing through it. There's an article about Hawaii I turn to.

Hawaii. That sounds good. Pretty much anywhere but right here sounds good. Michigan—I hear it's lovely this time of year. Or Pittsburgh.

Okay, think. All right. So he's hungover. Which means, right now, according to my brother Jamie, that's bad because . . . shit! Why is it bad? I need to get ahold of Jamie and find out how to act around a hungover man you have a desperate crush on.

Which means I need to get out of here for a minute. Now, how to do that?

I look over at the closed door and yell, "How about if I go down to the lobby and get you some aspirin?"

"No. Just give me one more minute," Jordan yells back.

Damn it. All right, I know I'm obsessing, but I need to figure out how to handle a hungover man. Where would Jamie be right now?

Okay, he saw Kate this morning. He's had a crush on her since he was thirteen. She is now available for the first time since he became legal, therefore, he is saying and doing anything he can right now to get past the velvet rope. And he's known her for so many years, he should know exactly what to say and do.

What the hell? I'll give it a shot. I pick up the phone and press the button for the front desk. "Can I have Kate Lopez's room, please?" I ask in a whisper.

Kate's phone rings. And rings. I start to put down the phone. Darn, I was sure they would have . . . "Hello," Kate says.

"Hi!" I say, putting the phone back to my ear. "It's Charlie. Um, I hate to bother you, but I was wondering if you knew where Jamie was. See, I'm with Jordan right now, and I—"

"Hey, sweetheart. What's up?" Jamie says.

Sweetheart. You know he's with a girl when he starts sounding like Sam Malone to his own sister. "I need some dating advice," I whisper into the phone, hoping to God Jordan doesn't open the door and hear me obsessing. "What do you do when you're with a guy who's hungover, but he won't let you leave?"

"Whisper the name Kobe Bryant into his ear," Jamie responds.

"That's not funny. Besides, I didn't sleep with him. What was that thing you said guys have when they're hungover, and it makes them depressed?"

"Dopamine," Jamie says. "But when they're hungover, they don't have it anymore. That's why they're depressed. That's why you should never sleep with a man the first time when he's drunk."

"Oh my God, I totally read about that," I overhear Kate say to Jamie. "That is so cool you know about stuff like that."

"Well, I have two sisters. It makes me very sensitive to a woman's feelings," Jamie lies to her.

I can hear him starting to kiss her. And her kiss back. Now they're making out, and I'm just the idiot on the other end of the phone listening to it.

"Hello?" I yell into the phone. "A little advice here."

"Oh, sorry," Jamie says. "Okay, it's Jordan, right?"

"Duh."

"Okay, well, right now he's hating himself, not you. So go have breakfast with him, then let him sleep it off. Tonight, I'll make sure we all do something together, and you can try hitting on him then."

"Okay. That sounds like a plan," I say, nodding my head even though he can't see me. "Now make sure when you talk me up to him tonight you tell him . . ."

And I stop talking, realizing Jamie has already hung up.

I hang up the phone just as Jordan opens his door.

All I can think is—damn. Even sick as a dog, and just wearing jeans and a T-shirt, the man looks good.

Jordan runs his fingers through his damp hair. "So, where do you want to go?"

"Well," I begin. "Caesar's Palace has an all-you-can-eat buffet. . . ."

Jordan clutches his stomach. I stop talking. He takes a deep breath (presumably to stop from dry heaving) and says, "I'm sorry. Right now, all-you-can-eat sounds a bit . . . overwhelming."

"Fair enough," I begin again. "Then we could go to a regular restaurant. There's a nice restaurant at the MGM Grand we could walk to that has—"

"Walk?" Jordan interrupts with a tone of voice that adds, *Please, God, no.*

"Or," I say brightly, "we could go somewhere in the hotel, so we don't have to walk."

"Better!" Jordan says, and it's the first time he's sounded happy since I got to the room.

Our trip down to the lobby was pretty much silent, save one

"You look very nice today" from Jordan on our way to the elevator, and one "Thank you" from me.

Once in the lobby, we go to a gift shop that sells aspirin in packages of two tablets per pack. Jordan buys three packs, and some Alka-Seltzer for good measure.

I keep trying to start up a conversation. I go everywhere from politics to photography, from Aristotle to Christina Aguilera. I get nothing back.

We head to the hotel café for breakfast. The hostess leads us to a table, hands us menus, asks us if she can get us coffee (we both answer with a resounding "Yes!"), and leaves us to our nonexistent conversation.

"So," I begin awkwardly, "Andy called Hunter last night after you left. He drove out here with all his bachelor party guys, including my brother."

"I know," Jordan says as he opens his packets of aspirin. "Your brother's going to be camping out with us in our room tonight."

"Oh," I say, quelling the urge to say, *No, he won't. He'll be camping out with Kate.*

Jordan puts all six aspirin in the palm of his hand and drowns them with the glass of ice water already set on our table. "So," he says pleasantly, "what's your story?"

He hasn't asked it in a belligerent way—more like he's making conversation. I try to craft a good response as a waitress with the nametag MARCIA puts down our coffees.

"You guys know what you want?" Marcia asks cheerfully, pulling out a pad and a ballpoint pen.

"Oh," I say, quickly glancing at the menu even though I know exactly what I want. "I'll take the ham and cheese omelet with extra cheese, and a side of bacon."

"What kind of toast?"

"Wheat. Lots of butter."

"Hashed browns?"

"Definitely."

"Great. And you, sir?"

Jordan coughs into his fist, looking like he's going to throw up. "Wow," he says to me. "That's a lot of food." He turns to Marcia. "I think I'll just have a bagel."

By the way she looks at him, I can tell Marcia sees this all the time, and can feel his pain. She leans in and whispers, "Can I make a recommendation?"

"Sure."

"Bloody Mary. A little hair of the dog, plus the tomato juice has something in it that helps the dehydration."

Jordan smiles, embarrassed. "That sounds perfect. Does it come in a supersize?"

Marcia laughs politely, takes our menus, and leaves.

And we're back to our awkward silence. Jordan rubs his eyes. I'm afraid he might go back to sleep right on our table.

"In what sense?" I ask, trying to get some sort of ball rolling.

"Hmm?" Jordan asks, sounding like I just woke him.

"You asked me about my story. In what sense?"

"Oh," Jordan says, as if he just remembered the question. "Well, your younger sister's getting married next week, you've just turned thirty . . . some women would be overthinking their life right now."

Ouch. I take a moment to wince internally, then give what he's saying some thought. He's right, of course. I have been overthinking my life. "Truthfully?" I begin. "Yeah, I'm a little sad that I'm thirty, and I'm alone, and that I haven't figured out everything in my life yet. But I'm not that sad. Most days, I'm pretty happy with my life. I like my job, I like my friends, I like the direction my life is going in. So I try not to dwell on the bad stuff."

Okay, not completely true. But it sounded good, didn't it?

Jordan eyes me suspiciously. "So, when you say 'alone,' what do you mean by that? I mean, obviously you have a lot of dates. A lot of guys interested."

"Getting dates is never the problem," I say, and I mean it. "Finding someone to love for the rest of your life—that's the tricky part."

"Hmm. Are you still seeing Dave?"

Again, very pleasant. No accusatory tone.

"No," I answer back just as pleasantly, but emphatically. "I haven't dated him since well before the wrap party. His phone call the night you were over was just an unfortunate coincidence."

Jordan smiles. "Glad to hear it. What about Doug?"

Shit! I had forgotten all about Doug. "Hmmm. Doug," I say, stalling for time.

When all else fails, try the truth.

"Well, honestly, I was interested, and then I wasn't."

"Why the sudden loss of interest?" Jordan asks, stirring some cream into his coffee.

I smile. "There was someone I liked more. And I just can't seem to get him out of my head."

I swear, he blushes.

"So what about you?" I ask. "Tell me about this ex-fiancée."

Jordan fidgets in his seat. "Okay. What do you want to know about her?"

Everything and not a damn thing at once. Of course, I don't say that.

And before I can ask anything, he interrupts my thoughts. "You know what, I'm having a really good time this weekend, and I'd prefer not to talk about her. Is that okay?"

"Okay," I lie.

And we don't talk about her for the rest of breakfast.

We do talk about colleges, art, Paris, the Mets (okay, no, I don't talk about the Mets, but I'm a very good listener), Drew, other stars we've worked with, *Queer Eye for the Straight Guy*, politics, Chinese food, and *Jeopardy!*

The conversation wasn't bad, but it wasn't great, either. Jordan was pleasant, but the look on his face let me know that he'd rather be anywhere but here.

We finish breakfast, Jordan pays the bill, and we head out to the lobby and casino floor.

"Did the Bloody Mary and aspirin help at all?" I ask weakly, ready to give up on my hot new romance.

"Yeah, it did, actually," Jordan says. "Although I could really use a nap. Particularly if we're going out again tonight."

Phooey. Well, maybe I can find someone to hang out with at the pool.

And then out of the blue Jordan asks, "Do you want to come up with me? You look like you could use a nap yourself."

"What, are you saying I look as bad as you right now?" I joke.

Jordan smiles bashfully, looks down at the carpet, and shakes his head. "No. I'm saying I came all the way to Vegas to hang out with you, and that's what I want to do. But I'm not feeling well, and if I don't take a nap, I won't be any fun tonight. So, I figured if you joined me, I could do both."

He looks up at me. I smile. "I would love to go take a nap with you."

Jordan smiles the most beautiful smile, takes my hand, and walks with me toward the elevators. "You know how to spoon?" he asks.

"I do," I say in a voice that's a little too high and cute.

And we head up to his suite.

Twenty-seven

Take lots of naps.

I wake up from my nap to see Jordan staring at me from his pillow. Suddenly I am self-conscious. "What?" I ask.

He smiles. "Nothing."

I sit up. "I hate it when guys watch me when I'm asleep."

"Oh," Jordan jokes. "Does that happen a lot?"

"No," I say with an irritated tone, pulling out a pack of cigarettes from my purse on the nightstand. "Do you mind if I smoke?"

He winces. "Sure. Go ahead."

"What was that?" I ask.

"What?"

"That look. You just winced."

"Hey, it's none of my business," Jordan says, sitting up with me and rubbing the sleep out of his eyes.

"Bu-u-ut . . ." I say, because, let's face it, that sentence had a big *but* at the end of it.

Jordan looks down at the covers, takes a deep breath for strength, and lets me have it. "Well, I don't smoke. Never did. And I'm sure it's a really hard habit to break and all . . ." His voice trails off.

"A-a-nd . . . ," I continue for him.

Jordan shrugs. "A-a-nd . . ." He kisses me softly on the lips. Then he kisses me a little more. I am turning to jelly, delighted by this sensual moment, when he finishes his sentence. "And when you kiss someone, and they smoke, they have really bad breath."

I want to scream, *Oh, God! Why didn't you say something sooner? I'm so embarrassed!*

Instead, I take the pack of cigarettes, crumple them into a ball, and throw them into the trash can. "Did I mention how I just quit?" I say, smiling flirtatiously.

He leans over to me. "You hadn't mentioned that, actually," he says, and kisses me again.

We start rolling around on the bed, fully clothed, and I am bliss-ful. After all, this is a much better motivation to quit smoking than, say, January 1st of every year.

As I contemplate whether or not to start unbuttoning his shirt, there's a loud pounding on our door. "Dude? You up yet?" my brother Jamie yells from the other side.

"Uh, yeah. Just a minute!" Jordan says, silently looking at me as if to ask, "Should we tell him?"

"Is Charlie up yet?" Jamie yells. "Am I disturbing anything?!"

I should have smothered him in his crib when I had the chance. "No, we were just taking a nap," I yell through the door, smoothing down my shirt.

Jamie bursts in. "We're having dinner at seven-thirty at that restaurant in Paris. You're supposed to go get ready, and meet Drew and Dawn in the cocktail lounge at seven."

"What time is it?" I ask.

"Six."

"Oh, no," I say, grabbing my purse and throwing on my shoes. "Is Andy pissed at me for not being the dutiful maid of honor all afternoon?"

"Are you kidding? She just woke up ten minutes ago," Jamie assures me. "But Drew's got a table for twenty, and he wants us all there on time."

I look at Jordan, and ask, "Are you feeling better?"

"Much," he says, smiling. Then he looks at Jamie. "Can you turn around for a second?"

Jamie makes a show of turning his back to us. Jordan gets out of bed, grabs my waist, and kisses me lightly on the lips. "See you at seven?"

"Be there with bells on," I say, and head out the door.

"Take a shower," I admonish Jamie as I pass him. "You smell like sex and candy."

And I confidently make my exit, feeling giddy and totally in control of my life.

Twenty-eight

Go to Paris at least twice in your lifetime.

And if you can't make it to Paris, France, for the weekend—head off to Paris, Las Vegas.

Every large casino/hotel/resort on the Strip has a theme, and Paris, Las Vegas, is no exception. Its theme is not only Paris, but all things French. You can walk on cobblestone streets, pick up a *pain au chocolat,* and stroll around the shoppes under a painted light blue sky.

This large hotel located in the middle of the Strip not only includes a fifty-floor replica of the Eiffel Tower as well as a small replica of the Arc de Triomphe, but it's got some decent French food as well.

Between six and seven o'clock, I took a quick shower, shaved my legs again (just in case), brushed my teeth (twice), and slipped into a slinky black dress and my Jimmy Choo shoes. (Yes, again. I'd wear them with my sweats to the grocery store if I could get away with it.) At 6:45, Jordan picked me up.

When I open the door, my perfect night begins. "You look stunning," Jordan tells me.

"Thank you," I say. "You're looking pretty dapper yourself."

And he does. In his charcoal gray Hugo Boss suit, white shirt, and red silk tie, he looks like one of those models you see in the black-and-white ads in *Vogue*.

Jordan leans in to give me a quick kiss, and we spend the next ten minutes making out in the doorway.

Realizing we're now late, Jordan takes my hand and leads me downstairs to the lobby.

He doesn't let go of my hand for the next hour.

First, we're the obnoxious couple making out in the cab. Yay! I get to be part of the obnoxious couple for a change.

Then we race into the hotel, dash through the casino (still holding hands), and make our way to the base of the Eiffel Tower elevator.

The Eiffel Tower Restaurant is located in—you guessed it—the fake Eiffel Tower. The glass elevator whisks us up to the eleventh floor and opens up to the kitchen, which I thought was a bit odd, but it's sparkling clean and running smoothly.

Jordan pulls me by the hand to the cocktail lounge, where Drew and Dawn are sipping martinis and listening to a wonderful pianist play some light jazz. Overall, the atmosphere is incredibly romantic. I could throw Jordan down on the piano and take him right here and now.

Jordan and I take a seat as a waiter magically materializes, asking us if we'd like some martinis. We would.

"I'm getting us some caviar before the evening begins. You have to try this stuff," Drew says, turning to the waiter. "Jonathan, can we get an ounce each of beluga, osetra, and sevruga? And a few extra bellinis, please?"

"Very good, sir," Jonathan, our waiter, says.

When the caviar arrives, Jordan spreads some sevruga on a toast point and feeds it to me. I smile and say "Mmm . . . ," but only because it's wonderful to have him feeding me. In reality . . . fish eggs? People pay one hundred dollars an ounce for fish eggs? And, I'm sorry, but when a man talks about how good caviar "explodes in your mouth," I don't see that as a big turn-on. I think of it as a reminder to suppress the gagging reflex.

But I digress.

Anyway, at seven-thirty, we meet everyone from the respective bachelor/bachelorette parties, and head to our intimate table for twenty.

The table has an exquisite view of the Strip. You can see all the colorful neon lights from the hotels, as well as the dancing fountains in front of the Bellagio Hotel. The tablecloth and napkins are crisp white, the china and silver sparkle. On the whole, a setting worthy of Napoleon and Josephine.

I start with the Maine lobster salad appetizer and a glass of champagne. With my first bite, I am in heaven (although the champagne and martinis have a bit to do with it, as does the company).

Jordan goes with black pepper–marinated raw beef, with mustard aioli, olive oil, and parmesan, which is also delicious (and he fed me again, which is delicious in and of itself).

For dinner, I have the filet mignon in a bernaise sauce and some potato gratin, and Jordan goes with the roasted rack of lamb and mashed potatoes.

What did everyone else eat? I have no idea. What was everyone else talking about that night? No clue. This was, by far, the most romantic night I had had in ages, and, boy, did I have tunnel vision. Or Jordan vision, as the case may be.

While he talked to others, Jordan either held my hand or had his hand on my leg. While he talked to me, he looked at me as though I were the only woman on the planet.

Over dessert of crème brûlée and café latte, Jordan put his arm around me while talking to Drew about work. While we waited in line for a cab to take us to Studio 54, he had his arms around my waist while he talked about sports with my brother. During the cab ride over, he discussed wedding planning with my sister while caressing my arm.

At Studio 54, he danced with me to Justin Timberlake without looking self-conscious, and when he slow-danced with me to Eric Clapton, I melted into his arms.

And anytime he didn't think anyone was watching, he'd give me a quick peck on the lips.

At one o'clock, Drew suggested we all head out for a nightcap at Napoleon's, a champagne bar back at Paris. It sounded like a perfect nightcap, and everyone agreed to meet there.

Don't trust drunk people when they say they will meet you at the next destination.

"I think we've been ditched," I say to Jordan. We have made ourselves comfortable on a plush red sofa, waiting for the others to get here. They haven't. I'm on my second glass of champagne. Jordan's having a Cognac.

He looks around the posh bar. "What makes you think that?"

I roll my eyes. "Honey, eighteen other people were supposed to meet us here. Not one has shown up. We've been ditched."

Jordan smiles sheepishly and looks down at the polished marble floor.

"What?" I say suspiciously.

"Nothing."

"Oh, no. You've got something on your mind. Why are you smiling like that?"

He keeps smiling stupidly, staring at the floor and averting his eyes. "Did you just call me honey?"

I roll my eyes again, but I smile. "Why? Does that bother you?"

He looks me in the eye, smiles, and leans in for a kiss. "No . . ."

We kiss again, and man, life is good! Tonight is perfect. The food was perfect, the environment is perfect, the champagne is perfect, the man is perfect . . .

"Why don't you call them?" Jordan says after he pulls away from the kiss.

"Huh?" I say, snapping back into reality.

"Call and see where everyone is. I mean, this place is really nice. But if no one's coming, I'd like to go back to my room and get some sleep."

Some sleep?! Did I miss a meeting?

"Okay," I say, wondering what I did wrong that made him suddenly want to cut the night short. I take my cell phone out, and dial Drew first. The phone rings forever, and then I get his voice mail. I leave a message. "Hi, it's Charlie. We're at Napoleon's, and no one's here. Where are you guys?"

Then I call Dawn. Endless ringing. Voice mail. Me leaving a message.

Next is Kate, who actually answers. "Hello?"

"Where are you two?" I ask, knowing she's with Jamie.

"Ummm . . . we got lost. We'll find you tomorrow, okay?"

And she hangs up on me.

I click my phone shut. "Kate and Jamie aren't coming."

"Oh," Jordan says, looking at me awkwardly. "Okay . . . maybe we should get the check."

"No, no," I say quickly, not yet ready for my perfect night to end. I hastily open my cell phone back up. "Let me call Andy."

Ring. Ring. Ring.

"Hello?" It's Andy. I think I woke her.

"Where are you?"

"Back in the room," Andy answers, like it's the dumbest question in the world. "Why? Where are you?"

"I'm at Napoleon's. With Jordan. I thought we were all going to meet here."

"Oh. I didn't think that was definite. Anyway, don't you want to be alone with Jordan?"

I look over at Jordan, who's now flagging down the waitress. "Yeah, I did, but . . ."

"Well, then, you're welcome. Good night," Andy says, then hangs up on me.

I try Drew one more time, to no avail. By now, Jordan has asked for the check. Maybe I can nurse this glass of champagne until three A.M. . . .

My phone rings. I click it on. "Hello?"

"Where are you?" Dawn asks, irritation in her voice.

"We're at Napoleon's. Where are you?"

"In Drew's room in the suite. Nobody was actually going to Napoleon's. That was a code so we could all leave graciously, and be alone with our dates."

Now Jordan is giving the waitress his credit card. Rats.

I lean into my phone, and whisper, "How in God's name was I supposed to know that?"

"Because it's social convention?" Dawn says sarcastically, like I've asked the stupidest question in the world. "Like never getting to a party until at least thirty minutes after it has officially begun."

"I'm sorry. I didn't realize flakiness was encoded in L.A."

"Sweetie, we don't have time for this right now. Drew and I are in his room for the night. Jamie's with Kate. Why don't you two come back here, have a nightcap, and see where it leads you?"

I start to whisper again, "Because I . . . Hello?"

She's gone.

I slam my phone shut, pop it into my purse, and sigh out loud.

"What's up?" Jordan asks.

"It appears we've been ditched," I say. "By eighteen people."

"Looks that way." He grabs my waist and pulls me into a long, sensuous kiss. "So, you wanna go back to my room and get some sleep?" he asks, pulling me onto his lap for more kissing.

I do. I did.

And sleep was the last thing we did that night.

Twenty-nine

Before you go to sleep at night, make sure you wash off all of your makeup.

I awake to my eyes glued shut from last night's mascara. That's always a pleasant way to start your morning. I use the palm of my hand to break my lashes apart from each other, and accidentally rub the gunk from my eyes all over my face. Men love this look, by the way. Nothing like raccoon eyes and greasy foundation to really get their blood pumping.

Jordan rolls over and opens his eyes. He looks like an angel—his eyes are dewy, not glued; his face isn't oily, it glows. I am torn between having a massive crush on this guy, and hating him for looking so great. I go with the crush.

"Hi," he whispers ever so quietly, like he's talking to a sleeping baby.

"Hi," I say just as quietly—worried that we are about to cross the line into baby talk.

"God, you were great last night," Jordan says as he crawls on top of me. When he kisses me, I realize I wasn't just drunk last night—I really like him. He's cute, and funny, and nice and . . .

"I think I need to tell you something," Jordan says, sounding a little worried.

I start to kiss his neck. "Okay. Tell me something."

He rolls off of me and sighs. "It's kind of complicated, and I don't want you to get upset. So you have to promise me you won't get upset."

"I won't get upset," I say, cheerfully moving down his neck to kiss his stomach. "Well," I joke, "I suppose if you told me you have a girlfriend, I'd get upset. But not if you told me anything else."

As I kiss his stomach, I feel it tense up.

Oh. Shit.

I look up at him. He's bristling. "Do you have a girlfriend?" I ask, pulling away from him cautiously.

"No . . . ," Jordan says, struggling with his words. "Yes . . . I don't know."

If you ask a man if he has a girlfriend, and his answer is, "No, yes, I don't know," that means "yes." Or, at the very least, the woman he's seeing has a boyfriend—him.

I immediately turn my back to him and grab my dress from the floor.

As I throw the dress over my head, Jordan puts his hand on my back and starts to stroke my back lightly. "I didn't mean that," he says softly. "I mean no. It's just complicated."

I quickly grab my underwear from the floor and shimmy back into it, careful to let my dress fall over my nude backside before I pull them all the way up. "Relationships are complicated. Having a girlfriend, and sleeping with another woman, that must be very complicated."

"I don't have a girlfriend. Okay?" Jordan says suddenly, sitting up in the bed. "Look, can we talk about this? Please?"

I roll my eyes to stare at the heavens, and silently ask God why I'm so stupid. Then I turn around to face Jordan. "Okay, fine—talk," I say, in the most pissed off "don't talk to me" voice I can muster.

Jordan takes a deep breath and looks down at the sheets. This is not a good sign. "I did have a girlfriend. Actually, she was my fiancée. I told you about her that night when we were online talking."

Swell. I don't say that out loud, of course. Instead, I say, very calmly, "I thought you said she stopped being your fiancée a few months ago."

"Well, that's the tricky part," Jordan says, pensive. He kisses me lightly on the shoulder, and continues. "I guess it was about two months ago, yeah."

"You guess?" I ask.

"Yeah . . . See, she hasn't given the ring back yet, and I've had to see her a couple of times to get the ring back, and I still haven't."

"Did *you* break up with *her*?" I ask. "Or did she break up with you?"

"I broke up with her," Jordan says.

"Then she doesn't have to give back the ring," I say, hoping he will understand that what I really mean is, *And you don't have to see her ever again. She is an ex—she is exiled into the photo album part of your life.*

"Like I said, it's complicated," Jordan says.

Then he sighs. And he looks like he's going to cry, and I hate myself, but I still like this guy.

I blow out a big sigh, and ask, "All right, I'll bite. Why is it so complicated?"

"It was my grandmother's engagement ring. My mother's mother.

And my mom didn't like Janet, my ex, to begin with, so she really wants her mother's ring back."

"And Janet doesn't wants to give it back?" I ask, knowing the answer.

"No. She thinks we're just having some problems because we're in a long-distance relationship. She wanted to go into counseling."

"Where the first thing you would do was tell the counselor that you wanted to break up and wanted your ring back?" I say, possibly a bit harshly.

Jordan smiles. "Actually, kind of. Janet thought even if I went in saying I didn't think the relationship was working out that we might have a chance at a reconciliation. Her thinking was that if I could get some of my reservations about the relationship out in a safe environment, we could talk about them, and hopefully fix whatever problems I was having. Or we were having. Whatever . . ."

His voice trails off. I don't say anything for a while. I just stare at the wall. I'm so mad right now that I can't even look at him.

I finger-brush my hair, more out of nerves than anything else, and bite my lip. Still not taking my eyes off the wall, I ask, "So, is that why you've been seeing her—to go into counseling?"

"No," he says softly. "Look, do you want to go get some breakfast?"

"Why?" I say, hoping to God I don't start crying in front of him. "So I won't cause a scene when you tell me the truth?"

Jordan takes my shoulder and turns me around to face him. He looks me right in the eye. "Charlie, I like you. I didn't go into therapy with *her* because I liked *you*."

I meet his eyes, but I can't think of a thing to say. Feeling a headache coming on, I look down at the carpet. God, please let me not cry. Just once can things go my way enough that I get to keep my dignity with a man I've slept with?

"Remember when I was gone that weekend after we talked?" Jordan continues in nearly a whisper. "Janet came down for the weekend, and I broke it off completely. I told her there wasn't anything wrong with the relationship, that she was a great girl, and that I would always love her in my own way, but that she wasn't the girl I was supposed to spend the rest of my life with."

Emotionally, it's better to be homicidal than suicidal. When you're upset with a guy, at least know which way to point the gun.

As I continue to stare at him, I start to get angry. Which is good in this case. "Did you sleep with her that weekend?" I ask. I stare right at him, knowing that I will get my answer without a single word.

He turns away from me, and I don't need the verbal answer. "Great," I nearly spit out, shaking my head, and putting on my shoes.

"Look, in my defense, you and I weren't dating yet . . . ," Jordan begins, but I interrupt, because a worse thought has occurred to me.

"Last weekend, after we made out at the wrap party . . . Did you see her then? Is that why you disappeared?"

"You mean the weekend I heard a guy giving you a booty call while we were making out?"

"Oh, so it's my fault now?!" I yell, grabbing my purse from his side table, and standing up to get the hell out of there. "Some guy I'm not seeing anymore calls me, so that gives you the right to jump into bed with your ex-girlfriend?"

"Ex-fiancée," Jordan corrects me. "Look, I told you, all I was trying to do was get the ring back. She hadn't brought it down the weekend of the final breakup, so I had to—"

"Did you sleep with her last weekend, too?!" I scream, already knowing the answer. I mean, let's face it, a woman desperate to win a guy (or, worse, win a guy back) pulls out all the sexual stops. And few men choose to say no.

Jordan opens his mouth to speak, but I put up my hand stop him. I have that moment of clarity, and I become inhumanly calm. "You know what? There's no point in answering, because all you're going to do is give me excuses about why it happened, and I don't need those. I've been through this before. I don't date men who lie to me."

Now Jordan looks like he's going to cry again. He almost whispers, "Charlie, please don't do this. I like you. I made a mistake."

I look at the ripped-open condom wrapper on the floor. "You know what? Me too."

And with that, I just walk out of his room, and out of his life.

And he lets me. There's no drama as I walk out the door, no one follows me down the hallway. When I get to my room, there's no one calling me to ask me to come back.

Which tells me I was right to leave.

Men aren't stupid, and you don't need a complicated set of rules to find a good one who loves you. Here's the only rule you need: if a man loves you, he will do anything he can to keep you around. Anything.

To be honest, it was pretty hard to leave. I desperately wanted to turn around, and tell him everything would be okay. That I adore him and I trust him and that I'll stand by him while he goes through this tough time.

But I'm just too tired. I'm thirty years old. I'm tired of relationships that are always painful. I'm tired of hurting. I'm tired of waiting by the phone, and second-guessing what a guy says and trusting someone not to hurt me. Again. I've been storming the relationship castle for fifteen years, and I still don't have my prince. I've got a bunch of battle scars from the field and I want to go home and nurse my wounds. I don't want to fight anymore.

I throw myself on my bed and stare at the ceiling.

I know I will hate myself, but I pick up the phone and dial.

"Hi, this is Jordan," I hear as his home answering machine picks up. "I'm in Las Vegas this weekend, so please call me on my cell at 323-555-9457. Or leave a message, and I'll get back to you soon." *Beep.*

"Hey, it's me . . . listen, I'm still really upset but . . . if you ever get your ring back, let me know."

Thirty

Breaking up is hard to do. Do it anyway.

Sunday morning, after our fight, Jordan took an early flight home. I was relieved to see him go.

But by Sunday night, I missed him, and had replayed the morning scene in my head a hundred times.

And, by Monday night, I had almost called him.

Tuesday night, I consoled myself with videos and an entire Sara Lee cheesecake, followed by a pint of Ben and Jerry's chocolate fudge brownie ice cream.

Wednesday night, I almost called him, and had to stick one of those damn Post-it notes on the phone to tell me not to. Then I called him from a payphone (so as not to trigger his caller ID) and got his machine. I hung up.

On Thursday, I decided to get a little advice from the enemy camp. So instead of calling Jordan, I called Jamie.

"You're a pig," I say calmly on the phone to my brother after I've explained the whole Jordan story.

"Maybe so," Jamie concedes. "But if a guy says he's in the middle of a breakup with his girlfriend, fiancée no less, what he really means is he's dating someone else, but wouldn't mind a little nookie on the side. Provided, of course, you don't blab to your friends about what an asshole he is."

"Why do you assume every guy in the world wants sex without responsibility?" I ask him as I scrounge through my cupboard, searching for depression snacks.

"Why does the sun rise every morning?" Jamie asks. "By the way, what does it mean when a girl says, 'I'm really swamped with work lately, and I don't think I can start anything serious right now.'"

"Kate say that?" I ask.

"Yeah. When I called her Monday night. What's it mean?"

"Depends," I say. "Did you see her Monday night?"

"Yeah."

"Well, then, it probably means, 'I like you, I may even love you. But I'm not in love with you, and if you're waiting for that, it's never going to happen.'"

Jamie's silent on the other end. "That's pretty much what I figured," he says. "Hey, but at least I've got a date for the wedding, right?"

"Right," I say, trying to sound encouraging.

I can't tell from his voice if he's sad and covering it up, or if he's just being his usual "Jamie Edwards: lousy boyfriend, perfect fling" self. "You okay?" I ask.

"Yeah," he says, then changes the subject. "So, you're depressed. I'm guessing you could use some company and some ice cream."

I smile. "Indeed I could."

"Are you 'I'm slightly depressed, but I've been binging all week, so bring frozen yogurt'; 'I've just started my binge, so bring a pint of Häagen-Dazs'; or 'It doesn't matter how fat I am anyway—I'm just going to become your kids' bitter, fat, chain-smoking aunt, so if you bring less than a quart I'll send you back out to the store?'"

I put my hand up to my heart and sigh happily. "You know me so well. I'll take door number three. And bring Oreos."

. . .

It's Friday now, and I still haven't heard from Jordan. But now I'm not sure if I care. I'm not sure if he's still dating Janet. I'm not sure of anything anymore.

I am sure that I didn't want to hear from my mother this morning, or pick up her parents and her mother's mother from the airport today.

It all started this morning at six A.M.

Drew had kept his word, and had given me the week off to help with the wedding. I had avoided my family most of the week, so that I could wallow in self-pity.

Really, I was doing them a favor. What is more cliché than a bitter maid of honor? (Oh, right—one that just turned thirty.)

Anyway, the phone range at six (or 5:57, to be exact), and I saw from the caller ID that it was Mom. I tried to ignore the call, but unfortunately, my answering machine is right by my bed.

"It's time for you to pay back those nineteen hours of labor I went through for you," Mom begins.

I light a cigarette, pick up the phone, and say in my "Elmer Fudd, I just woke up" voice, "Would now be a good time to point out that you got drugs the entire time?"

Don't worry about labor pains. There's this wonderful invention called the epidural. Get one in the parking lot on your way into the hospital.

It's always been a pet peeve of mine when women talk about how long they were in labor. When my cousin Jenn was in labor, she had so many drugs pumped inside of her, the only way she knew she was having a contraction was to see it on the computer screen.

But I digress.

"Your sister says you're depressed, and that some guy dumped you. She also told me that you finally quit smoking," Mom says.

I take another drag from my cigarette. "I'm not depressed."

"At any point this week, have you eaten whipped cream straight from the can?" Mom asks.

"I won't dignify that with a response," I say, although we both know that means yes.

"Are you still smoking?" Mom asks.

"Are *you* still smoking?" I respond belligerently.

"I'm raising you. You're not raising me," Mom says. "Speaking of, Grandma and Grandpa are on the noon flight with your Mawv. I need you to come with me to get them."

My grandparents are good Midwestern folk who never understood why their daughter moved to Sodom and Gomorrah to follow her dream and write sitcoms. My Mawv is my great-grandmother (grandma's mom), and my favorite person in the world. She's ninety-five, smokes two packs of cigarettes a day, and drinks really bad whiskey. Her lifelong dream was to smoke two packs of cigarettes a day and drink really bad whiskey. So she respects anyone who follows their dream.

She's the ginchiest.

Anyway, so I trek off to LAX and meet my mother in baggage claim. (You can't go up to the gates anymore for security reasons. Which I think is a good thing—think of it as five fewer minutes with your family.)

I spot Mom, pacing, holding a venti Starbucks coffee in each hand, and chewing vast quantities of gum.

"Thanks for meeting me," Mom says, handing me one of the two large cups. "I don't think I could have handled my mother on my own."

"It's not going to be that bad," I say, taking a sip of the coffee Mom bought me.

Mom nearly chokes on her cappuccino. "Oh, that's easy for you to say! She's not your mother." Mom pulls out a fresh pack of orange-flavored nicotine gum. Her hands shake as she tries to open the plastic wrapping. "She's judgmental, she talks too much, she gives a ton of unsolicited advice, and she embarrasses me every chance she gets."

Well, if that isn't the pot calling the kettle "Mom."

My mother starts ripping at the plastic packaging madly. "God-damn it! What's wrong with these people making it so fucking hard to open their product, knowing damn well how much you need it." Mom puts her teeth up to the box and tries to rip it open that way.

"Mom," I say, then calmly take the package of gum out of her mouth. I open it easily, and hand it back to her. "How much nicotine have you had this morning?"

"I don't know. A box, two . . . I can't keep track. These people just make me a nervous wreck."

"Ya think?" I say sarcastically.

Mom looks around the airport, her eyes darting around like a hummingbird's. "Maybe I should take a Valium. I'll have your father bring some by the hotel later. By the way, I haven't told your grand-parents that your father and I are living together again, so don't mention it."

"Okay," I say. But then I think about it. "And that would bother them because . . . ?"

Mom rolls her eyes and shakes her head, visibly astonished that I could ask such a stupid question. "Because they don't want me liv-ing in sin with a man."

"You mean the man you're still married to in the eyes of our

Lord?" I say sarcastically. "In the eyes of our Lord" is big with my
grandmother.

"Don't you take that tone with me, young lady," my mother says,
wagging a finger in my face. "You aren't so old that I can't still take
you over my knee."

"The only time you ever took me over your knee was to read to
me."

"And do I get any appreciation for that?" Mom asks in a screech,
nearly bursting into tears. "No! All the unconditional love and kind-
ness I gave you all through your childhood, and all I ask is that you
not tell your grandparents that I'm shacking up with your father! Is
that too much to ask, after all I've done for you?"

People are starting to turn and stare at the crazy woman.

"Mom?" I say calmly.

"Yes?" Mom sniffles back.

"She's making you crazy, and you haven't even seen her yet."

"I know," Mom says, inhaling a deep breath and chanting her
mantra, "nee-who-mah, nee-who-mah" several times. Her shoulders relax ever so slightly with the final deep breath. "You are so
lucky you don't have parents who make you crazy."

Before I can ask my mother what deluded universe she lives in,
we see my grandparents and Mawv coming down the escalator.

Grandma and Grandpa look like a couple of Protestants on vacation. They're dressed head-to-toe in L.L. Bean, including the shoes.
If they were visiting New York, they'd have been mugged already.

My Mawv, on the other hand, is dressed in a beautiful pink dress
that I swear I saw this spring at Bloomingdale's, and three-inch-high
heels.

A ninety-five-year-old woman in three-inch-heels. If that sight
doesn't cover the cost of admission, I don't know what does.

Grandma holds Mawv's hand, treating her like an invalid who

could break at any moment. "Are you all right, Mother?!" Grandma screams into Mawv's left ear.

"Rose," Mawv responds in her normal voice, "I bought a hearing aid so that people wouldn't shout at me."

"Bernice!" Grandpa screams into her right ear, "Your hearing aid isn't working! You couldn't hear a word I said on the plane!"

"No, I was ignoring you!" Mawv (aka Bernice) mockingly screams back into Grandpa's ear. Then she returns to her normal voice. "I bought this damn thing because it said on the box that it filters out unwanted noise. But I can still hear every damn thing you say." She sees me and her face lights up. "Munchkin!"

"Hi, Mawv," I say brightly as I pull her into a hug. Then I whisper in her ear, "Was it awful?"

"Dreadful," she whispers back. "I have got to be the only one I know in my retirement home who hides when family comes to get her."

"Hi, Mom," my mother says sheepishly to Grandma, putting her arms out for a hug.

Grandma eyes her up and down. "You're wearing that?"

Mom throws her outstretched arms in the air in exasperation, then plasters a fake smile onto her face. "Nice to see you, too. You're looking good."

"Well, I've been doing my power walking four times a week," Grandma says, walking past Mom to hug me. "I've lost five pounds since January. And your father and I don't eat bacon anymore."

"*You* don't," Grandpa says as he kisses Mom on the cheek. "If the Good Lord didn't want us to eat bacon, we'd have been born Jewish." He walks over to me and gives me a kiss on the cheek. Grandpa's a big "kiss on the cheek" kind of guy. Hugs are just too damn personal. "So, Jacquie, is that worthless son of a bitch ex-husband going to be at the wedding?"

"Yes, Dad," Mom says, struggling to keep her patience. "He's giving the bride away."

"You mean he's actually in the wedding?" Grandpa asks, pulling out a pack of Marlboros and a book of matches.

"You can't smoke here, Father," Grandma admonishes him.

Grandpa looks perplexed. "Ah hell, Mother. I knew when we came to California, we were going to the land of fruits and nuts, but I didn't think they had outlawed smoking altogether."

"No, you dipshit," Mawv says. "You can smoke in the state of California, just not in the airport."

Grandpa looks so incensed, he can barely speak. "What the hell?" He turns to my mother. "I told you you shouldn't have bought us plane tickets. This wouldn't have happened if we'd have driven."

Mom's about to respond, but Mawv talks over her. "If we'd have driven, I'd have put a bullet in your ear by Kansas." She turns to me. "Please tell me you brought your own car."

"Yes."

Mawv turns back to the others. "I'm going with Charlie. Can you get my bags and bring them to the hotel? What's it called again?"

"The Hotel Bel Air," my mother announces proudly. "It's gorgeous. You're going to love it."

"The Hotel Bel Air?" Grandma nearly screams. "Ah, we don't need to be anywhere that fancy. Just take us to the local Holiday Inn."

"No, Mom," my mother says. "It's already paid for. Besides, I want you to have a really nice trip, and the Hotel Bel Air is one of the nicest places in the city."

"How much did you pay?" Grandpa asks, an unlit cigarette now dangling from his mouth.

"Only ninety-nine dollars a night," Mom lies. The cheapest

rooms at the hotel run three hundred a night, and most are much more expensive than that.

"Ninety-nine dollars!" Grandpa nearly spits out in horror. "Jesus, Jacquie. With our AARP discount we could have got it for half that. Sometimes you just don't think."

However, Grandma's face lights up. "Oh, but Dad, it must be really nice for that kind of money. Remember when we got that place at Cedar Point for ninety-nine dollars? It had cable *and* room service." She turns to my mother. "Do you think the room has cable?"

My mother sighs. "I'm sure it does. But Mom, you're on vacation. Why would you want to waste it in a hotel room watching TV?"

"Very nice, coming from a TV writer," Grandpa quips. "Don't give me that highfalutin city snobbery. You're not too old for me to still take you over my knee."

"Dad, I just meant—"

"We read about what you TV types call us in Missouri—the fly-overs. Well, let me tell you something, missy—"

"Charlie! Cover your eyes!" Grandma yells, looking over my shoulder.

Naturally, I turn around to see what she's looking at. "What is it?" I ask.

"Two men—holding hands!" Grandma says. "Honestly, people said if we came to Los Angeles, we'd see the gays, but I didn't think we'd see them so soon."

"Imagine," Mawv quips, "gay men taking a plane. Just like normal folk. What are the odds?"

I look over at the "offending" couple. "Grandma, those aren't two men."

Grandma pops her head over my shoulder to get a better look. "They're not?"

"No. Actually, they're two women."

Grandma nearly faints, while Grandpa sucks his unlit cigarette and says, "Eh, the lesbians never bothered me so much."

Midwesterners can be just as snobby as Hollywood people or New Yorkers. It's just a different kind of snobbery.

An hour later, we all made it to the valet of the Hotel Bel Air, where the lecture on good Midwestern values continued.

First, Mom and her parents argued over whether or not to pull up to the valet ("never give a stranger access to your trunk"). Then Grandpa tried to carry in his own bags ("if you carry them in yourself, you save a dollar a bag").

Next came check-in.

As we cross over the stone bridge and into the gardens, I am immediately at peace with the world.

The hotel does that for me. I look around at the red tile roofs and the soft pink walls, and all is tranquil in my world. The hotel is done in the architectural style of the old California missions. Unlike other nice hotels in the area, none of the buildings are higher than a few floors up. And the landscaping is designed to resemble Hawaii, with colorful flowers everywhere, and wonderful, soothing scents. I am happy. I close my eyes, breathe in the smell of flowers, and smile. Ah, and there's the small lake, off to the side, next to the gazebo where Andy and Hunter will be married tomorrow.

If you ever (God forbid) need to check into a detox center, skip Betty Ford. Spend the same amount of money and check into a fabulous hotel, spend your days at the pool, and order lots of room service. You'll feel so refreshed and spoiled, you won't need drugs or booze.

Mmm, this place is so gorgeous, so peaceful, so romantic—and I'm stuck here with my mother and bickering grandparents.

"Edwards. Checking in, please," my mother says to the front desk clerk, Mike, as my grandfather looks around the lobby suspiciously.

Mike smiles warmly. "Good afternoon, Mrs. Edwards. Three rooms. Yours, one for Mr. and Mrs. Wharton, and one for Mrs. Geoghen. Correct?"

"Yes. Mine, my parents', and my grandmother's," Mom says.

"Can we get mine as far apart from the others as possible?" Mawv asks as I help her to a green velvet sofa.

Grandma looks out the window, then runs to Grandpa, hits him on the arm, and whispers. "Oh my God! That's Arte Johnson! You know, from *Laugh In*?"

"No!" Grandpa says as he runs up to the window and stares at a man walking past, toward the dining room.

They both run out of the lobby to get a better look, then come back self-satisfied. "Well, I'll be damned!" Grandpa says cheerfully. "Making his way to the dining room just like any normal joe."

"Wait until I get home and tell Marcia we saw a real-live celebrity," Grandma beams.

Mom signs some forms as Mike cheerfully asks, "Would you like smoking or non-smoking rooms?"

"Smoking," all four demand in unison.

Mike is a little thrown by the chorus, but continues to smile. "Smoking it is."

Grandma turns to me accusingly. "You're not still smoking, are you?"

Before I can respond, Mom pipes in proudly, "No, Mother. She quit on her thirtieth birthday."

Rats. The truth is, I took the habit back up Sunday night. Yes, it's a disgusting habit, blah, blah, blah, and yes, I did tell myself that I was going to quit on my thirtieth birthday. But my main impetus to quit smoking was to kiss Jordan without tasting like an ashtray. Now that he's gone, I need the cigarettes even more than I did before. I mean, come on, aging, single maid of honor? How am I going to get through this weekend without smoking?

Grandma looks at me suspiciously. "Is your mother telling the truth?" she asks accusingly.

"Of course she is!" I respond back self-righteously. I can't help myself. Her tone is pissing me off.

Grandma sniffs, and that sniff is just like her tone of voice. "Well, I hope you're not like your mother about it. She's never done anything she ever set her mind to. Must have quit smoking a hundred times." Before I can respond, Grandma turns to Mike. "Do you have a Jacuzzi here?"

"No, I'm afraid we don't. But we do have a very nice pool."

"We're paying ninety-nine dollars a night for this place, and there's no Jacuzzi?" Grandpa says, sounding appalled at the lack of hotel services.

At first Mike looks confused, but when my mother bulges out her eyes and shakes her head at him ever so slightly, he seems to get the message.

"Okay, here are your room keys," Mike says with a smile, handing my mother all three keys. "Josh can show you to your room. I'll get Charles and Glen to show your other guests to their rooms—"

"One valet will be fine," my mother says quickly, knowing full well my grandparents will insist on carrying their own bags, then won't tip, and she would only want to be embarrassed by her family in front of one employee. "Has my daughter checked in yet? Andy Edwards?"

"Yes, ma'am," Mike says, still smiling. "She's in Room 208."

"Great," Mom says, and we all head for the hotel rooms.

The next few hours are a blur. I went with Mawv to her room, where we hung out until the wedding rehearsal.

We were only interrupted by about twenty phone calls in a little under three hours. Mawv refused to talk to anyone (her soaps were on), so I got to pick up the phone all twenty times.

"Hello?" I answer.

"Don't order room service! They charge fourteen dollars for soup!"

Yes, ladies and gentlemen, it's time to play the game, "Guess which relative I'm talking to." (That first one would be Grandma, by the way.)

The next call: "Hello?"

"Goddamn it! Tell your Mawv she can order whatever she wants. I'm paying for this, not your grandparents."

Number three: "Hello?"

"All right, we talked to the concierge, and there's a Catholic church called Saint Monica's a few miles away. There's a nine A.M. mass on Sunday, so if we all meet at eight-thirty in front of the hotel, we can get good seats, and be out in time for brunch."

Followed by number four: "If they think I'm getting up at eight o'clock the morning after my wedding night, they're crazier than Mom."

Number five: "Tell your Mawv to turn on Channel Sixteen. They're doing a documentary on FDR."

Number six: "You do not have to go to church."

Number seven: ". . . and thirty-nine dollars for a filet mignon. We can get one at the local Kroger for seven bucks."

Number eight: "Your Mawv called, and asked that I get her a bottle of Canadian Club whiskey. I'm at the store now. What size does she want?"

Actually, Mawv sort of took that call. "Mawv, it's Dad," I say to her while I have Dad on the phone. "He says you called him and asked him to pick up a bottle of Canadian Club whiskey?"

Mawv doesn't take her eyes off the TV. "I did indeed."

"He wants to know what size?"

"Remind him that I am spending all weekend with Rose and Joe."

I return to the phone. "She says to remind you that she's spending the entire weekend with Rose and Joe."

"Right," Dad says. "Biggest one they got."

I hold the phone and look at Mawv. "Dad says biggest one they got?"

"Tell him he's a doll."

Number nine: "And there's a three-dollar service charge for every item ordered, so a fourteen-dollar soup is really seventeen dollars. . . ."

Number ten: "Goddamn it! If you and your Mawv want to order from the fucking room service menu, you can! This is the fucking Hotel Bel Air, not a fucking Howard Johnson's!"

Number eleven: "We just saw Oprah Winfrey by the pool."

Number twelve: Is there any way we can avoid Hunter's family meeting our family this weekend without it looking weird?"

Number thirteen: (whispered) "Can you call your father, and make sure he's bringing pot?"

Number fourteen: (mechanical voice) "You have no new messages."

All right, so I called home to check my messages, and see if Jordan called me.

Number fifteen: "And they charge eight dollars for a beer!"

Number sixteen: "This is why I left Missouri."

Number seventeen: "Are you hungry? Because Grandpa's going to a local A and P to get a twelve-pack of Budweiser, so we figured as long as he's getting that, he should get snacks."

Number eighteen: "I'm taking Mom and Dad to Santa Monica Beach. They want to get a picture of the Pacific Ocean, so they can say they've been there."

Number nineteen: "How far is it of a drive to San Francisco? We're thinking of going up there before the rehearsal dinner."

Number twenty: "I called room service. I ordered you the soup."

The wedding rehearsal took place without a hitch, mainly because the wedding coordinator wouldn't take any crap from our family.

I wish I could have said the same about the rehearsal dinner.

Hunter's parents, nice upper-class East Coast folk, decided to host the bash at a beautiful seafood restaurant on the beach in Santa Monica.

They rented out a gorgeously decorated room with a view of the ocean, there was a full bar, and the food was wonderful. All of the ingredients for a spectacular night, where the two families could bond in a relaxed, gracious atmosphere.

It was a disaster.

Let's start with Grandma and Grandpa meeting my sister's new in-laws. They were "dressed up" in polyester blends. Joan, Andy's future mother-in-law, wore a stunning pink suit, which Grandma immediately comments on: "Wow. That is one nice-looking suit. Where did you get it?"

"Oh, thank you," Joan says, her mouth barely moving. "I just popped over to Neimans this week. It's silk. Very comfortable in this climate."

Grandma grabs the tag behind Joan's neck, and her jaw drops. "It's Donna Karan. Dad, check out Miss Fawfawfaw in her Donna Karan."

Grandpa slaps Bill, Andy's soon-to-be father-in-law, on the back. "Well, you two must be doin' pretty well. What did that set you back?"

"Excuse me?" Bill asks politely.

"The old ball and chain. What did the suit cost you?" Grandpa says.

Startled, Bill looks over to his wife, "Ummm . . . well, I'm not sure. We really don't discuss her clothing purchases."

"Oh, big mistake. Big mistake. Mother gets fifty dollars a month for her clothes, and that's it. One penny above, and I will tell you, we have quite the rumpus!" Grandpa laughs, and hits Bill on the back again.

Grandma laughs, too. "It's true. And, you know, that's a good thing, because it forces me to keep an eye on my purchases. You know, I got this skirt on sale at the outlet store. Ten dollars, and it's a cotton blend. The sale was so good, I bought four more in different colors."

Andy looks mortified.

" 'Course, ten dollars times five, that's fifty dollars, so I didn't go over my monthly limit," Grandma continues proudly. She whispers into Joan's ear conspiratorially, "You know I've had these for almost fifteen years. A classic like this, it never goes out of style."

Joan smiles, confused. I'm sure she would have knitted her brow if the Botox hadn't kicked in.

I walk over to my father, who's been hanging out on the other side of the room, avoiding my grandfather. "Andy needs your help. This is not going well."

"What does she want me to do?" Dad asks.

"Go say hi to Grandma and Grandpa. Get them away from Andy's new in-laws."

"If you think I am going to subject myself to the wrath of that man, you're out of your mind."

"Would you prefer Hunter's parents get to know the real us? They are seconds away from being schooled on the wonders of polyester."

Dad rolls his eyes. "Okay, but if I'm going to get through this, you have to go get me a drink."

"Done," I say. I grab Dad's hand and pull him toward Grandma and Grandpa, who are now onto real estate discussions. "You mean you spent over a million dollars to live in a place where you don't even own the land?!"

"Well, co-ops in Manhattan are complicated . . . ," Bill begins.

My father and I quickly intervene. "Good evening, sir," my father says pleasantly, looking up at Grandpa's large form.

My grandfather glares at him. "You knocked up my firstborn," he says, sounding like a hick farmer behind a shotgun.

"Yes, sir. I did, sir," Dad says cheerfully, then turns to me. "And would the product of that knock-up please get Daddy a Jack Daniel's?"

"Um . . . yes," I say, then turn to Bill. "Bill, my father's a member of the Century City Country Club. They have a fantastic golf course. I understand you're an avid golfer."

"Indeed," Bill says, his face lighting up over the prospect of discussing something other than money. "What's your handicap?"

"Nine," Dad says. "But that's because I don't play as regularly as I used to."

"And God knows she could have done better than some two-bit costumer, and I told her so at the time . . . ," Grandpa says loudly to Dad.

"A double," Dad says to me, then starts pushing me toward the bar.

"He's gay, you know," Grandpa mock confides to Bill. "All them men costumers are."

Dad turns to me. "You know what? Tell them to fill a highball, and not to waste any room in the glass with ice," he says, giving me a shove toward the bar so hard, I nearly trip on my way there.

I walk up to the bar, where Jenn is arguing with her sons. "I want a Roy Rogers," Alex demands.

"Me too," Sean concurs.

"That's what the bartender just gave you," Jenn says, sighing out a deep breath of irritation.

"No, he gave me a Shirley Temple," Alex insists, putting his glass up for her to inspect.

."A Roy Rogers *is* a Shirley Temple," Jenn rebuts, making it clear he's working her last nerve.

"No, it isn't," Alex continues to insist.

"Okay, fine. You tell me—what's the difference?" Jenn asks.

Alex rolls his eyes. "A Shirley Temple has a cherry in it. A Roy Rogers has a lime in it. Like Daddy has in his drink."

"No, it . . ." Jenn begins, then stops herself. She pulls the cherry out of Alex's glass, pops it in her mouth, then looks at her son Sean. "Do you need a lime, too?"

"Yes," Sean says with such intensity I'm sure he'll one day play Hamlet on Broadway.

Jenn takes the cherry out of his glass, eats it, then grabs two slices of lime from a plastic container on the bar, and throws them into Alex's glass. "Here's two. Knock yourself out." She grabs two more and throws them into Sean's glass.

"Now, can you bring Daddy his drink?" Jenn asks, handing Alex a vodka tonic.

"Yes."

"Thank you. Oh." Jenn leans down to be at eye level with them. "And what's the special rule for tonight and tomorrow?"

"We don't talk about Grandpa's or Great Aunt Jacquie's funny cigarettes in front of the new family," the boys say in unison.

"And if the new family brings them up, what do we say?" Jenn asks in a soft motherly voice.

"They both have cancer. It's very sad," the boys say, again in unison, not a trace of sadness in their voices.

"Good boys," Jenn says proudly, and gives them both a hug. "Now, go find your father."

The two run off. "I'm afraid to even ask," I say to her, then turn to the bartender. "Quadruple Jack Daniel's, please. No rocks."

"Just a preliminary precaution. Earlier tonight, my father asked

Andy's soon-to-be mother-in-law if she knew what it was like to be high on cocaine," Jenn says as the bartender hands her a club soda.

"Oh, shit," I say, grimacing.

"Wait, it gets better. So she looks confused, and I quickly say to him, 'No, she doesn't, and neither do you.' To which my father then looks confused, so before he could talk again I stuck a cigar in his mouth and told him to go smoke outside, and that I heard a rumor there were Cubans floating about."

"Fast thinking," I say, impressed.

"Yeah," Jenn said, sighing. "Unfortunately, then Dad said, 'I thought tonight's herb was from Maui—not Cuba,' and I had to push him outside, then explain to Joan that mother had recently bought some Hawaiian sage and rosemary from Penzees, and that's what Dad meant by 'herb.'"

"Do they even grow sage and rosemary—" I start to ask.

"I have no idea," Jenn says, sipping her soda.

I sigh. "Well, I don't think that's as bad as Grandma telling Joan they shouldn't have picked this place, where the shrimp is twenty-two ninety-five a plate, because if they had held the rehearsal dinner at a Sizzler we could have had all-you-can-eat shrimp for twelve ninety-five, with bread included."

"And why your industry applauds child molesters!" Grandpa booms in his loud Midwestern voice to Dad. Jenn and I both slowly turn our heads around. "I mean, how you can show your face in public!"

The bartender puts the glass of Jack down. Andy walks up to us, takes Dad's drink, and downs it in one gulp. I put my hand out to the bartender. "You know what? Just give me the bottle."

He does. I refill Dad's glass with the bottle of Jack, gently take Mawv's hand, and lead her toward them.

"Dad needs help," I tell her. "And Grandma and Grandpa are embarrassing Andy in front of her future in-laws."

"I'll take no prisoners," Mawv tells me.

We get back to Bill, Joan, Dad, and Grandpa. A group has now formed around them that includes my mother. Mom begins, "Dad, this is not an appropriate time—"

"The hell it isn't!" Grandpa says, then points his finger at my Dad's chest. "You know, if you were giving my little girl enough sex in the first place, she wouldn't be dating that child."

Hunter's parents gasp. Mom shakes her head. "Chris is twenty-nine, Dad."

"And how old's Andy?" he asks accusingly.

Mom looks at her shoes sheepishly. "Twenty-nine."

"Which is the same age as one of your children," Grandpa says to her.

I bring Mawv over to the group. She doesn't lose a moment. "Rose, we just saw Charles Nelson Reilly coming out of the men's room."

"Charles Nelson . . . Father, get your camera." And the two of them scramble off.

The rest of the rehearsal dinner bordered on depressing—for me, anyway.

After all of the romantic toasts to the soon-to-be newlyweds, and all of the toasts about how love makes you whole, and about how you only get one true love in life, and about how it's God's plan that we each go through eternity with our one soul mate (that would be Grandma's toast), I go home to an empty house.

First, I walk up to my bedroom and check the answering machine. Two messages! Yay! The first message is from Drew, telling me that he'd see me tomorrow, and was looking forward to the wedding. The next message was from Andy to commiserate over how nuts our family is.

No message from Jordan. Not that I care.

Much.

God, I'm gonna die alone. No, worse, I'm gonna die surrounded by cats with stupid names like "Wuggles," "Kitty Carlyle," and "Catmandu."

All right, stop it. I am not going to dwell on my singleness, I am going to enjoy it.

I bring a bunch of white candles into my bathroom, line them around the room, and light them while I draw a L'Occitane Lavender bubble bath. I strip out of my clothes, slip into the tub, and bask in the silence.

And the phone rings.

For a woman, listening to the phone ring is like being a cat watching a string dangled in front of it—we can't help ourselves, it is in our genetic makeup to go grab that phone!

I immediately jump out of the tub and head to the bedroom, leaving a sudsy trail out of my bathroom, down the hallway, and to the bedroom phone. "Hello?"

"You should be reveling in your singleness right now," my cousin Jenn says sternly.

My shoulders slump, and I take the phone back to the tub with me. "Yeah, that's me," I say, without a hint of glee. "Glorious single woman. Woo-hoo."

"You haven't taken up smoking again, have you?" Jenn asks.

"No, I haven't!" I say, sounding appalled that she would think so little of me. When, in reality, the only reason I haven't taken it up again is because I don't want Grandma smelling cigarettes on my breath tomorrow. By Sunday night, I intend to light up like a three-week-old Christmas tree.

"Hold on," Jenn says, and I hear her yell to her husband, "Rob!

Has it occurred to you that if you let the boys leap off the couch, one of them is going to crack his head open, Superman cape or no?"

"Is that Auntie Charlie?" four-year-old Alex asks in the cutest voice ever. "I wanna talk, I wanna talk!"

"Charlie, someone wants to talk to you," Jenn says, and then I hear her number-one son come on the line. "Auntie Charlie, I'll walk down the aisle with you."

"You will?" I say, my voice immediately softening. "Well, that's very nice, but I think you and Sean should walk down the aisle together."

"Why?"

"Well, the ring bearers are supposed to walk down the aisle first, and they're supposed to go together. The maid of honor is supposed to walk down the aisle second to last."

"But then you'll have to walk down the aisle alone," Alex says, his voice dripping with worry.

"Well, that's okay," I reassure him.

"But . . . Daddy says the reason you looked so sad tonight was because you had no one to walk down the aisle with."

"Shit!" I hear Jenn yell before her voice goes back into calm Mommy mode. "Sweetie, give Mommy the phone."

"But I want to walk down the aisle with Auntie Charlie."

"That's very nice of you," I hear Jenn say in a mild panic. "Now can you give Mommy the phone back?"

"I love you!" Alex screams as I hear Jenn rip the phone out of his hand. "I am soooo sorry," she says.

"That's okay," I say, but really I want to drown myself in my lavender bathwater. "Did I look that depressed tonight?"

"What? No!" Jenn says, like that's the silliest thing she's ever heard.

"Then why are you calling me?"

"Because I love you. And Rob loves you. And the boys, too. And . . . we just wanted you to know that."

I get back in the tub. "I love you, too. Very much."

We're both silent, as Jenn tries to think of something comforting to say. "Marriage isn't a panacea."

"I know."

"Sometimes it downright sucks."

"I know that, too."

More silence. Finally Jenn says, "What are we babbling about? You're totally going to find someone."

"Yeah."

More silence. "I'm sorry I screwed up your night even more," Jenn says.

"You didn't. Hey, thanks for calling. You actually made me feel better."

"Really?"

"Yeah. See you in Andy's room at ten tomorrow?"

"Of course."

"Good. Now if you'll excuse me—I'm taking a bubble bath and must go."

"Wow. I'm so jealous. I love you."

"Love you, too. Bye," I say, then click off the phone and let it fall to the bathmat.

Okay, so I lied. Truth is, she made me feel so much worse.

Thirty-one

Truly great sitcoms only have two really great seasons—Season 2 and 3. Before that, they spend too much time establishing characters. After that, it's all downhill.

Right now, it's three A.M. and I'm watching a *Cosby Show* rerun. I think once the grandchildren tried to be cute, they should have packed up and closed down the shop.

But, that aside, my favorite scenes are always the ones with Heathcliff and his wife Claire. I want a husband like that. He's cute, and sweet, and funny, and even though they've been married for almost thirty years, he's still totally in love with his wife.

And he's a fictional character. And, right now watching him, I start crying.

I miss Jordan. I know, I shouldn't. I know, really, that it's not him I miss, it's the idea of him. It's the idea of having a guy to spoon with at night, a guy to go to weddings with, a guy who I want to share my day with, and who I want to know everything about. I know it's not him.

But it is him. I miss the way he smells. I miss his flirty e-mails. I miss knowing how he's doing.

I walk over to my computer and check my e-mail. Still nothing from him.

Oh, what the hell. I write him a quick note.

> Hey, it's me. I just wanted to tell you that I miss you, and that I hope everything is working out for you.
> love,
> Charlie

And I hit SEND.

Love. What a loaded word. But, I reason, I always write "love, Charlie" with anyone I care about. Because I might die tomorrow, and if I do, I want everyone I care about to know that I love them. So "love" is okay.

Damn it. I don't want to look like a stalker. I go back online and check the status of his e-mail. "Unread." Good. I hit UNSEND. Then I start over.

> Hi, it's me. Just wanted to tell you that I was thinking about you, and I hope all is well in your kingdom.
> xoxo
> Charlie

SEND.

I turn the computer off.

It's done, don't think about it anymore.

Twenty minutes later, I check Status, then hit UNSEND. I try writing again.

> Hi, it's me. Was wondering if you were free for a drink sometime next week.

> Let me know.
> Cheers!
> Charlie

SEND.

Yes, that should be fine. Now go to bed.

Ten minutes after that, I turn my computer back on. What the hell am I thinking, asking him out for a drink? Even if I do miss him, he's a creep, and I need to get on with my life. I hit UNSEND without even bothering to check on the e-mail's status.

"Cannot unsend mail that has been read."

Been read. God. Damn. It.

I check the status. He just read it five minutes ago. No response back. Maybe he's online.

I try to IM him—he's not online.

Okay, stay calm. Think. I know, he has that automatic download mail function, so it just automatically downloads mail to his computer every few hours. So he might not have even read it yet. That's probably why he hasn't responded. Yeah, that's it.

So, he'll respond in the morning, and there's nothing I can do about it now, so I should just go to bed.

I try to go back to bed. But after ten minutes of staring wide-eyed at the ceiling, I call him. And get his machine. "Hi, I'm out. Leave a message." Beep.

"Hey, it's me . . . Charlie . . . Um . . . I saw you just read my e-mail. I thought maybe you'd still be up . . ."

I wait. No one picks up. "Okay, I guess not," I say awkwardly, waiting for the earth to swallow me up. "Well, I just wanted to tell you that I missed you, and that I hope everything is okay with you, and that I'd love to see you again sometime. I mean, just as friends if you want . . . we don't have to do anything. I just meant . . ."

Beep.

The fucking machine cut me off.

And I can't even unsend the stupid message.

Final advice of the day:

Never call a household between 10 pm and 8 am.

Thirty-two

Feeling that my book of advice had recently become depressing, not to mention one-sided, I decided to ask everyone in Andy's wedding party to give my future great-grandniece one golden nugget of advice.

I don't think anyone was taking me or the book very seriously.

There's no such thing as a romantic dinner that includes a booster seat and a high chair.

"That's what you're writing?" I say to Jenn incredulously.

"What's wrong with it?" Jenn asks.

"You can write anything you want to a future generation. Anything at all! And that's what you choose?"

"It's no worse than what your Mawv wrote."

"Why?" I ask, grabbing my book of advice. "Mawv, what did you write?"

Bridesmaid's dresses are supposed to be hideous. Wear them anyway.

I look up at her. She shrugs. "Tell me I'm wrong."

Well, I can't say much, dressed as I am in my silver lame ruffled hideous bridemaid's dress.

We're all in Andy's room, the "bridal suite," getting ready for the wedding, just us girls. My mom (who's excused herself to the balcony at least three times to smoke pot), Mawv (who's excused herself at least three times to go smoke cigarettes), Jenn (who's excused herself to go to the bathroom to throw up), Grandma, and me, who's dying to excuse myself for any reason, but I can't think of a damn thing.

A makeup artist is putting the finishing touches on Andy's makeup in the other room, which is giving us ample time to dish on Andy's fashion choices.

"I think Charlie looks gorgeous," Grandma says, which is the first compliment she's paid me all weekend. Then she gives a pointed look to my mother. "Much better than that artsy-fartsy crap you put *your* bridesmaids in. But then again, your choices have always been weird."

Mom glares at Grandma, grabs my book of advice, then scribbles down the following:

There comes a point in your life when you should choose who you're comfortable with, and spend the holidays with them. Don't see your family if they're not nice to you.

"Oh, please. What's normal?" Mawv counters, lighting a new cigarette with the one she's just finished. "I've been on this planet almost a hundred years, and I've never seen a decent-looking bridesmaid's dress. And you know what really gets me is when you hear the bride say, 'She can wear the dress after the wedding.' Where is Charlie going to wear that? A *Star Trek* convention?"

Later in my journal I will write the following advice:

Save all of your bridesmaid's dresses for your wedding. That way, they can be "worn again" by the brides who made you wear them to their weddings in the first place.

"How do I look?" Andy asks, opening her bedroom door.

I turn to see her in her white dress and veil, and she is truly breathtaking. Her dress sparkles, matching her sparkly, happy eyes. "You look perfect," I say. And I mean it, she does. Her hair is up, her skin is glowing. I've never seen her look so happy. This really is her day.

"You're beautiful," Mom says, clasping her hands together.

"Stunning," Jenn concurs.

"How much did that dress set you back?" Grandma asks, pulling back Andy's collar to check the tag.

"Ninety-nine dollars," Mom, Jenn, Andy, and I say in unison.

"Good," Grandma says, lightly patting Andy on her shoulder. "Because I have a surprise for you. Your grandfather and I would like to help you pay for your dress."

Grandma walks over to her purse and proudly pulls out a check. "This is from us," she says, proudly handing Andy the check. "Fifty dollars. Use it to help pay for your dress."

Andy reads the check. "Oh, this is much too generous," she says, like she's just been given the Taj Mahal.

My mother walks over to Andy, looks over her shoulder to read the check, then rolls her eyes.

"Nonsense," Grandma says. "Your grandfather and I are happy to do it. Besides"—Grandma gives me a pointed look—"it's not like we're going to be giving out any more wedding checks anytime soon."

Mawv whips her head over to me, then back to Grandma. "What the hell's that supposed to mean?"

Which is exactly what I was thinking.

Grandma narrows her eyes at Mawv. "Oh, Mother, let's be honest . . ."

"Mother," my mom interrupts Grandma. "A wedding day is not the time to start being honest."

"Well, forgive me for calling a spade a spade! Back in my day, we had a word for women over thirty who weren't married. And do you know what that word was?"

"Spinster," Mawv says.

"No," Grandma tells her.

"Old maid?" Mom asks.

"No. Lesbian," Grandma states emphatically.

Swell. Then Grandma looks right at me, and glares. "And I love you, Charlie, but I don't believe in gay weddings, and I won't give gifts."

We are all so stunned, the room gets amazingly silent. I am speechless. Utterly speechless.

"That is the biggest load of crap I've ever heard," Jenn belts out at my grandmother.

"Jenn . . . ," I say quietly.

"No!" she says to me, then turns to my grandmother. "Rose, what kind of narrow-minded bullshit is that?"

"Jenn . . . ," I try again.

"You don't get to pick who you fall in love with! Love picks you. A wedding is a celebration of two people finally finding each other, and loving and supporting each other and getting to spend the rest of their lives together. How can you be against that?!"

"Jenn . . ."

"You know what? I hope Charlie doesn't even invite you to her wedding. You don't deserve to be included!"

"Jenn . . ."

"What?!" Jenn snaps, turning toward me.

"I'm not gay," I remind her.

"Oh . . . right." Jenn grimaces at her mistake, then lifts her chin in defiance of my grandmother. "Well, you're still wrong."

Before anyone can say anything else, the phone rings.

Welcoming the interruption, Andy picks up the phone. "Hello . . . Yes, she is. Hold on."

She hands me the phone. "It's for you. It's Dawn."

Still flabbergasted, I stare at my grandmother as I take the phone from my sister. "Yeah?"

"Come to Room 150. Now," Dawn says.

"Where is it?" I ask.

"It's along the left side of the hotel, right in front of a water fountain. Hurry. You gotta see this."

Desperate for any excuse to get away from my family, I leave my sister's room and head out for Room 150.

I knock on the door. Dawn answers. She stares at me in my dress. "Fetching," she deadpans.

She opens her mouth again, but I put up my hand in a "stop" motion. "Before you say anything else, I would like to remind you that, one, I did not pick out this dress, and two, having been with my family since ten o'clock this morning, I am in a piss-poor mood, and you do not want to be on my bad side right now."

Dawn continues to stare at me. She's dying to make a comment, but knows to keep her mouth shut.

But she keeps staring.

The silence is deafening.

I cross my arms and roll my eyes. "Okay, fine. One more. Just one."

Dawn smiles. "There's a drag queen in Reseda who wants his dress back."

"Very funny." I storm into the hotel room and stop in my tracks.

This is not a room, it's an apartment! There is a large living room, with velvet couches and a real fireplace that uses real wood. (You'd be amazed how many Californians have gas fireplaces with fake, nonflammable ceramic logs. You press a button, and blue flames shoot out of a few highly visible jets. It's like turning on a gas stove for ambience.)

"This is amazing," I say, walking around to examine the décor.

"And this is just the living room!" Dawn says, sounding uncharacteristically impressed. "Come see the outside." She takes my hand and pulls me through some French doors out to a private courtyard, beautifully landscaped with colorful, fragrant flowers and a private Jacuzzi. "Wow," I say.

"Wait! There's more!" Dawn says with the enthusiasm of a five-year-old as she pulls me back through the living room and over to an exquisitely appointed bedroom. "This is your room tonight."

"My room?" I ask, stunned. The room is gorgeous: a king-size bed with a white comforter, shiny dark wood tables and dresser, and an entertainment center with a DVD player and state-of-the-art speakers. And everything's immaculately clean.

This is what my dream bedroom looks like—when I dream I'm the princess of Monaco.

"What do you mean it's mine?" I ask, confused.

"Welcome to the 'too drunk to drive' room!" Drew says, walking in with a flourish. "Believe it or not, this is the small bedroom. Dawn and I have the larger bedroom, on the other side of the living room. It's outstanding. I'm telling you, there are days when I'm really glad I'm rich."

Dawn and Drew show me their room, which is even more fabulous, and the three of us retire to the living room, where a bottle of Dom Pérignon chills in a bucket of ice.

"So, what do you think?" Drew asks as he fills a flute and hands it to me.

"It's wonderful," I say sadly, taking the glass. "But I can't stay with you two. I'd be the third wheel."

"Don't be silly," Dawn assures me. "Drew and I brought you a few

things: jeans, T-shirt, pajamas. This way we can keep the party going after the wedding, and you won't have to drive home tonight,
then come back for brunch in the morning."

I stare at my glass, ready to cry. "You know, I think it's going to
take all my strength just to get through the wedding without bursting
into tears. Somehow, I don't think I could take a party afterwards."

"What's wrong?" Drew asks me.

"My grandmother gave my sister a check for fifty dollars," I say.

They look at me blankly. I take a deep breath and continue. "My
grandmother, who has never given any of us a check for over
twenty dollars in her life. Ever. And not only does my sister get a
check for fifty dollars, but I get a lecture on the evils of gay marriage . . . You know what? Never mind. It's hard to explain."

I take a sip of champagne. "I'm sorry . . . it's just . . . Drew, what
did you get them for their wedding?"

Drew darts a look at Dawn, as if wondering if he's in trouble. "I
got them the twelve champagne flutes on their registry."

"The two-hundred-and-fifty-dollar-a-pair champagne flutes!" I
exclaim.

I point at Drew, as I turn to Dawn. "See? My sister finds her soul
mate, and not only does she get rewarded with love and happiness,
she gets free champagne flutes, and dutch ovens and fifty-dollar
checks. And what do I get? What do I get on a day when I still
haven't found anyone to love? When I'm waiting by the phone for
some jerk to call me, and acting like a crazy woman, e-mailing him
at three A.M., clutching at straws that I might ever find anyone? Do I
get gifts? No! I get condemnation from my grandmother, and I get
to wear a dress that makes me look like a baked potato."

Drew and Dawn stare at me in silence. I can tell they're trying to
think of something comforting to say. They won't be able to think of
anything. I've been trying to think of something comforting to say
to myself all morning, and I'm still at a loss.

I fall onto one of the couches, and stare at my champagne flute. "It just doesn't seem fair that not only do I not get a soul mate, I don't get champagne flutes, either."

Dawn pulls out a pack of Marlboros from her purse. "Would you like a cigarette? It might calm your nerves."

I glare at her. "I quit smoking."

Dawn looks confused. "Today?"

"No. Yesterday."

"The day before your sister's wedding?" Dawn asks.

"Yes," I say angrily, setting my champagne flute down on the table.

Dawn's looking at me like she heard me wrong. She turns to Drew, who shrugs. Finally, she asks me, "How's that working out for you?"

"Argh!" I scream, pulling one of the couch pillows over my face.

And, with that outburst, the phone rings. Dawn answers. "Hello."

By the change in her tone of voice, I can tell immediately that she is talking to my grandmother. "Yes, ma'am . . . This is Dawn, ma'am . . . Yes, ma'am . . . No, ma'am."

Dawn has a phone trick I have to include in my book:

When you don't know what kind of person you're dealing with, always address them with "ma'am" or "sir." It immediately conveys respect—even if you're not feeling any.

"No, ma'am, I'm not Charlie's girlfriend . . . Well, ma'am, you don't have to believe me . . . Ma'am, not everyone in Los Angeles is gay. . . ."

"Oh for God's sake," I say, standing up from the couch and grabbing the phone from Dawn. "Hello, Grandma."

"Where are you?" Grandma asks accusingly.

"I'm in Room 150. Where you called me," I say, with the first hint of irritation she's heard from me all weekend.

"With another woman," Grandma states, like she's proven her point.

I sigh. "Grandma, did you call for a reason?"

"Yes, the photos are starting in a few minutes. We need you back here. And try to add a little blush to your face. You don't want to look washed out in the pictures."

God grant me the serenity to accept the things I cannot change.
—Serenity prayer

Thirty-three

No matter what kind of drama is going on before your wedding day, somehow, on the actual day, people will calm down, and it will all come together and be wonderful.

The wedding is beautiful and magical and all the things you dream your wedding will be when you're a little girl. Despite Andy's insistence on salmon and silver, the wedding coordinator had somehow convinced her to switch most of the silver decorations for white (except, of course, for my dress), and convinced her to go with peach instead of salmon. The results are spectacular.

There are white and peach flowers everywhere: dripping from the gazebo, hanging from the aisle runners and chairs. Peach and white rose petals are sprinkled over the white silk aisle draped over the grass. Two swans silently swim around the lake.

While the guests look on, the groom and his party take their places in front, and the bridal party stands in the back, waiting for the wedding coordinator to signal each of us to walk down the aisle.

As the string quartet plays "In My Life" by the Beatles, Hunter's two nieces walk down the aisle, looking adorable in white satin flower girl dresses and throwing peach-and-white rose petals down the aisle from their peach and white baskets.

Sean and Alex come next, walking down the aisle in their white tuxedos, each holding a peach satin ring pillow with a fake ring sewn on. (Jenn said giving them the real rings was begging to have two hundred wedding guests on their knees in the grass, looking for a dropped ring.)

Next comes Jenn, waddling down the aisle, looking like a giant peach.

And now it is time for me. The wedding coordinator throws her index finger forward, signaling "Go!"

I take one step forward, when Andy grabs my arm.

Turning to face her, all I can think is, Please don't be a runaway bride. Grandma will blame me. But I don't say it aloud. Instead, I tilt my head, giving her a quizzical look.

Andy smiles and kisses me on the check. "I love you."

"I love you, too."

She takes my hand and swings it. "No, I mean, I really love you. I know I've been a pain in the butt these last few months, but I want you to know . . . well, I think you're the best sister a person could ever have."

I smile and give Andy a hug. By now the wedding coordinator is yelling "Go!" loud enough for the guests to hear, so I go.

As I walk down the aisle, I turn around to Andy and mouth the words, "I love you, too." Then I make my way to the gazebo and stand in my designated spot.

The wedding march begins.

As Dad walks Andy down the aisle, I see Hunter is both smiling and crying.

Which makes me tear up a bit myself.

They did the traditional vows:

Don't write your own vows, unless you intend to subject your guests to really bad amateur theater.

And the ceremony is over in less than twenty minutes.

Party time!

At the reception, Andy is gracious enough to seat me nowhere near my family, except for Jamie, who managed to get his seat changed when he found out where Kate was seated.

I get to be with the cool people. Drew and Dawn sit next to me at Table 9, along with Kate and Jamie, and some friends of Hunter's, who are all our age and equally cool: Margie, a college friend who just moved to L.A. from Boston, and Susan and Michael, a newly married couple who aren't the least bit smug about it.

"Are you my date?" Margie asks we seat ourselves for dinner.

"Excuse me?" I say nervously.

She takes the seat next to me. "I was just told by Hunter's mother, and I quote"—her voice goes into a perfect Manhattan socialite accent—"'since you're a single gal, too, we figured we'd seat you with the maid of honor. She's single, and just turned thirty, and she's so funny about it.'"

"Yeah, that's me. I'm a regular laugh riot," I say sarcastically, and we clink glasses in a toast.

Overall, the conversation is pretty good, and it even allows me to forget about Jordan for a while. Despite having three couples at the table, no one asks Margie or me if we are seeing anyone special, or asks the dreaded question, "So, how come a woman like you has never been married?"

Never ask a single person if they're "seeing anyone special," an unemployed person if they've found a job, or a married couple when they're planning to have children. You're not making conversation. You're starting someone on the road to Prozac.

Our table stays with safe topics, like politics and religion.

I'm almost having a good time. Yes, I'm still craving a cigarette.

Yes, I'm still craving Jordan. But as I watch Hunter and Andy on the dance floor, I am genuinely, 100 percent happy for them—without the least bit of jealousy.

And that's a step in the right direction.

Of course, I should have known that even a semi-state of wellness couldn't last long with so many family members lurking about. Right after Hunter twirls Andy for the final crescendo, my grandmother appears at my table.

"So when are you going to introduce me to your friends?" Grandma asks, her autograph book in hand.

I know who she really wants to meet, but I introduce everyone else at the table first, saving Drew for last.

"I just loved you in *The Last Samurai*," Grandma tells Drew, thrusting her autograph book in his face. "Do you mind?"

"Not at all," Drew says, smiling graciously as he takes the book and signs it. "But, you know, I wasn't in *The Last Samurai*. I believe you're thinking of Tom Cruise."

"Oh, you're such a kidder," Grandma laughs, slapping him on the back. "So"—she addresses the table with a big smile—"do any of you know any available men for old Charlie here? All offers considered."

"No, no. Charlie's my date tonight," Margie jokes. "Hunter's mother said so."

Grandma narrows her eyes at me. "I knew it."

I see Dawn give Drew a pointed look. He quickly hands Grandma her book back, while placing his arm around my shoulder. "Grandma Rose, she's kidding. The truth is Charlie and I have been a couple for quite a while now."

Grandma looks at him, confused. And, when I say confused, what I mean is I could have picked her jaw up off the floor. Heh-heh.

"But," Grandma points to Dawn, "isn't she your date?"

"No, no. That's just for the press. You see, since Charlie and I work together, we have to keep our relationship hush-hush. You understand."

Grandma looks at me, trying to figure out if he's lying. I respond with a shit-eating grin of confidence.

"Of course," Grandma barely manages to eke out to Drew.

There's an awkward silence at the table for a few moments.

"Where are my manners?" Drew says, quickly standing up and offering his hand to my grandmother. "May I have this dance?"

And Grandma actually giggles. "Well, aren't you sweet?"

As they walk out onto the dance floor, I overhear her say, "You know, we loved you in *Ocean's Eleven*."

"Well, thank you. Of course, that was George Clooney."

Once they are on the dance floor and out of hearing range, I pat Dawn's hand. "Thanks for letting me borrow your date."

"No problem. And, hey, she's not so bad. You should hear my Jewish grandmother on the subject of my not being married. You Catholics ain't got nothing on us Jews when it comes to annoying grandmothers."

As I laugh, the wedding coordinator leans into our table and urgently whispers to me, "May I have a word with you?"

Uh-oh.

"Of course," I say, following her to a quiet corner.

"I was wondering if we could convince you to give the first toast?" the coordinator begins. "I'm afraid the best man is, um . . . indisposed at the moment."

No fucking way.

"I don't think that would be a very good idea," I say. "See, I'm not very good at public speaking. And, when I say I'm not very good, what I mean is, it makes me want to throw up."

"I understand completely," the coordinator says, smiling. "However, from what I understand, apparently the best man actually *is* throwing up. Rather violently, I might add."

Andy races up to us. "So, can you do it?" she asks me.

"Do what?"

"Give the toast. Talk about how happy you are for us . . . blah, blah, blah."

"I don't understand. What happened to Hunter's brother?"

"He and Mom had a drinking contest, and he lost. Big time," Andy says, sounding more than peeved at Mom. I open my mouth to ask for more information, but Andy puts up her palm. "It was Kamakazi shots. Apparently Mom drank him under the table. I don't even want to go there. Can you just do the toast?"

I sigh. I have nothing prepared. I've been drinking since ten this morning. Yeah, this is gonna go well.

"No problem," I say.

"Great," Andy says, and hugs me.

The best impromptu speeches are written well in advance.

About five minutes later, I stand up on the stage, slightly tipsy, desperate for a cigarette, all eyes on me. Everyone probably thought I'd spent days writing and rewriting my speech for two hundred people.

So I do what great orators have done for centuries.

I wing it.

I stare at my champagne glass. "The moment I knew that Andy had found her true love was at her bachelorette party," I begin.

There are titters from the audience, and Andy looks at me, wide-eyed and petrified. I laugh with the titters. "Now, now . . . contrary to what you might hear about bachelorette parties, most of them are quite tame. No, what I was going to talk about was Andy's choice of lingerie for one of her last nights as a free woman. She had stolen one of Hunter's T-shirts to wear with her flannel pajama bottoms."

I raise my glass for the toast. "Here's to finally finding the one whose T-shirts you want to steal for the rest of your life."

Everyone clinks their glasses, applause, applause, applause, and I am done for the night.

A few minutes after the toast, I take my glass of champagne and sneak outside for a breath of fresh air.

That's a total lie. I need a cigarette.

After tracking the wedding coordinator down and bumming a Marlboro and a light from her, I head toward the lake and away from the loud party.

I light up. Aaaahhhhhhh . . .

I can feel a slight chill on my shoulders as I walk around the grounds, dreaming of the day when I get to wear the white dress and be the center of attention and get all the free champagne flutes and fifty-dollar checks.

I finish my cigarette, stub it out in a discreetly placed ashtray, then start to walk back toward the reception.

On my way, I see Mawv sitting on a bench in a gazebo near the lobby, all by herself, also sneaking a cigarette.

"You know, those things'll kill you," I say as I walk up to her.

"Not soon enough, dear," Mawv tells me, and takes a slow puff, exhaling small cigarette donuts.

I take the bench across from her.

Mawv's glassy eyes seem to stare into space, even though she's looking right at me.

"Penny for your thoughts," I say.

"How about a kiss?" Mawv says, smiling.

I smile, and kiss her on the cheek. She smells of Chanel No. 5 and baby powder.

"I was just thinking that in my day, a woman defined herself by whether or not a man loved her enough to marry her. Then we had women's lib, and you all went to college, and you got jobs, and you worked your butts off so you could buy your own houses, and have sex with whomever you wanted. And you want to know where it's gotten you?" Mawv asks.

I shake my head, smiling the way you do when you talk to really old people.

"A woman now defines herself by whether or not a man loves her enough to marry her."

I'm not saying I totally agree with her, but there's something to be said for what comes with the wisdom of age.

"I'm sorry, where are my manners?" Mawv says, and quickly pulls a Winston from her silver cigarette case. "You want one?"

"Thought you'd never ask," I say, taking the cigarette greedily.

She hands me her sterling silver lighter, and I light up, enjoying the second cigarette I've had in five minutes.

"The grandkids are in the back, sneaking pot, if you want to go there instead," she tells me.

"Nah, I'll stick to the legal stuff."

Mawv smiles a grandmotherly smile and pats me on the knee lightly. "Good girl."

We silently smoke our cigarettes while listening to the wedding music drift from the ballroom.

"Whatcha thinking about now?" I ask.

"I was actually thinking about you, dear," Mawv tells me.

"Oh?" I say, surprised.

"I worry you're sad it's not your day today."

"No, I'm not," I lie. "My day will come."

Again, she smiles and pats me on the knee. "I'll bet you don't remember your cousin Jenn's *Charlie's Angels* baseball cards."

"Can't say as I do," I admit. "I'm notoriously bad about sports."

Mawv laughs at that. "No, no. When your cousin Jenn was about five, she loved this TV show called *Charlie's Angels*. You know, before it was a movie."

I nod. "I know. I've seen the reruns."

"Nice little show. Of course, it was on at ten o'clock back then, and even in 1976 I was old, so I didn't watch it much, because I went to bed early."

I nod, already worried she's about to go off on a tangent.

"*Baretta* was on before that, and I didn't like him, even before he killed his wife. I did like that *Carol Burnett Show,* though. She's such a funny woman. . . ."

"Mawv," I say gently, patting her knee.

"That Lyle Waggoner was such a handsome fellow. Very pleasant on the eyes. You know, he was on *Wonder Woman,* too . . ."

"Okay, Mawv . . ."

"That was the show with that actress whose husband was accused of stealing all that money. . . ."

"And we're back to the baseball cards," I remind her.

Listen to your elders' stories. They have a lot to teach you.

"Yes. Baseball cards," Mawv continues. "Your cousin wanted all the *Charlie's Angels* cards. They were like baseball cards, and each had a picture from the show on one side. Then, on the other side of the card, instead of statistics, there was a picture that was a piece of a puzzle. If you collected all the cards, you could make a picture of the Angels on a beautiful beach in Hawaii."

I continue to nod politely, but honestly I don't know what this has to do with me.

"Anyway," Mawv continues, "Jenn collected all of the cards—except for one. Her mother must have bought her fifty packs of bubble gum just to get this one card, but she never got it. So, her puzzle was always missing Jaclyn Smith's hat."

"Hmm," I say, figuring the story was over.

And pointless.

Suddenly, Mawv gets more animated, and more desperate to make her point. "But it was just one piece of the puzzle. Do you understand?"

"I do," I say, lying.

Mawv sighs and shakes her head. "No, you don't."

And then she gets me with a zinger. "I worry about you because you have a good life. And you spend too much of it sad that you don't have Jaclyn Smith's hat."

Ouch.

I wish I could assure her that that's not the case. But I can't. Because it's true.

For the next minute or two, we smoke our cigarettes in silence, listening to the sounds of an early Beatles tune coming from the ballroom.

Suddenly, my mother comes running out of the ballroom. "Charlie?!" she screams across the courtyard. "Where are you?! Your sister's about to throw the bouquet!"

I roll my eyes, and Mawv bursts out laughing.

Reluctantly, Mawv and I head back to the ballroom, and over to the center of the dance floor, where all of the single girls huddle in a pack near Andy.

I stand between Kate and Dawn. "Well, girls, time for the most humiliating part of the evening."

"Why do you say that?" Kate says, totally excited. "This is my favorite part. You know, I've caught the bouquet three times."

Dawn shakes her head. "That just says so much."

As Andy makes a big show of turning around so as not to see anyone, Dawn leans into me and whispers, "Hey, can you do me a little favor later?"

"Sure. You want me to make myself scarce tonight?" I ask, because, let's face it, who wants to be in an insanely romantic hotel room with your best friend next door listening to your every smooch.

"Not exactly," Dawn says, and she starts chewing her cuticles, which is her one nervous habit in the world.

"What's wrong?" I ask, slightly concerned.

"Well, it's Drew. See, we've kind of hit that point of, you know, fish or cut bait."

I stare at her blankly. "Meaning?"

"Meaning we haven't slept together."

"You haven't . . ." I say loudly, then catch myself. I lower my voice to a whisper. "You haven't . . ."

"No, and tonight's kind of the night," Dawn says. "So I'm going to break up with him."

She's what? I stare at her in astonishment as—

Bam! The bouquet hits me right in the face.

"Shit!" I scream, but I'm drowned out by the yells of disappointment from Kate and the other girls, and applause from the wedding guests.

I touch my cheek lightly with my finger. "I'm bleeding," I say to my sister. "What the hell's in this bouquet?"

"Just roses and lilies," Andy says, then walks up to check it as I grab a linen napkin and put it up to my face. "Ooh, it looks like a thorn hit you."

"Because, you know what they say," Dawn enlightens us:

A rose by any other name still has thorns.

I glare at both of them as we get off the dance floor to make way for the single men and the garter toss.

Yeah, here's another fun tradition.

The first time Hunter throws the garter, it falls about five feet short of the group of bachelors, and not one guy walks over to pick it up.

Swell.

The next time, it's caught by a twelve-year-old, whom I get to dance with. Finally, my prince has come.

The second the song is over, I race over to Table 9, grab Dawn, and tell her she needs to join me in the ladies' room. All jokes aside, I need to get her alone, so I can find out what's going on with Drew.

Because, you know what they say:

If you can't get laid at a wedding—go into a monastery.

Note to self: Call monastery Monday morning. Book "get to know" meeting for Drew.

Thirty-four

You don't choose love, love chooses you.

Once Dawn and I get to the ladies' room, I try to be the understanding friend that everyone deserves during a painful breakup.

"Are you out of your fucking mind?!" I yell at Dawn. "You're going to break up with my boss at a wedding?!"

I said I *try* to be an understanding friend.

"I know," Dawn says, pulling a lipstick from her purse and applying it in the mirror. "I picked a bad time, and I'm sorry about that. But there really never is a good time to break up."

Kate charges in. "Did I hear right?" she says to Dawn. "You're breaking up with the Sexiest Man Alive?"

"No. I'm breaking up with Drew," Dawn says, now irritated. "If Denzel calls, I'm open."

I stare at them, speechless.

Dawn finishes with her lipstick and hands it to Kate, who applies some in the mirror. "You're nuts," Kate says. "The guy's gorgeous."

"Do you want him?" Dawn asks.

Kate hands back the lipstick. "Actually, no. I kind of like this fuckbuddy thing I got going with Jamie."

Ewwww . . .

"Please don't refer to my brother as a 'fuckbuddy,'" I say to Kate. "It's going to take three more cocktails just to get that visual out of my head." I turn to Dawn, who puts away her lipstick and pulls out a powder compact. "I don't get it. You like him. What did he do wrong?"

"He didn't do anything wrong. It's just not working out," Dawn says apologetically. She puts on some powder, staring at her reflection in the mirror, consciously not looking at me.

Dawn finally looks my way. I guess I must be looking like a kicked puppy, because she seems genuinely upset to be hurting me. "It's just not working out," Dawn says, putting away her compact. "I mean, I'm at this incredibly romantic wedding watching people recite their vows, and I know he's not the one. So, rather than getting all depressed about it, I think it's better for all concerned if we just call it a day, so to speak."

I blow out a big sigh. I hate it when she's being reasonable. "Okay, fine. But do you have to break up tonight? I mean, have a heart. And why do I have to be here for it?"

"It has to be tonight because he's expecting sex, and I don't want him in that way. I tried, but I ain't feelin' it. And you have to be here because he's going to get all depressed afterwards, and you're his friend and you should be here for him."

And I hate it when she's being logical. Logical and reasonable. Goddamn her. We spend the next few minutes arguing, but I already know I've lost.

And when the wedding is over, I say my good-byes to everyone, tell Drew and Dawn I'll be back in the room at one o'clock, and head for the bar, knowing Drew will be calling me any minute.

Thirty-five

It's the friends you can call up at 4 am that matter.—Marlene
Dietrich

Thirty minutes later, my cell phone rings. I check the caller ID.
"Hi, Drew."

"Where are you?" he asks.

"The hotel bar."

"Any photographers there? How's the lighting? Is it a place to be
seen?"

"No, the lighting's fine, and no."

"Are there any women there?" he asks.

I look around. I'm the only woman here under forty. "A few," I
say.

"Good. Pick one for me, and bring her to my room."

"I don't think that's a very good idea."

"Why?"

"Because tomorrow morning, on top of dealing with a hangover
and a breakup, you don't need to be dealing with a starfucker."

The older couple at the table next to me turns around to glare. I
smile back at them.

"I suppose that's a good point," Drew concedes. "Okay, call my driver. I know a pretty good strip club we can go to. . . ."

"How about if I just come back to the room, and we'll talk?" I suggest.

"Talk? Why?"

"Because you're upset," I point out.

"I'm fine," Drew insists, shrugging me off with his tone of voice. "You know what they say—best way to get over someone is to get under someone. Now, who do we know that's cute and available this time of night?"

"Me," I say, sighing. "So I'll be right over."

"Really?" Drew says, audibly perking up.

"I'm kidding. I'll see you in a minute."

I hang up, pay the check, and make my way back to amazing Room 150, and knock on the door. Drew opens it. "You think Paris Hilton is available?" he asks.

"I don't know. Check your Pay-Per-View schedule."

He steps aside so that I can walk into the most romantic and decadent hotel room on the planet, designed to make even Queen Elizabeth want to do the horizontal mambo. So, naturally, a woman dumped him here.

As I walk in, Drew points to the coffee table, where I see a big box beautifully wrapped in glittery silver paper. "I got a wedding present for you," he says offhandedly.

"You mean to give to Andy?" I ask, confused.

"No. I mean for you." He walks to the table, picks up the box, and hands it to me. "I got it for you earlier tonight."

I carefully unwrap the present to see a bright red Baccarat box. Inside the box are two baccarat champagne flutes and a card. As I open the card, a check for fifty dollars falls out—signed by Drew. And he signed the card with my favorite new mantra, and one that will soon go into my journal of advice:

You needn't be married to drink champagne.
Love, Drew

"I love it," I say.

"Good. At least I made one woman happy tonight."

There's a bottle of Dom Pérignon, unopened, in a silver cooler next to the couch. He gives the cork a quick pop, and pours champagne into my new glasses.

We sit on the green sofa and clink our glasses in a toast.

Drew toasts, "Here's to finding someone who doesn't make us completely nuts."

We exchange sympathetic smiles. I rub his shoulder and ask, "What happened?"

He shrugs. "We were making out, and then she didn't want to go any further. And she looked so sad. She wants to like me in that way. But I'm not the one."

He shrugs. "We have a good time together. She wants me to be the one. But, you know, whatever . . ."

His voice trails off and he takes a sip of champagne.

I rub his shoulder. "You're gonna find someone," I say.

"Oh, sweetie, please let's not do the 'you're gonna find someone' speech," Drew says, turning on the TV.

"Okay," I say. "What speech do you want?"

Drew flips through the channels, settling on an old golf game. "How about the 'I won't say one more word about dating tonight. Let's watch ESPN in our pajamas instead' speech?"

When men say they don't want to talk about it, what they really mean is—they don't want to talk about it.

"I'll go get my pajamas," I say quietly, heading to the smaller bedroom.

I walk to the doorway, then turn around. I look at the back of Drew's head as he watches the old golf game. You know, for all his nuttiness, and all the times I want to wring his neck, I sure have a soft spot for him. He's one of the most good-hearted people I've ever met, and he deserves a soul mate just as much as the rest of us.

"I really like my champagne flutes," I squeak out quietly, trying to get him into a conversation.

"Good," Drew says, not turning his head from the game. "Next time we go to London, we should get you some china to go with them."

I'm silent for a while as I try to think of something else to say. Something that would make him feel better. Something like he deserves better than this, or that some day his princess will come, or that he doesn't need Jaclyn Smith's hat.

Instead, I go with an old standby. "I hear Jennifer Lopez might be available again."

Drew turns his head around slowly, grinning. "Really?"

Thirty-six

At almost any moment, you have the power to change your destiny.

Sunday morning, after having brunch with Drew and my family, and saying good-bye to all of them, I came home, changed into my comfy Eeyore pajamas and slippers, threw my hair into a ponytail, and opened *War and Peace* to page one.

I lie down on my purple couch, grab a cigarette from my pack on the coffee table, and pull out a lighter.

I stare at the cigarette. After about ten seconds' more thought, I break my Marlboro in half and toss the two unlit halves of the unlit cigarette into an ashtray.

What the hell? So I'll put on a few pounds. It's not like there's anyone to lose them for, anyway. Besides, I've decided I like my life. I want to live to be a hundred.

An hour later, I've cranked my way through twenty pages of *War and Peace*. It doesn't sound like much, but already Tolstoy has mentioned a mother who falsely thinks her fourteen-year-old daughter is her best friend—as so many mothers have done before her. This guy Leo was onto something. I write in my journal:

Read classics like **War and Peace** *once you're out of school. They're much better when there's not a quiz. Don't ever read* **Ethan Frome, The Sound and the Fury,** *or anything by Kafka. You're wasting your time.*

I forgot to include *Lord Jim*. God, it's amazing what English Lit. teachers do to make us hate reading for so much of our adult lives.

My doorbell rings. I walk over to the door and look through the peephole. Shit! It's Jordan.

Suddenly, I remember my stupid middle-of-the-night phone call.

There should be a phone service that turns off your phone between midnight and six A.M. every night. And if you want to make a call, you have to pick up the phone and talk to an operator: *Put me through to AAA. My car battery's dead.*

Yes, ma'am.

Put me through to Pink Dot. I need vanilla Häagen-Dazs toute de suite!

Yes, ma'am.

Put me through to my ex-boyfriend. . . .

I'm sorry, ma'am, the operator would say. *That would be a bad idea. Now you go to bed before you do anything stupid.*

And my call had been stupid, and now God was punishing me by making me see the man I have a crush on while wearing Eeyore pajamas and no makeup.

I open the door. "Hi . . . ," I begin, ready to shout a monologue to him about why I shouldn't have called, because he's scum, and I have no intentions of becoming a mistress, so he can just turn around right now, mister, because . . .

"I thought you might want to see this," Jordan says, holding up an engagement ring.

I stare at him, dumbfounded.

"I'm sorry I missed your call," he tells me as he puts the ring in his pocket. "I was in San Francisco getting it back."

"How was it?" My voice quakes when I ask.

Jordan smiles warmly. "Brutal. I don't want to talk about it. How was the wedding?"

I smile back. "Brutal. I don't want to talk about it."

I pull the ponytail holder out of my hair and fluff my hair up. "I did, however, get a fabulous wedding gift. Would you like to come in and have some champagne?"

"I'd love to."

I let him in, and we talk all night. You know the kind of talk you have that's half kissing and half talking? And you suddenly realize this person's going to be in your life for a while?

It was a good night.

And the following day, I finished my journal of advice:

I was never Jennifer Aniston. I never cooked as well as Julia Child, wrote as well as Tolstoy, was as funny as Lucille Ball, or as rich as Oprah Winfrey. I was never as beautiful as Beyoncé, as famous as Princess Diana, as good of an actress as Meryl Streep, as driven to a cause as Elizabeth Cady Stanton. I'm pretty sure I never learned physics, or how to speak Chinese. And I can almost guarantee you I never figured out the new math.

But I got to go through this life, and this century, as me. And that's a hell of a lot more than I ever dreamed.

Well, great-granddaughter, I hope reading my book has inspired you to write a book of your own, for your own great-granddaughter. I only wish I could ask you this question—because I'm dying to know: What will you write?